Mary –

Lessons

in

Disguise

Kate Porter

KONSTELLATION PRESS

Thank you so much for
your support – I hope you
enjoy! Kate P.

Konstellation Press

ISBN 13: **978-0-9987482-1-4**
ISBN 10: **0998748218**

Additional Praise for *Lessons in Disguise*

Kate Porter takes the reader on a tour de force spanning 150 years and the width of the American continent. An old book serves as a guide through time and space from Virginia to Minnesota and finally to California. Brilliantly written in the voices of the people who owned it from 1820 to the 1970s, it reflects the personal history of these ordinary citizens. A bookbinder, a suffragette, a former slave, a Norwegian immigrant, and a Black homeless vet are placed in the context of broader American history. Themes of slavery, women's emancipation, the Vietnam War, and bi-racial relations weave through the pages of *Lessons in Disguise,* like the quotes from the old book that sprinkle and sometimes shape the life stories of its owners.

—Cornelia Feye, author of *Spring of Tears*, 2012 San Diego Book Awards winner for Published Mystery; and her newest novel *Private Universe*

It is a credit to Porter's writing ability that each character's voice is so distinctly different from the others, with great attention to the vocabulary, culture, and jargon of each time period and social class. In the background, she adds the context of the larger political, social, and historical events of each era, as they impact the characters. This is not only one of those books you can't put down and don't want to end, but is as endearing, and often as comforting, to the reader as the fictional book it portrays is to the characters in this novel.

—Delin Colon, author
Rasputin and The Jews: A Reversal of History

Kate Porter's *Lessons in Disguise* is a book within a book, centering around *An Easy Standard*, a primer of sorts meant to help people learn to read, and to guide their moral development. In its 150-year history, the book goes from its pristine hand-gilded beginnings to a tattered clump of pages as it is handed down from a young orphan girl to a black friend and from there to a wide range of others: from a Norwegian immigrant to a disaffected suburban wife, to confused and vulnerable young people finding their way through the era of the Vietnam War. The poignancy of the book's messages about love, morality, ethics, kindness, and the good life are valued more by some owners than others, but its wisdom and the stories of its previous owners make an indelible mark on everyone lucky enough to have inherited it. Porter does an excellent job of distinguishing each character's personality and social milieu.

—Laurel Corona, author
The Four Seasons, The Mapmaker's Daughter

Kate Porter's debut novel, *Lessons in Disguise,* is a masterful tale about a beautiful, wisdom-filled book and the generations that are influenced through reading its pages. Porter has blended current events, strong characters, and old-fashioned values into an unforgettable story that resonates with depth and substance. Each era is skillfully portrayed and blends with and enhances the story of the generations that follow.

—Tamara Merrill, author
The Augustus Family Trilogy

David, Andrea, and Rustin

Acknowledgements

The writing of this novel began in 1998, and countless individuals and groups have helped me along the way. I am pleased to send my deepest gratitude to those who influenced and assisted me as I am forever grateful.

To my dear husband David, daughter Andrea, and grandson Rustin, you allowed me time to make writing a priority. For your loving support, I thank you with my entire heart. Without you, I may not have the courage to send my book into the world. You inspire me every day to create and to concentrate on what is most important in life.

To my birth family, even our ancestors, you have loaned me some of your stories, at least my fictionalize versions of them, so thank you for being an interesting group who think and feel deeply. To my siblings, aunts, and a few cousins who read an earlier version, some of which ended up being deleted, your encouragement moved me forward. You gave me permission to include bits of nonfiction within my story. A special nod to my stepmother, Ellen Carey. After reading the novel, you shared your knowledge of family secrets, which opened a door to healing, enabling me to edit this into a much more cohesive story.

To my other early readers: Gene Hughes, historian, artist, teacher; Donna Ferguson, talented writer; and Kim Glossip, voracious reader, your feedback was incredibly valuable and I hope someday to find a way to repay the favor.

To the leaders of the writing workshops and classes I've attended: Nicki Toler, Jody Lisberger, Donna Boyle, and Esteban Ismael Alvarado, I want you to know that your inspired lessons were heard. My book would be much less polished without your guidance. To the countless members of those workshops and classes, as well as critique groups in Rhode

Island and San Diego, your friendship, support, and willingness to share your own writing have brought clarity, depth, and fewer "ly" adverbs and exclamation marks to my story. We've struggled through but also enjoyed this journey together. Without Nicki Toler, editor, my book would be a ragged, less-organized, shabby façade of a novel. Your mentoring and our friendship mean the world to me, and I sincerely thank you. To Delin Colon, proofreader, I appreciate your thoroughness and accuracy as well as your encouraging feedback. To Erik Johnson, artist and graphic designer, the cover would be marginal if not for you. We had a grand time working it through. I appreciate your patience in tweaking our many revisions.

To Konstellation Press, especially Cornelia Feye and Tamara Merrill, thank you for your feedback and support in getting the book to print and for pushing the process to a conclusion. I look forward to our continuing relationship and friendship and for your ongoing support through the next phase.

Finally, dear readers, thank you. Without you, my characters voices would never be heard—they live because of you.

*"Mistakes made in life are our lessons in disguise.
And sometimes, the best lessons learned
come from the worst mistakes made."*

Unknown

I

Virginia, 1820
Alden Masters

Six years of drudgery under Father's tutelage would soon be laid to rest like a corpse in a churchyard. The chiming mantle clock brought my attention away from the sleet striking the window beside me. I picked up the wooden handle and pressed the tip of the gilding tool along a chosen path. My left eye followed the edge of the line, and my breathing became shallow lest the delicate gold leaf be stirred. Such a mind-numbing chore. Still, I envisioned myself an artisan, not unlike Charles Lewis, the finest bookbinder in all of London.

This was not London, however. I was Alden Masters, American, born and bred. My father spoke little but wished upon me concentration enough to finish the books as instructed. "One line of border is the single requirement of your labor," Father said. This reminder was deserved, for I spent more time pondering the bare tree outside the shop than on my work.

Together with the other men employed by Warren Masters Bindery, we had nearly completed our latest commission: six crates of simple texts to be distributed among those wishing to better their English. Along the coast, new immigrants arrived daily. Those volumes would guide them in their quest for betterment as the uneducated masses would learn how to read and how to live in their new country.

As the population increased within Virginia, however, I

longed to flee our state. The life of a seafarer whispered in my ear as waves call to the fisherman. Feelings churned within my bosom because, at twenty-one years of age, I knew I must decide my own lot.

Still, a final work of more distinction demanded attention. After reaching into the underbelly of the worktable, I brought out the volume I had secreted away. Pressing another row of gold into a hollow, I grasped the burnisher and rubbed the book's leather until the gold became firmly embedded. Remainders I brushed into a shallow slag bowl.

On this particular volume, though the interior was the same as the others, the design had become more intricate than even I had anticipated. The interlacing lines revealed several heart shapes. As I worked, three true-lover's knots appeared, surrounded on either side by half-knots. Sailors bound for sea gave their wives rings thus knotted, so pleasure filled me in believing the design might evoke in my beloved Mary what I felt deep within my soul. As eternal as the book's cover, our hearts would remain entwined—just as our bodies had been twice within the last fortnight.

Remembering her beauty, my heart raced. A deep sigh escaped my lips and finding the slag bowl, the breath sent a cloud of glittering fragments aloft. I spun on the workbench stool to check on Father's whereabouts. Luck was on my side. "The Warden" was nowhere to be seen. My heart settled to its normal rhythm while I swept up the stray gold bits back into their place. I opened the book to its title page and read: *An Easy Standard.* What a plod of a title. Even though I had sewn the book to this fancier binding, I saw it as a plain thing, not deserving of embellishment upon its calfskin cover. Still, I held it to my chest and murmured, "You are the finest I have fashioned. Your cover bears no resemblance to your dull words. I shall steal you away in my waistcoat." My father could not know, nor would he be bothered if he knew. The book was to be my gift to her. Thoughts of Mary made me feel warm, deep inside, and although the north wind had found a path around the window's drafty sashes, sweat glistened upon my brow. "Ah Mary, you boil me to a steam," I whispered.

Unfortunately, she could not be mine. Mary was the wife of the stonemason, Mister Sherman. For a time, he seemed content with his status of cuckold. Most men did not tolerate a wife's indiscretions, so perhaps he had not been aware. But of late, there was no chance he would keep this secret, though he could be bound to an even lesser station upon the telling. Perhaps this quandary occupied his waking hours. To be without a wife was surely a pox on any man, especially one whose child could then be denied her mother. I knew the entire truth of this as I had grown up without a mother, she having been lost in the act of my birthing.

Would my beautiful Mary be disgraced and her daughter ripped from her? Along with a recent event, this question was hastening my seafaring plans. You see, Mister Sherman might not have known of our actions but for the prior Wednesday, when his early arrival home had availed to him a discovery—us, lovers abed. Mary's husband had sat in a chair just five paces away, with his calloused hands stroking his forehead, waiting for me to dress. As I left, he kicked the door shut behind me.

Mister Sherman knew.

I wiped my brow against my sleeve. Passage to England had to be found, soon. Mary's future could then be secure. Again, I

3

stared through the window and saw the sleet had stopped. So dreary, the endless winter.

The view across the narrow street held the apothecary, a tree bereft of leaves, and a short saltbox lean-to with a small stage to one side. My eyes focused through the wavy window glass and searched the hut and the darkness within. Metal accoutrements hung upon one wall, which was lit enough to view. While glancing at the recesses, I detected a slight movement then the whites of someone's eyes. The person stood, and I saw it was a child of perhaps ten years, a slave boy wrapped in a blanket.

He walked a few steps toward me until his shackled foot was caught short. We stared at each other. He seemed to be asking for something; however, I knew his ability to think for himself was limited by his inferior race. Perhaps he was cold, just as a dog might be when tied within the shelter of a barn.

I felt some pity for his plight but turned away to my task. I opened the book to its back-most page where, before stitching the final signature together, I had inserted two empty pages, a site for inscription. I picked up a nib, dipped into the inkwell, and wrote in my finest calligraphic script:

To whomever shall open my pages and read my words,
may thy life be abundant with beauty and grace.
Alden Masters, Bookbinder, Virginia, 1820

After blotting the ink, I closed the book. My hands caressed the leather. Gilt letters shone bright, even in the dusk of the lantern-lit room. When raising the book and angling it toward the light to make certain the gilding was uniform, I could find no line breaks. This book was ready for its own journey.

Glancing again at the hut, looking for the boy, I could not detect him nor any other chattel within the darkness. Perhaps he slept, for the auction would be held the next day. His fate? I would never know, for I had my own to consider.

The following morning, I sat upon a wet tree stump and felt the wintry cold seep through my wool trousers. I had carefully chosen that spot, so I could be hidden from view from Mary's front door. The previous night had seen snow, but the icy mantle had melted into a mess of soggy crumbs. The morning light thrust its arms wide to my perch, but I felt no more comfort than a hound sitting on an icy pond. With knees fully bent to where my chin rested and my hat pulled to hide my face, I believed no one could recognize me. I peered over a rock wall. My teeth chattered and a strong shiver traveled through my body. This cold did not compare to the cold of the North Atlantic. I knew I must learn to stivver through, for complaints would not be tolerated aboard ship.

My plan was to board the frigate, *Alina*, scheduled to be docked in Philadelphia on Thursday next. It would take nearly all the remaining days to ride to the coast from my home in Wilton's Hollow, Virginia. I would miss our sleepy town nestled along the Potomac. It sat where the riverbanks widened, allowing for a slow path for the water flowing toward the sea. Other shores beaconed, however.

This day, though not often aware of fashion, I wished to look my best. I had donned a washed shirt and more than combed my fingers through my brown curls. I had trimmed my beard. Alas, after all these careful preparations, a wet spot must have soaked my trousers from my icy perch. It would surely be visible upon standing. I rose to inspect.

As though beckoned by invisible messenger, at that very moment, Mister Sherman emerged from his home. Luck was on my side, however, for just as the mason came into view, when he certainly had clear sight of me, a gust of wind sped through the dooryard. His hat lost its roost. As he quickly bent to retrieve it, I ducked down to escape detection.

My heart beat in my throat. I held my breath and waited, motionless, for the man's shout. None arrived. Instead, the sound of plodding hooves came from his horse team as it wheeled around a bend and headed away toward the main road. The mason's cart laden with stones thumped behind. After silence recaptured the woods, I stood, strode to the back window of their home, and tapped. My breathing sent a plume of white vapor into the cold air.

Mary opened the door and stepped onto the outside stoop. "Why Mister Masters, what brings ya here today?" She looked about and spoke louder than necessary.

"Our lessons," I replied in equal volume.

Mary shook her head and furrowed her brow. "Elizabeth and I will be on our way to market, just now. Lessons are not to be till mornin', Mister Masters." Her auburn tresses swept across her face. Her cheeks flushed.

Moving closer, I reached into my waistcoat. The leather book felt smooth to my touch. I longed to draw her close and wished to stay through to the following morning, to lie with her just once from one dawn to the next. Lessons with Mary contained more than my teaching her to read. Older and more experienced, she had taught me in turn.

Mary's daughter, Elizabeth, appeared from behind her. The girl with the alarming pale-green eyes stepped between us and faced me. Her smile glowed so similar to her mother's that I thought of kissing her, though refrained. She was still of a tender age and about to have her tenth birthday that spring. Hints of the young woman she would soon become, however, were visible to anyone but the blind. Mary braided Elizabeth's long tresses in a thick rope then handed the end to her daughter. "Find the red ribbon, the one on my dressin' table. We'll be leavin' after Mister Masters departs."

When Elizabeth's steps could no longer be heard, I reached for Mary's hands and placed the book within the nest they formed. Whispering in her ear, I said, "You are my love. This, the best of myself, is all I possess other than the beating of my heart. They are yours."

Mary's smile fueled my desire to stay. To stay forever.

I guided her backward into the great room that, though smaller than Father's bindery, held the home's cooking, living, and eating spaces within four walls. The large hearth behind her held a smoldering fire and steaming pot. The air smelled of stew. I wrapped my arms around her waist.

"Tomorrow, kind sir—"

My ardent gaze interrupted, and my lips found hers and lingered.

She pushed me back and whispered, "We musn't." Holding up the book as though it could halt my advances, she shook her head. "We must not," she began again, louder.

I felt proud when she remembered to not combine "must" and "not," which she had learned from our last lesson on faulty diction. The desire she felt for me was obvious in her gaze and flushed face, but the familiar sound of floorboards creaking in the bedroom arrived.

7

"Thank ya kindly, Mister Masters. I been tryin' to read more words. Practicin' what you taught me. I used 'must not' in the proper way. No?" She only glanced at my gift then slipped the book into her knitting basket. She hurried to the fire to stir the stew. Red cheeks near the hearth were as common as robins in the yard after a soaking rain.

"Yes," I answered and stifled the urge to retrieve the book from its hiding place. I longed to once again declare my love. I would not be returning. I spun around to where Elizabeth now stood and said, "Your mother will teach you to read. She has learned enough to begin."

"But my papa, he not be wantin' me to learn. I'm only a girl, Mister Masters."

"Girls will someday go to university. You are, pardon me for saying this, you are clever enough to learn."

Elizabeth's gaze dropped to her practical brown shoes.

Mary's expression turned scornful. "What Mister Sherman sees fittin' is what we be expectin'. If a husband cannot be found to take her, Elizabeth will go to service. That will be her station, Mister Masters. A better lot is for someone else to hope for."

Though Mary's words brimmed with conviction, I knew they did not tell of what she believed. Her truth had been entrusted to me one afternoon as we had walked along the Potomac's eastern edge. Sunlight had streamed through the sugar-maples, the grove standing as tall as a city courthouse.

"If only I could, I'd be leavin' this life. I would," Mary had said, frustration dripping from her words. "Will Elizabeth be findin' somethin' better?" Her eyes brimmed with tears.

My hands had cupped her face. Nervous that someone might witness this advance, though, she had turned away. Her action did not stop me. "Yes, a different life shall be . . ." I began but strode quickly into position to halt her steps. Standing in front of her, I made certain our eyes became locked in a fixed stare, lest my words be forgotten. "Yes, a different life shall be hers—if she learns to read.

Kate Porter

II

1820-1825

Elizabeth Rose Sherman

My name is Elizabeth Rose Sherman, and in due time it will become clear why I must tell my story by traveling around the barn and back. Others laying claim to an equal number of years may find themselves doing the same. We see the impatient eyes of the young gazing skyward when we do so. I beg patience. For you see, in my early years, I had not one but two objects of which I could say ownership was mine, and before I speak of that dear little book, I must tell of the other—a quilt. The one Mama stitched for me.

That cherished thing began as a much smaller version of its full-grown self. It was nothing more than a swaddling blanket. Mama cut and stitched each piece out of work-worn clothing, taking care to salvage the cloth least rotted by sweat and sun, avoiding the patches made threadbare by farm use. The sides of dresses and tops of sleeves would hold fast longer than the knees of Papa's soiled trousers. Even his Sunday-best fell from grace to become farm clothes, then they died a pauper's death as cleaning rags.

Now, looking back nearly eighty years, I can imagine my five-year-old fingers poking into that quilt seam from which I pulled bits of wool. I rolled tiny rolags and stuffed them into a

toy I sewed in my first attempt at fancy-work. It resembled a
dog, not the wished-for doll. Still, I slept with that mongrel every
night and played with it each day. In the quilt, however, my
poking left a void where winter's cold would invade.

"Eliza Rose, what made ya do such a thing as this?" Mama
said upon the discovery and in the roughest tone she could
muster. When Papa arrived home she told him of my reckless-
ness.

I hid beneath the dining table but could still hear his harsh
words. "Eliza, the last sheering from your ma's black-face sheep
went into that quilt. Now I best be takin' it outa ya. Come now,
and I'll give ya but four, not the six ya deserve." His enormous
arms lifted me. The sting of Papa's strappings hurt me far deeper
than my tender flesh.

You can be certain, Elizabeth Rose Sherman never poked
again at her quilt. No sir.

I grew, and the quilt grew too. Length and width were added
as I worked and played my way through the adventures of
childhood. With each passing year, Mama also stitched scraps to
cover over tattered areas. These patches created a thicker quilt
under which I felt secure and loved. Its weight held me to bed in
swaddled dreams. Even around my shoulders, not a breath of air
could pass, its warmth as close to heaven as a young girl could
expect on this earth.

Then, on my tenth birthday, the seventh day of April in the
year of our Lord, 1820, tears streamed down my cheeks as I
unbound Mama's present. She had sewn a new cover for my
quilt. I cried at its beauty. She had made it from store-bought
cloth, the pieces going together like the stone fences Papa
built—not like those that less-skilled farmers erected throughout

our county to clear their fields. The crazy coverlet of my earlier years lay hidden beneath colors snipped directly from springtime. No happier a quilt could be seen in the state of Virginia. Not only did it contain the soft colors of lilac, pale green, and daisy yellow, but the cloth's flannel surface bade me each night to snuggle as though I were a baby lamb next to its mother.

Mama had never done such an extravagant thing before. Store-bought cloth! The Sherman family could ill afford such luxury. But Mama reminded me of Papa's near-double hay harvest that had allowed her to indulge in a bit of spending. Along with cloth, she had purchased a ready-for-Sunday hat. Yes, indeed, she looked fine in that hat. I recall it to be black velvet with a row of pansies hugging its crown. Papa bought practical items: an axe blade, iron rims for the wagon, and even though he could forge them himself, a ten-pound keg of nails. "The frivolous spending, I'll leave to the women folk," he had said, then reminded us not to expect such extravagance again.

Yes, the spending slowed to a trickle like a drought-starved creek. That is why a few years later when my thirteenth birthday arrived, I was again halted in wonder at what Mama gave to me, a mere girl. A leather-bound book. Oh, it was but a wee thing, for certain, only as big as my hand flattened upon the table. However, its interwoven design and gold lettering, the silk ribbon marker, and the soft calfskin leather combined to make it the finest thing I had ever held. A few books, not nearly as fine, could be seen at the mercantile. Those I was never allowed to hold, nor even to touch.

Papa thought it a waste of time, but Mama's sharing the joy of reading was a gift she worked hard to bestow upon me. In the beginning, two days of every week she gave an hour to her own study tutored by our neighbor, Mister Alden. His father owned the bindery where the book was made, so perhaps he even had a hand in crafting that particular volume. I do not know. What I do know is that when Mama deemed me old enough, and her own ability could inform enough, she turned her attention to me. Evenings of learning with Mama are among my most treasured memories of childhood.

The books we read most often were more than slightly worn. Many smelled of rot and made me sneeze. Others had missing pages in places where the story collapsed from their lacking. My heart sank at never knowing the end of one plot.

"No, Mama!" I shrieked. "Was the girl ever forgiven? It wasn't her fault. Was it?" I frantically asked her as well as everyone I knew. Did they own the same book? Did they know the ending? No one did. And most looked at me with scorn. They seemed to believe that I had been tainted by such a needless endeavor.

All the books Mama and I read were borrowed from Mama's tutor, our neighbor, now wait . . . his name? Not Mister Alden, no . . . Alden was not his Christian name. Was it? Memory serves me poorly in this my eighth decade; though, I can easily recall his face and the looks of adoration that passed between Mama and him. They laughed at humorous things, and I felt joy in hearing them. He often winked at me and sent a blush to Mama's cheeks quicker than a fox could raid the henhouse.

Mister Alden's father brought most of those books to our eastern shore, all the way from England, and he had them shipped inland by overland carrier. Most of the tomes succumbed to sea air and damp, making their leather as crusty as burnt toast, but they still contained words I strove to read. Mama had read aloud to me, as many as she could.

I carefully unwrapped the cloth from Mama's gift. A new book! I could hardly believe it true, yet I held it in my hands.

"This book'll show ya how finer folks speak and live," she said and smiled and wiped a stray tear from her cheek. "Someday ya'll be livin' away from me and Papa, and ya need to know more of the world than what we're able to give." She folded the cloth wrapper to save for the next occasion.

My eyes brimmed with tears. The book was so grand that I hesitated, but soon the draw of words won me over. After opening it, I read aloud through joyful tears.

All animals are fitted for certain modes of living. The birds which feed on flesh have strong claws to catch and hold small animals, and a hooked bill to tear the flesh to pieces; such is the v-u-l-t-u-r-e and the hawk.

As I was unfamiliar with vultures, the word halted in my throat. But after sounding out each letter, Mama smiled and reached over to touch my arm. I turned to Papa. He stood, walked to the door, flung it open, and said, "I'll leave you to it. I must see to . . ." He slammed the door behind him as his words fell to silence.

"What's he to see to, Mama?"

"Your papa doesn't need to be tellin' his reasons." She also stood but came to my side. Her arms enveloped me as her words hugged my soul. "Eliza, my heart's full of gladness at your likin' the book. Your readin' is comin' along nicely."

***

Why do memories I would rather forget scurry in when least expected? They seem to cling to one's heart the way lichen takes hold of a stone. One such day arrived just weeks after Mama folded the giftwrapping cloth and placed it in the oak bin kept beside her bed. No one could have known there would never again be an occasion to use the cloth.

Even now, as I did back in those tender-most years, I often find myself dreaming the same recurring nightmare. In it are contained true events that feel more horrid than the daylight memories from which they were spawned. There does indeed live in my soul a haunted place, one where I struggle to catch my parent's wagon as it disappears from sight, where imagined water swirls about my ankles, where the more I seek to escape the mire, the farther my beloved Mama and Papa drift away. I strive to scream, but muted cries fail. At long last, the promise of a new day does break the bonds of slumber. I do awaken. However, within that dream lies truth—the absolute truth of the real event.

Many mornings I tug on the quilt to bring it over my head, just as I did on that daybreak, two years after receiving the book. The sun beat through the eastern-most window, sending rays of warmth to release the comforting smells of fifteen years of slumber. Could I detect a bit of the rose-oil Mama rubbed into her hands? I imagined it to be true.

Two years had passed, you see, the longest years ever lived. I was finding it difficult to recall what Mama and Papa looked like. The color of their eyes, the shape of their noses, the reassurance of Mama's touch. Neither tintypes nor even a painted portrait existed.

"They've gone to be with God," is what everyone said, those words echoing within my empty heart. The intended comfort could not ease the pain solidified around me like stone and mortar. Yes, two years had been wrested away since the river, swollen with a flood of snow-melt, had swallowed Mama and Papa along with his wagon. The Hollander Bridge had been crushed by a sudden upriver dam break. The wagon and stone surely became rubble, adding further fury to the raging torrent.

I could still picture them waving goodbye through the misty fog as they departed the dooryard. My mind knew it to be true, yet my heart could not believe their bodies lay rotting on some far-off riverbank—their souls called home to heaven.

"They have gone to be with God, dear. Pray for them, and all will be provided." Yes, that is what Alden Masters' father had said. Yes, I am now quite certain that was his name. Alden Masters, the son of the bookbinder, the man who could halt Mama's chores and bring quick laughter. So rare had been her smiles. My parents had been such dutiful people.

Darker days followed. The thirtieth of April, 1823, arrived with a sudden gust of unseasonable air, when the Reverend Mills drove his wagon up the main road and stopped at the door. *Boom.* The loud knock resonated through to my bones. I opened the door a crack, and he burst into the emptiness of the house. "You'll be ridin' with me, young one." As he talked, thick jowls nearly obscured his mouth.

What else could be done? I knew a young girl, alone, one lacking any family, would not fare well. My station dictated a life of servitude—or worse. So I gathered my precious book, Mama's quilt, and even though my thirteen years should have guided me otherwise, I held my tattered, handcrafted doll to my bosom and awaited direction.

The Reverend's stature was short, still his presence commanded respect. He tugged at the doll until my hold was broken. "Where you're going, you won't be needin' the likes of that. Tis a fine home with fine people." He threw the doll across the room and began pulling at my quilt.

I attempted escape, to run after my toy, but his grasp on my arm was like Papa's workbench vise. That was the very moment I became convinced. Mama and Papa would not be returning home.

Seeing my arms locked around my quilt, and unknowing of the book secreted away in my apron pocket, I felt thankful when the Reverend at last relented. He emitted a grit-filled growl. I supposed that not even he could be so heartless as to take away every vestige of my home. We boarded his carriage and drove from the cottage, the one where Mama had given birth to me. Samuel and Mary Sherman had been my parents. This truth was evidenced by only two reminders. With my quilt and my book clutched close, I bestowed upon them a fondness given to only the most precious of all things.

***

Two years later, in 1825, while remembering those terrible days, I could often bury the sorrow. But on that one particular morning, no matter how ardently I tried, teardrops welled into pools and fell upon my pillow. "Enough of this," I said to no one. Peeking from beneath the quilt, I gazed toward the bed table where *An Easy Standard* lay. Sunlight glinted off its gilt-letter title. Where I had placed my book the previous evening, it remained in the morn. The thing had not vanished as had everything else held dear. I stretched my legs from under the covers and slipped out of my dressing gown. An icy dread struck as the morning air sent its cold eye looking for trouble.

"Oh no!" I yelled and snatched up a fresh pair of pantaloons, threw a camisole, petticoat, and cotton dress over my head. Since no corset was demanded of a girl of no means, this was thankfully avoided. While running from the room, I tied my apron sash behind my back. I thought of jumping atop the banister rail and pictured sailing to the bottom, but the mature age of fifteen anchored my feet to the floor. Instead, weighed down by layers of skirting, I bustled to the bottom of the stairs.

"Lord, I be late again." Those words escaped my mouth and flew heavenward.

Missus Turnbull, the mistress of the house, paced to and fro. Her wide skirt swept dust into a small storm. "Lizzy, we must not be waiting for you. We breakfast as the clock strikes six. Mister Turnbull left for town an hour ago. Sarah has started her studies. And here, you haven't even plaited your hair." She gave one of my curls a sharp tug.

I groaned.

"You will go without your morning meal," she continued. "'Tis a shame to miss Pearl's blueberry muffins, but perhaps that will teach you. Though heaven knows why I should think so." She paced, waving a finger in my direction but never squarely looked at me. If she had, my troubles would indeed have doubled, as my tongue wagged at her twice while she continued her tirade.

"Why I've a mind to call on Reverend Mills. Perhaps another placement . . ." I could feel her eyes on me then. "Lizzy, what do you have to say?"

"My name's not Lizzy." I did not return her stare.

"Well I declare, Miss Elizabeth, we shall see how you feel after a day's work in the barn." She placed her hands on her hips, the widest hips east of the Mississippi. They were nearly as broad as the doorway leading to the hall. Her skirt, in a style that may have been the most sought after, only added to her immensity. She grabbed my arm in such a violent manner as to throw me off kilter, forcing me to step upon her right foot.

"Pardon," I murmured.

"Head to that barn before I whip you," she screeched, her flabby face jiggling inches from my own. After two years of daily word lashings, I had learned to ignore Missus Turnbull. Mama would have called her an "old bully." Even Papa, who demanded that I respect my elders, would never have seen Missus Turnbull among the deserving.

I ran from the house as fast as my legs could go. The air contained a hint of autumn, but bright Virginia sunshine washed over me. Missus Turnbull did not know me to the slightest degree if she thought time in the barn to be a fitting punishment.

Near to the bottom of the hill, I slowed to a walk and twisted my hair into a long, thick braid then tied it off with a ribbon, which I had tucked into my apron pocket. Upon entering the barn, I quickly found Mister Luke, the eldest Turnbull slave. A gray halo of curly nap, along with his white beard, framed his face, reminding me that I was in the company of a living saint. He stood combing Essie's mane. She was a black mare with none but a single flaw, a stray white spot painted on her cheek. Her eyes shone with a friendly spirit. She was the one I most often pretended was mine.

"Mornin', Mister Luke. I'm to be helpin' today. Hope I won't be a bother." Essie nuzzled into my arm. "Oh, Essie, no apples today, sweet thing," I said and stroked her soft nose. "You's never a bother to me, child." He smiled and handed me a comb. "Essie and me been wonderin' if ya'd be out today. Now tell me, did ya get up late, or did ya forget to make yer bed?"

I moaned but combed Essie's mane. "Both, I'm afraid. Mistress will be havin' herself a conniption when I go in at noon time. I'll sneak upstairs and make the bed 'fore she notices."

"Ain't no way to fool an old fool like the missus. I's afraid ya got to learn to turn the other cheek." He spun his backside to me, showing which cheek he was meaning. "Is what all us old slaves got to live with. Laughin' be the way of it. When ya get on yer own at night, ya need be lettin' out a good howlin'. Why some nights, ya can hear the whoopin' from the Wilson farm clean down here, though it be a ways up the road. Those Wilson fellers, they has loads of mighty fine howlin' to do, after the way they's been treated." He continued onto Essie's other side then after a pause added, "We's lucky here. Mister Turnbull be a fair man."

At the sound of approaching footsteps, we turned toward the door to see Willy.

"Good day, Willy T.," I said.

"I was hopin' ya'd be in trouble soon," he said, barely glancing in my direction. He had turned the corner to fourteen and had finally begun to grow. There was a hint of whiskers atop his lip. Still as stovepipe-thin as ever, he attempted to master his own voice. Most times, he spoke in mere whispers to hide the sharp squawks that threatened. The frequency of these events was diminishing. Soon, the transition to manhood would be complete since his voice promised it to be so.

"Let's set to cleanin' this place," I said, "so your uncle won't be doin' it all himself." I traded the comb for a rake then followed Willy T. who was heading off to the next stall with a shovel in his hand.

Much satisfaction could be found in the work. It was no small change from the normal dreariness of learning what was expected of a young lady: stitchery, setting a fine table, proper grooming, and in what seemed like an afterthought, letters and numbers. Mama had begun to teach me, but as my instruction had ended so abruptly, I still had much to learn in that regard. In the barn, however, I could give in to feeling joy, which in those days was indeed a rare flower. I can recall that day as if it were yesterday: the cool, breezy air; the smell of hay so sweet; the ease I felt amongst friends.

I had never known a slave before living with the Turnbulls. At fifteen, I was old enough to hold strong opinions on such things. Owning another person seemed plainly wrong. Against the Bible, of that I was certain. In a way, Mister Turnbull owned me as well. All of us who toiled in the barn that day knew our lives were not our own.

A day was approaching, as quickly as a steed without a rider, when I would most likely be turned out. But poor Luke and Willy T., well, they were destined to die working the Turnbull estate as so many before them had—Willy's mama and papa, and Mister Luke's wife who died among the corn stalks with an unborn baby still in her belly. Countless generations before them had died under the cruel hands of Mister Turnbull's father and grandfather. The passage of time had not diminished their cruelty. I had heard the stories and knew of the barbarous dividing of families. Knowing the sting of my own losses, I could not wish them upon any soul, not even upon these people I'd been told didn't have souls. Weakened by years of toil, some had succumbed to the fever. Perhaps most had just curled up and died from a broken heart.

Willy T. and I fell into silence. Ours was a comfortable kind of friendship, the best kind, where the clutter of chatter was rendered unnecessary. Now and again, I looked up to catch him staring at me. His gaze would dart away as a fly does when swished by Essie's tail.

Mister Luke continued his way through the stable, giving each of the twelve horses his full attention. He had a way with them. All seemed to sense he would be firm but gentle. The old man needed them to be gentle in return, for his fingers had become twisted with age. Now and again, loud thuds could be heard as he dropped the brush to the floor. "I ain't be worryin' bout a little pain at my age. I's fifty after all, Miss Beth," he said. I stared at his mouth. The three missing teeth were always a distraction.

Oh, the things that bother a young girl. Having passed that fifth-decade mark myself and the next three too, I know the pain of my own rheumatism, a burden on my years of late.

But I must say, those infirmities didn't slow Mister Luke down. Even Titus stood still to allow him to comb him clean. Titus was the only brute in the barn. Rarely ridden and simply stored, he seemed to be rotting. No one had set his bridle, since he took off with Missus Turnbull in tow a few years before, her carriage nearly flipping as it flew up the long maple-lined drive. She had threatened to shoot Titus herself, but Mister Turnbull had put a halt to her empty words. "Woman, I've no doubt you drove him to it. Now stop your whining," he had said right there in front of me, not even softening his words for my young ears. His stinging remarks had set my skin to shivering, but he got the job done. For that I was thankful.

When I finished mucking out the last few stalls, I searched for Willy T. who would often sneak away and hide in order to goad me into hunting for him. I soon discovered him lying in the fresh hay he had spread across the floors of the milking stalls. The barn's back door stood agape and Willy T. gazed skyward.

"Someday I be leavin' here," he said. This nearly broke my heart as the truth seemed to be that he could never be free.

I made certain no one was within sight then flopped down beside him. After sinking into the scratchy hay, I noticed dark clouds were gathering, appearing as menacing as shadowy thoughts collected in the mind. Reaching toward him, I took ahold of Willy T.'s hand. Our fingers entwined as I brought his hand to my lips. I gave it a feathery kiss and felt him tense, but soon he relaxed. His fear, normally so close to the surface, seemed to melt.

"I know you'll leave, and I as well, Willy T.," I whispered back, attempting to believe my words.

We lay side-by-side while I looked down at his fingers mingling with my own. His hand, as rough and hardened as tree bark, made mine appear white and fragile like that of a fine lady's, which is forever-gloved. Bringing my other hand up, I spread our fingers and held his hand between mine to compare. They were nearly the same length but his was certainly larger, stronger. My thoughts drifted to Papa and our final embrace. Those arms had been strong too. A powerful feeling of longing flooded in, mixing with memories of being protected and loved. Someday, might I be away from this place? Would I find a man as strong as Papa? Too bad that man couldn't be Willy T. We were already the best of friends. But he could never be Willy T.

"Do you ever want to have a family, Willy Turnbull?" I asked, my gaze moving to the clouds.

After a bit of silence he answered. "Yup, I does. But not 'til I's a freeman. I's lived it and couldn't stand by watchin' this happen to none of mine. Bad 'nough seein' Uncle Luke gettin' tore up."

"You'll get there. You'll be free," I said. "I'm believin' it all the way to the softness between my toes." I don't know where my conviction came from, but the wish was pure.

He squeezed my hand, stood up, then reached down to lift me toward him. Our eyes met as he plucked a few pieces of chaff from my hair. His fingers brushed my skin as tender as music sings through a summer's night. My heart skipped about in my chest, and I am certain my face flushed as red as it ever could, but then he abruptly let go and stepped away.

"Best be gettin' to it," he said and picked up the shovel.

I watched him depart then continued to work where I had left off. The rest of the morning passed at a stubborn pace. Time announced itself frequently as hunger rumbling across my belly. Even though I welcomed time in the barn, the gnawing grew as biscuits do in a hot oven.

Ah, hot biscuit. At long last, the supper bell rang.

"Good luck to ya, Miss Beth. Remember what I tells ya," Mister Luke said, slapping his backside. I smiled and glanced at Willy T. who poked at the dirt with his brogans. They headed toward the crude shack they called home. I turned and plodded up the hill to the Turnbull's three-story brick house.

***

Missus Turnbull and Sarah sat stick-straight in the belief that slouching was as sinful as greeting a man in the parlor without a chaperone. I attempted to slip unnoticed into my chair. Dinah, the cook's daughter, swirled about the table in an elegant dance. Though she listed to one side from the weight of the iron stew pot, her skirt moved to her internal music. She grasped the ladle with graceful fingers and served up the steaming liquid into each bowl. Looking at her, I smiled a silent thank you. The thick broth laden with venison, carrots, onions, and parsnips spread over the daisies of the Turnbull's everyday china. The aroma reached my nose as the floral design disappeared.

A basket of golden biscuits, a plate of butter, and a pot of raspberry preserves waited on the table, an offering that increased the desire for food to nearly beyond my control. I swallowed hard and forced my hands to reside in my lap.

"So there you sit." Missus Turnbull spat her words, each syllable an opportunity for venom.

"Yes Ma'am." My gaze veered away from the food.

"Go clean up. Do not dally." She waved her hand toward the kitchen.

I rushed to the servants' basin while Pearl, the cook, stood nearby plucking a large goose.

"Ya has hay in yer hair, Miss Beth," she said, wiping her hands on her apron. "Keep to yer washin'. I'll tend to it."

"Thank ya," I said, watching the clear water before me mix with grit from my hands and face turning it to a murky gray.

Pearl pinched out the bits and tossed them aside while I peered at my reflection in the looking glass. My pale skin and freckled cheeks looked clean enough for the matters at hand. "I'm as hungry as a hog. Pearl, the stew smells good 'nough for the President. What's his name, ya told me it just yesterday? Monroe?"

Pearl nodded. "That be right, Miss Beth. None other than Mister James Monroe."

I smoothed my dress with my damp hands and sped back to the dining room and dropped back onto my chair.

"Thank ya for waitin' on me, Ma'am," I said.

"I am not waiting 'on' anyone. I was waiting 'for' you. Your faulty diction is a curse upon this house."

I might have said something in turn, but since no response appeared to be required, I chose to keep my lips tight for fear I should err, yet again. Moreover, blathering was about the last thing on my mind. The stew's aroma washed over me as though I'd jumped in for a swim.

At long last, Missus Turnbull bowed her head and clasped her hands. "We thank thee, Oh Lord, for the gifts of thy bounty. Let us be ever mindful that a bad life will make for a bad end. We must to live well so we might die well. Amen."

Missus Turnbull's blessings never strayed far from a dose of vinegar. I mumbled an "amen" and shoveled in some stew, barely taking a breath between mouthfuls. Halfway to done, I glanced up to meet Missus Turnbull's glare. A stern look, equal to that of her mother's, was thrown in my direction from Sarah. Perfect Miss Sarah Turnbull.

"Apologies, Ma'am." I slowed to a more civilized pace.

Dinah waltzed about the table, pouring milk, then planting

biscuits with silver tongs upon each of our plates. Her body was so slender and lithe. If caught in a gentle breeze, I imagined she would twirl away to the clouds. Though nearly of the same age, Dinah and I were nothing alike. I was large-boned and a little too tall and took after Mama who would never have been called fair. Mama's kind ways had offset what she lacked in appearance, and I hoped to someday lay claim to a bit of her character.

I buttered a biscuit and slathered on a thick layer of preserves. Ah, raspberry, that splendid mixture of sweet and tart. Dealing with pesky pips was only a slight price to pay for the pure pleasure of the flavor. The biscuit tasted fine to be certain, but I saw it simply as the means by which the preserves arrived at my mouth.

Every now and again, perhaps once a fortnight, I had snuck to the kitchen. Eating a spoonful was always my intent; however, there had been a time when I had eaten an entire jar. Afraid of being found out, I had hid the empty vessel under the back stoop. No one seemed to take notice, so later, when fortune showed me a way, I pirated another full jar from the pantry and wove a path through the night to the barn. To this day, I can recall the disbelief on Mister Luke's face. His smile was so wide that if his ears could have, they would have joined in. That grin made me forget my initial shock at finding him and Willy T. still toiling by lantern light. They opened that jar and ate the contents at a most furious pace. Over the years when I have searched in vain for sleep, I have engaged that particular memory. Of late, there are too many such fitful nights.

"Lizzy? Elizabeth...Elizabeth!" Missus Turnbull's near shouts called my attention back from the biscuits. "The rest of your day will be spent in study. I am weary of the way you talk.

You do not speak better than the ignorant ones among us. Listen to Pearl and Dinah for such evidence."

I glanced at Dinah who stood with her back against a wall, awaiting her call to clear. I hated Missus Turnbull for talking so. My own cheeks turned red, as though it were I who had thrown that hateful comment. Did she not know Dinah could think for herself? That she could hear? Mister Turnbull was no better. Dinah did not flinch; though, with each acrid comment, her sweet insides must have shriveled.

"Ma'am, I beg forgiveness, but I didn't finish up the chores. Luke will be expectin' me. I could start fresh in the mornin' with my studies."

Missus Turnbull sneered. "In the 'mornin', as you say, more chores will need to be done, the first being the ones you did not choose to do this morn-I-N-G. Cleanliness walks hand in hand with Godliness. Remember this Lizzy, lest your soul be buried deeper than your earthly body when you are called home to your maker." She tugged at the lace collar noosed around her thick neck. "You are fifteen," she shrugged but continued, "so we must do our part to endeavor a job well done. Therefore, you will study that book of yours. I took the liberty and read it myself. Don't just read the words, Lizzy. Think!"

I pictured her holding my precious book, and my blood boiled. How dare she look through my things?

Missus Turnbull hoisted herself by leaning on the creaking table. "You are excused, girls. And Lizzy, Sarah shall be your tutor. You are the elder by three years, but my own daughter is more learned in such things. Off you go." With a spin of her heavy skirt, Missus Turnbull left the room by stepping sideways through the door since her girth barely missed the doorjamb.

"My name ain't Lizzy," I said, knowing my words meant nothing.

***

Table I

ba be bi bo bu by

This simple lesson was already behind my level of reading, so I grumbled and flipped to the middle of the book. I chewed on the tail of my braid—a habit picked up while waiting for dinner, waiting for someone to dictate what I must do, waiting for my life to begin. The rarely read pages of *An Easy Standard* opened, and I began to read.

Table XIII
Lessons of easy words, to teach children to read, and to know their duty.

Be a good child; mind your book; love your school, and strive to learn. Tell no tales; call no ill names; you must not lie, nor swear, nor steal.

As for those boys and girls that mind not their books, but play with such as tell tales, tell lies, curse, swear, and steal, they will come to some bad end, and must be whipt till they mend their ways.

I glanced at Sarah, who sat squarely before a pedestaled frame, concentrating on her embroidery sampler. With dainty fingers and pouting mouth, she was a girl I both envied and loathed in the same moment. Fashioned in pink cotton, her dress was adorned with eyelet collar and cuffs. Not a speck of dirt, nor even lint, could be seen.

I asked, "Sarah, have ya ever been whipt?"

Startled, she dropped her needle to the floor then glared at me. "Pardon?" She bent over to search for the fallen needle. "What are you asking of me?" Each strand of her hair was contained in perfectly aligned ringlets. I supposed nothing could disturb the perfection, evidence of her birthright.

"It says here in my readin', if ya swear or steal, ya must be whipt till ya mend your ways."

Sarah paled and flopped to her knees to look beneath her chair. Having found the stray item, she placed the needle between her front teeth and gathered her skirt with one hand and pulled herself up with the other. "My muver ant fuver have not reashon to whip me." The needle wagged up and down with every word. I became distracted by the hand nearest to me. Sarah never chewed her fingernails.

"It also says the same for tellin' lies," I said, peering down at my ragged nails. "Are ya sure you've avoided a whippin' your entire life?"

"I do not have to tell you that." Sarah blushed and re-threaded her needle.

"No, ya don't. But we're stuck in this dreary room. We could be findin' some pleasure in talkin'."

"Mother says we are to study. You must quit your 'talkin' about 'whippin' and such, and start adding 'Gs' to the end of your words." She smoothed her skirt and straightened her back.

"Oh Sarah, life ain't always the way your mama has it planned. She loves ya sure enough, but there's more to life than embroidery and fancy dishes." I placed the ribbon marker within its pages, closed my book, and slid it into my apron. Through the window, I could see the clouds still threatening, but no rain had yet fallen. "When was the last time ya went runnin' outside, free and easy? Ya must remember the sweetness of fresh air in your hair and dirt in yer toenails." I gazed toward the window where an unfettered view of the orchard, and beyond it the sloping field lined by trees, curved away. The terrain beckoned.

I whispered, "Why don't we sneak out and visit my Essie."

Sarah's eyes grew wide. "If I were to listen to you, Elizabeth Sherman, I would be in some fine trouble. The thought of Mother being mad enough to whip me sends me a chill. I cannot—"

"Oh hush, Sarah Turnbull. Ya just think too much, that's all." I stood, grabbed her dainty hand, and pulled her off the chair.

"Come on. No one'll see us if we go out the back way."

Before Sarah could utter another word in protest, we were outside flying down the hill away from the house. We ran under the apple tree growing a few hundred yards from the back door, and without missing a step, I snatched an apple with my free hand. A low branch caught a ringlet of Sarah's hair.

"Let's make a run for the woods," I called over my shoulder.

The midafternoon clouds cast a silent shadow on the forest. The cover of trees, thick with healthy underbrush, did not beckon us into its fold but nudged us along its rim. Placing one foot after the other down steep terrain, we wove our way through brambles and tall grasses, until finally, the stone wall border forced us to turn toward the barn.

"Come on, Sarah. We can make it." Panting from the effort, I slowed to a brisk walk still pulling Sarah after me. Having followed along the forest's edge, we had traveled past the barn, but thankfully our approach would bring us in from the rear; though, we had to climb two stiles to do so. Hidden from view of the house, I felt some relief. But still, the barn's back doors were some distance away. The muffled thudding in my breast was an immutable reminder of a growing dread. In my moment of bold spontaneity, I had given no consideration to the uphill trip we would eventually need to travel. Time had sped by at a furious clip. The shadows had indeed grown long.

"Slow down," Sarah moaned. Tiny beads of sweat glistened on her upper lip.

I quickly bounded over the last stile and turned to watch Sarah. She raised one foot to the top of the bridge, looked up, and turned slightly. Her foot found a protruding rock, and without warning, she was airborne, her body shoving me backward. We landed in a ruffled heap. She rested on the protective blue bed of my skirting. One knee missed the edge, however, and hit a moist patch of dirt.

"Mother will have me," she said, as we both stared at the imperfection on her dress. Several ringlets had strayed along her left cheek, giving her a lopsided look.

"We'll think about how to clean that later. Come on." Wiping my hand against her dress, the smudge remained. It was a large, brown blotch on a field of pale pink rosebuds. When we finally arrived at the barn's back door, we picked our way through the cow stalls, pushing the milkers aside as best we could. Sarah's shoes, indoor satin slippers, accumulated dirt around their edges, further evidence of the trouble I was heaping upon myself. Then she stepped on a fresh cow patty.

"Eeew," she shrieked, her shrill voice sending my hands to

my ears.

Arriving in Essie's stall, I ran my hand along the animal's soft flank. "There, there, easy now, girl. Look what we has for ya." I handed the apple to Sarah. "The two of ya can get acquainted. I'll go see if Mister Luke's nearby."

Upon my leaving, I heard Sarah's loud whisper, "Elizabeth Rose Sherman, come back here at once!"

I ignored her pleas and peeked into each stall while moving through the breadth of the barn. The floorboards creaked with displeasure. The old building felt as cold as a root cellar. A dog barked in the distance, sending its voice winding through the knotholes in the outside wall. Squinting through one such hole, I attempted to see if anyone was about, but the view held only trees and rocks.

"Where ya headed?"

I jumped at the unexpected touch and harsh tone of those words. "Oh, lordy, Mister Luke. Ya half scared me out o' my skin." In turning around, though, I discovered that the man in front of me was not Mister Luke, but a stranger. "Sorry, you're not Luke," I said.

"Well, I's not sorry one lil' bit. Why, he be dead and buried long 'fore me." The man bent over to pick up a shovel.

I shrunk back, worried he might use the tool as a weapon. When he stood upright he gawked at me. Standing as tall as I could, it was plain to see this foe would not be hampered by someone of my stature. His shoulders were broad and his neck thick. By not wearing a shirt, his muscled torso displayed row after row of whipping welts. The long bumps of skin were painful to see, though they appeared to be healed. He also wore an angry scar across his face, and his nose was half gone. As my imagination conjured up several horrid ways in which that particular wound could have been inflicted, I winced. Once or twice from afar, I had seen a person that could have been this man. He had been splitting cordwood. "Pardon, aren't you Dinah's papa?" I asked, relaxing just a bit.

"Yes, Ma'am. And yer sure to be Miss Beth." He bowed so low his hand swept the floor. "I's Jax, that's what my Pearl calls me, and it seems to be stuck to me like pine pitch." With one eyebrow raised, he mirrored my stare. "Now, where is you headed?"

"We were just comin' to feed Essie some apple, and Sarah fell, and now I be in more trouble than—"

"Slow down, Miss Beth. Is we talkin' 'bout Sarah, the Massa's young'un?"

"That's right, me and Sarah, we should be studyin' our words right now, but the day was callin' to me. How am I to get her back without Missus Turnbull whippin' me?" I felt like crying but held fast.

"Well, whippin' be somethin' Jax knows 'bout. There won't be no whippin' today. I'll get ya back home."

Back home. His words flung me afar, to my mama's end-of-the-day comforts. "You're safe at home, Elizabeth. Sleep now, tomorrow's another day." She had whispered those words every night, unless of course I had been the cause of some real trouble. How I longed to be back in her arms. Back home, if only to hear her again. A tear fell from my cheek, and I gazed down to where it landed and watched as it disappeared into a hoof-worn plank.

Just then Sarah came into view, followed by Mister Luke and Willy T. "Lizzy! Elizabeth Sherman, we must go home!" With each of Sarah's words, her eyes roamed wide in an attempt to cast a silent alarm. I was certain she had never been surrounded by so many unfamiliar black faces. She continued, "At any moment, Mother will be coming to find us. I want to…to save her the trip. We must go now!"

"Oh, Sarah, your mama won't be comin' to save ya, not this time. Besides, there ain't nothin' to save ya from. Luke and Willy T. are my friends. And Jax, here, was sayin' he'd find us a way back to the house."

I reached a hand toward her, but Sarah slapped it away and seared me with her glare.

"God willin'," Jax said, and everyone turned to him and waited for his plan. He thrust his glance from one corner to the next, until all corners of the barn had been covered by his searching thoughts. Minutes passed as we waited for the rafters to reply.

Hope dwindled.

"I think I has the idea," Willy T. said, interrupting the silence. "How 'bout we go apple pickin', Jax? I think there be near to a cart-full close to the big house. We load Miss Beth and Miss Sarah in, and haul 'em up. Bring a load in for Pearl." He stepped into an alcove and rolled out a little two-wheeled cart.

Feeling some relief, I stepped forward and blurted out, "Willy T., I think you're the smartest person I've ever met." My hands, as though they had a will of their own, simply reached out and found themselves resting upon his shoulders. I looked directly into his eyes and continued, "Maybe ya can't read, but ya think quicker than any of the rest of us. That's what I believe."

He bristled and stood straight as a dried cornstalk. I was certain he'd quit breathing.

"Elizabeth Sherman! Of course Niggers can't read!" Sarah's shout brought my attention back to an awareness of everyone's discomfort.

I dropped my arms and looked toward her. "Maybe not, but no one else has got a better idea. We best get back before anyone notices we're gone." I spun around.

A collective sigh was exhaled. Without hesitation, Jax and Willy T. wiped off the cart. Leaning his weight into the task, Luke slid the large barn door open along its track. He fetched a milking stool and placed it on the floor near the rear of the cart. As if he were a coachman about to aid a lady aboard a proper carriage, he extended his left hand and bade us to come aboard. I made a slight curtsy, gave Luke my hand, and stepped up gracefully. Sarah gathered her pink skirting in both hands and attempted to get in without assistance. The stool wobbled. With nothing to balance against, she fell backward into Jax's open arms.

Just then the clomping of hooves arrived, and to everyone's horror, Mister Turnbull rounded the corner into the barn atop his dapple gray.

My heart leapt to my throat.

In a moment of astonishing composure, Jax didn't drop Sarah, but eased her to the floor as though she were his infant being laid to bed. Sarah's shock was evidenced by her inability to extend her legs to stand. She looked like a dollop of pink foam spilled upon the floor. Luke came forward to take the reins from Mister Turnbull, and Willy T. stepped backward into a shadow.

"Oh, sir, you scared us all half to death. This be my fault," I said, jumping off the cart. "Jax was just gettin' Sarah into the cart. Isn't that right?" I glared down at her for a response, but she

37

the same fate? I had no avenue by which to know. Instinctively, my hands plunged into my apron pocket, hoping to be soothed by the familiar. The book rested against my thigh. But then, I remembered what I had read that very morning.

"Sarah, is he goin' to . . . must they . . . must they be whipt? Oh, Sarah, they were only tryin' to help. Why didn't you . . ." My legs gave out and I dropped to the ground.

"Elizabeth, did you consider what just happened to me? Those sweaty, black-skin arms, that disgusting chest. He touched me." She wiped her brow with her dirty hand, leaving a smear across her forehead. An exaggerated shiver traveled across her body. She then turned square to the hill and continued her assent. "I will call on Pearl to draw a bath. Sit there if you must. I will not be part of any more of your trouble, Elizabeth Sherman."

With her words fading from my ears, my emotions descended into a twilight that matched the approaching night. My mind was set adrift with violent thoughts. No glimmer of promise nor enough strength to stand could be found. As rain began to fall in earnest, small rivulets collected and amassed loose soil in a downhill rush. Despair washed over me, and I curled into a ball in the deepening mire.

Perhaps I will drown, I thought. If I do, I will not care.

***

Time stopped. A persistent drone pulled me deeper into a wet fog of fear. I had no way of knowing how long I lay there.

Then, hands lifted me from the mud. As I was slung over someone's shoulder, a bone wedged into my ribs. My body hung as limp as tree moss. My hands thumped against a man's back while he trudged up a hill. Off to the side, a morsel of light grew, and with each step, bits of that light shone on the cloth where my cheek rested. Through squinted eyes, I stared at how the cloth's warp and weft crossed each other. A door shut. Again I swung back and forth. We scaled stairs. The familiar sound from the hall clock struck the half hour and chimed through a world of shadows. A dark silhouette placed me on a dry blanket, slid my wet dress over my head, and lifted me onto a bed.

I felt a hand brush away my hair. "Rest now." The whispered voice seemed to set me free, so I closed my eyes and floated into an enveloping slumber.

***

Some hours later, my eyes opened. Darkness still claimed the night, but a glow from a window sent blue moonlight dancing across the bed and found its final resting place on my bedside table. It lit a protective doily and the book, which rested atop the lacy edge.

An Easy Standard, the gilt lettering announced. Someone had removed it from my pocket. I could no longer hear any rain. The clock chimed five. I closed my eyes for just one more moment.

Next thing I knew, my heart was beating wildly. I thrust my feet to the floor. Sunlight poured into my room. "Oh, beans in a bucket shop, I only just closed my eyes." I groaned, forgetting for only a moment what had transpired the previous night. My teeth set to chatter as the cold October air hit. I was wearing my nightdress. Someone had redressed me without my knowing. I blushed picturing the man's coat, the man's silhouette, and hearing his whispered words. I quickly changed into new sit-down-upons and donned my red dress with the golden stripes, thinking that perhaps the bold color would make me stronger.

A paper sat atop my book that read: "Stay in your room until you are called."

I needed something to hold my attention, for dread sat nearby awaiting any calm to crumble. Such worry lay within my breast. I picked up the book. The poor thing was drenched. The ribbon marker was blotched with mud, and the leather cover felt like a soggy old shoe. A few pages in the front were even soaked through. Tears clouded my eyes as I gingerly pried the title page away from the front end paper. It tore in two. My stomach retched as I laid the half-leaf on my table and turned a few more pages. I felt some relief upon discovering that a little further in, everything appeared unsullied. How could I have been so careless?

Cradling the book in my hands, I flipped through the endless lists of words used to drill pronunciation skills. They wore headings such as "difficult and irregular monosyllables" and "easy words of four syllables, accented on the second." However, on page ninety four, I recognized the engraving of a man lying on the ground with a large menacing bear lurking nearby. A second fellow hid behind a small tree. Looking at that picture previously, I had feared such a scene, so I never had read the story. Believing that the fable could take my mind from my troubles, however, I chose now to read.

The Bear and the Two Friends

Two friends, setting out together upon a journey,
which led through a dangerous forest, mutually

promised to assist each other, if they should happen to be assaulted. They had not proceeded far, before they perceived a bear making towards them with great rage.

There were no hopes in flight; but one of them, being very active, sprung up into a tree; upon which the other, throwing himself flat on the ground, held his breath and pretended to be dead, remembering to have heard it asserted that this creature will not prey upon a dead carcass. The bear came up, and after smelling to him some time, left him, and went on.

When he was fairly out of sight and hearing, the hero from the tree called out—Well, my friend, what said the bear? He seemed to whisper you very closely. He did so, replied the other, and gave me this good piece of advice: Never associate with a wretch, who in the hour of danger, will desert his friend.

I inhaled sharply. Tears welled once more and clung to my lids. "Please Lord, let them be unharmed." I began to pace, then finally stopped to peer out toward the orchard. Though the red fruits hung ripe, not so much as a glimmer of hope could be found amongst that sweet promise, until a glimpse of someone drifting through the grove caught my eye. At first, there was no discerning who it was only that their clothing was that of a slave, drab in color. It was a female. She moved closer to the house, picking apples. As Dinah's graceful form came into full view, she glanced upward.

Our eyes met and she waved, then smiled.

I thought that surely she wouldn't be happy to see me, if she knew me to be the cause of her papa's whippin'. Did she not know? I waved back as footsteps approached in the hall. A loud knock came at my door, followed by words hissed as if by an angry cat.

"Lizzy, come now, to the library." It was Sarah.

"I'll be right along," I replied, watching Dinah place the fruit she picked into a bushel basket. I tried to motion to her that I must go, but she did not seem to understand. I turned away and left the room.

I had caught a glance of the library once, when a door had been left ajar, but never had I been invited to enter its woody interior. As my skirt swished along the hall, the absurdity of being so overdressed made me wish I had chosen the everyday gray Swiss dot. Glancing down at the gold brocade stripes, I saw the damp book remained in my right hand.

The cavernous room smelled of lemon oil and musty paper. I stifled a sneeze. A sliver of light shone through a break in the floor-to-ceiling draperies, and dust swirled in the beam as it forced its way through the darkness.

"Sit down," Mister Turnbull boomed. He did not stand when I entered as was his custom when any female approached. My eyes adjusted to the darkness enough to see him motion to a chair. Sarah and Missus Turnbull sat together on a bench before the fireplace where a few embers glowed. There was little warmth to the room. I thought of how a small fire could never heat a room such as this, especially with the bitter cold emanating from the Turnbull family. Their stares stabbed icicles into my heart.

"I have come to a decision. You are to leave the estate." Mister Turnbull's chair faced the library windows. No charity could be seen in his expression. He held a book in his lap. It was a large volume with lettering and decorations gilded along its spine, and his right hand stroked it as he talked. "Soon you will be sixteen, the age beyond which a young woman of your station will have any hope of marriage. You are not like us, though Missus Turnbull tried to teach you to no avail. It has been folly to think we could mold you into someone you are not. You were raised by John Sherman, an honest man to be certain, but your mother's people were thick with trouble. None of them even saw fit to take you. Missus Turnbull fears there is too much of the Callahan in you."

I'd never heard anyone speak ill of my mother's family. My remaining determination scurried away.

Mister Turnbull stood and straightened his waistcoat. He positioned his book on a platform, one not unlike a dais found in a well-established church. His hair looked like waves on a rocky sea, and his eyebrows drew together forming one long line. Watching his face, I felt unable to breathe, but I knew I must find the strength to speak. I held tightly onto my book. Its words echoed within me. I would not forsake my friends.

"Sir? Please. I'm . . . if I must pay this price, then, so be my penance, but—"

"That is not all!" he interrupted. "My daughter has been grievously molested. One of our most valuable slaves, oh what is his name . . . Willy, yes, Willy Turnbull must pay for this indefensible act. He is to be sold at tomorrow's auction."

"No, I beg you! Please, Sarah, tell them how—"

"She has done so," Missus Turnbull interjected. She walked to the heavy draperies and swung them to the side. The light slapped my face and she continued. "He laid black, filthy hands upon her White Christian skin. Surely, even you cannot condone such an action. For many years, she has felt his eyes upon her. Thrice, I have caught him looking through this very window."

I jumped up. "No. That didn't happen. He didn't touch her. I swear it on my mama's grave."

Sarah stood up as well and said, "How would you know? You left me. Oh, Mother . . . I was alone." She collapsed back onto the bench, shaking with exaggerated sobs.

"But I do know. It's Willy T. He'd never—"

"That is all," Mister Turnbull thundered. His stare bore straight into me. There seemed to be no distance between us. "What is done is done. Go now. You will be leaving this evening."

My glance shifted from him, to Sarah, then to her mother. How could this be? Where would they take me? And Willy T. was to be sold? I felt my stomach begin to heave. I swallowed hard and tasted only bitterness. Mister Luke could surely die from the loss. My eyes overflowed. Shame and anger stifled my voice, leaving my throat to burn with muted sorrow.

"Go now and pack your trunk. We shall call you in time." Mister Turnbull lowered his eyes to what I assumed was the family bible. He pounded his hand upon it as a judge might slam his gavel. "You will learn to accept this day as you would any other. I prayed for guidance, and this is what I know to be God's will."

No words were worth the breath it took to utter them. Not if "God's will" was on his side.

I trudged upstairs to my room then changed out of the red and gold dress into the more practical gray one. The chore of packing my steamer trunk took over my attention. The red brocade and the green calico both had long sleeves, which I stuffed with stockings. The other two dresses, a pair of slippers, and leather ankle-boots I wrapped in my light summer cape. Knotting my black bonnet under my chin, I set out my warmest winter cloak then packed a few personal items: my underclothes; the bone-handled button hook; the tortoise-shell comb and brush set, which had been the only Christmas present I received from the Turnbulls. The handles were silver with cherubs dancing and strumming harps. These I nestled in a woolen scarf.

Then, smoothing its surface with loving hands, I stowed away my quilt that still smelled of rose oil, the essence of better days.

***

I waited.

Twice tiptoeing into the hall and peeking down the stair-well, I confirmed that my view only reached to the front foyer. Muffled talking was heard, but whose voices they were and what was said could not be discerned. The angry tones, however, pushed my dread deeper. The view from the window beckoned while the clock struck each quarter hour. The day turned into the sort that all northern Virginians covet. Any hint of summer seemed to have withered overnight, every leaf now painted gold or crimson. Its beauty was lost to me, however, as my vision became blurred with tears. Even eyeing the puffy clouds overhead, which usually brought contented memories of hanging laundry with Mama, sent my thoughts to conflicted feelings. Where would I be tomorrow? Would my lot be worse? What of Willy T. and the rest of them? Not knowing was torture of the same ilk I had known only when my parents had gone missing. The wait for word of Mama and Papa had lasted two entire days, the longest hours I ever spent on this earth. The impact of Mister Turnbull's words rivaled the thunder that had exploded in my head when I had learned my parents' fate.

How could turning me out and selling Luke's last relative be God's will? I ran to my bed, retrieved the thunder jug from under it, and relieved my body of any nourishment it contained. After wiping my face and rinsing my mouth into the washbasin, I flopped onto the bed and snatched my book from the table. Opening it, the leather cover shifted along its spine. The glue, meant to last forever, had let go. A tear fell from my cheek and landed on an open page. I quickly wiped it away. Once again, the words drew me in as I read aloud.

Example III

Words formed by adding ing to verbs, and called Participles.

allay	*allay-ing*
beat	*beat-ing*
fight	*fight-ing*
faint	*faint-ing*

I spat out each word, stabbing the "ings" with my teeth clenched. "That is for you, Sarah Turnbull. I may drop my Gs, but I don't drop from the truth like you. A lyin' milksop, that's what you are," I said, hoping she would hear but knowing she could not.

Leafing from one page to the next, I willed the book to remain intact. The gutters creaked as the leather floated upon the book like an ill-fitted glove. I brushed dried soil from the ribbon marker and swung it near to the back of the book. Two bold words leapt from the page:

OF ANGER

Yes, in a swamp of anger I swam but knew my heart would soon return to gut-wrenching fear. With the book clasped in a firm grip, I felt a snapping somewhere under the cover. A stitch must have let go. I returned to the words.

Q. Is it right ever to be angry?

A. It is right in certain cases that we should be angry; as when gross affronts are offered to us, and injuries done us by design. A suitable spirit of resentment, in such cases, will obtain justice of us, and protect us from further insults.

Heat rose to my ears and colored my cheeks. I untied my bonnet.

Q. By what rule should anger be governed?

A. We should never be angry without a cause; that is, we should be certain a person means to affront, injure, or insult us, before we suffer our- selves to be angry. It is wrong; it is mean; it is a mark of a little mind, to be angry at every little trifling dispute. And when we do have cause we

*should observe moderation. We should never be in a
passion. A passionate man is like a madman. We
should be cool even in anger; and be angry no
longer than to obtain justice.*

"I'm so mad I could spit," I said and walked to the window
again. The sun was well past noon-time. A soft tap came to the
door, and I ran to it and swung it open. There Dinah stood. She
held a small tray of food, and after looking warily behind her,
she stepped into the room.

"Hush," she whispered. "Be still, Miss Beth, so as I can tell
ya what I has to say. We don't be havin' much time." She hurried
past me, set the tray on the dressing table, then closed the door.
"It'll all be clear to ya right soon." She motioned for me to sit
beside her on the bed. Dinah's dark eyes gazed into my green
ones. "Massa Turnbull ain't what ya think he be. He been helpin'
us Negroes ever since I be a wee child. Ya see, we's a safe house
for runaways tryin' to get up to North. We's hid scores o'
travelin' folk—without the Missus or Sarah knowin' 'bout it."

My mind whirled with this unexpected turn. My breath
became trapped within a near-bursting chest.

"Now, Missus say ya must be gone, and Willy sold, and my
papa be whipt. But don't be worryin' none, Miss Beth. Massa
Turnbull he ain't like that. No. He ain't never whipt nobody, not
since Willy's papa dies. Now, the Massa he tells my papa to stay
out from them fields till time enough go by, if he been whipt, he
be mended. And for Willy, he sees what we all sees. We know he
be more smarter than the rest of us mixed into our stew. Now,
Massa Turnbull he says he gonna take him so's he can get some
educatin' proper-like."

"But what about—"

Dinah raised a finger to her lips. "Now, I knows you be thinkin' on ol' Luke, but don't ya be worryin' 'bout him neither. We loves him like our own kin, and he loves us the same. We's all sorry ya must go, Miss Beth, but where ya goin' can't be bad. I's sure, 'cause Massa Turnbull he see to it."

Relief washed in. Tears flowed from my comforted soul.

"Now, my mama says for ya to keep warm and your heart joyful." Dinah leaned in close. "I'll miss ya, Miss Beth. I knows how fair ya be in yer thinkin'." She wrapped her arms around me and squeezed. "Yer feelin' be on yer face like dirt on a muddy boot. Always is. We didn't get much time, but I knows it."

"Thank you," I managed to say, wishing I could hold on to her forever.

"I best be goin'. Mama and I gots twelve loaves bakin' tonight. Miss Beth, you be one of 'bout twenty-six mouths we to feed." Dinah wiped her cheeks with her apron as she stood and walked to the door. She turned around. "What I been tellin' ya? Ya see to it, not a word to Sarah or Missus." From the doorway she looked back at me. Her expression acknowledged our missed opportunity for friendship along with a deep sadness.

It was odd that we had been able to become friends at all. With but a few chances to speak to one another, and she being a kitchen slave and me being a ward of the Turnbulls, we had spoken mostly through gestures and glances. Few moments of conversation arose away from judging eyes. Very few.

"Dinah, thank you," I had said one day after breakfast when rushing into the kitchen to deliver a bolt of cloth to Pearl. It had arrived that morning, from England.

"Lizzy, tell Pearl to come to my room when she has finished

cleaning up from breakfast," Missus Turnbull had said. "This is enough blue brocade for a gown. There is to be a ball for the mayor next Saturday. Pearl will need to rush, but her stitching is better than any other in this county. I will have the best and newest gowns this season."

Dinah had stopped me when she saw the cloth. "Wait, Miss Beth. We can have ourselves some finery!" She had pulled on the cloth, unfurled it like a flag, draped it over one shoulder, and twirled. The fabric had wrapped around her as we giggled until our stomachs ached, until the sound of footsteps arrived, leading us to quickly refold the cloth.

We could have been friends. I know it, for that regret, to this day, still weighs like a heavy burden.

***

Night fell in the time it took to load the wagon with six days of provisions for four passengers. Along with the sundries needed for a trip such as ours, five bushel baskets of apples were crammed into the wagon bed. Behind these, Willy T. and I sat in a layer of straw. Beside us lay his meager belongings, wrapped in a grain sack, along with my comparatively huge steamer trunk. As the wagon lurched forward, Mister Turnbull tipped his hat to wife and home. Sarah was nowhere to be seen. Though the thought was most uncharitable, I was thankful we did not see each other again. My tongue would have lashed out in a manner that lacked civility.

To the east, clouds drifted in front of a sunflower moon. And as Mister Luke maneuvered the six-horse team and wagon down the drive, my attention turned to where my heart lived. I focused on the barn, a silhouette against the darkening sky. We traveled to where we were broadside, where I could then see a crowd gathered in a final farewell. The figure that could not help but leap about had to be Dinah, and Jax was clearly identified being larger than the rest, but the other faceless forms could not be distinguished one from the other. Perhaps sixteen in all stood hidden from view of the house. I struggled to make out Pearl, yes, Dinah's mother, but also the woman who was as close to a mother as I found at the Turnbull estate. My heart ached at the parting; though, I knew my feelings were mere shadows of what Willy T. must have felt.

He stood and waved frantically. He was leaving home, and as I assumed, would never return.

"Sit down," I pleaded. "You'll take flight and land up north before the horses."

As though on my cue, the wagon hit a bump, and Willy T. landed in the hay. He then shrank as though his precious life had been forced from his body. A crisp breeze caught the maples overhead and rustled several leaves free. They floated, dipped, and swirled in a blur to the ground. Mister Luke steered in a hard right onto the main road. His being our driver brought some relief, as my thankful heart was temporarily pardoned from one of my most difficult goodbyes.

A wavering courage strangled my voice as I glanced back up the hill to the brick house. I hoped my future would hold something beyond what I had found there. The Turnbulls had provided safety, food, and shelter along with a small amount of education. The charity they showed me, an orphan of meager means, could not be denied.

I turned away, however, and never looked back.

"You have a bit of explainin' to do, Willy T.," I said, gathering my voice and pulling my cape closed against the cold. "Dinah tells me how you've been helpin' those able to run."

"So, ya knows. Good," he said. "I be feelin' rotten but couldn't tell ya. That night ya bring the jam to the barn, ya near found us out. Uncle Luke and me, we's eat so quick cause we gots to, so as you'd leave us be. Two shakes later our shipment comes. With ya livin' up in the brick house, it be better to keep ya in the dark 'bout all that."

"I suppose I can't blame any of ya." I patted his knee. "I'm just angry 'cause I was always out danglin' by a thread. Every day I was ready for . . . well, especially yesterday, I thought it all was fallin' apart. Willy T., if you'd been whipt, I don't know what I would have done."

"Uncle done tell Adam, I mean Massa Turnbull, he find ya up the hill, all muddy and cold. Adam, he carry ya on in," Willy T. said.

Adam? I had never thought of my custodian as having a first name. In private thoughts, I had shortened his name to "Mister Bull" for it seemed right and fitting. "Mister Turnbull brought me in?" I asked as my cheeks burned red with the thought of him removing my wet clothes.

"Is true, Miss Beth."

"You don't have to call me 'Miss' any more, just 'Beth' will do." I thought about how gently Mister Turnbull had treated me, how comforting were his words. "I might not've hated him so, if I'd known what the truth be."

"Don't ya see? That's why we couldn't tell ya? Adam had to keep appearin' like the Massa he always been. After Papa was killed, Adam makes me a promise, right that night. He tells me, I be fit and able to leave someday—be set free. He says he seen too many of us get dead or broken. He knows up north people be workin' to end all that. It'll be done, he says. Things never the same after that. He even starts hangin' out the lantern so we helps others along the way."

Willy T. and I sat silent for a time. The moon seemed to chase us from behind the trees. Then the forest became so thick that almost no light shone through.

"Still, it must be horrible hard for you to be leavin' home," I said. "Do you know where he's takin' us?"

"I don't know 'bout you, but I's goin' to some place they calls New York. I's goin' to some schoolin' up there." He sounded so proud, even though nothing had yet taken place.

I smiled, but my stomach churned. Was I to be left there too? Or somewhere else? Alone? Stories were plentiful of young women being forced to care for the children of their keepers, and of sometimes being beaten when those children misbehaved. Would I be forced to marry some old man needing a wife and scullery maid? For a White woman, that would be servitude bordering on slavery. Inside my cape, I clutched my book with such strength that the cover became molded into a shallow arc. Upon discovering that fact, I thought of how learning from its pages had of late become tedious. The pronunciation and spelling of most of the words it contained I knew by rote.

I glanced at Willy T., at his small form huddled in the hay, his pants too short, the toes of his shoes cut away so they could fit his growing feet. "I want this book to be yours," I said, holding it out toward him. "It's the only thing I has that might be some use to ya. Our friendship . . . well, it's meant so, so much. We're like family, Willy T. But sorry . . . look . . . it's soiled and bent." I flipped the pages a bit and felt the binding shift, yet again. The leather was no longer attached to the book in even a small way. "At least the words might still teach ya somethin'."

He lifted the book to his face. In the near darkness, I saw him sniff at the leather and then feel the surface of the ribbon marker. We came into a small clearing and moonlight burst through the trees. He was studying the letters. Though, of course, he could not read. "Thank you, Miss Beth, I mean Beth." He ran his fingers along the book's spine. "It's so fine a thing. I loves it already."

He turned to look at me. Our eyes locked.

The force of so much longing bade me to speak, or he might have kissed me right then. "Please, Willy T., don't . . . just don't forget me. We cannot. We'll be partin' ways so soon. Everyone who has cared a thing about me has been snatched away." Tears began to well in my eyes.

I suppose he did not know how to respond. We both simply turned away to stare at the road. Trees towered overhead. The rutty track beneath the wagon hastened away as though we navigated a dirt river that was contained by stone fences along its banks. Daybreak would arrive, and with the dawn our lives would change forever. Perhaps that is why Willy T. turned back to me and placed his lips on mine. No one could have been more stunned than I, but then, by meeting his kiss with my own, I expressed what came directly from my heart. We had never dared to show what can only be described as love. I felt an urgent desire to repeat the moment, but we quickly drew apart.

Looking back with seventy years having past, my heart still holds longing for that moment. We never had any other. Indeed, I saw Willy T. only one more time.

Kate Porter

Lessons in Disguise

III

1825-1880
Willy T

Yes, *An Easy Standard?* Of course I remember that book—the first thing I ever owned. The first thing I owned as a freeman. Starting off, I didn't find the book's words to be easy, no sir, not easy at all. Plus, being a Virginia slave, freed or not, I could have been strung up by my boot straps and beaten in a prelude to a hanging, just for looking at such a thing. If caught reading, why I hated to think. They'd have been within their legal rights to do whatever they damn well pleased.

Those days are indeed a long time gone. I find myself living in Minnesota of all places, among folks I could never have imagined—Norwegians. They are a stern breed. Many struggle with their English, but at least they accept my living amongst them without offering up much of a fuss. I've been trying on their favorite curse, "uff da." It seems a good and mild, yet jabbing expression, saved up for times when wanting a word to make some point heftier. As when I've eaten all my stomach can possibly hold and someone is offering more, I might say, "Not another bite. Uff da, no more."

Yes, sixty years have passed under these shoes, well, not these very ones, these fancy things I bought just five years ago. Up until this last year, I've had the money. But back when I'd just received my freedom I'd have said, "I don't have nothin'."

Yes, sir. Some would wonder if I might wish to forgo the memories of those bleak days. I do revisit them just the same, lest horrible actions are doomed to be repeated. Slavery was an evil pushed upon me, my family, and in hindsight, yes, I'd say it was thrust upon some who leveled the deed upon us. I can and do bring those times to life, though only when asked. Always, I include the facts related here, for they speak of my own pain, for mine was an enormous price paid.

You see, after Massa Turnbull Senior died, we were deeded to Adam, along with the livestock. It was that young man's snobbery and stubbornness that led to my papa's lynching.

What a hotheaded bully Adam was back then. All of us, even I a boy of ten, knew that riding that maverick stallion to be the act of a senseless scallywag. Sure enough, Midas bolted from the dooryard with Adam, a marginal and cantankerous rider, bouncing in his saddle. As they sped down the drive, my papa, Matthew, watched that fool being pounded like beef on the chopping block.

So Papa, the only man who could rein in the other stallion, Titus, took off after them. That was the last anyone saw of my papa alive. Yes, he rode off to save his master without considering his own life. Perhaps he thought himself unworthy of saving. It still hurts to think on it. Still hurts when I think of how fast Titus galloped. I can still see Papa's house-slave coattails wagging behind him, like an obedient dog's tail.

Later, we surmised that he must have found Adam dangling from a stirrup, or some such, or beaten and unable to be roused. When Midas returned empty of rider and saddle, a search ensued. Directly, we found Papa dangling too, but from a tree, swinging dead. Nearby, Titus lay shot in the head. It appeared my papa had been caught by pattyrollers, and with no pass in hand, he was sure to be labeled a runaway and hung on the spot. All I knew was that his life paid the price for a rich man's folly.

My mama was dead but a year, so Papa's death hit me with the force of ten-thousand lashes.

Two years passed before I could trust the changes everyone else began to see in Adam Turnbull. He did veer from the ways of his forebearers. Perhaps that rocky road had shoved some sense into the man. He never was the same. But, truth be told, it was Uncle Luke's ability to forgive him, and Adam's agreeing to pass out clothes to the runaways, which availed to me the same path. Without those actions, hate for Massa Turnbull would still beat in my heart today.

Those final days of travel with Beth were cloudy, yet gloomy I was not.

The moment Beth handed the little book over to my care, it felt like a companion, one able to spill facts of a wider world. After knowing only a narrow space, the Virginia estate, hours sped quickly while she began teaching me what the lines, dots, and symbols all meant. Discovering some twine, I tied the book together so the leather would not fall off and get lost along the roadside.

Beth rode with us for most of the following day. She drilled me on letters and taught how each letter contained a sound, and that they all got secured together like knots in a rope to form words, some so glorious that they tumbled from the lips. "Frothy, commendable, future." We found words for which neither of us knew proper definitions. "Apropos, gewgaw, gherkin." The book contained phrases as well. Linking those strings together told stories that taught lessons. From then on, my attention became bound to that book.

Hindsight is sharper than a vulture's talons, however. I do wish my mind had been more focused on Beth than on her book. She may have wished the same, for it was not long after that when we were forced to deposit her at her new home.

***

"Keep to the right up ahead. I believe we're crossing over about now," Adam said, pointing into the night. "At long last, New York."

I remained hidden behind the apple barrels, alone, struggling to read. As the wagon bumped along, Uncle Luke and Adam Turnbull sat perched upon the driver's seat.

"How far does we have?" Uncle Luke asked, tightening his right rein and driving the team onto a well-traveled thoroughfare.

"This road will take us clear through. We'll be there by tomorrow evening, God willing. We meet up with friends in Oneida. There, I will be relieved of my worry and a bit of the debt I owe your brother," said Adam.

From where I sat, I could see Uncle Luke scanning the road. Trouble came often to those country byways, disguised as fellow-travelers. Yes sir, back in the 1820s we lived in fear of slave snatchers. They did not see a difference between runaways and freemen; we were all the same dark-skinned chattel to them. Hard to imagine this occurring—especially in a northern state. But, there you have it. I'm still alive to say it did. Yes sir, that's the God's honest truth.

"Are you certain you do not want to stay with Willy?" Adam asked. "I could tell Missus Turnbull you up and died along the way."

"I's sure. The boy needs to find a place to set his goods without his old uncle hangin' 'round."

"I brought your papers. Should you change your mind, just say the word."

"Who'd look after ya?" Uncle asked. "We been at it too long for me to scrap on ya now. 'Sides I couldn't be livin' in the land of steady habits. I hear what they says 'bout New York." Uncle scratched his head and glanced in my direction. I closed my eyes so he wouldn't detect my eavesdropping.

"I just want you to be . . . Oh, hell, you're a stubborn man, Luke." Adam paused and adjusted his hat. "My father's teachings . . . we both know there was a time I followed directly in his wake. Admit it, Luke. I treated you worse than the animals in the barn."

"Don't go blamin' yer own self."

"But it took Matthew's life." Adam hit his knee in frustration. "I swear, sometimes I can be thicker than dirt."

"Sometimes?"

I chuckled silently to myself.

Adam didn't laugh but wagged his head from side to side. "In death, Matthew led me to the proper path. He pointed out what I was blind to."

"He had a way of showin' a lot to a lotta folks. Me, I's the followin' sort too. Like you." Uncle Luke looked back toward me, again. In the darkness, he didn't see that my eyes were open, but a slit, so their talk continued. "The devil, he be pullin' at a lot o' men. White folks ain't the only ones who got the hold on it. What I's sayin' is, we's all got to eat the corn."

How could he say such a thing as this? Slaves had a part of

the blame? Or was he just saying that men could act with evil in their hearts. My mind simply could not wrap itself around my Uncle believing such a thing as that, so my thoughts drifted away from their conversation. It pained me to think of how my papa was born and died a slave. He had been devoted to family, and beyond reason, to the land though he never could lay claim to even the smallest slice of it. I vowed silently to myself, "My life'll make more bacon than a sow's rump. I'll be havin' somethin' for it."

The wagon lurched, and I brought my attention back to the men. "Well, I'll never forget Matthew's sacrifice," Adam said, placing his hand on Uncle's shoulder. "You can be certain of that. And, you know, I am quite hopeful for his boy." I shifted forward to be able to still hear his lowered voice. "Have you noticed him working over that little book Elizabeth gave him? You would think he could read. Luke, I see two things in Willy that will keep him in line. His father's steadfast eye for justice and his own God-given tenacity."

"Tenacity? I don't be knowin' what that be. But, if you say he's got some, he do. I just say he got the spunk."

"Yes. And he will need that spunk. He has a lot of growing to do. Do you think he's ready to be on his own?" Adam asked.

Uncle steered the horses easily around a sudden sharp turn, and as only a well-matched team could manage, the wagon was glided through unperturbed. The pause between the men lengthened, and I wondered if Uncle had forgotten to answer. Finally he did so. "The way I looks at it, he is or he ain't. He's all full of his self, as much a young buck can be. But he don't know nothin'. He'll do what he does. I can't be sayin' a lick 'bout it."

Dawn began to lighten the eastern sky. Rising from a small

group of nearby houses, wisps of wood smoke filled the air with the smell of home. Uncle Luke hesitated until he found a way to express his final words on the subject. "He be fine."

"You're a kind man, Luke."

"I thank ya for lettin' my nephew go."

Hearing them talk made my heart miss them, though we had yet to part company. I shifted around, knocking my head against one of the apple barrels.

Adam heard the thud and asked, "You still with us, William? You've been asleep nearly twelve hours."

"Yes, sir, I is." I sat up and stretched my stiff legs. My left foot had fallen asleep. Ankles, as skinny as chair slats, poked out from my trousers, which set my skin to shivering. Along the last few days, I had said goodbye to the whole of my boyhood and to Beth, the one person I had called friend.

In Dawsontown, Pennsylvania, we had bid her farewell at her new residence. We delivered her to a mansion, a more massive one I could not have imagined. The size of five Turnbull estates stacked on one another: three anchoring the bottom and two piled up top. Beth looked to be a wee thing, so alone standing before the imposing front door. Creatures carved into the top of the wooden portico glared down from above. They spoke of fears that I attempted to stifle. A servant who greeted us seemed kindly enough, a woman of perhaps forty years with soft eyes and a hint of a smile. Still, a portion of me wished to stay right there, to protect Beth from what might await her.

Our last words were rushed and we stood at a respectable distance. "Willy T., learn your path to a better life. I'll be keepin' my mind on what's in front of me . . . but . . . but know I will be rememberin' ya every day." Tears streaked her cheeks.

I looked away and simply replied, "Yes, Miss Beth." As we departed, I did not look back at her, until finally, not able to withstand the draw of a final glimpse, I turned. The massive door had closed. I was too late.

I knew some fortune would find her because Adam Turnbull would have seen her placed among educated and connected guardians. My heart, though, wished that she find people of kindness. I hoped educated and connected people could also be kind, but at the time, I did not know if they could be even charitable.

To this day, our last morning together remains clear to me. Upon rising, I had tiptoed to where Beth slept, intending to stow my bedroll into the back of the wagon. Her head rested on her quilt, and I took notice of her face. Lord, she'd changed to be a woman. Her body had filled in. No boy could miss that. Striving to push away such thoughts had become a difficult trial. A no-account buck such as me could not wed, nor even bed, a White girl—not and live. Not even an orphan, possibly heading for servitude. Therefore, I had never before dared to look directly at her, not often, fearing my thoughts would be found out. Sweetness hovered about her, and I allowed myself time to gaze at her face that morning as the light grew. I forgot about the walk I intended to take, about the morning fog, about my uncle and Adam Turnbull.

Her eyes opened.

"Mornin'," I mouthed but let no breath utter a sound. Her eyes brightened as they stared into mine. She sat up, faced the morning breeze, quickly braided her hair, then hopped down from the wagon. We walked the opposite direction from where the horses were tied. Uncle and Adam slept near the team to keep at bay any would-be thieves. We knew my uncle and master would soon awaken.

"What's goin' to happen, Willy T.?" she asked, her voice barely above a whisper.

"We's goin' to live out our lives, apart. But we be holdin' this memory from now on."

There it was. Neither of us smiled. Beth, not being one to dwell long on the unpleasant, picked the little book from my pocket. The feel of her being close enough to reach for it sent me a deep, warm shiver. We walked to a nearby creek and sat on a boulder. Beth opened the book to a simple verse, one she'd read to me before, the one in which I saw no appeal. It was so trite and odd. Birds, what nonsense. No human could know the thoughts of a bird or why they acted as they did. Still, my ears listened to the tone in her voice, I noticed wisps of her hair caressing her cheek—as I longed to—and I watched her lips as she read.

The Bird's Nest

Yes, little nest, I'll hold you fast,
And little birds, one, two, three, four;
I've watch'd you long, you're mine at last;
Poor little things, you'll 'scape no more.

Chirp, cry, and flutter, as you will,
And simple rebels, 'tis in vain;
Your little wings are unfledg'd still,
How can your freedom then obtain?

What note of sorrow strikes my ear;
Is it their mother thus distrest?
Ah yes, and see, their father dear
Flies full and round, to seek their nest.

And is it I who cause their moan?
I, who so oft in summer's heat
Beneath yon oak have laid me down
To listen to their songs so sweet?

If from my tender mother's side,
Some wicked wretch should make me fly,
Full well I know, 'twould her betide,
To break her heart, to sink, to die.

And shall I then so cruel prove,
Your little uses to force away!
No, no; together live and love;
See here they are–take them, I pray.

Teach them in yonder wood to fly,
And let them your sweet warbling hear,
Till their own wings can soar as high,
And their own notes may sound as clear.

Go, gentle birds; go, free as air,
While oft again in summer's heat,
to yonder oak I will repair.
And listen to your song so sweet.

She closed the book and handed it back to me. "Willy T., we must be passin' along to new lives. We've no choice."

Something weighed heavy upon me, and I couldn't let the morning pass without bringing it forth. "Beth," I began, "must ask ya for somethin'." The problem was, I didn't know how to ask. It seemed such a backward thing to do. Yes sir, I prodded along as if digging a hole with a stick. "Papa's name, it be forced on him, and his papa too. 'Turnbull' be tacked to the tail-end of our family. We not havin' want for it. That be makin' no difference. Turnbull's our owned name, not our own. Do you know what I's sayin'?"

I hesitated. Perhaps I wanted her to answer, but she didn't. Maybe there wasn't anything for her to say, so I continued. "I wants to choose a name to carry free, when I goes free." I kept my eyes looking anywhere but at her, until the moment I knew I must look directly at her face, to see her reaction. "Beth, would ya let me borrow yer name to live as the freeman, Willy, uh, I means, William Turnbull Sherman?"

Our eyes then met. Her smile scattered all doubts. "I'd be honored, Mister William T. Sherman. But ya don't have to be borrowin' it, Willy T., I'm givin' it to ya free and clear."

I liked the sound of that. So let it be said, that on an autumn day in the wilds of Pennsylvania, I became William T. Sherman. I had not a penny, nor even shoes that fit, but I acquired a valuable thing. With that name, I could become a man of distinction or property. I knew it the second I heard the thing flow from my mouth. And it has served me well. That is, until about fifteen years ago. Up to then, I had suffered no ill-consequences of my action. On the contrary, each time someone called out "Mr. Sherman" my name offered up respectability. In the year 1862, however, the gravity of my decision slapped me upside the head. No one, not a single one, could have known that The War Between the States would bring forth a man with whom I shared a name. Though we never met, General William Tecumseh Sherman's fame became the bane of my very existence.

***

Each story has a way of begging to be told, and to get to the telling of how my name made my life hell, I must first tell of days when it made my heart sing. It began in Oneida, New York, where Adam Turnbull and Uncle Luke deposited me. Those two grown men had looked pained beyond what I could stand to witness. They lingered far longer than was customary. I even gave a two-handed shake to Adam Turnbull while saying these words, "I be thankin' ya for lettin' me go."

He had grunted, handed me my papers, and began checking the wagon for wear. I watched him, willing my feet to stay on the ground, for they longed to jump back onto the wagon.

Somehow, Uncle Luke found the words for our difficult goodbye. "Willy T., remember now, you's the hope of us. And don't ya be thinkin' 'bout me, I's fine. Pearl been askin' me to move in, when I gets back. Won't be alone. I be findin' myself a lil' corner." While he spoke, he straightened my shirt and jacket.

"Stop yer fussin', Uncle. Ya ain't my ma," I said, flicking away his hand and immediately wishing I hadn't. "Sorry," I said. "But I won't never . . . never be forgetin' ya. Never."

Tears fell like rain that day, until he cleared his throat and enveloped me with one final embrace. Then they boarded the wagon and drove away. My chest felt like I'd been kicked by a horse, but I held my head high, yes sir, lest my new guardian see. I lifted my sack and turned to Mr. Withers, the headmaster of the school that I would begin attending the following day.

Wire-rimmed spectacles rested low on the man's long nose. Wispy hair flew in all directions but the one he may have chosen. "Well, we best go inside before you run off after them," he said, looking me up and down then added, "Do not worry. No one has ever claimed my bite leaves much of a mark."

Mr. Withers opened the door to a stone cottage consisting of three rooms: two for sleeping and one for living. A large hearth centered the room, and the table and chairs were arranged to bring everyone as close to its warmth as possible. The house would seem small to most, but to a boy who'd never lived anywhere larger than one room, my new home felt near to a palace.

Withers moved not in one fluid motion, but in gestures with added jerks thrown in where they didn't belong. The rest of the man was as long and lean as his nose. He would not be called frail, but rather knobby, pale, and awkward. It appeared he might topple over if given the slightest nudge. He removed his long cloak and hung it on a hook beside the door.

After opening a pantry cupboard, he began prying lids from tins. "Where'd I put . . . I just can't find . . . Oh, hell to a handmaiden . . . Ah ha! Here it is." His face disappeared into a large container, and he inhaled deeply. "My boy, have you ever tasted coffee before?"

"Yes, sir, I has."

"Yes, sir, I 'have'," he corrected. "Well, not like this you 'have' not. I bet no one 'has' added a shot of brandy to it to warm what ails you." With one eyebrow raised higher than the other, he turned to me and peered over his spectacles.

After a short pause, I realized he expected my answer. "No sir, I has—" I halted, choosing not to continue this simple sentence, one that suddenly seemed impossible to navigate.

He answered for me. "No sir, I 'have not had' any brandy in my coffee to warm what ails me."

So it began, living with my teacher. Not a day passed without him riding herd on my every word. We discussed and pondered over many things: things of value, and things long forgotten. I came to believe he so brimmed with information that the weight of it was why his body couldn't operate evenly. Too top heavy. He stood tilted on his own axis as the earth spun under him.

The following morning, my formal education began in a tiny classroom with my eyes, and those of twelve other Negro boys, concentrated on our teacher. "William Sherman has joined us!" Mr. Dresden Wither's classroom-voice roared as though volume were needed to fill the small room.

"They calls me Willy T., sir."

"They 'calls' you that, do they?"

"Yes, sir."

"My boy, here you will be William Sherman." And so it was that with those simple and few words, Willy T. was buried and William was born.

Weeks passed quickly into months as my time filled with decisions, ones I made for myself. Freedom was something I bathed in, basked in, and drank up with an insatiable thirst. It seemed I could reach out and touch it like a person, animal, or desk. Better yet, it seemed as immense as the bounding sea and as embracing as the endless warmth of the sun. The vast feeling of freedom grew much too large to grasp, though I knew it to be mine.

"Mr. Sherman, are you with us?"

"I's sorry, sir."

"I 'am' sorry is what you mean. Yes, Mr. Sherman, my boy, you are." Somehow, his calling me "boy" didn't rankle me, since the addition of "my" softened it a bit.

The class laughed as I pulled at my collar. Wearing stiff and unfamiliar clothes felt abnormal. Handed-down ones, patched and broken-in ones, those were what I'd known, not the new-to-me-and-the-world-at-the-same-time clothes. Still, each day, I survived the crisp new trousers and starched white shirts, until after the noon-time meal when we were dismissed to change into our working trousers and shirts. In the afternoon and often late into the evening, we answered the call to the manual-labor hours of our day. Though I hungered for worldly knowledge, digging and hoeing felt more natural to me. Habits were hard to break.

It wasn't till long after the sun went down that I fell into bed, most nights forgoing the change into the final set of clothes, those set out for the job of sleep. After waking in the morning, I would once again don the starchy whites. Because I lived with Mr. Withers, one of our two teachers and the headmaster, I had but a short walk to school, only about a mile. That brisk morning jaunt, in total darkness half the year, would jar my mind and body awake enough for early lessons. By midmorning, though, I'd be found drifting off. With a loud smack to my desk, or worse to my head, Mr. Withers would bring me back to the fore.

That first year of learning sped by with little time to see beyond the work at hand. My classmates accepted me well enough; however, I lived with their teacher. They supposed, perhaps, that my accomplishments were not my own but handed to me at the dinner table along with my supper. Rightly so, yes sir. The truth being that Mr. Withers did hold me to a higher standard. His relentless prodding pushed me to heights I might never have otherwise attained.

One day, Mr. Withers handed me an envelope and said, "The post office had this for you. If your knowledge is too shallow to read this letter, ask for my help. First though, William, endeavor to decipher the words without me. My boy, I will not always be here to help you."

I gazed at the envelope, the first post I ever received. It was addressed to Mr. Withers with my name under his. A stamped date was in the upper right corner. With my heart pounding within my chest, I tore it open not knowing who had sent the letter.

"My dear Willy T." With this salutation, I knew immediately who the writer was. Letter by letter I worked my way through the words. Beth explained how her life was opening to her, just as, she was sure, mine was to me. She loved her school and teachers. Soon, she would be sent to another of higher learning, one in New York. She hoped that her new home would be close enough for us to visit. "But I worry, Willy T., the distances in these states be too large to allow us to meet." To me, however, the most important lines were her final closing.

"You are always in my thoughts for I love you. Your friend forever, Beth"

Her address in Pennsylvania was included within, so after taking up my graphite and using lesser penmanship than she had mastered, along with Mr. Wither's help for the envelope, I crafted a return letter. What I remember of this were the many drafts it took to spell correctly all the words, to place them in the right order, and to express rightly what I held in my heart. Would she read and reread every word just as I continued to do hers? I believed she would.

Mr. Withers posted my letter after I pasted the envelope and kissed the paper where it was sealed. Two days later I asked him, "Were there any letters for me, sir?" as I knew he had gone to town.

"Your letter will get to Pennsylvania in a week or two, William," he said. "Do not be asking every day for the post. Letters come when they get here. No amount of asking will bring one sooner."

I turned my attention to school to push the time to pass faster. At first all was new, and my mind drank in every word of the book learning. Soon, though, the progression seemed too slow. My attention would often stray, and still, my exams received excellent marks. I advanced through the grades, approaching then passing students older than myself. My other teacher, Mister Jansen, was angered by what he perceived to be my laziness, especially when subsequent test scores received high marks. "Intelligence is no excuse for a lack of diligence," he repeated daily and demanded I pen those very words a hundred times over on my ledger.

My mind grew to be a thirsty thing. Knowledge poured in my direction, first in the basics of mathematics, reading, and spelling, and much later in the subjects of chemistry, physics, literature, and history.

Most evenings while I studied, Mr. Withers drafted plans in a book he called his *Insane Idea Index*. "Write down what's in your head, my boy, before it leaks out and disappears. You never know which idea will be the most important of your discoveries. There may be one due to change the world in some manner. Mark my words, if you do not write them down, why they get lost to you and get picked up for someone else to claim as his own." His advice turned into a lecture about Leonardo Da Vinci, and about machines that fly, and paintings on ceilings by that other Italian fellow, Michelangelo. Later, when resting in bed and staring at the wooden planks overhead, that very notion stirred me to think of a scene I would paint above, if I were so inclined. It would show Uncle Luke standing in the doorway of the barn, and our cottage nestled in the woods nearby.

In the dark of night, loneliness for home washed in and pushed sleep away. I thought of Dinah's surprising strength when we played toss the rock as young children. How her father's scarred, muscular body grew heavy with sweat while cultivating the potato field. And how my heart still dwelled within the comfort of Pearl's bosom when she hugged me and treated me to an extra chicken leg. How my own mama and papa rested outside the Turnbull's family plot with an unmarked fieldstone to mark the spot. The most difficult memories were those of Uncle Luke's gray beard and his grin appearing within its reaches. And of Beth. Her lips. Our one kiss that caused forbidden longings. Thinking of her, sleep never could come. I would instead reach for her book, hold it in my hand, get up, and pace the room's edges.

Owning the book did bring some comfort. Its lessons, so firmly fixed on practicality, rescued me from yearnings. First, a sprinkling of relief was found from reading passages aloud while struggling to unlock the code of the barely known letters. Then later, as I read silently skimming from word to word, I would begin to relax. When finally asleep, longing for Beth brought recurring dreams. One night in the dark of slumber, what came to me were the feel of her skin, my thigh touching hers while in a forbidden embrace, then a view from on high as though floating above the apple orchard in Virginia. I reached for her and we faced each other, held our hands in front of ourselves, placed them palm to palm, and compared our hand sizes. I awoke with such a feeling of excitement that once again sleep evaded me.

Even after I grew much older, and my abilities deserted the book's simple language for loftier material, I still returned to the pages of plain-spoken truths. It became a way to quiet my soul. Within the words, a restful place was found where my loved ones lived. One passage, even as I recited it by rote, easily transported me from grief.

Love him that loves his book, speaks good words,
and does no harm: For such a friend may do thee good
all the days of thy life. Be kind to all as far as you can:
you know not how soon you may want their help; and
he that has the good will of all that know him, shall not
want for a friend in time of need.

I did change what was written as I read and thought of dear Beth. "Love her that loves her book."

***

Letters of the alphabet materialized everywhere. One evening while engaged in after-supper cleaning, I discovered a few hidden words. I deciphered what the letters meant and shared my find with Mr. Withers. He sat at his small corner desk. A lantern lighted his work.

"Sir, did ya know yer name's on the bottom of a bowl in the cupboard? The one we hasn't . . . I mean, we haven't not never used the thing. Not never. I mean, not ever. What was yer mama thinkin', I mean thinking 'bout, when she named ya after some empty bowl?"

He turned to me and peered over his spectacles. "What my dear mother thought was to deliver unto me a name, Dresden, by which she could recall Dresden, Germany. The bowl was made there, and her father hailed from there as well. My father gave the bowl to my mother on their wedding day, with this solemn vow, 'Forever, I will endeavor to keep it full.' My boy, they had known hunger, and the promise of plenty contained cherished words. Later, their wealth far exceeded . . . well . . . the end does not justify what he . . . what he did." Mr. Withers' mind drifted to where only his thoughts traveled until he cleared his throat, wiped his spectacles with his fingers, and spoke again in a raspy voice.

"Never you mind, Mr. Sherman. Just do not forget. There are souls near at hand whose plight is of an ilk that should never be dealt from one human to another." He hesitated, tapping his forehead with his index finger. "William, here is tonight's word: Inhumane. I-N-H-U-M-A-N-E. I expect you to use it properly in a sentence before we breakfast."

He headed to bed without saying his customary departing words, "Morning comes early, dream plenty." I had grown to expect this nightly farewell, so as the lantern light dimmed into his bed chamber, he left an emptiness in me and the room.

Warming my backside near the fading fire, I just stood there.

On that night and others, he had spoken of his parents' need to justify something. But I didn't know of what, at the time. My wanting to know left a hole. Mr. Withers often left voids in our conversations. I wondered if his father had been someone of stature. Yet, there was no evidence of wealth in his tiny home. In fact the opposite was true. The house contained threadbare flour-sack curtains, tin drinking vessels, and oak furniture so beaten that splinters often snagged at our clothes.

I stepped over to the table, picked up a few crumbs, and flicked them into the fire. Though our dinner of smoked ham and parsnips had filled my belly, my mind was not sated. It's inhumane to what? To whip a man. I wondered if Mr. Withers, or his family, had ever owned a slave or whipt one. Had a slave raised him like Pearl had raised Sarah and Elizabeth? Those questions somehow felt wrong to ask. Is it inhumane to die young? I knew that humans could die young. My parents had met that fate.

As I fell into bed exhausted, I knew there was much to learn, perhaps more with each passing day—not less. The world held complications. The way people were treated, simply because of the color of their skin and birthright, and the misplaced thoughts they had toward each other, questions of why these existed were what I wanted to learn.

***

Those three years of early learning sped by. Just after turning seventeen, on June, 13, 1828, I graduated with the rest of my class of twelve, all of us Negro boys. We had received more education than any of us had hoped to find. I was lucky to attend that school, fashioned in the image of The New York African Free School. Upon graduation, we were expected to return to Africa, to rid America of our race and to educate the "heathens" who were, we were taught, begging to become Christian. Neither I nor any of my classmates cared to do so. None of us had lived in Africa, no sir, and we had all been slaves and now were freemen.

My goal was to change others' notions about the capacity of a Negro boy's mind. I had been educated beyond the use of a pickaxe. My faulty diction had been righted. "Ya" had been replaced with "you." Most grammatical rules I held within my grasp. Geography of the world, the rhythmic beauty of a poetic phrase, and what art had been created during the Renaissance were embedded in my mind. What good would come of that knowledge, I wondered, if I lived among the "uneducated hordes" we'd been told inhabited the "dark continent"? When I shook Mr. Withers' outstretched hand and received my diploma, I said, "Thank you, kind sir, for everything. I am forever in your debt."

"I am not done with you, William Sherman," he said. "I hope you continue your studies as we have discussed. College awaits you."

"Yes, sir. That is my hope as well." It was difficult to believe such a short time had passed since Uncle Luke and Adam Turnbull had deposited me on Mr. Withers' doorstep.

Upon graduating, I left my childhood to face other challenges. My first action was to post a note to Beth of what my new address would be. Our letters had dwindled to a mere trickle as we had both concentrated on our education. In my final year, a new teacher had arrived, a woman who had graduated from the same school as Beth. They had not been friends, but I saw an admirable strength of will in this teacher, and because Beth was receiving the same instruction, I knew she would be well-prepared for her adult life and would most likely become a teacher too.

For the next three years, I attended the Oneida Institute in Whitesboro, New York. In 1828 there were just a handful of colleges admitting Negro men. Oneida was one. The first two years, I was dead-on-track to becoming the brightest among the students. My final year, however, was of dubious distinction, and though it does pain me to tell of it, even these sordid details must be told.

My tale may seem only to be that of an ex-slave and his book, but life is never that simple.

Prior to the start of my third fall term, and sparing no expense, I bought the finest hat fashionable to the day—a seal-fur stovepipe. It was the richest, mellowest brown, and felt as soft as ground wheat flour. Of course, the purchase of such an extravagance on my meager allowance meant that, daily, I wore the same set of street clothes. I could afford no others. The sacrifice was of no consequence to me since the hat's rigid bowl made me taller. Strutting through town and bowing to all the young ladies, the fair-skinned ones often crossed the street or quickly turned away. The others nodded in reply, but not one would meet my gaze.

Then one day, with a flower adorning my lapel, I saw a girl who looked directly at me without hesitation. No shame, nor pleasure, could be seen in her expression. She was fine, and I watched as her skirts swayed down the street. She was on the arm of an older man, whom I assumed to be her father. I vowed to return to that very spot to meet her again. Though I still loved Beth, I knew the next time I saw this beauty I would not remain silent. Beth and I could never wed, so I allowed my affections to wander. Returning daily for nearly a week, my desire ripened like peaches in sunshine.

Then, while standing in my customary place and leaning against a hitching post, a commotion grew around me. At first I took no notice, but my attention was brought to the fore when two quarreling men came to blows. One fell against me, sending my hat twirling off into the gutter. To my dismay, it landed on a pile of steaming horse dung. As I stepped over to retrieve it, the man who had pushed me was tossed again in my direction. We fell in a heap, upon the heap, and everyone within spitting distance stopped and snickered. I looked up, and you can believe it, there the young lady stood looking plumb at me with a look of pure pleasure.

Instead of sulking away, I pushed the man off, picked up my hat, placed it on my head, and walked straight over to the young lady and knelt beside her. "William T. Sherman, at your service," I said. My eyes became fixed on hers. To complete this forward action, I proclaimed my intent by speaking so quickly that I don't really know how the words came to me. "Do not forget my name, dear lady. Before a fortnight has passed, I may be your husband. And in the years to follow, you will birth our many children."

I detected the beginning of a smile. Still, our eyes remained locked while the howling around us swelled to enormous proportions. The odor of the dung must have been detected by the young lady and by everyone else within ten rods. She raised her handkerchief to her nose but did not laugh at my actions. Tipping my befouled hat to her escort, I sauntered away, trying to regain a dignified air. As I walked past the lumber mill, I scooped up some sawdust and carefully worked the dung from my hat.

Later that night, I thought of her smile, her delicate hands, her smooth, black skin, her eyes that matched my gaze. My desire grew. The following morning, though due in classes, I returned instead to the same spot, hoping to find her. And indeed, there she sat upon a bench. Her long, black hair lay twisted over one shoulder, and her cheeks and lips were painted crimson.

"Are ya a man of your word, Mr. Sherman? Or are ya all show and no action?" She stepped forward and entwined her arm around mine.

She smelled delicious and rendered me speechless.

"Let's move along, before ya lose your nerve. A young man like ya'self needs a woman, don't ya." Her dark green dress swished as she walked. Her hand rested on my forearm.

Walking down the street, we were one high-falutin' vision. All decked out in finery we were. Peering down at my shoes, though, I wished they were not the brogans I'd worn for the past three years. We turned the corner onto a side street, and my beautiful companion approached a door. She knocked twice in quick succession, then again after a pause. The door swung open, and a woman, with hair sprouting from a large mole on her chin, poked her head into the daylight.

"Lordy, Grace, this's him? I thought he'd be riper. Why, he's barely sprouted." She threw her head back and let out a beastly laugh, the raucous sound akin to a feral cat slaying its supper. "Grace, you'll have somethin' fer him, to be sure, but what does this young dandy have to give back? Nothin'." She pivoted out of our way. "Watch yer step now. Don't want ya fallin' in any shit." Her laugh echoed down the long hall as we entered.

Leading me up a narrow staircase, Grace pulled me by the hand.

"I'm talkin' to ya." The woman was still yelling when we arrived at the landing. "Don't be fallin' fer him. If he don't be handin' it over, kick him in the ass."

I'd never heard a woman speak with such foul language. Her words, however, passed without comment since I wanted to appear worldly.

We entered a small bedroom, and Grace sat me down and began to remove her clothes. The slap of truth hit me broadside. "No, Grace, I'm not . . . oh . . . I'm not here for . . . for that." Try as I might, I was unable to avert my eyes, unable to watch her body without a steam rising within me. While I attempted a bit more of my pitiful protest, she continued to unveil herself. Uff da, if my skin hadn't been as dark as a Black man's could be, she would have seen the blood rush to my cheeks. I was so green, I had ignored all the signs, most obvious being the naked woman standing before me. When I realized what Grace was, what she wanted as she held out her hand, I should have walked away. But you can bet I paid for her, yes sir, I paid everything she asked. Every time she asked.

***

I could not deprive myself of visits to Grace's room. With cash, I bought all pleasures imaginable. Yes, I did. But saying so now only brings forth pain, not pleasure at all. You see, the sting of regret, like nettles grasped in the hand, began to rise as my college marks plummeted. My clothing took on the shabbiness of shame. Avoiding classes and classmates, I returned nightly to her waiting embrace. I didn't just want her but suffered a raw hunger for her. Fooling myself into thinking I could make her walk away from that life, I spent all that I had, every last cent. She will be my wife, I vowed to myself. I even had my silhouette cut for her birthday. After all, she was only seventeen. Her life didn't need to be trapped in that little room, her own form of slave quarters. Poor fortune could change. Mine had.

On a late-October evening, one flooded with desire and whisky, I fell asleep beside her. Sometime later, untwisting myself from our tangle of legs and arms, my mind awoke enough to hear voices. The comforting aroma of smoke, laden with the promise of food and warmth, filtered through the dark room. I wondered if Grace had ever cooked a meal. Had she ever tended fires other than those of the flesh? An image of her plucking a goose came to mind, but I couldn't truly see her ever doing the chores of a wife. Chuckling, I marveled at how that reality could be so confused by sleep. Grace's cramped room lacked a working fireplace. Seconds later, I heard yelling, and dread thrust its hand against my throat.

I leapt out of bed, coughing. "Grace, wake up!" I shouted. Smoke was billowing from under the door. Calling her name several times, I sped to the window and thrust it open. The night air streamed in but pulled smoke under the door in equal measure. I picked up the drunken Grace and carried her to the window. There was nothing between us and the ground, twenty feet below.

The door. It had all but disappeared in the choking haze. I

held my breath and rushed over to feel it. The wood was nearly hot enough to ignite. Back at the window. I began to hack from a depth that reached down to my insoles. I coughed into the night and gasped for fresh air. Flames engulfed the door and were quickly spreading across the ceiling. No choice. We would have to jump.

Grace mumbled incoherently as I lifted her onto my shoulder. Balancing her as best I could, I climbed feet first out the window, lowered us as far as possible, then let go. Hugging her head to my chest, I tucked in my legs, and braced for impact.

I heard the snap then felt it.

Somehow, I had protected Grace from harm; however, the shin bone in my right leg thrust straight through my trousers. The pain was beyond reason. My screams and the fresh air entering Grace's lungs brought her back from her stupor. She was coughing and appeared confused, then terrified. She began to shriek then stumbled away. My mind drifted into darkness.

**

I don't know how long my soul roamed. If I brought myself closer to my body, pain drove me away. Now and again, my eyes opened enough to see light. But whenever possible, I chose to live in the murky gloom eased by laudanum. Unrelenting pain lived within me as a monster does: lurking, hunting, burning, and stabbing when it damn well pleased. Thankfully, the only sensation still vivid in my mind now is the ghastly taste that took up residence in my mouth, something akin to the smell of rotting fish.

One day, a voice filtered through the haze, "Hi there, sweet stuff." It was Grace.

Breaking the crust that wanted to keep them closed, I forced my eyes to open.

"Please, don't go away again," she said. The sound of her dress rustling against her shoes reminded me of the smoldering fire. Fear released a moan from my throat. "Doctor, he be awake now," she called out.

I squeezed my eyes shut.

"Well, there you are at last, Mr. Sherman," a man said. He lifted my right lid, then the left. "Everyone here at the hospital thought you might be done for. You are indeed a lucky man."

I struggled to roll to my side, away from human interruption. My legs, wrapped in a tangle of sheets, hindered any progress. While lifting the bedding slightly to set myself free, I gazed down. One leg was there. The other leg was not. A gauze-wrapped stump protruded beyond my right thigh.

I thrust the sheet back down and beat my fist onto the bed. "Lucky?" A pitiful scream arose from my throat.

"Better a cripple than six-feet below," the doctor said.

His comment left me breathless and wanting to thrash him with a whip. I bit my tongue and concentrated on the roaring sound of blood rushing in my head. A lump rose in my throat. Bile spewed from my mouth. Why couldn't I return to the darkness? That relief never came, just the ghostly throb from a leg that no longer existed.

"Please, William, ya needs to get back on your feet . . . I mean . . . back to yer schoolin'." Grace, now ill at ease, shifted in her seat and looked about the room. She could no longer meet my gaze.

I never felt more alone than in that moment. I pretended to

lose consciousness. Slumber helped form the hours into days, the days into weeks. Grace came less and less often, until finally I was rid of her.

***

Weeks later, they lifted me from bed and set me in a chair. Drinking a stiff coffee and staring out a window so dirty that my mind could remain empty, I suddenly felt a hand on my shoulder. That old book, *An Easy Standard*, dropped into my lap.

"There you are, my boy. I will be taking you home," Mr. Withers said and sped away, all the while calling over his shoulder. "Do not argue with me, Mr. Sherman, the decision is made. I'm fixed on it tighter than a rusted nail in an oak plank."

The hospital's pace usually moved as slow as my dark thoughts. But no one sat idle that day, not with Mr. Withers on task. Except for me, of course. I looked down at the book, which I hadn't read for over a year. The water damage had taken its toll. The gold lettering had begun to rub off. Tying it with twine, my own action in trying to save it, had furthered its decay. The cover separated from the book anyway, and where the string rubbed, the calfskin had eroded down to the inner wooden boards. I unleashed the whole mess. Bits of desiccated leather, looking like dark tree bark, flaked off onto my lap. Unfettered, what was left of the title page drifted to the floor and slid under the bed.

The book fell open where the ribbon marker rested. The silk stuck to the page and needed to be peeled from one side. I stared at the letters that tracked across the paper and wondered, could I have forgotten how to read?

I looked about, hoping no one would witness my struggle. I

paused several minute to gather my strength, my gumption, and my faculties. Finally, deciding the time had come to find out, I stared at the exercise on the open page.

Common Compound words

Ale house	*cop per plate*	*gin ger bread*
bed fel low	*drip ping pan*	*fer ry man*
chain shot	*moon shine*	*ink stand*
land tax	*lap dog*	*Yale col lege*

I quickly realized, of course, my knowledge had not abandoned me. Below that list was the following line:

> *The most necessary part of learning is to unlearn our errors.*

I pulled at chin whiskers and wondered if Mr. Withers had planted the ribbon on that page. Surely, he would not have approved of my visits to Grace's bed. In fact, he most likely disapproved of me all together. After Grace had halted her visits to the hospital, I had requested no visitors be allowed. The missing leg was my penance. I deserved to be less than whole.

"Here we go." Mr. Withers interrupted my self-loathing. "They are preparing a method of transport to my carriage. At home, I have built a ramp and procured a cart, so we can push you inside. A surprise awaits you in the form of a nursemaid. You seem to be keen on the ladies, so I found one who actually wants to take care of you."

"Grace?" I mumbled.

"No . . . and you will see soon enough. Save your breath, William."

The ride home was a trial of bumps, but the outside air felt crisp and much cleaner than the inside of the hospital ward. Death, blood, and moaning had filled that room, day and night, but I tried to begin to leave those memories behind while my skin became warmed by the early winter sun. Arriving at Mr. Withers' cottage, my mood lifted further at seeing smoke rising from the chimney and braided pine boughs hanging around the door frame. Christmas was a holiday never celebrated by the slaves at the Turnbull plantation. It had always felt like nonsense, until that moment; my heart began to lift from its cavern of shame and despair.

"Mr. Withers, when did you take up holiday decorating?" I asked.

"It is not of my doing, William. And if we are to be living together, this time as peers, you must call me Dresden."

I pondered making peace with this change, when the front door swung open. Out rushed a vision I could never have expected. Dinah, my childhood friend, dashed over, climbed aboard the carriage, and threw her arms around me.

My mouth fell open.

Dresden stood with arms folded. "You have a few folks living in Virginia who would not be denied," he said. "Had I not explained that my house contains only three rooms, the total of the Turnbull slaves would be here." Dresden carried my bundle of clothes and a few baskets of food into the house.

Dinah and I stared at one another. Time had changed her. Or perhaps it was I who had changed. When we had last seen each other, she was only thirteen. In no part of our childhood did she stir me the way she did that day.

My heart leapt and fell in the very same instant. Dinah represented my entire family. Tears fell, but they did not sting. It is a moment forever engraved in my mind. Our words were simple.

"Mr. William T. Sherman, you be home now," she said, her voice a soothing elixir.

I whispered in her ear. "I am. Yes, I am."

***

Healing came in fits and starts. Just as I would gain strength of spirit, my body would head the opposite direction. Dinah and Dresden tried to push me, but to be perfectly honest, my heart was not convinced of the ability to be better.

Not much thought had gone into restoring my stump to a useful end. The lumpy mess hurt like hell when Dresden attached the wooden leg he had crafted. The added pads of lambskin helped, but still, it felt like an assault of stones grinding into an open wound. If my misfortune had followed the Great Rebellion, perhaps then the wound would not have festered so. You see, war surgeons learned volumes from the sheer number of soldiers losing limbs. But back in the 1830's, when there were fewer fellows in my condition, doctors merely sawed and sewed, and I had to live with the consequences.

"That God damned thing. It hurts!" I swore at Dresden as he fitted the peg to my leg. "Who proclaimed you an expert? Shit!" I tried to swat away his hands.

He absorbed my verbal and physical assaults and said, "You may quit your hollering, William T. Sherman. I don't care three beans about whether you like this leg or not. And quiet! The entire state of New York hears you." I winced as he cinched the strap another notch. "This is the peg you've got, and no other will be floating along the Erie Canal to come knocking on our door."

He called it a peg-leg, but it was truly a work born of genius. The idea had come to him while writing in his *Insane Idea Index*. Six years would pass before the clapper leg would come along, with its straps and noisy hinges. Dresden's leg had a far-superior design to even those later models. He hollowed out the core, and yet it remained sturdy. Its light weight made it easier to maneuver. Dresden explained, "It's in the wood, William. That's the secret. Ash contains a long, strong grain."

After a few months, I attempted a return to my college studies. In just three days, however, it became clear I could not keep up. The work, both physical and mental, felt beyond my ability. When failure was certain, my demeanor turned even more foul. I spat out words like sour milk and attempted to retreat from the world.

When I look back on it now, the following two years seemed to fly by. However, as I lived it, they plodded by as do long-winded sermons. Life was an endless series of dull, aimless tasks. Where I was stubborn, Dresden was relentless. When he was in need, he forced me to be his driver. If marketing was ordered, he sent me to the Mercantile where the grocer's oldest son would load the wagon. Upon my return, Dinah unloaded the heavy sacks and bushel baskets. I hated sitting by as she labored under those heavy burdens, but lifting fifty pounds of grain, bushels of potatoes, and ham shoulders were tasks she did without complaint. Even if I had no need to relieve myself, I would rush to the back house to avoid watching her toil.

One bright spot existed. I grew to love Dinah, you see. With certainty, though, I could not envision a life together. No, sir. Heaping upon her back the care of a cripple, I refused to do. To avoid troubling her further, I fought to hide my feelings. Doing so proved a difficult task as we lived in close quarters. Dinah's bed was just steps from my own chamber, in a corner of the great room. Though "great" was the name, the room could not have measured more than a twelve-foot square. Each night, after placing my head on my duck-feather pillow, visions of her flooded in: her bending to sweep crumbs from under the table; her fingers gently tucking her hair behind her ear; the graceful gathering of her skirts before stepping onto a chair to reach the high shelf. If the winds fell quiet, I could hear her restful intake and outflow of breath. The most cumbersome to me were her heavenly sighs and the sounds she made turning upon her creaking pallet.

During the day, I prayed silently, to no god in particular, for the strength to arrest all urges. I could not allow them to overtake what I knew was right. She would not be saddled with my care any longer than necessary.

One late-winter day while she carried a large pail, Dinah tripped over the loose floorboard on the front stoop. I heard the thump of the board, the one which always fetched up when least expected. The filthy mop water spilled onto her dress, so she came inside to change.

In her haste, she must have forgotten my whereabouts. The contrast of the darkened interior of the house, so opposite from the bright sun outside, must have dimmed her vision. She began to undress as though she were alone. Within my view. Unlike hers, my eyes were adjusted to the bit of light. Just the smallest ray entered through the curtained two-over-two window and fell upon her silhouette. Instead of looking away, I lost my wits. My wooden leg was strapped on; I could have walked into the other room. But I felt propelled to do the opposite.

I stepped from the shadow and began to aid in the unlacing of her dress.

She jumped at my touch. "Oh, Willy, I'm . . ." She began then stopped as I caressed the nape of her neck.

I longed for a moment of tenderness. Longed for the touch of her skin. The taste of her.

She turned toward me and accepted the passionate kiss I offered. Perhaps if she hadn't leaned on me, toppling us over onto her bed, we would have halted. But a love had been born between us, stronger than any I'd known. This love was not forbidden like the feelings I still held for Beth. With Dinah, rules were only self-inflicted.

Finding the back openings in her cotton layers, I slipped my hands inside. Dinah's inexperience and need for gentleness did not deter my advances. Before I could stop myself, we tasted of one another.

We ate heartily that day.

Once the afternoon had passed, we arose and smoothed our clothing. By the time we heard Dresden's arrival from his tutoring visit at a nearby home, our secret was concealed. I snuck into Dinah's bed that night, grateful that Dresden slumbered as deep as the dead, for my "sneaking" sounded more like a stampede of cattle. *Thump, thump, thump* echoed through the house as my weight fell upon my crutch—nothing akin to the melodic hum of the frogs and toads outside.

"Dinah, can I stay with you?" I whispered.

"Mama wouldn't . . . we ain't jumped the broom, Willy," she said, but her arms reached around me just the same. I breathed in her scent. My stump did not stop her from wanting me to take all of her. She did not object to my caresses, to our rhythms that continued until light began on the horizon. In that soft light, I memorized her details then arose and hobbled back toward my own bed. While doing so, I stumbled over a stool and remembered. In fairness to her, I once again vowed to not visit Dinah's bed. Not again. Though it pained me as sharp as a razor cutting flesh, I renewed my determination not to look at her.

My longing, however, grew to a suffering misery.

Dinah did not understand and asked, "Willy, why won't ya tell me? What did I do?"

"Nothing Dinah, we just cannot . . . I mean, *I* cannot." After picking up my crutch, I knocked on my wooden leg with it to accentuate the point. She turned to her chores. The cast iron pot she stirred became a reservoir for tears that slid silently down her cheeks.

***

A neighbor, Mr. Phipps, a lawyer, one day observed me on my route between town and home. He called out from his front door to catch my attention. "Boy. Yes, you there. Come."

Grumbling something I care not to repeat, I pulled the wagon up short.

"Could use a Nigger such as you to bring my mail from town. I find my time better spent with clients than on doing what a lesser man could do. Two cents per week should cover it."

"I am not your 'boy' nor anyone else's, sir." Heat throbbed in my ears. "You can keep your pennies and your offer."

The man's nose, as large and bulbous as an October turnip, turned red as he drew up his walking-stick and threw it in my direction. "You'll rue the day you said that to me. I know you're Withers' boy because I know the horse you're using today, and I don't care if you're his. I'll get you."

I slapped the reins firmly, and the mare sped away pulling me in the wagon behind. I hobbled into the house and threw down my crutch. "God damned cursed imbecile."

"Ya look to be bothered, Willy. I get ya somethin' cool. Then ya can tell me 'bout it," Dinah said, smiling and reaching into the root cellar for a cider jug. She was all sweetness.

I wasn't in the mood. "You can go on back to Virginia. Your ma and pa are likely needing you more than I do. I'd consider it a favor if you'd just go."

Her smile faded, and I did not deserve her kind reply. "I only seen ya was hot on the fringes. Like ya could use somethin' cool."

"Just stop, Dinah. Please. Go unload the wagon before the damned flies find the salt pork."

Silence descended around us. She stood there. The poison I had flung seemed to etch her face. I longed to take back my hateful words and to touch her again. To show her I still loved her.

With her head held high, she walked out the door and quietly went about the chore of unloading our provisions. She didn't utter a single word to me and continued her silence for four days. Yes, four long days she and Dresden spoke only of the weather and of what to plant come spring. She refused to talk to me.

Dresden kept himself occupied and out of the way, probably sensing something was amiss, or perhaps too involved with some new idea to notice.

At the close of that fourth day, Dinah spent the evening thumbing through the little leather book. I had taught her to read, at least a little. Always, we had used daylight hours because being next to her at night, in candlelight, would have been torture for me. Through endless exercises and simple sentences, she struggled. Without complaint. That night, instead of helping her, I watched her lips forming each word.

ne gro	sa cred	pa gan	so ber
cri er	gru el	stu pid	cru el
tu tor	du ty	li ar	ru in

Then she fluidly read the next sentences. She obviously had practiced them without me. Her voice was as sweet as apple-pan-dowdy.

> No man can say that he has done no ill,
> for all men have gone out of the way.
> There is none that doth good; no, not one.
> If I have done harm, I must do it no more.
> Life is not long but the life to come has no end.
> We must pray for them that hate us.
> We must love them that love not us.
> We must do as we like to be done to.

"Oh, all right, Dinah, just dig me a shallow grave. I'm sorry," I blurted.

"Well, Willy, it only took ya four days. I knew ya to be one sorry fool since we was back home." She gently closed the book and peered at me. "Even when ya thinks yer too good fer me, bein' educated and all, I still loves ya. So I suppose I's a fool too."

"Is that what you think?" I reached for her hand, but she pulled away. I continued, "I do not think you are less than me. Dinah, the opposite is true. The burden of this body is mine. I simply cannot wish upon you a moment more of hardship. The continual load would soon darken the light in your eyes. If we were to give in to what I feel, you'd lose the dance in your step."

"Willy, ya not the one put the dance there, but ya sure be the one keeps it alive. Don't ya see? I never be as happy as now. I's here with ya 'cause I wants to be. We's family, Willy T. Sherman. And I's hopin' we keep on bein' family. Only thing is, ya got to make yerself a choice." She stopped and stared at me. "I be leavin' now, if yer gonna keep pushin' me away. If ya be wantin' me, I's here. But later, ya can't be drivin' me out."

She sat back in her puddle of red calico fabric, the fanciest of her dresses. A knot of concern formed on her forehead. "Willy, ya be the one planted the wee child I has sleepin' here." She smoothed the fabric over her belly, and I noticed a small mound. "So ya best be takin' back all the poison ya sendin' my way. Or I will. I'll be leavin' to go back to Mama."

"The what?"

"Ya heard me with yer own ears. I's to be birthin' a baby 'bout five months from now, if I has it right."

"But, Dinah, we're not married."

"Married or no, baby still comin'. 'Sides, that ain't my fault, Mr. Sherman. Ain't it a man's job . . . the askin', I mean? Does I have to do that job, too?"

My thoughts swirled in such turmoil.

"So, what do ya think, Willy? Will ya marry me?" she asked. Halfway through that question, in the midst of the most telling portion, Dresden burst through the door. He took one look at us, turned a shade of crimson touching on purple, then retreated without a word.

Our laughter filled the house and tears streamed down our faces. All the tension of the last months just squeezed from us. She strolled over and sat on my lap. I stroked her wet cheeks.

"I was the one who needed to say the words," I said, catching my breath. "I couldn't."

"How long's it gonna take for ya to gather 'em up? I can't be waitin' for ya to get over the hurts, no more. Your body's as mended as it's gona be, and fightin' like a mule to keep yer eyes off me ain't gonna get ya nowhere. I can't be settin' here without the answer."

"No, I suppose not," I said. I thought of Dinah's mother and father, Pearl and Jax, and how their home and life on the Turnbull estate might be a more fitting place for Dinah and our child. Our child. That thought blew through like a summer storm, one which clears the humidity from the air. No child of mine would be born into slavery—even if freedom was promised.

I bent forward, and we kissed one of those wondrous kisses traded in the orchard of young love. Lingering there, I felt all the ice inside me melting. The chair squeaked on the floorboards as I urged her to stand and face me. My heart thudded in my chest. "I love you Dinah. And I want you something fierce. I will marry you, but only if you are certain of . . . of your want for me. You'll be saddled with the burden of a cripple."

"Well, I'll be blessed. Yes, I'll marry you, Willy!" She stood and twirled around, her red dress wrapping itself about her ankles. "Only one thing we has left to do," she said.

"What is that?"

"Ask our papas, I mean, Dresden and—"

"Ask my 'father' and yours," I said, finishing her thought.

She planted a quick kiss on my forehead and sprinted to the door. "I'll be gettin' ol' pa Dresden," she called. I waved my hand and smiled, but she was already out the door.

***

Wind howled from the north that day. As I strained to hear, the tiny window across the room rattled. Only that sound, along with the wind, reached my ears. Overnight, a small pile of dust had blown through the crack under the door. The whisk leaning beside the hearth beckoned to me since I did not wait well.

Lately, living here in Minnesota, I haven't minded quiet hours, but that day, sitting made me fidget like an impatient child. I grabbed the whisk and swept up the nearby dirt. I could have strapped on my peg or hoisted myself up on my crutch, but I knew Dinah and Dresden would be arriving soon. I hoped she would bring Dresden inside before telling him our news. Of course, he had most likely guessed what was transpiring when he had arrived unannounced. At any moment, they would burst through the door. I smiled at the image of Dresden's hair flying in his face.

"Dinah," I called out, not expecting her to hear. The wind grew louder.

After what seemed far too long, I cinched up the straps

holding my peg, grabbed my crutch, stood, and limped to the door. I pushed it open and could not comprehend what I saw.

On the opposite side of the road sat a figure in Dresden's cape, crumpled in a very unlikely posture. At the edge of my vision toward the main road, I turned just in time to see a group of perhaps five men riding away. In front of one rider, I spotted a flash of red cloth draped over his horse's neck.

"Dinah! Oh, no! Dinah!" Perhaps my screams were carried far enough. Perhaps they fell short. Perhaps my beloved's ears could no longer hear.

I hobbled closer to Dresden. He was still alive. That fact, though fortunate for me, was painfully unlucky for him.

"Phipps . . . Shepherdstown," he said in one expelled breath. Then he managed to force out just three more words. "Under . . . step . . . Will . . ." Struggling for air, heaving in agony, his chest caved in. No breath would come. I dropped to the dirt and cradled my friend while his life drained from him.

Night overtook the day while I watched the moon rise over the trees. I moaned and rocked but could not budge from that spot. Our road, only a laneway cut first by deer or savages and later worn smooth by horses and men, was not well traveled. Even still, it seemed odd that not a soul rode or walked by. Looking skyward, I blamed the threatening clouds as I thought of Dinah and of what could be her fate. The pain of that was far too difficult to ponder. Dresden's final words stabbed at me as I agonized over what to do. Rescuing Dinah, though my highest priority, seemed beyond the moment. I had to keep my mind clear and move in such a way as to maximize the possibility of finding her. And oh, dear God, our baby.

Moving Dresden into the house became my first task. His

body had not appeared heavy in life. In fact, I would have said the man was lean. Held by the clutches of death, however, his weight felt like boulders heaped upon a lifeless body. Using my crutch to drag us forward, I hauled him over the loose boards of the step and into the house.

Filled with a consuming weariness, I lay on Dinah's bed, dreading that sleep would be beyond reach. The lavender pomade she combed through her hair still lingered on her pillow. You can bet I festered while smelling her around me. I must have dozed a bit, however, for I awoke with a start from a dream where she had said, "Willy, my love, my love. Please."

"I will find you," I breathed into the darkness.

***

Morning slid in as I mustered together what was needed for travel. I donned the trousers Dinah had fashioned. She had created a large pocket on the right side, by turning up the leg and stitching it near the waist. Within its reaches, what little money was mine, a knife, a graphite stick, and Elizabeth's book could all be carried. Below the pouch, I strapped Dresden's peg leg. I couldn't believe he was gone.

Elizabeth, now also in New York, seemed to be my only resource. Risking a return to family in Virginia felt unthinkable. Loss of my freedom would be near certain, and with my movements slowed by my impairment, I'd be easily snared.

Dresden's final words carried great importance, I knew, since he had struggled so to free them from his lips. Following his cue, and wondering what I might find in prying up the loose floorboard on the front stoop, I sat down to accomplish the task.

Fleeing spiders did not welcome my intrusion as I reached into the gritty darkness. Patting about in the dirt, I hit something solid. Its edges revealed it to be too bulky to remove through the opening, so I pried two more boards loose.

I lifted a metal chest and found it surprisingly clean, which indicated someone had recently moved the container. It weighed far more than the size would dictate. After carefully unbuckling the leather strap around its girth, I lifted the lid. In the chest were some papers along with currency and coins of varying sizes and denominations, some silver, but most gold—hundreds or perhaps thousands of dollars—certainly more than I had ever seen before. On a better day, I might have shown some excitement at the sight, but I did not allow myself that luxury. Instead, I quickly scanned through the papers. A deed to the house, Dresden's certificate of birth, a death notice for each of his parents were held there. Below was a pouch labeled "Last Will and Testament."

Inside the pouch lay a small envelope. It was sealed with wax and stamped with a crest. I was familiar with the emblem's design as it adorned a few dishes in the kitchen. On the front, in Dresden's perfect penmanship I read, "William T. Sherman, upon my death, Dresden Withers." I put the Will aside, broke the seal, and opened the envelope and read this:

Dear William,

No rest shall come to me until I have settled my affairs. I believe this amount is enough for you to start a life with Dinah. Always listen to her, for she has a heart equal to the glitter you see before you. My boy, I know you will be married before the year is done, but in recent days, trouble has begun to stir.

I am not proud of the manner in which this fortune came to be mine. You see, I am the son of a slave trader. My father was a very successful man, if you choose to call selling humans a success; certainly, there was no man richer nor meaner than he. Adam Turnbull's father and mine were partners, along with Joseph Phipps, the attorney in town. I could not bring myself to spend a cent of this shame on my own comforts. Instead, over the years I supported several ex-slaves, you included. The others are well and away, living on their own in Canada. What is left is what you see. Someday, you may find a method by which to help someone to escape from the darkness of their birthright and to find the air and lightness of freedom.

Mine was a legacy I do not wish upon my worst enemies, and the burden partially lifted when Adam brought you and the others into my home. Save for your recent youthful indiscretions, I look on your years here with pride.

Please accept this gift. This is the only way I have to atone for the suffering of those less fortunate than I. You are worthy of it, William, but always remember from whence it came.

Perhaps one day, you will find a fitting use for it.
Dresden Samuel Withers, III

Dresden had known I loved Dinah. He'd seen my future

even before I did. And Phipps, the old reprobate who had denigrated me that recent day, I knew I'd have to confront him. Would he know of Dinah's captors? My grief shifted aside and made room for anger.

I read the legal mandates in Dresden's Will, trying to grasp what they meant. Key phrases jumped off the papers such as "and to William T. Sherman, I bequeath my entire estate and property." I'd only known a little of what lawyers call business. They might have seen themselves as reputable people, but I saw mostly hot air with little substance. My memory spun to this fable in Elizabeth's book:

Fable VI
The Partial Judge

A FARMER came to a neighboring Lawyer, expressing great concern for an accident which he said had just happened.

One of your Oxen, continued he, has been gored by an unlucky Bull of mine, and I should be glad to know how I am to make you reparation.

Thou art a very honest fellow, replied the Lawyer, and wilt not think it unreasonable that I expect one of thy oxen in return.

It is no more than justice, quoth the Farmer, to be sure; but what did I say?

I mistake—It is your Bull that has killed one of my Oxen.

Indeed! says the Lawyer, that alters the case: I must inquire into the affair; and if—

*And if! said the Farmer—the business I find would
have been concluded without an if, had you been as
ready to do justice to others, as to exact it from them.*

***

Six half-eagles wrapped in cloth, a hand full of silver coins,
and two pouches of documents joined the other items that
knocked against my thigh. The rhythmic clanging mirrored my
uneven gait. I strode to the door and hammered it with my
crutch. The sound boomed as though a spike was being driven
into a thick timber.

Phipps opened the door. "Go away, boy," he snorted and
attempted to close the door. It did not shut, though, as I had
thrust my crutch into the gap.

"You have business with me, sir," I said as I stepped
uninvited into his home. The old swine's startled look gave me a
hint of pleasure. "I am here to inform you of the death of
Dresden Withers and to ask for your services in the reading of
his Will."

"Withers . . . dead? Oh, you mean Withers, Senior, of course,
that happened years ago," Phipps said, not looking at me while
he rubbed the sparse hairs atop his head.

"No. I meant Dresden Withers III. He died yesterday, and his
estate must be settled."

"Well I . . . uh . . . you've come to the right place, boy." He
motioned for me to have a seat, but I remained standing. "What
do you know of it?" he asked.

Even though I'd seen Phipps about town many times, words
had only been exchanged between us when he'd offered me a

servant's wage. The man showed no recollection of who I was. "I know much," I said and reached into my coat. "His Will is here in this oil bag." I held out the parcel.

"Well, let me take a look at her." He grabbed with his fleshy hand. Three gold rings flashed on his fingers. Phipps scanned the pages. "I say. It looks to be in order. A man, a Mr. Sherman, is to inherit what is left of Withers' legacy. Indeed, he is." A slight smile curled his lip. "Withers was rich . . . well . . . it isn't common knowledge, he lived like such an indigent." Drawing the gray hairs of his thin eyebrows together, he scowled at me. "Boy, do you happen to know this Sherman fellow, what is it . . . uh . . . William T. Sherman? And why do you have Withers' papers?"

I ignored his question. "I do know Mr. Sherman. But before I tell you where to find him, I must have your assurance that what is justly his must prevail as the Will decrees. Do we need more witnesses to the rightfulness of this document?"

"No. I am fully licensed. This is a simple transaction. It has all been legally documented and signed."

I took two steps forward. "In that case, sir, I am the very same William Turnbull Sherman."

Phipps' face flushed as he snarled like a rabid cur. "You? I don't believe you. I won't—"

"I have my paper of freedom and school diploma to prove identity, along with gold to pay you." I jingled the coins to prove it.

"Gold? Where did you get that money, boy?"

"It is none of your affair. I have more than this, and will pay double your fee for services. But you must first tell me what you know of the slave snatchers whom yesterday raided Dresden

Withers' home—our home."

"You're Withers' Nigger? Slave snatchers? I am unfamiliar—"

"No!" I thrust my crutch into his chest. Phipps fell backward onto a small rocking chair, splintering it beneath his bulk. I moved closer, my weight now on his throat. "There will be no further lies!" Phipps paled as I drew in a deep breath and continued. "I know your past. I also know you had it in for me and Dresden, both. There is gold, yes, an abundance of it. You may even believe some share of it belongs to you. I will give you a piece of it for the information I require." I leaned on him even harder. "Now let us begin again."

"Alright, alright! God knows I didn't mean for them to kill anyone. I'm a civil man. I'm no murderer. I just wanted those boys to stir things up, to teach him and his chattel a lesson. You all look the same, I did not recognize . . . and whatever you've been told, I was no slave trader. I just wrote up some papers. I did the books. And listen, boy, if I had known you were Mr. Sherman, I wouldn't have—"

"You wouldn't have what?"

Phipps did not dare to say.

"I'm no fool, Phipps. You hate me and those who would help freemen. You may want to justify what you did, but you still procured money selling people in to slavery. You cannot simply wash away the stench of what you've done. You reek of it, sir." I pushed harder on my crutch, making him wince. "Now, tell me where they have taken her."

"Taken her? Who?"

I lunged weight into him, this time pinning him with all my strength, my hands trembling at his throat. "My Dinah, you old dough-faced soul driver. I am not leaving till you divulge her whereabouts."

Drool oozed down his jowl, and sweat poured from his contorted face. He squirmed beneath me, coughing as he struggled to loosen my grip. Finally, he raised his arms in surrender. My hold eased but only enough to allow him to speak. "Shepherdstown. They're from Shepherdstown, Virginia." He rubbed his neck and wiped his forehead with his sleeve. "I don't know if that's where they'll go. And I don't care. To be sure, your girl will be sold before the week is over."

I pushed into him to lift myself off the floor. He let out a yelp then rolled onto his knees and brushed off his waistcoat. Trying to escape, he scuffled over to the farthest corner. As he flopped down on a small bench, he adjusted his collar and the wooden frame moaned beneath him.

Right behind him, I wedged myself beside the startled lawyer. "Now we're getting somewhere," I said, pushing into him. The lion-shaped walnut arm surely was jutting into Phipps' spine. He winced. Color drained from his sweaty face.

"Now where were we?" I planted my crutch in the center of his left foot.

I managed to get out of him what little he seemed to know. He did not regard himself as an evil man; however, I saw the cost of his actions. They were perhaps worse than those done by someone convinced of their validity. This man knew better. He wasn't ignorant. Still, he took part simply for the wealth it afforded.

Wherever Dinah was, I had to find her. In the end, Phipps saw it my way. He agreed to provide a release of Dresden's estate, and I agreed to not contact the authorities about his part in

Dinah's abduction. Time was short. Getting the magistrate involved would have slowed my progress and accomplished little. After all, she was a young Negro woman. No one would have cared about her safety—except me.

***

Somehow, I found the strength needed to perform the next tasks. First, I had Phipps dig Dresden's grave. While he did so, I retrieved my book and turned to page ninety.

As a slave on the Turnbull farm, what I knew of money had been sparse. Thankful that the book contained some information on the subject relieved me of having to ask and show my ignorance. The complexity still confounded me, so I set about to review what the book contained.

The dollar is one hundred cents; but the value of a pound, shilling, and penny, is different, in different states, and in England. English money is called Sterling—one dollar is four shillings and six pence sterling—in New England and Virginia, it is six shillings—in New York and North Carolina, it is eight shillings—in New Jersey, Pennsylvania, Delaware, and Maryland, it is seven shillings and six pence. But these differences give great trouble, and will soon be laid aside—all money will be reckoned in dollars and cents.

With no mention of gold, the value of what the trunk contained would need to be later calculated. I hoped it would be enough for what would come.

After the grave was dug, I insisted that Phipps stand by while I prayed aloud for my friend's departed soul. Next, we counted the cash and coin. The gold and silver, it turned out, would to be enough to provide comfort to nearly the end of my days. I paid Phipps the fee for his services, in silver. A journey to Virginia was about to begin. The anger, which I used to get that far, began to drift away. Sagging in my seat with fear and grief, I boarded Dresden's wagon in Oneida, New York, but before I headed toward the South, I had one last stop.

***

The Rockaway coupe, a carriage of fine character with sleek lines and superior comfort, would hopefully afford me safe passage. Knowing the deal was slanted in favor of the seller did not halt my purchase of the vehicle. The day contain-ed too little time for haggling. Yes sir, I spent a reckless sum of money, but it would make the journey to Beth quicker and more comfortable.

Two days later in the early afternoon, after pulling the carriage to a stop, I shifted in my seat. An itch still existed where there once were toes. An ache of regret slid into my heart because I had never disclosed to Elizabeth the truth—that I was one leg shy of whole. In my reply, to the letters received from her after the fire, I had written of my fall from the window, about my growing love for Dinah, and how I held admiration toward my mentor, Dresden Withers. No words followed of what some might think of as my most important, yet despised, detail.

If the truth were written in my own hand, I could never deny that truth. She still thought of me as whole. In my own illusive dreams, a complete man still ran along the wooded paths of my boyhood. Beth could see me there as well, mucking out the barn and resting in a hay mound. If she knew the truth, the disappearance of that undamaged person would be complete.

Soon, the real me would be reflected in her eyes.

On that warm day, the sun seemed brighter as it reflected off the white-washed building before me. I could see no one through the four even rows of windows dotting its stately facade. Many of the buildings in Troy, New York, had nearly this same exterior. I rechecked the number from Beth's last letter. Building after building marched along the stately street.

A fitful growling in my gut arose and brought a retched taste to my tongue. I tottered to the door and tapped quietly upon it. Perhaps I did not want anyone to answer, and indeed no one arrived for a few moments.

Finally, a young girl opened the door and greeted me with a curtsy. "May I help you?" she asked.

"Miss Elizabeth Sherman. Is she in?" I tipped my hat.

"Why, no. Miss Sherman should return sometime soon. If you check again after supper, you're sure to catch her. Might you have a card to leave?"

"I do not, but please tell her to expect a caller this evening." I gazed past her into the huge foyer. A plush, ornate rug swept through the middle of a marble floor. The door closed and I turned around.

A group of young ladies walking toward me, along the elm-lined boulevard, came into view. One held a stick and was bumping it along the wrought-iron pickets. The racket she created did not fit the air of the place. "Beth," I whispered. While gazing directly at her and tucking my wooden leg solidly beneath my frame, I held my crutch close at my side. I could see she had matured into beauty. Sickness in my stomach began to roil.

"Oh lord, what a beautiful thing," said one of the ladies as she walked alongside my carriage. Her golden dress swirled about her ankles. Her gloved hand slid on the glossy black side panel. "Perhaps one of us shall be seated beside the gentleman who owns this fine carriage." She peered into the side window and reached in to touch the leather seat. "Maybe the Governor is calling. I'll ask the driver," she said, motioning for the others to follow. She turned in my direction. They jostled toward me, each nudging slightly to be in front. Beth hung back as her attention focused on stroking the mare's mane.

"I am a disappointment to be sure," I said. "This carriage belongs to me. As you can see both driver and passenger are under the comfort of cover, which suits my sensibilities." No hint of recognition crossed Beth's face as I spoke. Her smile, which had captured my young heart, was spent on the horse.

"Of course, if Uncle Luke were here he would take us for a turn."

Hearing those words, Beth spun around. She strode forward, searching my face. Then her attention was drawn to my wooden stump. Her smile faded. "Willy T.?" she asked, lifting her inquiry back to my eyes.

I was used to that change in people, the one making its way across her face. It took root in a flicker of discomfort, and, without fail, there followed a recognition of what I lacked. The awkward silence would be mine to break, for suddenly the observer had nothing to say. Beth, however, hesitated for such a fleeting instant that perhaps it was only my anticipation of the moment that sent more of that vile taste to my mouth. I swallowed.

"By the look of it, you have quite a story to tell, Willy T. But first, let me introduce you. These are my sisters in learning: Elizabeth Cady, soon to be Mrs. Stanton; Martha Browne; and Emily Swift. Ladies, this is my oldest and dearest friend, Mr. William T. Sherman."

My fears began to thaw as we bowed and smiled in the proper manner. The young women then excused themselves, leaving us alone, as alone as two people could be on a busy street in the bustling city of Troy.

She led me to a nearby park bench. We began to share stories of what had occurred since our parting. Beth had lived with the family of a lawyer and abolitionist, Arlan Theel, who spent much of his time abroad. In his absence, his home still bustled with political activity. The debate raged between those abolitionists who wanted slavery stopped but Negroes sent back to Africa, and those who saw us equal to themselves in God's eyes. "Willy T., some women are even starting to voice their own opinions. They think we should have the right to vote. I join them in leaning to that side; though, I would not want Mrs. Turnbull to be among those to vote on any issue."

I smiled. Her tone sounded familiar, but her words were foreign to what my memory held. Education had changed her just as mine had changed me. My attention wandered while watching her hand brush a stray hair aside. The memory of our one kiss presented itself. Her lips curled in her own soft smile, making me wonder if similar thoughts were visiting her in the same moment.

"During the first few years, I was tutored by Mr. Theel's wife and also by their eldest daughter," she continued. "Now,

Mary and I are both here at the Troy Female Seminary. Though I wished to find a different vocation, most of us, and we number nearly three hundred, will be teachers. All but a few are from elite families. I was given some charity, in free tuition, because of Mr. Theel's connections."

Ladies in lacy silk dresses strolled by, many on the arms of men wearing stovepipe hats and satin vests. There was a slow steadiness to the place.

"Of all the subjects I study, by far History is my—"

"I beg your pardon, Beth, it is Dinah," I interrupted. The ease and tempo of the day would be comforting to most people, but worry was sapping my patience. "I'm desperate to find her."

"What do you mean, find her? Is she not at your home in Oneida?"

I related the violence and crushing grief of the last few days. How travel had been slowed by mud and early spring rain the likes of which no one could wish to encounter. How my only comfort was in knowing that Dinah's captors were surely hindered by the same conditions. And how I had deposited a portion of Dresden's money in a bank, naming her and Dinah and myself for withdrawals. I also needed to keep alternate funds in another location, since placing trust in one institution seemed foolhardy.

"Beth, of late, the banks prove to be terribly risky. I was told the notes Dresden had held for years have been rendered non-redeemable. They were drawn on banks now closed. The suffering endured for that fortune now drained of value, by further greed and thievery, turns my sight red."

"You said there is some gold, Willy T., surely that will be usable. Will it not?" She patted my hand.

I pulled it back, feeling eyes already staring at the young White woman and Negro man who sat side by side. "Do you know of someone I may call upon? I need to lighten the load further, and I don't know anyone else. Someone you trust?"

"Yes, of course. But Willy T., I . . ." She paused, placed her hand upon her breast, and tears appeared at her eyes. "I must go with you."

"No, I will not let you. I wouldn't even ask this favor of you, were it not for my lack of connections. You must finish your studies, Beth. Though I do not know how a woman might use knowledge, other than to teach, perhaps a direction will avail itself. Besides, a White woman traveling with me would only raise—"

"Yes, of course. But—"

"No! We will not speak of it again." The words came quick and sure, but my heart bled at the thought of denying her. I still held love for Beth, you see. She still came into my thoughts daily—even while I loved Dinah. No future could ever be ours, however. Not together.

"You have become a stubborn man," she said, her tears flowing, which she did not attempt to hide.

I turned on the bench to look at her. "You must understand. Here, you are sheltered from what the world is still like. Not everyone is so refined. Wealth is worn on this street like a comfortable overcoat. The places I will need to travel, if I pranced around like these men do, someone would strip me and sell me for what they could get. I have to go back. Shepherdstown may only be at the border, but it is still Virginia."

"But Willy T., you do need . . . if not me . . . some assistance. Don't you?" She wiped at her tears as two men stopped across the street, conversing and looking in our direction.

I stood so the onlookers could see my missing limb. Most, upon seeing the wooden peg, would walk away, believing I was incapable of movement and no longer a threat. My action brought about the desired result. "Beth, you are right of course. I do need someone willing to do what is necessary. I have gold enough to buy almost anyone's services. However, the right person must have shrewdness gathered from experience. Perhaps you know of safe houses between here and Virginia? Or of someone willing to take risks as well as to travel with me?"

She stood and paced, so I sat back down. "Yes, what you say is right," she began. Her hair sparkled in the sun. Her concerned expression made me love her even more, but seeing her also bade thoughts of Dinah. I discovered right then that it was possible to love equally more than one person.

"I believe your first stop should be the Theel estate," she said. "Mr. Theel will know where to send you." She kicked at a cobble, which jutted up higher than the rest. "I cannot imagine. It will not be simple to . . . well . . . to say goodbye to you, again."

"Every day, dear Beth, I carry your book in my pocket. You see, it is here. This is how I hold you close in my thoughts." I reached into the deep folded pocket and handed it to her.

She opened the cover, and a few leather flakes drifted to the ground.

"The water damage took its toll, in particular here on the back," I said, reaching up to run a finger along the scaly surface. "Most pages are still legible. Perhaps it would be safer if . . . do you wish to keep it?"

"No," she said and thrust it back into my hands. "It was my gift."

I reached into my pocket again, handed her the graphite, and opened the book to its final page. "Please sign and date it here to show the book had once been yours."

As she did so, her tears fell upon the page. "The warmth this gives my heart, when I picture you reading it, is enough," she said. "Someday, when you find Dinah, you might use it to teach her to read."

"We had begun lessons when . . ." Caught in a painful lump, my words faltered.

Beth sat back down beside me. "And you will continue those lessons. You must believe in this."

My attempt at remaining stoic wavered as Beth wrapped her arms around me, right there on that stately boulevard across the street from the town square. Tears stung my eyes, but I did not allow them to fall. At any moment, the sight of us might be cause for a small riot. However, I could not move. Elizabeth's embrace held me to the bench.

Finally, when I was able, I stood and said, "I must go."

"I will be here when you return. Promise me, Willy T., please. Bring Dinah to visit, won't you?" I wondered if my love for Dinah gave Beth any cause for heartache. Her mention of a future visit felt so natural, as though my having someone else to love made her content. Perhaps.

"I promise, Beth. We will both return." Her expression relaxed. My brow remained furrowed as I had no right to make such a promise, especially regarding Dinah's future. While driving away, I could not look at her, but with a level of certainty, I knew she had waved me out of sight in a final farewell.

Somehow, I was able to recall her directions to the Theel

residence. I sped along the road as quickly as my carriage could travel and lingered at the Theel Estate only long enough to obtain what was required. I also deposited the monies not presently needed. Having to trust that these strangers were honorable was a tall order, but I shoved my fears away and left. Upon my departure, the road was as good as could be expected, worn smooth by local traffic and maintained by some politician who apparently had money to spare. Neatly trimmed trees and hedges lined the way, their branches as manicured as the beards of the men who rode the route. Perhaps Arlan Theel himself saw to it. Not one traveler looked askance at me, a black-skinned man riding alone in an expensive carriage. I appeared to be a servant, running errands at his master's bidding. The distance between slave and servant seemed to be a short one.

Long about noon-time, however, and as directed, I veered onto the narrow lane marked by a sign reading, VISTERS WIL BE SHOT. The superior road gave way to rarely traveled ruts pocked with stones. Like a ship in a hurricane, the coupe bounded through the woods. I held to the reins to keep aboard until my arrival in a clearing. A small wooden shack-like cabin draped in briars stood before me. Even though the sun shone high in the sky, the house appeared dark and vacant. My thoughts strayed to the hidden compartment under my seat, the one containing gold within its reaches. There I had stored but a fraction of Dresden's fortune, enough for the remainder of my journey as well as a sum deemed necessary to buy needed services and Dinah's freedom.

I drove around the back of the building and halted before a small shed. The roof sagged in the center. To even a casual observer, it was easy to predict that before the end of the coming winter, the building would finish decaying to rubble.

Mr. Theel had assured me. "Many runaways travel through that unlikely place, more than through my own mansion. The hovel's location, being on a direct route from Virginia to Canada, makes it a timely respite." Anyone able to arrive there from the South seemed to have a degree of certainty of reaching freedom.

Dismounting from the coupe in my customary fashion, backward, I heard footsteps in the dirt somewhere behind me.

"You there, state yer business."

"Mr. Odber Perkins?" I asked.

"Hold on, don't you be movin' another inch. How do I know ya?"

"If you are indeed Perkins, you do not. Arlan Theel sent me."

"Who the hell's Arlan Theel, you say?"

"Perhaps I am mistaken. Are you not acquainted? I have a letter of introduction."

"Well, let's see it, boy."

I finished landing on the dirt from the carriage, turned around, reached into my coat, and eyed the rifle pointed in my direction.

"Slow it down, boy. I'd just a soon shoot ya." He raised the gun to aim at my heart.

"You have nothing to fear, sir. Do you expect that I will beat you with this?" I shook my crutch at the ground. "I have no match to your weapon." While I spoke, I studied the man. "Odber" was a fitting name for the odd, little bump-of-a-man who stood before me. A baggy, woolen cap drooped over one side of his head. His waistcoat was frayed around the edges and appeared far too tight. The buttons pulled, and his shirt, which peeked out from behind, was soiled by a large oily stain. Yes, I believed he would shoot me. His sign had told the truth.

After handing him Mr. Theel's letter, Perkins' eyes stared and barely moved along the paper. It seemed the man could not read. He spat into the dirt and wiped his chin upon his sleeve.

"So what's your story, boy?"

"My name is William Turnbull Sherman and—"

"Turnbull? One of Turnbull's Niggers?"

"I am not anyone's slave. Perhaps you are the wrong man." I turned the coupe's foot plate to begin re-boarding.

From the corner of my eye, I perceived Perkins to be lowering his rifle. He spat again. "Now, hold on there. All depends on your troubles, I suppose. For some I'd be a right-good fit, others best be movin' down the road to look for another." He scratched his head, and in so doing, revealed the side his hat had concealed. No ear, only a scar, one nastier and newer than my own, lay where the ear should have been. He tore the hat completely from his head and threw it to the ground.

"God damn thing. Hurts like hell." He growled, literally, as though he were a bear rising to attack.

"Sir, if you are an acquaintance of Adam Turnbull, then we have at least two things in common," I said and knocked on my wooden leg.

"Yes, I suppose that stump means you're missin' somethin' more than me," he said.

"Might I ask? Can you hear from that side? Or did you lose your hearing as well?"

"It ain't clear, but ya bet I can hear somethin'. Sounds like my head's at the bottom of a frog hole. I got fish wadin' through, and the bubbles set my head into some fierce itchin'. Course if I itch, hurts like hell. Not sure which be the worst of it—the itchin' or hurtin'.""

"I am indeed familiar with having an itch and nowhere to scratch."

"So what're yer troubles, boy? And why'd ya come to think I'd be the one to see about 'em?"

I described Dinah's abduction and why I was heading to Virginia. "You can plainly see that I need a traveling companion. However, my other needs are more than what is obvious. I require the services of someone with a lighter complexion and more sagacity than I possess."

"Well, I don't know if I has any sagacity lyin' around here, but if I do, yer welcome to 'em, boy. I's shades lighter. Squared up on that account. But what'll the cost be to me? I just don't know how much spendin' money to bring along."

"None, sir. In fact I will pay you handsomely," I said. "I do need to retain enough for Dinah's freedom, but the rest of what I carry, I assure you, it will be yours."

"Hmm . . . well, I suppose I could be countin' on more than say . . . twenty . . . or no thirty eagles? A trip like what you're proposin' could be costly, not knowin' what's around the next turn and all."

"Yes, that would be right."

"What? The thirty eagles, or the not knowin'?"

"Both."

"Both? Well then . . . hmm . . . I'll need to see what ya have. Seein' it would turn this bastard into a believer."

With a small rod hidden beside the driver's seat, I pried up the cushion, then lifted the small trunk, and placed it on the ground in front of Odber. With less than one quarter of its original content, the container was much lighter.

"Oh, now, ain't that pretty." Perkins knelt down and dove his hands into the cache and sifted the coins through his fingers.

As he did so, my imagination drifted to what such a sum could do. For Dinah, I could purchase a home with windows, even with shutters. We could raise a family, and somehow provide aid to others. However, such a dream remained in danger as Dinah could already have been sold. My life was, to that moment, a series of misfortune and poor choices. If the trend continued, perhaps trusting Perkins would prove to cause even more trouble. I no longer wished to be swayed by circumstance. There appeared to be no flat ground to stand on. Would this odd man turn thief and leave me stranded? Or worse?

"Mr. Theel assured me you would be honorable. Might I have your word, Perkins? You will not rob me some night while I sleep. Swear to it on this bible," I held out Beth's little book.

"No need to get God involved." Odber spit at the dirt. "This gold'll be awful temptin', but I's not the theivin' sort. Not lookin' for handouts, no siree. Just knowin' where this is at, that'll be enough." He lifted one coin above his head..

"Then, might we begin?" I asked, grabbing the coin from him and tossing it back into the trunk. "Now. While we still have daylight remaining? We won't be able to travel as many miles at night." I stuffed Beth's book back into my pocket and stowed away the trunk. I looked down at Odber. He stood only as tall as perhaps my shoulder. "I shall be the driver," I said.

He spat yet again and glared at me. "Boy, there's a thing or two we've got to get straight. First, I's the boss, 'Massa' to ya, boy. Surely ya know this. I has some years on ya, and by the look of ya, I's gone to a different sorta school. Are ya willin' to do what yer told? We'll be heading to the South, after all."

I hesitated. Giving up my freedom to this stranger seemed more than a few steps in the wrong direction. However, I would need to succumb to more than this degradation to retrieve Dinah. "I will agree to your terms; however, you may not address me as 'boy'."

"Yes sir, I can call ya 'Willy', wouldn't sound right to say 'Mr. Sherman'." He flicked my hat off my head and caught it midair. "Next, you gotta lose the finery. We'll head into town and sell that fancy carriage straight away." He stroked the smooth brim of my stovepipe, and felt the satin lining. "Loads of folks has passed through here, so I's sure to have somethin' that'll fit ya. We're the stop where the alterations get done. We divvy up the new clothes and send 'em along. Yer trousers and boots be good to go south, but this here hat, your shirt, and coat have gotta go up to the North. Just the shine on them buttons is enough to set men to wonderin'. These'll outfit someone goin' to Canada. Yes siree. My partner ain't here just now, but he'll find them a fittin' heir."

Odber opened a shed door, dug through a horse feeding trough, and found a shirt nearly as stained as his own. He handed it to me along with an overcoat with holes at each elbow. They would fit my frame. As though he were a fine clothier, he estimated my size by sight. Hairs from unmet heads lined the hat that I lifted to my head. What Southerners expected of a slave is what I became as I traded my attire for those rough-sewn scraps.

I spent the following half-hour ridding myself of everything else that seemed even remotely expensive. When my attentions reached Beth's book, I admired what remained of the leather, gilt letters, and ribbon marker. With knife in hand, I cut through the silk. Thinking the gold lettering and design on the cover could be removed by rubbing, I made a feeble attempt but soon discovered the entire binding already slid freely on its boards. Slipping the knife along where glue should have held the leather, I cut through a few stitches, then tore off the wooden under-boards. After throwing the wood into the room's cold hearth, I placed the leather cover and ribbon on the table. I thought of them as an altar at which to pray forgiveness. "Forgive me, Beth," I said. "In less than one minute, I have turned our dear book into a ratty untitled pad." I slid it back into my pocket where, without its hard corners, it settled in like a child against its mother.

I felt so sorry. I should have left it in her care.

***

As though we had done it a thousand times before, Odber and I packed his wagon with necessary food provisions. We added two bedrolls, consisting of two mats and quilts, which would offer sufficient warmth.

Odber insisted we hide my gold in a barrel of grain and leave the empty trunk in his shed. We drove my coupe as far south as Albany, where he sold it to the first person who showed an interest. I suffered a substantial loss, but the buyer threw in two chickens to sweeten the deal. Driving away from the town, we were at long last traveling in the intended direction: toward the border between New York and Pennsylvania, then on to Virginia.

"Odber, how many miles to the border? To Virginia?"

"Willy, yer remindin' me, I'm 'Odber', sure. But you don't be sayin' the 'r', it's 'Odba'."

"Odba?"

"Yes, Odba. Ya gots to say it the way my pa's people says it since I's named after his grandpa."

"I'm familiar with the importance of a person's name. Having the title of a relative honors the past. You have the right to be called what you wish, but do you think it best that I call you 'Massa Perkins'? Perhaps I should even call you 'Massa Perkins, sir'?"

"I know Odba's a funny name, but don't ya think it's more fittin'? 'Massa Perkins' sounds all . . . I don't know, just wrong. If ya call me by my last name, I'll think maybe Pa has stepped right outta his grave and joined us." He spat toward the ground but the glob landed on his boot. "Ah hell, probably only need to keep this up for a few days. Drop the 'sir', change it to 'Mister', and we have a deal. I can't stand all them stiff manners. Shit, I's stuck with Perkins, ain't I?"

I did not answer. When my companion spoke he seemed to not expect a reply. Perkins' jabbering was grating but provided distraction. If we had been more kindred spirits, my fears may have more easily taken root. With Odber's entertaining chatter flapping in my ears, the hours sped away at a gallop, not a trot.

We drove the horses hard and only stopped to switch who was behind the reins, and once to refresh the horses. I ran the team at a fast clip during the daylight hours, while Perkins did his part at night. For me, the only stretches fraught with difficulty were those when he slept because I had only his snoring to keep me company. During the first afternoon and evening, my head bobbed, and squinting against the setting sun, my eyes watered. After witnessing my fatigue, Perkins did not awaken me until midday the next. A sense of dread awoke me from a fitful sleep. We had stopped along a riverbank. Smelling of dirt and sweat, I walked to the water's edge and began an attempt at a bath.

"Willy, stop! What're ya doin'?" Perkins threw his hands skyward and ran down the embankment in my direction.

"Bathing," I mumbled.

"No, no! Damn, boy. Do ya have rocks for brains? Need to be ripe when we get where we're goin'." I opened my mouth to speak, but he held his hand up to halt the progress. "I want us so ripe that we can't either of us stand bein' within twenty rods of the other."

"I am near to feeling overwhelmed already by—"

"And by the way, Willy, start droppin' those 'G's of yours like ya said ya would. Come on, boy. Oh, sorry about that 'boy' habit o' mine, but ya told me it weren't gonna be a stretch to shift back to yer Southern talk. We's got to keep up appearances."

Most of our conversations went much the same direction as that one, with him yelling at me, lecturing me on what to do or not to do. Memories of Dresden floated in as my previous teacher had done much the same, only he had pushed me in the exact opposite direction, upward. Perkins shoved me down and away from learning, discretion, and respectability. Most other discussions centered on speculation of what we might encounter, even though we both knew planning any action would likely be worthless.

After one of the chickens decided to lay a few, we added boiled eggs to our diet of johnny-cakes and hard tack. The non-laying hen we roasted and ate on the third day. Being ever-closer to where Dinah might be stirred my inner turmoil. Eating anything felt as though I were forsaking the hardship she might be enduring. I needed strength for what lay ahead, however, so I did find a way to eat. On several occasions, I could not keep what I ate inside.

In a mere four days, we reached a point overlooking where the Potomac meets the Shenandoah. The town of Harper's Ferry lay far below, within the embrace of those two mighty rivers. Hoping to avoid suspicion, we planned to cross the Potomac there and approach Shepherdstown from the south. We would appear to be Southerners, a slave and his owner, arriving in town to attend the weekly auction. We would bid on a young woman needed for breeding stock.

A sudden loud crack was followed by a low rumble. I raised a questioning brow toward Odber.

"Some blastin' up ahead, I 'spect. Heard the railroad's comin' clear up here. Canal's just got built and now the train's gonna take over." Perkins scratched his head. "Stupid, God-damn politicians. Ain't enough havin' all them city-folk down along the seaboard. They gotta make it easy for 'em to move up to these parts. For what, I ask ya? For what? Why'd they want to move here for?"

Again, I did not answer his question. Conversing with a "massa" certainly could be cause for others to take notice. At that moment, it was safer to remain silent.

The road we traveled took a turn as we approached a small outcropping. Ahead stood four men, and one stepped forward to wave us down. "Better stop right here. You'll be blasted to kingdom-come if you go any farther. 'Sides, the ferry's closed for the next couple weeks. If you need to cross, can do it up at the Pack Horse Ford, just north of Shepherdstown. Go back 'bout a mile and take the left fork onto the Canal Road. If the sign's gone, don't worry none. It's the only road worth the time to piss on. Only take you one, maybe two extra days, dependin' on your ambitions."

And so, just like that, the one plan we had mutually decided on was quite literally blown to bits.

***

"That's the biggest stack o' logs I've ever laid eyes on," Perkins said later that day. "How many cord ya figure?"

I thought of the book's passage in this regard, but I was too afraid to take the book from my pocket to read it to him.

In solids, forty feet of round timber, or fifty feet of hewn timber, make a ton. A cord of wood contains one hundred and twenty-eight solid feet; it is, a pile four feet high, four feet wide, and eight feet long.

"It appears too large to calculate," I said. "Perhaps they have cut this much because of the rail?"

"Come on, Willy. 'It appears too large to calculate?' Do ya mean 'too big to be figurin', Massa.' Ain't that what ya mean to say?"

He spat in the dirt and continued. "Course. Seems so. Look at her, though." Perkins motioned to the other side of the wagon. "About half mile that-a-way as well. All the cleared land around here, ya think they wouldn't be cuttin' through the forest. Course they's all sittin' down in Philadelphia, around some big-ass table considerin' maps. Come up with this keen idea. Them boys don't know about the trees none. Not these ones up here. Some trunks has to be four-feet 'cross. I bet maps don't take no account o' the trees. Trees oughta have a place for livin'. Most folks think I's odd, even crazy in the head, and they figure much of what I say as meanin' nothin', but I's always thought trees oughta get left alone." He jabbed his elbow into my ribs. "More times than not, don't ya think, Willy? Hell, they're older'n humans, some of 'em. Ain't that so? Ain't they older'n us?"

"Yep, Massa, they be, Mr. Perkins, sir."

Perkins rolled his eyes. "Course ya can bet, some fella's makin' a shit-load-o' money off this thing. Yes siree."

Perkins' comment reminded me of his true motivation, and how it remained most prominent in his mind. Money—my gold to be precise. After the second day, I had decided to not look into the barrel to make sure that portion of my fortune remained within its depth. Bringing his attention to it might be a mistake. Suddenly, I wondered if it was there. Of course, if Perkins had stolen it already, then surely he would have killed me and dumped my body along the way.

A thought crept in and hastened the thudding in my chest. Perhaps he planned to sell me at auction when we arrive in Shepherdstown. I had no choice but to trust this man. Trust him with my life and freedom.

***

A day-and-a-half later, we approached the Pack Horse Ford. The spring thaw and groundwater fought for space through the passage. Trees entangled in briars floated by, halting our pro-gresssion for a time. Seeing the ford clogged with travelers expanded my fear into a fury. I wished to scream with impatience, but silence was demanded of me. When we came to be next in line, the snarl of wagons and carriages allowed us to hear the talk up and down the line. The chatter contained only one item worthy of consideration.

"Fred. Hey, over here! Is the auction delayed?"

My breathing halted as I awaited the reply.

"Sure 'nough. That there's the hell of it. Railroad's costin' me money, see, just like I was tellin' ya it would. That thang ain't even up and runnin' yet. If they's gonna cut through here, why I ask ya, why not do it next week after the sale? Why be sendin' logs down when they knows auction's comin' up?"

Perkins fidgeted in his seat and spat onto the ground from our high perch. He then leaned toward me and whispered, "That be a lick o' honey. We's in time." He grabbed the reins. "Willy, while we's settin' here a spell, ya need to . . . um, to take the leg off."

"What?"

"Way I sees it, we's got to play all the cards. Can't hold any aces, not now. We's got talents not bein' used, like the one that makes all fools edgy. We's gotta use your stump, and hell, even my missin' ear. Those lackin' body parts can throw people all off. Right away, there ain't no hesitatin' on their part. That's the good of it. We can count on it. Maybe we can get through this mess faster, if folks just don't want to be dealin' with a couple cripples. So, go on, Willy, toss that thing in the back. Shove her there under that quilt, the one sportin' little cornflowers. Oh, and here's my hat to go with her." Perkins shoved his hat at my chest and nudged me toward the edge of the seat.

Thinking about the knife I had moved into the hollow shaft of the peg, the one I planned to use on Perkins, if circumstances should dictate, I shook my head. "Rather not," I whispered. "I prefer my peg to be as near as possible. What if I should come to have need of it? You see, I never know—"

"Oh, right. Yer knife." Perkins interrupted. "And how do ya suppose that'd work?" He slapped the side of my head. "Would ya say somethin' like this here: 'Hold on, feller, I's got to take my leg off, see. Be a short while to get my knife out . . . now hold on . . . just a wee bit longer before I get to it. Oh, and after I get it, stand right there so's I can be stabbin' ya. Cause if ya be too far away, I can't reach ya.'"

He pushed me again, forcing me to teeter upon the edge and to grab ahold of his arm. "Willy, ya might learn somethin' soon. Just stick close. Ya ain't all full up in here, right?" He slapped the side of my head, again.

His words held some logic. Perhaps we could use the staring eyes and embarrassment that forced men to look away. Their uneasiness might indeed give us clearance. I never did learn how he knew I'd hidden a blade in my hollow peg. But the advantage I might have had over him was summarily taken away.

I climbed to the back of the wagon, causing onlookers to stare as my maneuvering could not be called graceful. And as though we had ordered them to do so, several wagons moved to the side.

Grunting loudly and grimacing, I unstrapped and stowed my peg and his hat. My face surely portrayed my growing impatience, for Perkins then spoke with a gentler tone. "We's only jammed up here a spell. Don't ya worry none. I's wagerin', we'll just get lost in this here crowd lickety-split-rickety-spit." He wiped his chin on his shirt sleeve.

Truth be told, we crossed the ford without much ado. We were simply another wagon wading through the river. If anyone took notice, we probably left no memory more than being a pitiful sight of one man missing a leg, the other an ear.

A short while later, Perkins pulled to a stop in front of a large meeting house. "Sit tight. I's goin' see when this thing starts," he said. "And Willy, for Christ's sake, don't ya talk to no one." He jumped down and easily parted the crowd. Under that crusty exterior, his heart beat in the same manner as everyone else's, I reminded myself. Although, I knew contact with the man would surely leave a mark. Others appeared to feel likewise. I hoped Arlan Theel's words would continue to be the truth. "Perkins may not be much to look at," he had said, "but he is a man who can weasel out of the most difficult of situations." Theel had then laughed in a way that had set my teeth in a clench. I saw no humor, but he had continued, "Perkins simply surrounds and befuddles his adversaries and is gone before they understand what he's taken from them."

Waiting in the wagon, I avoided looking at passers-by and instead stared at the leather reins draped over my knee. My hands began to sweat, not from heat but in apprehension. Only a hint of callous creased my palms, but the dent in my right finger betrayed what I endeavored to hide. I was a dark-skinned man who knew how to write. A keen observer would assume I possessed the ability to read as well, and in Virginia, those two abilities made me fit for hanging.

I clasped my hands together, and though I was not drawn to do so often, I prayed silently to myself. Lord, please let Dinah be here. Unharmed.

Perkins bumped his way back through the crowd. "We's in luck, Willy. Auction's tomorrow, and twenty-three mammies bein' put up. They get them outa the way, then the bucks, before they brings on the other livestock." Perkins clambered up beside me, the rush of his odor preceding him by several seconds. "Eight in the mornin', that's when we's gotta come back for it. Be campin' down by the creek, like the other men who's here for the sale. Got to get up with the chickens. Ah, hell. We ate 'em already!"

That night, while thrashing about, my thoughts remained ensnared by images as clogged as the Shenandoah. Dinah's face, weary and in pain, returned. If she had been beaten, I would not be in control of my rage. I pictured her wrapped in her torn red dress, cowering, but then I remembered her strength as she lifted sacks of grain. She remained so tender, though, as tender as a bud bracing against a late snow. Questions invaded my reverie. Had she been whipt or worse? Had some heathen defiled her? My heart beat so wildly that it felt as though it could burst from my body. There was no avenue to gain information about Dinah, not until morning. Or to even know if she would be at this auction. Had she already been sold? What if she was to be sold on some other day or in some other town?

I sat bolt upright. "Dinah, are you alive?" I said and pounded my fists against my chest.

"Everything's goin' to be all right, Willy," Perkins whispered through the darkness.

"What if she's . . ."

"Whether ya stew on it, or not, it's the way it'll be. Drop off to sleep, already." He rolled over, and soon his loud, deep breathing signaled his slumber.

I lay on my back, sleepless until morning, and left my bed long before Perkins. The creek banks were heaped with boulders, and I hobbled over to sit upon one nearby. The sun's first light danced on the water. After scanning the area for judgmental eyes, I reached into my pocket and pulled out the book. This fable caught my attention:

The Country Maid and Her Milk Pail

WHEN men suffer their imaginations to amuse them with the prospect of distant and uncertain improvements of their condition, they frequently sustain real losses, by their inattention to those affairs in which they are immediately concerned.

A country Maid was walking very deliberately with a pail of milk upon her head, when she fell into the following train of reflections: The money for which I shall sell this milk, will enable me to increase my stock of eggs to three hundred. These eggs, allowing for what may prove addle, and what may be destroyed by vermin, will produce at least two hundred and fifty chickens. The chickens will be fit to carry to market about Christmas, when poultry always bears a good price; so that by May day I cannot fail of having money enough to purchase a new gown. Green—let me consider—yes, green becomes my complexion best and green it shall be. In this dress I will go to the fair, where all the young fellows will strive to have me for a partner; but I shall perhaps refuse every one of them, and with an air of disdain toss from them.

Transported with this triumphant thought, she could not forbear acting with her head what thus passed in her imagination, when down came the pail of milk, and with it all her imaginary happiness.

As was often true, the book's words bade me to think. After reading, I was determined that my fears would not cloud my judgment. I looked about and took notice of the newly sprouted grass and the tiny lily-of-the-valley that had opened to the sun-drenched day. The air began to fill with smells from cooking fires being lit down the banks of the creek. I counted four curls of smoke within the scope of my vision. The smoke rose, then fell, and filled the little gully with haze. Perkins stepped within my view, casting his shadow from above. I looked up.

He ran his tongue over his lips. "Listen here, Willy. I know yer not gonna be wantin' to hear what I's about to say. But ya have to live by it. 'Cause of our agreed-upon agreement, see?" He spat, littering the freshness with a vile brown glop. "Gotta stay put, boy, while I get myself up to the sale."

"What? No, I—" I began to stand up.

He put a hand on my shoulder and pushed firmly, halting my attempt to rise. "Like I says, gotta live with what I's tellin' ya. On my own, this auction here seems simple, but with ya taggin' along, it gets all fouled up in my head."

"But, I must go. I just now considered it thoroughly. Rest assured, I decided fear will not cloud my judgment, and—"

"No. Ya might be thinkin' to be steady. But what happens when the girl calls out to ya, and ya bein' all keyed up. Somethin' stupid's gotta spill out. 'Sides, I's got a way of biddin' at these things. Ya plain won't get it. Somehow, I just know if ya be there, it's gotta end up costin' me money."

I grabbed ahold of my crutch, hoisted myself off the rock, and took a small step toward him. He held his hand high to halt me. "Look here, Willy. I's gonna bring her back to ya. No way

I's not payin' every last eagle, if need be. But fess up, ya give up everything, the second ya sees her—"

"So it is the gold, that is what you are—"

"No, it ain't the money, boy. A woman makes a man a fool, is all."

"But, I cannot sit here. I will not be able to wait."

"Well, ya see I's got yer leg in the wagon. And I's takin' the wagon."

"So, what was all that talk of using our talents?"

"Oh hell, I still be usin' my own, but that's all I rightly need." He scratched the side of his head and spat again. "Feaverin' festers, what I don't need is ya taggin' along ready to kill if things get ugly."

I lunged awkwardly toward him.

He lifted his rifle and pointed it at me.

"There's no need for that," I said and moved closer.

"Halt right there, boy. I's loaded and be goin', now." He backed up to the wagon and boarded. "Truth is, Willy, life ain't all messy. No matter how much worryin' ya do, things turn out how they maybe would've, anyhow. After today, be seein' a truth, ya will. Gotta be trustin' folks to do things for ya. Set back down right there and read that little book. Yeah, I seen it. Everyone'll be at the auction. It's safe here, now. I don't know what a man sees in pourin' over words, but ya seem to like it more than sleep. Stay put and outa sight. Yep, seems safe enough. No one's gonna waltz by on a casual stroll, too many briars along this creek."

As I watched him disappear through the trees, I felt as though my body was being dragged along behind his wagon. Angry, humiliated tears streamed from my eyes. The weight of the feeling rested on my own shoulders. "How could I have fallen for his ruse? Will he return? He's stealing the gold!" The empty alder forest did not answer my pleas, but I knew Perkins had plenty of time to rob me before, and did not. I scratched at the dirt with my crutch and stared at the trickling water.

Several possible plans began to form in my mind. I could attempt to find my way to the auction; though, my timely arrival was impossible. Furthermore, if he later did return, we might not find one another. I sat back on the boulder and considered the second option of agreeing to his terms, waiting and trusting this man of dubious character. The end *did* rest in someone else's hands. In Odber Perkins' hands. The notion was repugnant, and worse, it was like many previous decisions which had brought me to that moment. I would yet again be tossed about like the pebbles bumping along the creek bottom.

"It rests in someone else's hands," I said aloud, trying to convince myself. At least, the fear of my being sold had not come true. I looked down at Beth's book, and with nothing else to do, I decided to read, yet again.

Remarks

A wise man will consider not so much the present pleasure and advantage of a measure as its future consequences.

Those words, though true, did not seem helpful. I felt no single grain of pleasure, nor advantage. The dreaded future lay beyond my control. I read for an hour or more, not retaining what my eyes saw except this sentence:

The cheerful man hears the lark in the morning;
the pensive man hears the nightingale in the evening.

I looked about to reassure myself there were still no peering eyes then read the following line:

Elizabeth R. Sherman 1820-1825

Though I already knew I would later re-sign the book with ink, I took out my graphite and signed my name below her signature and began to date it.

William T. Sherman 1825-18

I wondered who would next be worthy of this gift, and when would I pass it to them? Or would I keep it to the end of my days. Beth's book seemed not to belong to me but to whomever might need it most. Finding the next someone . . . someday . . . perhaps it would be my future child.

"Oh Dinah, please be safe," I said, closing my eyes. The sun's warmth beat on my back. The rock I was perched on still held the previous night's cold and damp, which bit into my thighs. By allowing my thoughts to drift with the trickling sounds of the water, however, some comfort began to arise. Ideas came and departed, weaving in and out of my solitude. First, I heard the rhythm of my breathing, then the trees whispered as they were blown by a light breeze. The water bubbled and surged, and a woodpecker knocked on a tree. Then came the soft metallic chinking of a bridle and horses hooves upon a road. My eyes sprung open as I slammed the book shut and thrust it deep into my pocket.

"See, what did I tell ya," someone said from behind me.

I turned around. There was a wagon, and there, with her dirty cheeks streaked clean where tears had washed them, was Dinah. My Dinah.

"Like I's tellin' ya, Miss, I's no Massa just my own self. I don't need no Niggra-girl takin' up space in my house. Ha! Look there, would ya, Willy's lookin' like he can't move. Why don't that beat all. No, I's not contagious, Miss. Don't even think I snores at night. Only coughed and sputtered like I did, so other fellers would stop biddin'. Had to get things rollin', so no one would catch on to . . ."

Perkins continued his jabber, but Dinah came to me in a rush, and his voice faded away. It took a moment to gather my wits and respond. But indeed I did. We embraced as though we would never let go. The blanket draped around her shoulders hid that she was bereft of clothes.

"Oh Willy," she said and kissed me deeply. Then again another kiss. "I didn't know what to be thinkin'. He tells me ya'd be here, but I couldn't let myself believe in it."

We kissed with longing meant for those lost in love. Her skin felt warm in our sheltered embrace, and I could feel the bulge of her belly. Her engorged breasts nestled against my chest. She still carried our child. I melted in relief, wanting to hold her forever, wishing to make her see how much I had needed that moment. "I felt so afraid," I said, between kisses.

"Come on, now, ya's have plenty of time for that." Odber moved the wagon backward a bit, making the horses clang together like chimes in a church tower. "Right here, right now, we's got no time to spare. We got to git. Most important, we needs to find a dress. It just ain't decent walkin' 'round like that, no siree."

I stole one more look at Dinah before wrapping the blanket around her. Most likely, no one had known she was with-child because they were not as familiar as me to her shape. They had no way to know how lean she had been. Our desires were postponed. They would need to wait. They would have to wait.

Turning to Perkins, I nodded my head. He had been right. All of life was once again how it should be. My worrying had amounted to nothing and had made no difference.

***

Those days were so long ago. Living alone here in Minnesota, those times do not seem so far away, though, because love has a way of bringing what is most important into your heart, if you let it. First, Beth had shown me how love was a possibility, then my love with Dinah grew over time to be one large enough to sustain me even after she was gone. We had our child, lived in happiness, and survived the Civil War before that happy life with her was taken away. Reconstruction may have happened somewhere, but my life deconstructed at about the same time. Each day, thinking back on where I have come from, I know, though, that I would not change a thing. For I have known love, and it has known me. What more could I have wanted?

Kate Porter

IV

1880-1896
Johanna Kristoffersdatter Skauge
Nyhus

I am born Johanna Kristoffersdatter. My father's given name Kristoffer, so he give this name to me, his daughter. I given name Kristoffersdatter. Then change to Skauge our name, when move to Skauge farm by Trondheim in Skaun, Norway.

I hate name, glad to marry different one. Jens Ingebrigtsen Nyhus I marry on ship. Ship name *Tosso*. On cloud-fill day, water drip, drip, drip. In ocean we on ship from Norway to America. Two weeks this, uff da.

I am Johanna Nyhus, when land in Castle Garden in place they call New York. Change name again, Nyhus is "Newhouse." In my language, Norwegian, I say is right—in new house, in New York, in new country, in new name—Newhouse.

I think, *Jeg er så glad i å være i America.* Ja, I happy in America, no more name change.

When William Sherman give me, no, he tell me old-name story for him, I do not know this. William T. Sherman, name to him is life, freedom—but pile in trouble. I think big trouble, no. What does name matter? None. It comes and goes, like herring from *sildkjele*. "From herring crock," you say. With no elbow grease.

William he read. Nigger-man read! Uff da. In America all

need English, he say. He not quit, day and day in. No, "day in and day out" you say.

When on America land, I speak English little, but learn. Now I speak English more good. *Mange tokk*, thank you, William. Winter nights he read book. I try make English easy, no, easier. To, too, two? A mess this language. Ja? I read twenty-six states in book. William, he tell me people go to West. William old like old book. I think in him memory broke. This I read:

States	*People*
New York	*New York'ers*
New Jersey	

I see what this mean. America new country so "New" states. But in book I worry, does not tell what I should call "New Jersey" people. If I to meet "New Jersey" man, what I call? William he say "Jersey" mean cow. We laugh. We hurt from this laugh-out-loud. He say, "Johanna, call them new cows!" I forget English word for this. In Norway, word for "new cow" we say *kalv*.

I find in book this:

Country	*Adjective*	*People*	*Chief Cities*
Nor'way	*Nor we'gi'an*	*Norwe'gians*	*Bergen*

Trondheim chief city for Johanna Newhouse. No Bergen. When I see in book, my heart feel cripple. Like William, leg he miss. My Norway I miss. Sorrow in breast when goodbye over. On ship, I think life over. No fun, no love. I am nine and ten, only. Is America word nineteen?

It 1870 when go to America. *Rosemalt* trunks we carry. Ja, beautiful flower paint, wood carve. All *tolerkener, kjoler, hatter* in trunk. Someone take trunk when not our eyes look on. Is gone. All gone. No plate, no dress, no hat but one on head. I cry for *Mormor* her stitches. What you say, mother's mother? Greatmother? Beautiful Mormor her stitches, ja, beautiful color, flowers, animals. Better to all others. All gone. Ja, I see in eyes. I see Mormor beautiful stitches.

We look on dock, but must go. Must go from lost trunk. Must leave. Men hurry we push in big hurry. Trunk they take. We in *sykehus*. We not sick. Men use word, "Quarantine?" Not know this word. Angry words. They say we sick in "small pox." Mormor say, "*Ingen vi er ikke syke.*" She say we not sick. She throw medicine in toilet gutter. Six weeks in room, like meat in meat locker. I hate this. In sleep, Mormor *hun snorker*, you say, "snore." I not in marry bed where belong. I not with new husband. Jen and me wait, wait, wait. *Klokke tikker* tick tock, tick tock. Forever when young and love beautiful, no, I mean handsome man. I never see end. Then does. *Endelig!* "The end," you say.

We go from Castle Garden. Float in boat in canal, Erie Canal. Glad go but no trunks. Gone. Now to city, to train, to chosen state, Minnesota. Many friends wait on father. Trondhjem Lutheran Church he build. Stone rest on brick, then more tar.

In Northfield we live. Three child babies born. Bank robber men come. No money get. But good friend Nicholas Gustafson, Swede, imagine good friend with Swede. Uff da! He not English speak. Not know, "Get off street!" Bullet in head. Blood in dirt. Gustafson wife, she cry. I back rub her.

Most town men ride away. Look and ride to find robbers.

Days I wait for husband in home. Imagine this. Robbers, they get twenty six dollars with seventy cents. In 1876 not big money this. This, imagine, nothing for dead Gustafson. I wait with three babies. Wonder will husband kill or be kill? I in top of house window sit, wait, sit. I think forever. Not end. Three weeks I wait. They catch robber man. No Jesse James, no biggest bank robber. Littlest, weakest ones they catch.

Jens and me move to city. Safe now. He say, "Wheat farm, make little money this. Need more. We buy house, and open door." Take in *gjester*, you say "boarders." We smile on by four children more, all born to me. Seven babies . . . but . . . Ellen, Joseph, and Marie die. Uff da, tears I cry.

Ellen born sick, three days live, Ellen die. Marie, in six year, I wake to cold child. I shake. Eyes no open. I weep. Jens no, not ears to hear I cry. He say, "No more cry, Johanna." Joseph . . . I never can . . . I never can talk. Oh, my Joseph, big pain. Years he sick and moan. I more cry. I fill bucket in tears.

Julius, Isaac, Hanna, little James Marcus, they live. My husband say, "Johanna, four children for happy, busy house is good. Ja?"

House big, bigger, biggest we buy. More children, more *gjester*, more money, more work. Life fat in diapers, clothes scrub, food stew. Children little, need mother. *Gjester* need beds. *Gjester* need food.

No time. No time for book I find.

William book, he give me. He say, "You must learn, Johanna." His book, in shelf I rest. I never look. To *den minste gutten*, you say, to youngest boy, to James, I give him this book.

New cover I sew. Mormor beautiful stitches? No. Eight stitches in board, you say "good 'nough." This, most old thing in house. Old *søppel*, dirty *søppel,* you say "trash." Uff da!

Funny this old book. James Marcus in sleep, book he fold in arms. "Book sleep," I say, "it little bird in nest."

Kate Porter

V

1896-1958

J. Marcus Newhouse

Mother told me to stay away from William T. Sherman, the "Nigger-man," so no doubt about it, I was drawn to him like a boy to the herring crock. He would peek-a-boo a smile, then she'd slap me up-side the head, then I'd run away down the hall. Of course, people my age now say "those were the good old days." I don't know what the hell they're talking about.

Mother's rooming house contained three floors. Along the top two, on both sides, ran rows of coffee-colored doors. Behind each lived one to four people. I'd barely meet some before they'd be packing their trunks and heading down the road. Most went west. They'd up and leave so others could slide right in behind them. Slick as snot on a door knob.

I'd scamper down those halls just as fast as my five-year-old legs could, even though I'd been told half-a-million times to slow my ass down. Well, Mother would never use that sort of language, but in Norwegian she'd scream something with an "uff da" thrown on at the behind end of it. If she had a wet towel or rolled up paper, I'd get a good swatting. That is, if she could catch me. My legs got so strong and so fast, she'd miss me more times than not. But those "uff das" stuck to me, scarred me for life they did, like a real whipping.

One month, on the third floor, a man rented a room who had an ugly growth on his neck. From another room, a woman would peer out at me. She had eyes that darted every-which way, making me wonder who or what she was looking at. For me, those boarders were a scary business. So for a time, the easiest thing to do was to stay on the second floor.

That was when I started dashing to Mr. Sherman's room. I'd sit tight as long as I possibly could. The quiet there let me feel invisible. His room, also on the second floor but above the kitchen, wasn't above the parlor like our quarters. Mother gave him that wing because it had a different set of stairs. His door didn't need a number, everyone knew where to find Mr. Sherman—he being the only dark-skin man who ever boarded with us. Below him in the kitchen, my mother, along with four other helpers, swarmed around the black cook-stove like moths crowding around a gaslight. Toward the front of the house and to the right was the dining hall, and to the left the parlor. In the middle, the front foyer welcomed guests with a staircase that reached clear up to the rafters.

We, the four Newhouse children, weren't allowed to use the front stairs, instead we ran in and out through the kitchen alley, along with the help and Mr. Sherman. Did I mention he was the only Negro living with us—ever? We lived in Saint Paul, Minnesota, after all. Not too many Negro folk lived in Minnesota in the 1890s, maybe only about five hundred, or so.

Parading onto the red front-hall carpet came everyone else. "Stuffies," we called them. Yes, those stuffies entered through the front, folding their parasols and setting them down along with their canes in the rack beside the door. They strutted about like turkeys, proclaiming their right to space in the barnyard.

Their gobble-talk gave me a headache.

Most evenings, the parlor filled with those men and women playing games, reading, and chatting about nothing. Their kids drew on sketch pads and read parlor books. Girls, with ringlets like real pigs' tails, cut out paper dolls for the younger ones among them. Being the youngest in my family, and being a boy, I didn't care two hoots that I wasn't allowed into the room. I was saved from having to perform for all those adults who fluffed up their feathers when their children showed just a nibble of gumption.

Anyway, by splaying my body on the floor, and cracking the door open just a bit, I had a clear view of the wall where the piano sat. The instrument seemed cut from the same tree as the rest of the room's dark furniture. It was from that very spot that I first heard the syncopated rhythms of Ragtime. Rat-a-bang-bang, swoosh-a-doodle-doo.

It was during the month when the flaming Fairmonts lived with us. I called them "flaming" on account of their red hair. Father Fairmont wasn't a preacher but did sing gospel songs. In a voice that shook the fringe on the lamps, he proclaimed, "I'm telling you. Those new rhythms are sinful. Cover thy children's ears!" Because he spoke like God himself, my mother banned Ragtime from our home. But since she and Father didn't cross paths much, she was always in the kitchen, he always in the woodshed or painting the outside of our massive three-story boardinghouse, Father never heard the original proclamation— nor Mother's rule. One time, I spotted Father's foot jumping to the rhythms as he stood in the doorway for a listen. Of course, he didn't stand around long; he had too much to do. He kicked my shoulder when he turned and spotted me on the floor, listening. I let out a yelp. The next kick was harder, but I stifled any noise. Boys don't cry, you know. Uff da, indeed.

When I was about seven, I took up playing the fiddle. My brother, Julius, gave his attention to the banjo, and my sister, Hanna, the piano. We had ourselves a regular county band, all by ourselves. We played mostly show tunes. Mother swore something in Norwegian when she heard Hanna and me playing a ragtime duet. We'd picked it out special just for her: the "Gladiolus Rag." We thought maybe she'd favor it on account of the gladiola being the flower she most liked to pick from her garden. It seemed a better bet than Scott Joplin's "The Easy Winners." Nothing "easy" could ever fit our mother.

"James, life hard. I seven years, in Norway, potatoes I plant. No music. Want play? Here." She handed me the broom. "Sweep!"

If her life had been so bad, I didn't see why she'd want my life to be the same. At least she called me "James" not the Norwegian "Jens" like my father held to.

Wrapping around the back corner of the parlor, bookcases sat containing a mixture of odd books, mostly throw-away novels with titles like *Prisoners of Chance*, *The Wicked Marquis*, and *The Silver Horde*. They'd been left by previous boarders. Not one book was ever bought by my family. One of my chores was to dust them off and keep them standing upright by pushing in the cast iron bookends.

Now, I don't have clear memory anymore; I'm pushing eighty, so the exact day I spotted that old book is as forgotten as the book had been there, lollygagging on the bottom shelf as it was, looking all forlorn.

But Mr. Sherman's reaction? That I can see clear as now.

Most times when I'd enter his room, he would just stay sitting there with a sort of slouch. But that day, he seemed to grow as I walked toward him. He said, "Marcus, bring it over here what . . . whatever it is you have there." He always called me by my middle name. His large hands latched onto the book like a dog fetching an edition of the *Journal*.

"I thought this book might have been cast off with the rubbish." His fingers stroked it like it was the hair of a newborn babe. "Do not tell your mama I said this, Marcus, but in some ways, I wish I had not given it to her. Years ago, I did begin to teach her to read using this as a primer. Your mama stopped trying, though. She said she was too busy. But honestly, I do not think she saw any value in it." He held me on his lap. "Sit here a minute while I read to you. And do not judge your mama. Johanna is quite intelligent. She knows how to read in Norwegian."

I can almost hear his voice reading this passage because it triggered something new in me, a thirst for more written words.

> *Fowls which feed on insects and grain, have mostly a short straight bill, like the robin. Those which live on fish, have long legs for wading, or long bills for seizing and holding their prey, like the heron and the fish hawk. Fowls which delight chiefly to fly in the air, and light and build nests on the trees, have their toes divided, by which they cling to the branches and twigs; those which live in or about water have webbed feet, that is, their toes united by a film or skin, so that their feet serve as oars or paddles for swimming.*

My young mind couldn't hold my tongue, so I kept interrupting. "What's a heron? Mr. Sherman, isn't that a robin out the window? See it right there?" A few blocks away was a park, which ringed itself around a lake, so I knew about ducks and had seen Canada geese gathering in giant squalls acting like a school of fish in a river of air. They'd land there amassing until their numbers were such that the land and water couldn't hold even one more. Then, they'd just take off all to once. Seemed like they could talk because they lifted up in a single breath. They were such a rowdy choir of honkers.

Mr. Sherman read to me a ton, and his voice contained a tone as soothing as taking a warm bath, so fatherly. But it had no hint of the stern tones my own father always mixed in.

I remember that old book. Of course I do. Early on, for several months, I even slept with the damn thing. I don't mean to mislead anyone, I didn't fall asleep reading. Uff da, hell no! I couldn't read, yet. Just curled my little arm around it, hoping the words would slip into my brain while I stumbled away to sleep. You know, mostly the book was a treasure because it had belonged to Mr. Sherman, not because there was any real value in that ratty old thing.

Long about five years later, maybe about 1901, when I was ten, Mr. Sherman and I walked to that park nearby. He said, "Marcus, there must be close to a thousand geese over there, counting the little ones. They have returned. The winds carry them to the South for the winter, but they always find their way back to this exact nesting place in the spring. Yes sir, year after year. They are indeed a wondrous sight." As he hobbled closer to the lake, I held up some of his weight. We stayed there just breathing the air and watching the geese as they went about their goose business. But soon, we made our way back home. The carriage man and one of the stout kitchen maids helped carry Mr. Sherman back to his room.

His good leg had grown severely painful, making stairs impossible. Sad to say, but he and I would've stayed longer in the park, if we'd known it was his last trip out of the house.

On account of his color, he didn't fit in too well. Did I mention he was a Negro? Well, he sat in his room most days. He had lost the one leg, and the other was all knotted up around the knee. Somedays, it swelled to the size of a kick ball. He ate up there, and when I could sneak away, I'd bring my plate too and join him for supper. He never shooed me away, and he lived with us nearly fifteen years, five before I was born, and ten after, longer than any other boarder.

I asked him why he didn't have a traveling trunk like everyone else. "Marcus, I am not want for travel. I'm no carpetbagger. I do not wish to be anywhere but right here. I came here for a purpose, and that purpose has kept me in one place all these years."

"But why?"

He smiled and patted my head. "I was asked to move to Saint Paul to write for *The Western Appeal*. I know you have never seen a copy. It is a Negro newspaper. They started printing it way back, in 1882."

"But how do you do that? I've never seen you go to work." I chuckled because of not believing him. He never told fibs, that I knew of anyway. This one was a doozy. A Negro newspaper? There weren't enough of them around, plus most probably couldn't read. That's what I thought at the time.

"Until now, I wrote here in this room, then went once a week to the office. I had to quit, though, because of not being able to manage those stairs. Mr. John Quincy Adams' brother, Cyrus, came to be our editor a couple of years back, in '88." Mr. Sherman's smile broadened. "Besides the writing, the other reason to stay is that your mama's cooking is to my liking."

"Can I see what you wrote about?" I asked.

"Well, I do not keep any of those papers here, son, and I did not use my real name on any of the articles, since people would be confused by why General William T. Sherman is writing for a Negro newspaper." He let out a laugh.

I smiled and said, "That's okay. I get to talk with you, so I don't need to read what you wrote."

"Well now, truly, the main reason I stay in this house is to watch after you. Who would, if I was not here?"

I ran over to hug him. Though he was seated with his stump raised on a huge cushion, to decrease the swelling, I managed to burry my head in his chest as his arms wrapped around me. He always returned a heartfelt hug since he seemed to need them as much as I did.

Along with that feeling of home, his room was the only spot to go where there wasn't a crowd. Being the youngest, I even had to share a bed every night. In the winter, all four of us would line up on one mattress like corn cakes. With me squished somewhere in the middle, and our blankets all piled on top, my tiny space turned into an oven. Didn't have much to say when it came to the sleeping arrangements. I'd wake up overheated, force an escape, scrape the frost off the looking glass, and see my red-hot face. More than a few nights, I chose a cold chair over the heat of siblings.

Speaking of overcrowding, how about all those boarders

eating in a clang of dishes and then using the same back house. Uff da! A private moment was hard to come by. Someone was always waiting their turn right outside the door while you'd be trying to take care of your business.

In the solitude of Mr. Sherman's room, we played checkers, ventured on to chess, and then, don't hate me Mother, God rest your soul, a bit of card playing as well. Five card stud, nothing fancy. We played for matchsticks while he told stories. Many I remember to this day. I'm sorry to say, just as many are long gone from this old head.

"Marcus, you remind me of my boy Luke, all curiosity and spunk," Mr. Sherman said in the middle of a poker-packed day.

"You have a son?"

"Yes sir, I did." Mr. Sherman laid down a full house and gathered up all our sticks. "I buried my boy long ago. Back in 1866, such a sad time. My lovely Dinah and he died of the fever. That September, so many died as disease ran through our town. So many. The sickness came on the tail-end of a flood." He rubbed his bald head then his left eye.

"Sorry they died, but what flood? We already have enough lakes in Minnesota to drown a fish." I'd heard someone say that once and felt all grown up, being able to find a perfect spot to repeat it.

Mr. Sherman had a far-off look as he said, "It had something to do with the water." He cleared his throat, smiled, and nodded. "It was in Elmira. Elmira, New York." He turned and looked out the window. "It had been a beautiful town to live in, before the war. Some called that bloody mess the 'Great Rebellion.' All hell broke loose, and so did the easy life we had grown to know. Needing to do my part for the Union, especially with all the men gone to do the fighting, I wanted to help more slaves gain freedom, so I volunteered. However, because of my missing leg, they assigned me a job in the prison. Kitchen duty, 'slop duty' is what I called it. At least they gave me a stool to sit on, or I might have died from exhaustion in the first month. They worked us in fourteen-hour shifts, seven days each week. Not one day off. Somehow, I lasted the entire year before the place was closed." He sighed, turned back to the table, shuffled the deck, and dealt a new hand.

"You know, Marcus, 'hell' is a swear word, so do not repeat this or I will be in trouble with your mama, but the Southern boys called the camp 'Hellmira', and rightly so. Those exhausted men arrived, and the place killed them like hornets dunked in kerosene. That year, I would guess nearly three-thousand died while imprisoned there. In my estimation, they starved because Colonel Hoffman fed them a diet of only bread and water. In the winter he even rationed their clothes. He would not let them wear a stitch, unless it was gray like their uniform color had been. Men succumbed to cold while watching their blue, red, and black woolens rot in giant heaps outside the compound. You see it was late in the war, and they had been captured wearing whatever clothes they might have owned. Many did not have uniforms. Some had stolen clothes from dead soldiers. Many came to us wearing Union blues. Their bellies grew swollen with hunger-gas, and the rest of their bony bodies rattled around the yard like bare trees blown by a gale."

He looked at me and must have noticed the furrowed brow on my forehead. "I am sorry, son, if this upsets you. But what I am telling you is the honest truth, and someone should know what happened and never forget. Southerners were not the only ones who killed for no reason." He looked up from the cards he had fanned in his hand, and with a fierce look in his eyes, one that I had never seen before, he said, "You are ten, so you can understand what I am telling you. I was there to help, to do my part, but what I saw would offend the devil himself."

He picked up his hand and asked me if I had any discards. I shook my head since I had three tens and an ace and a queen.

"Do not misunderstand me," he continued, after he'd discarded three cards and divvied up three more into his own hand. "Every single day, I faced an onslaught of insults from the guards and prisoners alike. The guards would stir up trouble with each new batch of prisoners they brought in. They introduced me as 'William T. Sherman.' Or as 'the General,' you see."

He halted his story and filled me in on how much Southerners hated General William T. Sherman, the man who'd plundered his way into Georgia. "Those prisoner boys would say something akin to, 'Ya ain't no general, boy. Ya gotta lotta nerve callin' yerself William T. Sherman.' Once someone said, 'Yer tellin' me that General Sherman lost his leg in the fightin'? And I suppose it scared him so's his skin turned black. Now the North's too ashamed of him bein' a Nigger, so they's stuck him out in Hellmira with us.'"

My three of a kind beat Mr. Sherman's two pair, but I didn't have the heart to pick up my matchsticks.

"The worst that I can recall was the man who arrived with a gut wound. He lay there day after day, begging to die. Once, when I bent over to remove his slop bucket, he grabbed my arm and said, 'Sherman's troops killed my wife. I don't care if yer skin's the wrong color, just stay clear, Nigger. I might just forget ya ain't him and kill ya myself.' Marcus, even though I had clear reasons for not liking most of those boys, nary a one deserved the treatment he got."

"Nigger is a mean word, isn't it?" I asked.

"Yes, Marcus it is," he said. "I do not ever use it myself. I'm just now saying it, to let you know what others have said. The word is as hate-filled as one can be."

Right then, I decided to never use the word either.

Mr. Sherman kept some gentleness about him, which seemed no easy business to me, one for the record books. I don't know, maybe what he and his wife had shared was what kept him going. When he talked of her and, come to think of it, when he talked about that orphan girl, Elizabeth, he'd get this look and a smile that I didn't recognize. But now I know they were memories of love. He and Mrs. Sherman had helped runaway slaves, before the war, so seeing folks suffering worse than him probably kept his slant on the world coming in at a good angle.

One day, out of the blue, he said, "Mrs. Sherman, Dinah, and I were rich once. And not just in love, but in gold—slave gold. You see, it came our way back in '35, entrusted to us by Mr. Dresden Withers. Do you remember? I told you of my teacher several times. Ironically, that money allowed us to aid hundreds of people, and I still have enough today to pay your mama, to keep me in my old age."

He reached into his pocket and tossed a gold piece to me. "Keep this one, son," he said with a wink. "It's a four dollar coin—a Stella. They didn't make many of those. Some might say it is rare.

I recently traded a few slave gold pieces to buy that one off a congressman who was bragging about having one. Most of the Stellas were bought back by the government, so you will not ever see another one like it, no doubt."

"Can I keep it? Wow, slave gold!"

"You may, as long as you do not waste it on candy or gambling. Keep it. Find a safe place for it." Mr. Sherman continued on about how no one was supposed to have any Stellas. They were supposed to all be turned back in and melted down for some reason or other. Some political mess.

"That coin deserves a bigger purpose," he said.

I held the small coin in my hand and imagined slaves being sold and some fat, rich bastard getting a satchel full of gold in return. It downright made my skin crawl, just thinking about that dirty business.

Hard for me to believe Mr. Sherman was rich. But I did because I knew my mother. She would never have taken on any charity cases. Especially Negro ones. She called them "Niggers," which rolled off her tongue like spit into a spittoon. She usually added another word, "ignored," but I knew she meant "ignorant." Mr. Sherman, therefore, must have paid, somehow. Sometimes his stories seemed stretched far to the extreme, but I had no reason to doubt him about his gold. I do like to think he helped people with his money. At least I know he didn't gamble it away, like most men do, since he refused to gamble for money—only matchsticks.

***

One winter day, just after his birthday in 1901, Mr. Sherman just up and died. I found him. Even though I was only eleven, I knew he was gone on account of his being cold in the bed and smelling like piss. The stench was oddly familiar because one month earlier, I had found an old sot, in room twelve, in a pool of piss. But Mr. Sherman wasn't a drunkard. His heart just plain gave out, that's what the doc said. I suppose it's as good a way to go as any, but his passing left a hole in the food that fed my brain and heart. Uff da, it pains me still.

He had made it a point to get past his ninetieth birthday. Just a few days before, he had said something like, "Son, I am more than the number of years my mama and papa lived when you add their two ages together." He'd seen two centuries, and he was proud of making it into the 1900s. He celebrated his birthday on the day the thirteenth Amendment got ratified into our constitution, December sixth. Mine was the seventh, so I always thought we fit together like ham and applesauce. It wasn't his real birthday, though. When he'd heard about the amendment, way back in 1865, that's when he changed it. Right then and there, he told me.

His heart giving out seemed a fitting way to go. You know, he never complained, not once. He just got through it all. And in his last few days, he seemed sort of ready to go.

So there you have it. I had school and chores, but I missed Mr. Sherman something fierce. In one of our last conver-sations, I asked him why he called me by my middle name, Marcus, when everyone knew my name was James. He told me the word "Marcus" had its roots in Mars, being the God of War and the fourth planet in our solar system. "You must fight to find your place, otherwise, you may get lost in this busy family. A warrior's name is fitting for you, son."

He'd tried to sock me in the arm, but he was so weak that his fist only tapped me. "You must endeavor, as well, to own a bit of Marcus Aurelius, he being a tolerant emperor of ancient Rome.

Look him up in your school books," he had said and told me how Marcus Aurelius saw Man as a species made for cooperation and that war is contrary to his nature. "Aurelius gave us many words to ponder. Yes Marcus, promise me you will look him up." His comment did send me to the library. It seemed to me that if Mr. Sherman's skin hadn't been dark, maybe he could have been a teacher. I left his room that day amazed at how clear thinking a person can be when they're hovering with one foot over the grave.

Wasn't until they carried his body to the pauper's yard when it occurred to me, I should have tucked his old book beside him under his crossed arms. That thing was ratty enough, even back then, to deserve a decent burial. It would have been fitting. Couldn't bury his piece of slave gold with him, not in the pauper's yard. No Negroes were allowed burial in the nearby Whites-only cemetery.

Now, I get sidetracked even worse than my father did in his final years. Stop me if I don't stick to my story. It needs to be told before it's too late.

After Mr. Sherman died, the very same week, there I was picking up my first cigarette, lighting it, and smoking it. And now I've smoked un-filtereds for more than sixty years, so they're telling me that's why my lungs are spittin' up pink pus. Uff da. Doc says, "Newhouse, it's time to quit."

I don't see it. Not when he's saying that to me with his own cig wagging in my face while he talks. If my smoking caused the cancer, why the hell does he smoke? Then there's my pickled liver too. I've about seen my last sunset. Really want to tell, though, about the things I've learned from this pile of used up paper and ink. And why I'm giving it to my granddaughter, the one I can only hope will appreciate its story.

Holding the book was like holding an old dishrag. It had been scoured by so many eyes that the paper felt as if it had been scrubbed on a washboard. The corners? Pounded into curled edges. It's a wonder it survived in such a naked state. For nearly forty years, it had been knocking around in Mr. Sherman's pockets, and before him the girl, Elizabeth, had owned it. Mr. Sherman told me about her a bunch. Her story is faded away. Lucky she wrote her name in the back, Elizabeth Rose Sherman, or I wouldn't even know that.

Funny business, how they both had the same last name.

The book had seen all kinds of weather, and I don't mean rain and shine. No, it had survived a lot of history, is how I saw it. The first dozen-or-so pages were gone. Some of what remained had chunks ripped out. But at least my mother had given it a new cover. She hadn't used fine stitchery but had slapped it together and put the old thing back in business. She found some old leather and fiber board and attached them with eight or nine stitches. There were wood fragments stuck inside, so I figured the book might have had wooden boards, long ago. Well, my guess is as good as anybody's.

Too bad a person's body can't get fixed so easy.

But back to Mr. Sherman. A boy can dig up what he needs from anywhere. So I found my lot from what that black-skinned man could give me. He raised me. Really. No one else had time. Because his son was dead, and he had no other kin, all that's left of my friend was pasted into my memory. Mother told me how she'd let him stay on, during his final half-year, even though his money had run out. When she told me that, I actually hugged her. She stood there stiff as an ironing board and didn't hug me back.

It's a funny business how I loved my mother, since really she made herself so unlovable.

But that book, his stories, and one gold piece were all that was left of my friend. I refused to spend the damn thing. Instead, years later, after discovering a slit in the book's binding, I slipped it in there along with a Indian head nickel, which was about the same size, one I had found in a street gutter. I've been hauling them through the last fifty-odd years.

The book's weight felt comforting but heavy with responsibility. Seems hateful that someone like me, a man who's wasted most of what he could be on drink, should be in charge of Mr. Sherman's memories. But, there you have it. I am here to say, Marcus Newhouse did give a damn, even if he became a wasted old sot.

***

In the year 1906, I turned sixteen and was figuring to adventure my way out to California. To be on my own. But that damn earthquake shook San Francisco and the drive to leave right out of me. Disaster felt too close to home. Reading about a mother who cried out that two sons were buried alive and another who was made a widow with nine children, I just couldn't leave my family. Not right then, anyway.

My body still lived in the boarding house with my parents, but you can bet my mind had flown the coop. My patience aged from wine to vinegar. Though the book could be found bumping around in my jacket pocket, most days I'd forget it was there. Although, if I felt a need for advice, I'd crack it open. Not that it had any direct answers, not really. But I would find Mr. Sherman among its pages, in particular if I read aloud, which sometimes I did. Here's a passage that dumped shameful grit into my heart as I read:

> *Art thou a son or a daughter? Be grateful to thy father, for he gave thee life; and thy mother, for she sustained thee. Piety in a child is sweeter than the incense of Persia, yea, more delicious than odors, wafted by western gales, from a field of Arabian spices. Hear the words of thy father, for they are spoken for thy good: give ear to the admonitions of thy mother, for they proceed from her tenderest love. Honor their gray hairs, and support them in the evening of life: and thine own children, in reverence of thy example, shall repay thy piety with filial love and duty.*

The truth lived in all its ugliness. It didn't come in as a sweet gale of spices, no. Uff da no. "I hate my father," I said aloud. The more I pondered the idea, the more it seemed to be so. "Hate" might be too harsh a word, but sometimes it felt like the God-honest truth. You have to understand, back around the turn of the nineteenth century, folks were different. There were rules to follow, "strip-tures" I called them because they stripped all the drive out of my get-go. The weightiest among them was to "love, honor, and obey" your parents. The young men of my day, those teetering like sheep on a see-saw, knew change to be a-comin' round the bend.

America's old attitudes were fading as pale as Levis washed to a sky-blue. My parents, and others who'd grown up in

Norway, saw what was coming but wouldn't budge. My father in particular clung to old attitudes. He hated Swedes like a person hates bedbugs.

So I hated him.

"To you I tell, Jens, walk to other side of street," he said, slapping me upside the head. "Jens, no closer to filthy Swede church. Ten rods!"

"My name's Marcus." I hated how he couldn't even pronounce "James."

"Devil lives with Swede, walk to other side." Another slap.

I tried to ignore Father, but you add those comments to what happened a few days later, and my harsh thoughts were as clear as unsalted herring left in a crock for two weeks. All that's left are sour lemons and bitter onions floating on a briny broth.

"Boy, fetch hammer." Without looking at me, Father hadn't asked but spat out the order. His cigarette waggled up and down between his teeth, and his forehead bore a permanent furrow the size of the Ohio.

Since I was nearly a man, being called "boy" made my skin crawl. "I'm not a 'boy,' and I can't stop now," I said. "I'd have to wash my brushes." I was painting a sunset while looking at the one perfectly framed in the front-foyer window. "I'll lose the light."

"Now, Jens."

"Christ, Father, in a minute!"

"Ya, cannot—" He halted his words and grabbed the brush from my hand and threw it across the room. "No more, I say. These . . . these. Never do. No paint." He tore the canvas from my easel and stomped on it with his boot. "Men need work, no paint."

Even though it was winter, and there wasn't much to do, no fixing windows, no painting the back house, no re-shingling the roof, Father hated when I painted canvases. Art was what I loved, but he never commented on any of my work, not even the portrait I did of Mother. Her likeness hung in their bedroom, for Christ's sake.

Father was a painter of buildings, not pictures. He worked each day, beginning as the cock crowed, but during the boarding house's busy season, all of a sudden, he became part of our household again. During those times, he seemed like an intruder. Like a roach in the kitchen. Mother defended him by reminding me that when Father was young, in Norway, he had been an artist too. He had given it up for the rigors of adulthood. "You need follow in footstep," she said.

A frustrated artist is a hateful human being, so I swore I'd never be one of those ornery men wearing his grudge wrapped around his head like Christ's thorns.

My talent wouldn't be a childhood fancy tossed out with the garbage. I picked up my brush, threw it into the turpentine, found the hammer, presented it to him with a bow, ran from the house, and slammed the door. I slid my way down the icy street and skated to a stop in front of Auntie Maren's house. It was Uncle Ole's house too, of course, but Auntie Maren was definitely the queen. She was my father's sister-in-law, but everyone said she took after Farmor, Kristoffer Skauge. They weren't related, except through marriage, but she did have the same deep dent between her eyes, the one that the "scowling Skauges" were famous for.

Auntie Maren scared me, but she was the only adult I knew who agreed with the new ways. She was as Norwegian as they come, but she had Swedish friends. I spent as much time as I could at her house.

I burst through the door that day and found her standing in her seal-fur coat, her purple Suffrage banner wrapped around her thick body, and wearing her hat, which spewed a foot-high plume from its brim.

"Don't dally, Marcus. There's a rally at the courthouse." She imprisoned my hand while we marched down the street. Her grip was as strong as a man's. "I'll tell your mother I needed you to run errands for me. She'll never be the wiser. Women should have the right to vote. You agree. Don't you?"

Her question was a command, so I had no choice but to agree. I nodded my head.

Long before it was fashionable, Auntie refused to wear a corset. I know what that sounds like to someone now, in the 1950s, when women can show bellies at the beach. But back then, she was downright revolutionary. To my father, she was an extremist dressed like a harlot, but I think Mother secretly admired her. I did. Seemed to me that every woman would want to rid themselves of being tied up like a pot roast.

Mind you, Mother and Father were not ignorant. Just absorbed by their day-to-day business. I wish, now, I could recall their Norwegian. To young ears, they spoke a sweet gibberish sprinkled with rhythms of a faraway homeland. Except for "uff da" not a single word has remained in my memory. "Uff da", an acceptable swear word, was screamed by parents up and down our block as freely as salt was shaken on Northern Pike. Most likely the word was spawned from empty pockets. "Uff da, Jens Marcus, get out from my way," Father hollered when he was angry, which was most of the time.

The rest of their Norwegian had a way of moving like a ship on the sea, swaying, dipping, lapping at the shore just the same as an Edvard Grieg song. If you've ever heard one, you know what I mean. If you haven't, go buy a record, put it on the turntable, and give it a spin.

At the very least, our family had some music. Father was the only one who didn't play an instrument or sing. Mother made up for what he lacked since her voice rang with natural talent. When she sang were the only times Father smiled. He would stand in the kitchen, listening to her as she stirred onions in the giant spider pan. She sang while emptying chamber pots and in the early morning as she dipped her fingers into the sugar water used to keep her hair up like a twisted sticky-bun. Then, she'd sing when Father swatted away the summer yellow jackets swarming about her sweet-smelling head. Norwegian folk tunes and ballads were all she knew, never anything syncopated. But you know, her heavenly voice bathed me in comfort—the only comforting she gave to us.

Mother was thirty-eight years old when she birthed me, her youngest child, so she wasn't singing out of youthful glee. At about six, I learned of the death of my two sisters. One was just born, but my sister Ellen was six when she died. Both passed on before my entering the scene. Diphtheria and influenza took those baby souls. Confounds me why my parents had more children, even after Isaac was born a little funny. He was their second child and his eyes crossed, and he couldn't talk. Somehow, Mother kept him busy helping in the kitchen, or she'd set him out in the yard to pick weeds from the flower bed. He could be there for hours and never bother anybody. Just rocked back and forth, tending to his business while making moaning sounds. Once, we all forgot him until it was time for dinner. Someone finally asked, "Where's Isaac?"

"Uff da, uff da, uff da," Mother screamed, smacking each of our blond heads. She ran by and out the back door, scooped him up, and kissed him. I felt as green with envy as a spring pea. She never kissed me. Not that I remember. Maybe she just plain had too many kids to kiss. Only the most needy one got any.

Then there was Joseph. Didn't surprise me when he died. He'd been in and out of hospitals most of his ten years. We didn't talk about what was wrong with him. His sickness was just part of Mother's chores, tending to him and singing lullabies to calm him to sleep. He was a thing she took care of like the cooking, cleaning, washing, ironing, marketing, and bed changing. She did have some help, and most of us kids had our chores. When the house was full, she even hired more staff, but that was a job too, making sure we all took care of our business.

So on that day, when Auntie and I went to the Suffrage rally, a big chunk of me was searching for an escape route, away from Mother and Father, away from the hub-bub of the boarding house.

I struggled to free my hand from Auntie Maren's grasp. And as I glanced up, there she was, Ruth Olson, staring in our direction. Realizing it was me she was looking at, blood sped to my ears like a runaway streetcar. I'd spent many moments staring at Ruth. Every boy who ever saw her had to stare at her. Figured there wasn't a chance in hell to catch the eye of a girl like Ruth Olson. But still, she had me all tied up like the ribbon under her chin.

My heart pounded and beads of sweat formed on my forehead. Sweating in a Minnesota February? Uff da! I whispered to myself as she walked toward me, "Say something, you fool, anything. Anything. Come on, Marcus Newhouse, say something."

"Don't I know you?" she asked, her voice angelic.

"Yeah, sure . . . aren't you . . . um . . . Ruth Olson?"

She smiled at me. The world was ablaze. "I am, and you're Marcus Newhouse." My name drifted from her mouth, and I thought I heard birds singing, for Christ's sake.

A gust blew by, sending my cap scurrying up the sidewalk. I ran to fetch it and returned with it on my head. I tried to look calm, like one of the dandies who hung out at the local speakeasy. Silence. Then a little more. The lack of words spun around my tongue, which seemed to have swollen in my mouth and tasted like stale rye crackers. My ears burned.

Praise the Lord and pass the butter, she dug up something to say. "I didn't expect to see anyone I knew here. There's usually a few men here but none our age."

"I'm here with my aunt," I blurted out and stuffed my hands in my trouser pockets. Did she just call me a man? I need to say more. I want her to think I'm sympathetic to The Cause. She did call me a man, didn't she? Come on, Marcus, you dimwitted oaf, say something.

I just stood there.

"So you were dragged here by someone else?" Her hair was caught by the next gust, and the light beaming through it shined her up a halo.

"No. No, not at all. I just . . ." I was a buffoon.

Auntie Maren had been talking with someone who held a U.S. flag. She turned to us and salvaged what was left of me by asking, "Marcus, who is your friend?"

"Ruth Olson, one of the Olsons from 6121 Pine Street. That's down by the library. The Olsons go to my school."

Ruth looked surprised when I rattled off her address.

"Oh yes, Ruth. I know your mother. Is she here today?" Aunt Maren asked.

"No, I came alone."

"Alone? Well then. We will be leaving soon and can escort you home. You will join us." Because Auntie Maren stood at least six inches taller than Ruth, she looked down her long nose as she spoke. I knew Ruth would obey.

"I'm, I'm not supposed to . . . well, maybe, if Marcus agrees," Ruth said.

"Swell," I said. Marbles seemed to be rolling around in my mouth, fighting with my teeth.

Aunt Maren raised her right eyebrow.

I felt queasy but hoped to survive the next half hour without retching into the gutter. I did more than survive, didn't retch, and even managed to untangle a word or two. Mostly Ruth talked. I listened and found a few appropriate replies. Auntie chatted with almost every person we walked past, leaving Ruth and me to talk without fear of her listening; though, we were never away from her view.

I mustered up the courage to ask, "Ruth, there's a book I want to show you, could you meet me at the library tomorrow?"

"I'd be pleased to see you," she said in a near whisper. "Mother and I could be at the front steps at two o'clock."

"Swell," I replied. Swell? Can't I think of anything else?

When we arrived at her home, I watched as Ruth walked up her front steps, her white dress slightly visible below her velvet coat. I noticed the shape of her ankle where it entered her shoe and admired her slim fingers as they wrapped around the doorknob. She waved goodbye.

I stood immobile, but Auntie finally gave my arm a yank. "Come now, Marcus. Your father would never approve."

"What? I'm not—"

"You know. She's Swedish."

My heart sank into my boots.

***

"Luck has stopped this, ja. Maren tells of this. Your mistake to ruin family." Father poked his rigid index finger into my forehead.

"My friends aren't your choice," I said, stepping away from his reach, knowing what could follow.

"Not approve. Never. What this there lead to? Trouble. Boy young, will lose brain."

"I don't care if you approve of her."

Father lunged, and all in the same motion he belted me on the side of the head with his fist. He'd been angry before but had never hit me with a fist. And he hadn't spanked me since I was a small boy. "Not this Swede again. Uff da, Jens! What would come of this here? Mix-breed child? Little better to stray dog." He threw me to the floor. Then it happened. He kicked me—the worst of all insults.

My head throbbed, and my ears heard noises, a shrieking, a sound that only I could hear. Tears flooded to my eyes. In that moment, meeting Ruth Olson at the library became the goal, but also to marry her. Someday. I'd show Mother and Father that I was not like them. In my business, I'd make my own decisions.

A few months later I read this passage:

Of the Boy that stole Apples

> *An old man found a rude boy upon one of his trees stealing Apples, and desired him to come down; but the young Sauce-box told him plainly he would not. Won't you? said the old Man, then I will fetch you down; so he pulled up some tufts of Grass, and threw at him; but this only made the Youngster laugh, to think the old Man should pretend to beat him down from the tree with grass only.*
>
> *Well, well, said the old Man, if neither words nor grass will do, I must try what virtue there is in Stones; so the old man pelted him heartily with stones; which soon made the young Chap hasten down from the tree and beg the old Man's pardon.*
>
> ### *MORAL*
> *If good words and gentle means will not reclaim the wicked, they must be dealt with in a more severe manner.*

My anger swelled as I read that. There was no moral high-horse for a person to ride who would throw stones at a child. I would never hit a child, no matter what they did. I swore to it on the little book like it was the God-be-damned bible. A boy never forgets being struck by his father.

I felt stabs of loneliness poking in my chest for Mr. Sherman. The next day, by one o'clock sharp, I stood waiting. If the

Olsons arrived at the library early, they wouldn't be waiting for me. My tweed jacket and foppish cap barely kept me from freezing as I waited for the hour to pass. The weather didn't care about my discomfort and sent quarter-sized, wet snow globs onto my shoulders. I pulled my cap lower, turned down the flaps to save my ears, and flipped up my collar. There was a three-inch snowpack when I arrived, and as Ruth emerged from the near-blizzard, my heart somersaulted. No matter that by then my ankle boots were sunk up to the top button. I felt airborne.

She was alone. No chaperone.

"Marcus, you look like you've been standing here six hours," she said, and in what seemed like slow motion, she pulled off my cap and shook off the snow to the rhythm of a nearby clock bell. *Bong, bong.* When she returned my cap to my head, she ran a finger down my nose. "Let's go in, before this freezes off." She started up the stairs.

My feet felt heavy. "I didn't want you to wait for me," I said.

She turned to look at me. "I would have."

"Swell."

"This little blizzard couldn't stop me," she said and continued up the steps then turned to peer down at where I still stood and asked, "Do you need help? Or do you want me to stop?"

"No, please don't stop," I said and could feel a blush splash onto my face. Please let her think my red cheeks are from the chill. I swallowed and stomped the snow from my shoes then stepped up toward her. Only one riser away, I lifted her hand with mine. My heart leapt about like a rider on a runaway horse. "Please don't stop," I repeated, unsure if I had only thought the words before.

She stared at me. Her mouth puffed out clouds of misty air. Her face was the color and texture of fine porcelain, and her cheeks were pink round dots like on a China doll.

"Ruth, are you ill?" I asked.

Her eyes brimmed with tears. "Marcus, my mother has forbidden me to see you," she said. "Your family is from . . . you know . . . from Norway." Her cornflower-blue eyes remained glued to mine. "I'm so sorry . . . I'll go," she said and tugged on her bonnet ribbon while her other hand still rested in mine. "I thought I would just meet to tell you that I can't see you. I don't know." Our eyes met again.

I felt seasick.

"I can't seem to . . . to leave," she said. Her chin quivered.

I pulled her into the foyer of the building and removed my cap. The feelings jiggling through my body, from her hand to mine, were something akin to the shock I might get when removing my wool trousers and stepping on the floor-furnace grate. "Ruth, can I . . . ?"

"Can you what?"

I didn't answer, or ask again. I just kissed her smack certain on her lips. Her Swedish lips. No twittering springtime songbirds that time. Uff da, no. I could hear an orchestra playing the Hallelujah chorus. I stepped back. "Sorry," I said. "I just had to do . . . you know. My parents too . . . well they don't want me to—"

She stopped me from babbling by kissing my cheek. We smiled at each other. I guided her into the far corner for another smooch, this one lasting a lot longer. Her hair smelled of rosewater.

"Marcus, I had to sneak out. What about our parents?"

It didn't matter what she said; the path we'd started down was one I wouldn't stray from—not if she wouldn't. Finally, I knew what Mr. Sherman had been smiling about when he'd talked about his Dinah. It seemed to me he loved Elizabeth the same way. That's just a crazy thought, I know. But then Negro men seemed drawn to the white-skinned ladies. There's a mixed couple living down the street. They don't have any children; can't even imagine what those children would look like. An unnatural business, like a lion making a cub with a leopard. But then, I also know the strength of that draw to another human being. I could no sooner leave Ruth behind than cut off my own arm. Suppose Negroes have the same feelings. Mr. Sherman had showed me that truth.

I led Ruth through the doorway saying, "I want to show you something." We entered the library by way of the front ballroom-sized chamber. Our squeaky wet shoes echoed with every step. Afraid we would be seen by someone we knew, we nervously glanced about and made our way to the far reaches. The shelves protected a table encircled by chairs. We pulled out two seats with a *screech*, which no one reacted to, and I uncovered the little book from a pocket on the inside of my jacket. I felt as though Mr. Sherman prompted me as I began to tell Ruth his story. Starting with Elizabeth Sherman, the enormous weight of the little book's history began to spill from me like water. With each word, relief came as I was no longer the only person who knew the book's history.

Ruth considered every word and responded with care and cradled the book in her hands. The look in her eyes told me what I needed to know. She understood. More than that, she seemed to feel what I felt. "Marcus, I love that you carry this with you. It's a book containing many lessons in disguise. No one would know that it had any worth by looking at it."

A young boy came around the nearest bookcase and asked where the children's section was. I stood and pointed him in the right direction.

Ruth smiled and continued. "Mr. Sherman sounds like a good man, you must have meant a great deal to him. My parents hate Negroes too, and I'm surprised your parents rented a room to him for so long." She reached for my hand under the table. "He was lucky to have you, Marcus."

The feel of her touch sent shivers to places I didn't know were on the same track as my fingertips. "I loved him, more than my own father," I whispered. "And yes, my mother took a risk, letting him board. But he was wealthy, and he came and went by the back door. Someone had to be snooping around by the trash to ever see him. Would have thought he was one of our workmen." I couldn't believe that the words I formed made sense. My heart beat wildly.

We talked for hours until the library was about to close. That meeting stirred beginnings of courage and love; though, I didn't rightly know it then. By the time we left, my heart slowed to a normal *clip-clop*. Never felt love before. Didn't recognize it. Couldn't. All I knew was I would meet Ruth again the following day, and the next, and the next. She was the single goal driving my train down the tracks.

We sped ahead, you know, in the love business. Our first night together, we rounded up ourselves some stolen kisses in the back seat of Cliff's hupmobile. What a beaut. That old buggy's seats were as soft as the underside of Ruth's titties. Cliff let me borrow his car, and my girl snuck away from her home through the back door. Rusty hinges creaked loud enough for me to hear from inside the car, but somehow didn't wake up her folks. We drove out of town, put the top down, and parked at the far end of Lakeview Drive.

Yes siree, from then on, Wednesday was our night. Come hell or high water, neither of us would miss it. Every Wednesday morning began with Father peering at me over his coffee. His left eyebrow would curl up, and he'd say something along these lines. "Out tonight? Can ya see clear of it then, Jens? Uff da, Cliff not friend there, father drinks ya know, devil whiskey. Ja, just stay home. Leave pubs to rats."

The next morning, I'd tell Father I had lost another fin in a friendly game of chance, and he'd give me another talking to. His anger would be spat in my direction but was no match to what he'd have dished out, if he knew what I was really up to. A son's gambling problem and his drinking whisky couldn't compare to him gallivanting with the enemy—them dirty Swedes.

As time passed, Ruth and I began meeting behind the Golden Rule, then we'd run down to Main's Hotel. We were in love. You know the type, where you put your brain out to pasture, and what's in your britches plumb takes over. No other choice presented itself.

Thank the good Lord and pass the beans, Ruth's parents, the Olsons, were easing themselves into a different framework, noticing what was riding in on the rails. They sat miles ahead of where Father stood wallowing in his own drinking and hatred. But the Olsons were different, more accepting.

***

The war began to rage overseas, in 1914, and there was talk of a draft, enough men for what turned out to be World War One. In my gut, though, I was a pacifist. You see, I'd read all the great philosophers and poets, even those most chaps would have passed by. My favorite was a Chinaman, Lin Yutang. I saw myself following in the footsteps of the great artists, not picking up a gun, not spilling blood onto the ground. I had different landscapes in mind, ones to paint. Planned to be famous—not dead. And definitely not wrong in the head like my buddy, Cliff. Yep, he came home as shell-shocked as the best of them.

Ruth read a lot too, finding newspaper accounts of how the war carved out heroes from the grocer's son, or the iceman's brother. So I don't think she saw war from the same slant as I did. Still, she was too much in love to want to see me go. She read between the lines and saw the hints. Before that rotten business was all over, even married men would be pulled into the service. Sure enough, by 1918, men as old as fifty were drafted, old men, many of them leaving poor widows behind. Ruth and I didn't wait until then. By June of '16 when the National Defense Act was brought into order, Ruth and I planned our own attack.

We were making our share of bing-bang-floozy-do, and by the end of that month, she had our first little baby growing in her. Of course, I didn't object to all the trying we had agreed to. No. We tried and tried, every chance we got, we tried some more, if you get my meaning. That was a business we didn't mind tending to.

No more being careful about her cycle. No more last-second withdrawals. Some nights Ruth even snuck in the back window of my bedroom. The bed being way too squeaky forced us onto the wood floor. Well we weren't sleeping; that wasn't the point

179

now, was it. No, and we weren't bothered by the discomfort. We knew being married wasn't going to be good enough, we had to have children, loads of them to keep me from the war. The more the better, and quick.

If we'd been unlucky like my sister, and never birthed any live babies, well I'd have been labeled a coward and jailed, or worse, when I refused to go to that war. I knew where the truth lay behind the reports of glory. Europe was splattered with blood. Guts filled the trenches. I'd see no part in that. Do you know they even hanged a few poor saps, just for their refusal to cooperate with the draft. To me, it was a wretched business.

In order to get the full picture, you have to understand we'd kept up appearances before we got hitched, all the way to August 1916. That's when I hugged Ruth and noticed what felt like a watermelon between our bellies. She was pregnant all right, just like she swore she was. So we eloped.

Mind you, we weren't just a couple of young, senseless kids. I was twenty-six by then, and Ruth twenty-five. Mother had died a couple of years before, and it's a good thing because Ruth's condition and our lack of wedding bands would have killed her. Of course, Father's opinion still weighed on us like a sack of rotten potatoes.

So you see, Ruth and I executed life backward—got pregnant, then married, then told what parents we had left. Father's face turned red, like he might explode, then he poured himself a stiff belt. He swallowed it down quick and poured another. "Jens, ya sin, boy. I never forgive. God not forgive this here." He stormed around the room, hitting his fist on the furniture, his voice rising to a roar. "Ya safe for one thing. Mother in heaven. This shame, she not bear." He hurled his glass at me. It skimmed past my left ear and smashed against the wall behind my head. A shattering spray of slivers flew in every direction. One of those shards took months to fester itself from under the skin of my neck.

Father's last comments still bite at me. "How, Jens? Dirty Swede. This tramp? And baby, a devil. No bastard-child in this house."

Even though I never returned home, there was a hole drilled clear through me. Being the youngest, after all, I left my father alone and drunk. I abandoned him. He'd never meet my children, and still, somehow, a man's want for the approval of his father can never sway.

> *The eye that mocketh at his father and scorneth to obey his mother, the ravens of the valley shall pick it out, and the young eagles shall eat it.*

Yes, ravens picked at my eyes when I read that passage. They stung as if I'd poured alum in them.

> *Be not hasty in thy spirit to be angry for anger resteth in the bosom of fools.*

One day, I searched for a passage to relieve my pain, not to fan its fury. Finally my eyes arrived at these words:

> *Art thou a husband? Treat thy wife with tenderness and respect; reprove her faults with gentleness; be faithful to her in love; give up thy*

> *heart to her in confidence, and alleviate her cares.*
> *Art thou a parent? Teach thy children*
> *temperance, justice, and diligence in useful*
> *occupations; teach them the social virtues, and*
> *fortify thy precepts by thine own example.*

My father's example was one I refused to follow and yet, to this day, though he's been dead over thirty years, I still see his approval as something I'd have traded my right nut for. Well, maybe not. Isn't that a ridiculous state of affairs? I hoped to do better in the fathering business, but truth is I've made my own mess. That's the hell of it. Uff da, I say.

***

Cliff and I started slow. I felt sorry for the guy. He needed a drinking buddy to give a boot to his war-torn nightmares. Soon, we ended up meeting at Benny's or some other joint a couple of times a week. Well, maybe four or five. I'd drink myself piss-faced then open my mouth and let fly, "All you chaps, next round's on me!" As the guys stumbled away happy, they'd slug me on the shoulder and say, "Thanks, Newhouse." "You're the best Newhouse." "This bar would be a dive without you, Marcus." Most times, I'd owe the barkeep more than my pocket cash. Once, my handout happened on payday. I had nothing left for the week. I remember feeling the book in my pocket and considering selling the gold coin, but I didn't. Mr. Sherman's words kept riding me with guilt for even thinking about it.

When I arrived home, Ruth paced about. "I know you hate that I work, Marcus, but my ironing money is feeding this

182

family." She always started off saying something like that, but given a little time, her voice would crank up to an actual scream. I tried not to blame her, but her yelling made me head back to the bar to run the tab higher. More than once, I ended up painting a mural in a smoke-filled room to clear my bar tab.

One painting in particular I remember, not just because of what it looked like, but because of what it felt like to paint. As my brush moved against the wall, I loved the smell of the linseed oil and turpentine, the stroking of my brush against my subjects' skin, watching as what my mind held slid into view. That painting was my vision of how life should be—a family portrait. My kids and wife were sitting around a table, enjoying a lavish dinner by candlelight. My children's faces looked content, and Ruth wore the lavender silk crepe dress that had long before been stuffed into the dead-storage of our closet. The dress flowed from her shoulders and plunged at her neck. I lost myself in painting that image, and for twenty hours I forgot where I was, and why.

Actually, I painted clear through the night and part of the following day. Don't really remember the number of hours, but in the afternoon, the owner stood by the wall, staring at it. "I have to admit you've got talent, Newhouse. But pal, what the hell are you thinking?"

I was only half listening, still lost in completing the final touches of light coming from a window. I had made sure the light source entering the painting came from the same direction as the bar's light, up and to the right.

"No man with a family's going to sit here," he continued, "when you've reminded him of what he has at home. Jesus, pal, paint something else! Maybe tables of food to make them hungry. Or a parched desert to drum up some thirst."

My stomach churned and lurched while I painted over my dream with a raw umber wash. A damn-rotten business that was. The wall ended up with an image reminiscent of "The Last Supper," only my masterpiece contained barflies seated around the table drinking from beer steins. Everyone laughed and pointed when they recognized themselves. I cast the bartender in the role of Jesus. "Well, Newhouse, you outdid yourself. Next round's on the house. Thanks, pal," the owner said with a wink. My own face was that of Judas, the betrayer.

One night, our two oldest kids, Keith and Louise, or Lou as I usually called her, actually had to fetch me from a place six blocks from that month's home: The Barn Bar, a joint adorned with haystacks in every corner.

"Come on Dad, get up, we've got to go." Keith shook me awake. "Mr. Fenstermacher says if you leave now, he'll forget about the damage."

I couldn't tell if I'd been in a fight, or if I just broke something while falling off the stool. Who knows, but seeing Lou's young but fretful face shoved my heart into a pit. Ruth hadn't been able to retrieve me that night since she had just delivered Shirley two days before. Her birth rounded out our family at three kids, enough to keep me from any draft.

When I stumbled into our bedroom, Ruth sat up and hugged me. "Poor Marcus," she said. "I was wondering . . . well, just come to bed. I'm getting up in an hour with the baby." Can you believe that? Pity for me? She stroked my head while I drifted off.

The next day, Keith said, "Pop, I won't let Ma buy you any more booze." I swung at him, and we ended up in an actual fist fight. He was only, I don't know, maybe ten. In the middle of it, one of us knocked over a pot of stew, which had been cooling on the stove. We slid around in the meat and potatoes like two pigs in the slop. Ruth and Lou heard our yelling and ran in. "Stop! Please stop!" they screamed. Ruth's voice rose over Lou's and yelled, "There's no war going on, not any more. I'll have no fighting in my house!"

Not my proudest hour. Mr. Sherman must have rolled over in his grave.

My wife moved out for a spell to live with her sister. She packed a suitcase and bundled up the baby, Shirley, and walked out the door without much fanfare. Lou, who was only eight, cooked our meals, cleaned the house, and ironed. Keith took care of the shopping and washing since Lou was afraid of the wringer. I did my best to do my part, to sober up some. Ruth did come home, but in no time I was drunk. She left more than once but always came back. And I always started drinking again.

Even during the big dry spell, being sober didn't sit right with me. You'd think it would have made it easier, with booze harder to come by during prohibition. Somehow, my buddies and I never went without. Liquor was simply found farther back in the building, behind the launderer's shop, in the rear of the abandoned icehouse, or on the loading dock of the grocer's warehouse. Yes, there was a blind pig on nearly every block. Of course the quality of the offerings dove down deep. The worst jug I drained someone had dubbed "coffin varnish," a fitting name for that bottle of rot gut.

My friend, Fred, found his refreshments in all of his pals' kitchens. When he left our house, Ruth would shriek, "Damn that Fred, he's been here again. There's no vanilla for the cake." That report echoed down our block. I never got a taste for vanilla as a substitute for whisky. Probably what saved me from Fred's fate. Dead from poisoning his brain. When I heard he'd swilled alcohol from the cobbler's stash, I flew straight. For a while anyway.

In 1928, I actually landed a respectable job because a buddy of mine's father owned a company looking to add to their advertising department. Even kept it up for enough time that Ruth and I bought a house. That house on Brimwall Street, Minneapolis, was small but comfortable. It had three bedrooms, so Keith could have a separate room from the girls. I kept my drinking down to three-a-day and went to work every morning, just like a regular Joe. The family was happy and the neighborhood was filled with children playing. Our yard, no different from the others, had a clothesline and linens drying in the sunshine. In the summer, the girls organized parades of doll carriages. Lou dressed up herself and Shirley, decorated their carriages with crepe paper, and off they marched, streamers trailing behind. Keith joined the army of boys shouldering long sticks, pretending to be heroes home from a foreign war.

Then the stock market crashed. Lost my job and the house. Nothing was ever as good as life on Brimwall Street. Ruth spelled out her only demand. "We won't move too far, not out of the district, Marcus. I won't have these kids moving away from their school and friends." Sure, we moved within the school district, but we must have moved twenty times in four years. I'd come up with twenty-five dollars for the first-month's rent, but we'd get evicted after two months of not paying. I think the entire neighborhood rotated in a giant circle, with each family taking its turn in every house. It was a terrible business. Folks just couldn't keep up. A couple of times we were living in a house, and the bank repossessed it because the landlord couldn't keep up his payments. During the summer, when the windows were open, all you could hear was yelling. Frustration, like a disease, infected our neighborhood. And our home had it bad.

Idle time increased my drinking until I was burning a blue flame.

Those were some terrible days, but we always had haircuts. My friend Clayton was a barber, and he and I made a pact. I'd paint his signs, and the kids and I would never want for a haircut. It didn't hurt that Clayton and I made the deal over a bottle of malt.

"Shingle up the back and show the tips of their ears," Ruth said every time. The girls and Keith were treated to identical styles. "Look at Lou. She's a boy," I heard Keith snicker to his friends. I thought all three of them looked like they'd been trimmed by a hay mower. Clayton's being highly lubricated had a negative effect on the quality of our cuts.

Unlike lots of folks, we didn't go hungry, either. At Helgeson's, a dime would buy pork chops for the five of us. My friend, Edger, made sure to sneak us generous portions since we'd spent our evenings discussing beer-bottle philosophy out at The Barn Bar. In trade, I painted signs for his boss, so Edger didn't have to. I had a giant roll of butcher paper in the basement and rolled out twenty feet at a time. Keith held one end, and I the other, while Lou snapped a chalk line. That's all I needed to set the stage straight for my letters. A drunk with a steady hand is an unusual thing. "On Special: Chicken Hearts & Turkey Gizzards 5¢ per pound!" A few times I painted pigs, cows, or chickens, but mostly just the letters and numbers.

So we never went hungry, and we didn't look too shabby.

At some point, Lou started babysitting for a wealthy family. She made a lot of money for a kid. Their family lived in the biggest house in the district. They loved her and gave her tips. And even though Ruth yelled at her, Lou sometimes gave me money for drink. When she wouldn't, I tried to ignore that she had her tip money stashed in a piggy bank. I took a kitchen knife into her room, one day, and slid a few quarters out of the slot. From then on, I couldn't ignore that ceramic hog-o'-temptation. Lou was never able to buy the bicycle she'd been saving for. Like I said, those were tough times.

There may still be a bar somewhere in Minneapolis, with a painting on a wall signed "Marcus Newhouse." I hope so because we lost all the canvases I ever painted, during one of the times Ruth left. I didn't pay the rent and had to put everything in storage since we were staying at a buddy's house, and the locker's contents were sold when we couldn't pay the storage fee either. Ruth never forgave me for losing the few treasured things our family owned.

"You let my mother's china go, and her embroidered tablecloth, and you kept that ratty old book in your pocket? Marcus, maybe Mother was right, Norwegians do live with the devil."

There was no answer for that. I wasn't thinkin', no, I was drinkin'. I just kept my head down and my shaking left hand in my pocket. Could never tell Ruth about the gold piece. Figured she'd want to spend it on rent or food or clothes for the kids. That gold just seemed too precious to spend on ordinary things, plus what could it have been worth, anyway. Just a few bucks, probably. It was only the size of an Indian head nickel. It's not like I was following any of that old book's advice, or any of Mr. Sherman's words, either. I laughed while reading this passage:

Most men are more willing to indulge in easy vices, than to practice laborious virtues.

Not unlike this, is the history of the grog-drinker. This man wonders why he does not thrive in the world; he cannot see the reason why his neighbor Temperance should be more prosperous than himself—but in truth, he makes no calculations. Ten cents a day for grog, is a small sum, he thinks, which can hurt no man! But let us make an estimate. Ten cents a day amount in a year to thirty-six dollars and a half—a sum sufficient to buy a good farm horse!

This surely is no small sum for a farmer—But in ten years, this sum amounts to three hundred and sixty five dollars, besides interest in the mean time! What an amount is this for drams and bitters in ten years! It is money enough to build a small house! Suppose a family was to consume a quart of spirits in a day, at twenty-five cents a quart—in thirty years, two thousand seven hundred and thirty seven dollars and a half! A great estate may thus be consumed in a single quart of rum! What mischief is done by the love of spirituous liquors!

The practice of drinking spirits gives a man red eyes, a bloated face, and an empty purse—It injures the liver, produces dropsy, occasions a trembling of the joints and limbs, and closes life

*with a slow decay or palsy. Spirituous liquors
shorten more lives than famine, pestilence and the
sword!*

***

When I reached my fiftieth birthday, a huge event marked the day—one larger than my celebration of being halfway to one hundred. You'll understand what I mean when I say, "some things you don't choose, they choose you." You see, I was born on Dec. 7, 1891.

That beautiful Sunday afternoon, fifty years later, was one of those rare December days when there's an unexpected break from the normal winter. The sun blazed so bright I could pretend it was warm. We arrived at the Olson home for supper, and they surprised me with cake and candles. I had just huffed and puffed when Aunt Maren ran in from the back room, yelling for everyone to gather around the radio. Now Auntie running was an event in itself, but we soon found out what all the hoopla was about. Our world jumped into war again—the big W.W. II.

Forget about Pearl Harbor, we may have been four thousand miles away, but we felt like the bombs had blasted the ice in that Minnesota backyard. Keith signed up the next day, and the rest of us waited, listening to President Roosevelt's radio announcements, and reading dailies. The following Friday morning, I was scraping paint from a wooden sign, when Keith sauntered into the basement, wearing a God-blasted Army Air Corps uniform.

To the girls he cut a dashing figure, but my stomach did a flip-flop, then a slow burn. Within a month, they were training him as a pilot, and most of the war he was stuck in a bomber, flying runs over Europe. I suppose a father's pleading holds no weight in the end.

"Keith, the war can kill you. Or worse," I said. "Haven't you seen that old man who sits down at the depot, mumbling to himself? I knew him. His name's Cliff. He was like you: a strong man, when they sent him to the trenches. If you listen to him, you'll see. He's still in some ditch, listening for another bomb to drop."

"Gees, Pops. I'm going to be flying over, not digging myself into the dirt" was Keith's answer.

Nothing could sway that boy. At least our late night talks pushed me toward something besides drink. I stayed home more, drank less, and ramped up my other vice. I lit one unfiltered Camel at dawn, lit the next from that, and put the last one out before I went to bed. A man's got to have some depravity. Doesn't he? Besides, the bars weren't all that much fun anymore. My friends had sent their sons to fight, and they were all full of pride. "Our son's over there too; we're so happy he's found some direction." Direction my ass, more like, found a way to his grave.

As with many of our boys, mine wanted adventure. I suppose we were lucky he lived through that hell. But not a one of them went over there and returned without one scar or another. When Keith arrived home, Ruth and I drove downtown to meet him. The boys dragged themselves out of the buses like cattle being dragged to the slaughter. I couldn't pick Keith out of the khaki crowd. When his bedraggled body came in to view, I wanted to fall to the ground and sob, but I just held it in tight, shook his hand, and patted him on the back. Ruth flung her arms around our boy, hugged him tight as her knees collapsed, and her tears made a dark spot on his shoulder.

There was a hollow look, something missing in Keith's eyes that would never be refilled. Before his volunteering, he'd carried himself with some lightness. He had been quick to smile and joke with his buddies. But after, he was dragged down by the weight of whatever he'd seen. "Pops, I was talking to Denny. He was sitting right there beside me when, *boom*, just like that, the poor sap got a piece of shrapnel straight through his forehead. My ears still ring from it, but at least it didn't get me."

Denny was a kid who had spent more time at our house than his own. His parents argued nightly. They both drank, and his father beat him up. Losing him was close to losing Keith. But Keith's body came home alive, not in a bag like Denny's. You can't get over stuff like that. No way, uff da, no how.

One night, Keith and I sat around the kitchen table with our two wisps of smoke heading toward the ceiling. We played a little rummy, drank some scotch, and talked. He talked about how he'd seen planes shot down that had been flying right beside his plane, how he'd felt glad to be alive but also terrible guilty because he'd known the guys who were killed. I felt myself drifting away. My chair seemed to be on a glider, slipping me farther and farther from my boy. Finally, I stood up and said, "I'll leave you to it."

"Come on, Pops, I'll stop talking. It's your deal."

"No, I'll see you in the morning."

Somehow, we both knew. And we both knew that we both knew, if you know what I mean. He had gone to war. I hadn't. Don't be thinking that I'd wished I'd picked up a gun. No, none of that business for me. I did what was right and followed my beliefs, got Ruth pregnant, and we raised a family. But he had chosen something different, and I would never share in it. There was no faulting him for his choice, but he assumed I did. From then on, from where he sat, I had little of importance to say.

I had my girls though. Shirley was seventeen, and Lou twenty-two. Our youngest still had some growing up to do, but then one day she waltzed into the house with news that, after his divorce was final, she was marrying a doctor. He seemed nice enough. But I wondered how can you trust a cheat after they've cheated on someone else? Problem was that we knew from our own lives, there's no arguing with young love. So off she went. It didn't last forever, but he did give her two great kids.

Soon after, Lou married her beau, a frat-boy named Robert "Jig" Spencer. Ruth presumed our daughter would be taken care of. But Jig's reputation as a charmer didn't sit right with me. Reminded me of this passage from the old book:

> *Art thou a young woman, wishing to know thy future destiny? Be cautious in listening to the addresses of men. Art thou pleased with smiles and flattering words? Remember that man often smiles and flatters most, when he would betray thee.*

I'm sure Jig saw me for what I was too, an old souse who had, for years, been snatching his wife's money. Lou married him to get out of our house. I'm sure of it. In those days, girls replaced fathers with husbands. She simply packed a bag, got married, and unpacked that night in another man's house.

I could see why Lou got hooked by him. The guy was handsome, rolled in fun, and threw wild parties. Good times lasted for as long as they dated, six months. Then snap, it seemed like the honeymoon was over the second they got married. That's when all of us realized the guy had been living off his parents' money not his own wits. Jig changed jobs like most folks change their underwear. Among other things he worked as a meat vendor, advertising salesman, and as a journalist, which was what his college years had taught him. The guy drank way too much. I should know.

Eventually, they traded the Midwest plains for sunny Southern California, but his job switches didn't end there. One harebrained scheme after another, and Lou just went along for the ride. They moved many times in the first ten years after the wedding, but it must not have seemed all that odd to her, migrating from one place to another. Hell, we'd done it enough. If you ask me, though, it was a crazy business.

They finally settled into one place for a good amount of time, so Ruth and I decided to follow them and moved to Bakersfield, California. We lived in a little house just an alley away. It wasn't the bustling San Francisco I had wanted in my youth, but being close to my Louise made me feel wanted.

Most families enjoying the postwar years expanded, adding a child about every year, but Lou and Jig ended up with only one. I knew she wanted more, but life can be tricky. Lou's greatest gift to me was Maren, born Dec. 7, 1957. That sweet baby girl was born on my sixty-sixth birthday and was given my Auntie's name. I can tell you, she was cuter than a bug's ear.

But by the time she was born, as I said before, I was spitting up pink pus and coughing like there was no tomorrow. With a granddaughter who shared my birthday, it seemed, I could die and not be forgotten. She'd remember. Besides, being born on Pearl Harbor Day gave her the same sort of distinction it gave me. An "infamous" day, but a distinction none the less. She would never be neglected. Never. More like over-mothered.

While raking up leaves from under the pomegranate tree one day, I decided I wanted little Maren to have Mr. Sherman's book, after she'd done some growing up. Of course, the old thing was almost as used up as me. Its words were such relics that Maren might not ever view the book as anything special. But I'd leave it to Lou to explain the weight of it.

***

Every Sunday at 6:00 p.m. sharp, Ruth and I ate supper at Lou's place. We'd stay on, and after Maren was put to bed, Jig and I usually talked and played cards while Ruth and Lou cleared and did the dishes.

This one night was no different. "Time for a game?" I shuffled the deck on the cribbage board, and glanced at their console TV; the Honeymooners were on.

"Sure. You deal, Pop. I'll pour. Want one?" Jig asked, holding up the scotch bottle.

"Just a short one, I've got my smokes."

Until he sat down, I tossed the cards from one hand to the other then handed him the deck to cut. "I'm dying, you know," I said and took a healthy swig.

Jig cleared his throat and rapped his knuckles on the top of the deck, signaling there was no need to cut.

"Can you take me out fishing?" I asked, dealing six cards each. I fanned out my hand. "Tomorrow?" I clarified.

"Sure, Pop. It's supposed to be a nice day. Getting out in the air might do you some good. Put your mind off it."

"Might." My hand was one of those where you don't want to throw anything into the crib, but you have to choose two cards. I sighed and tossed a four and a five onto his two discards. "While we're out in your boat, I'm going to ask you to do something." I avoided looking at his face, but I could feel his stare. "It's like this," I continued. "We head out and put in a day. Then you leave me. You know, kind of like they say the old Indians used to do. You come back by yourself." I took a long drag on my cigarette and left it dangling on my lip as I looked at his face.

Jig started coughing. He had asthma that flared up whenever he needed it. His neck turned red, and he reached into his pocket for his snot rag. He hawked up something and stuck the rag back into his pocket. "Three," he said, tossing his first card on the table.

"Christ all mighty, I can't hold up to the pain. Cancer's eating me from the inside out." I played a ten. "Thirteen."

"Fifteen, two," Jig said, his reddish skin paling as he moved his peg two holes.

"Seventeen, for two." Our pegs ran neck and neck.

"Twenty seven. Pop, how? You can't ask me to do this."

"Thirty." I looked again at his face. Beads of sweat glistened on his forehead.

"Go," he said.

I laid down my ace and pegged two points. Jig placed his king on top of his other cards and moved his peg another hole. I glanced at my cards, then it hit me. Uff da. For the first time, ever, in all our years of playing that game, we had never forgotten to cut the deck for the fifth card. We had that time, though.

"Jesus, what the hell've we done, Jig? Cut the deck now.

You're a betting man. If it's higher than a nine, you have to take me out tomorrow."

He was calculating the odds. A salty drop slipped down his forehead. "What happens if it's lower? What do I win?"

"I won't ask you again."

He rubbed his eyes and cut the deck.

"Jack of diamonds. That's it, fair and square. I win," I said and took another drag, chasing it with another healthy sip.

"And, you get nobs," he mumbled.

"Uff da. My lucky day. That's a fine business."

He stood. His tall frame looked a bit shorter. "I don't know if I can do this, Pop. You're Lou's father."

"She won't know. Nobody will. The way I figure it, you just tell them I needed to take a wiz, stepped off the boat, disappeared into the woods, and didn't come back. Someday, they might find my body all rotted out. But if we're in the boonies far enough, I won't be able to change my mind and come waltzing back home."

Jig appeared withered. I could imagine what he'd look like when he was as old as me. "I'm going to die soon," I said. "That's true anyway you eat the corn. Pain's damned unbearable. Every breath feels like I'm hoisting a ton of rocks on my chest. When I cough, I think I'll never stop, and worst thing is— no sleep. I spend every damned night pacing around, trying not to disturb Ruth. It's taking a toll on her, too, you know. I've tried drinking myself into oblivion, hoping I won't wake up. But I'm not even strong enough to hold enough booze to dump myself into the grave." I took another puff. Just to underscore my point, my body took off on a coughing fit.

Jig sat down to watch me and probably hoped this spree

would just kill me. He'd be off the hook. It truly sounded like the final rales of death. The hacks and snorts went on and on, and I'm not sure, but I figure my lips might have turned gray. When it finally eased up, we just sat across from each other.

He seemed to need more convincing, so I continued. "Look, I don't own a gun, and I wouldn't use it if I did." I took another drag on my Camel, let the smoke linger in my mouth, didn't let it go all the way into my throat, then hacked out a gray cloud. "I'm not going to die by no gunshot wound when I've avoided two God-forsaken world wars." I glanced toward the kitchen door to make sure it was still shut so the women couldn't hear, then I bent toward him and whispered, "Hell, Ruth would be the one to find me. I just can't do that to her."

Jig appeared to mull over every possible option. He took another nip of scotch and let the twenty-year-old liquid swirl in his mouth. He swallowed noisily. His voice was barely louder than what my whisper had been when he said, "A bet's a bet."

"What?" I leaned closer.

"I lost."

"Yes you did. Good enough. We'll get up early and go by five, before anybody else wakes up. Don't want to suffer any tearful goodbyes."

"I can't promise what'll happen. When it comes down to it, Pop, I may not be able to, you know, leave you."

"Come on, Jesus H. Christ, I know what I'm asking. But we'll just go, throw our lines in a couple of times, see what we catch." I looked at him and waited to detect a hint of agreement. None came.

Finally Jig stood and said, "You don't mind if we quit this game, do you? It's all buggered up anyway." He walked to the kitchen door and pushed on it.

Ruth and Lou had to have only made a dent in the cleanup, so I was surprised when he offered to finish the dishes. "Mom, listen. Pop's ready to go home," he said. "Lou, why don't you walk them over. I'll stay and finish up here."

Lou kissed him on the cheek, stripped off her rubber gloves, and draped them over his shoulder faster than you could say, "Bob's your uncle." She said, "Thanks, I'll be right back," with a smile that made me wonder if I wanted to live forever.

Back home, I decided to spend a few minutes with Mr. Sherman's book, and before falling to sleep, I found this:

> *The time will come when we must all*
> *be laid in the dust.*

Yes, I was as old and crusty as a man could get, but not as old and crusty as that old book. Mother's cover was nothing to be proud of. She must have been in a huge hurry, like usual. Instead of opening it to read more, I placed it in my pocket. I'd stick it under my pillow, beside Ruth, before I left to go fishing. She'd find it later. That was the plan, but you know, life can be such a tricky business.

***

The next morning, before dawn, I walked into the kitchen and opened the cupboard under the sink and dove into the back to find the bottle of whisky stashed there. Not bothering to get a glass, I took a swig. Ah, nothing like a bit of a nip first thing in the morning. I took a few more then found my hat and walked into the alley to meet Jig. He pulled up in his truck with the boat on a trailer.

After kissing my hand, I blew the invisible smooch into the air toward Ruth's window, picturing her doing that dance she had done when the kids were little. They'd blow her kisses, and she'd reach high above her head, jumping desperately to catch the kisses floating over her. She'd nab one in her fist and release it onto her own waiting lips. The kids loved her playful side. Me, too.

At the lake, with Jig at the helm, his little rowboat skimmed into the middle of the body of water. The sun wasn't awake yet and there wasn't a lick of chop. Most days when I got up, if I had slept at all, I'd cough for an hour before breakfast. But that morning, I had escaped the torture. Maybe all my swearing to Christ, had finally paid off.

"You seem better," Jig said, thumping his chest.

"Just shut up. You're gonna scare the fish."

"Sorry, just thought you might change your mind."

"No chance in hell," I said.

He dipped the oars a few more strokes, then eased the anchor to the bottom. We fed our worms onto our hooks and tossed them in.

"Can you at least think about it, Pop? You're not the only one suffering here, you know."

I pulled out my Camels and lit one.

He glared at me, reeled in his hook, secured his line to his pole, and latched his tackle box. "Okay then, never mind. Why wait? Let's get it over with," he said. "Where should I drop you? Over there? Or no, in that poison oak patch? You can go out scratching." He pulled the anchor back into the boat. "Do you have enough smokes? You might last longer than you think. You don't want to be deprived when you're struggling with your last breath."

I wondered where all the talk had come from. Communicating wasn't his strongest game. "Jig, we can't do it now 'cause you'll be arriving back home too early. For Christ's sakes, it would be broad daylight. They'd send a posse out to pick me up."

"Quit whining, Pop. Why's it have to be on your terms? What about the rest of us poor slobs?"

"It's me that's dying."

"So?"

"So, I get the final say."

"Who died and made you dictator?" Jig asked and began rowing toward the far edge, away from his truck.

With each stroke, my heart pounded a little quicker. I snubbed out a nearly un-smoked cig on the rail and lit another. My hands shook more than normal, so the newly lit Camel flipped over the side. It sputtered out and floated past the stern. I detected a smirk curling Jig's lips. "Christ, I suppose you think this is funny?" I asked.

"Not at all. But, this just isn't the way it's supposed to work."

"Who died and gave you a brain?"

He started laughing. The stillness was shattered, and four ducks sliding along the edge suddenly beat their wings on the water, lifting their bodies into the air. As if this was the funniest moment in his life, Jig howled. He doubled over, and the boat bumped up and down. I couldn't help myself. I grinned. Then a slight chuckle escaped. Then I burst forth too. The boat rocked back and forth while we bellowed into the growing sunlight. Our gyrations eased up a bit as we each cut in with a few coughs, making us laugh even harder. We kept at it for quite some time, alternating between coughing and laughing, until he contained himself long enough to talk.

"What now?"

I put up my hand, unable to speak. My stomach muscles burned.

"Do you give?"

I shook my head, no.

He paddled toward the far shore.

Right away things went south. First, there wasn't much shore where we landed. For a distance up from the water, all I could see was a tangle of manzanita, sage, and briars. Not a nice spot for a final resting place. I stood up to get situated and nearly tipped us over. In the commotion, I waved my arms, and my right hand hit against my jacket. All I could do was watch as my open pack of smokes flew out of my pocket in a giant arc, hit the water, and floated away. I grabbed the oar and flailed at the pack, hoping to bring it to the boat. Instead, I sent it deep into the drink.

"Uh oh, you're in for it now, Pop," Jig said, looking smug.

I further surveyed the shore and saw a possible landing spot. "Hells bells, just take me over there and let me out." We paddled to a rocky spit that gave way to a patch of sand at the water's edge. The boat dug in and held tight. After hoisting myself onto the shore, I said, "There, you're done," and kicked the boat in a feeble attempt to send it off.

"Okay. I'm going." He shoved off using the oar and backed away.

I picked a path over some rocks then turned around. He was still just sitting there. "Go on. Get your ass outa here," I yelled.

"Okay, I'm really going now . . ."

"Me too, frat boy."

"I love you too, Pop."

I could hear the oars hit the water as I pried my way through the brush. The bushes out there grew hearty. They had to withstand dry spells that came over the land like giant Hoovers, sucking out any water from the sandy soil. The Manzanita grew strong fingers and had a way of snagging and scratching at anyone who might be traveling by. In two minutes, I looked down to see several rips in my trousers. "God damned shrubs," I growled.

My progress was slow until the undergrowth thinned. Jig and the boat had moved beyond my sight and hearing, or I had moved beyond his. Either way, I was done with him and the rest of it. I sat down and thought about lighting up. No smokes. I patted all my pockets, hoping to find a stray butt and found, you guessed it, the God damned book! "Shit sticks to shine-ola. Now what?" After whacking my forehead with it, I spread it open and read a little.

It requires but little discernment to discover the imperfections of others but much humility to acknowledge our own.

"I'm too old for this shit," I said, sticking the book back into my pocket, and I thought about how someone might find my body before it had time to putrefy. Shit, the book! Uff da. The book's journey will end with me? Here? This pile of paper gets

203

eaten by coyotes? Oh, hell. What if I can't make it back? This thought scurried up the back of my neck. "The gold piece!" I yelled skyward. "I'll be damned to hell, if that piece of slave money ends up in a pile of animal crap."

When I leaned on the dirt to stand up, I felt something crunch under my hand. Well I'll tell you, it was the most disgusting thing I'd ever laid my eyes on. I'd seen one of those critters once, in Ruth's rosebush border. But this one was bigger. They call them "potato bugs" also "children of the earth," I suppose because they have a huge bald head like the most grotesque human baby ever seen. This one, nearly two-inches long, was now a mass of slime and brown shell, stuck to the palm of my hand.

"Cheeerist!" I pushed my hand into the dirt to wipe off the muck. The thing hadn't bitten me, at least. With fragments of shell still stuck on my hand, I stood up and just started walking, well, marching really. I had to get back.

Had to get the book back. Couldn't let the gold go to waste. Didn't give much consideration to the direction except to keep the lake in view. I just placed one foot in front of the other, following the land as it went up and down, around the lake, slowing only when crossing some tangles. Started wanting a drink; thought a little bourbon would taste real good. Finally, after climbing up and over a few large sandstone boulders, I came around a bend. And there it was. Well, I'm embarrassed to say, it was Jig's truck parked where we had left it earlier. He was sitting inside it watching me.

I opened the passenger door and climbed in. "Let's go," I grumbled.

"Where?"

"Home." Picking a few burrs from my pants I asked, "What time is it?"

"Probably about nine. I almost left an hour ago. You would have had to walk home." He backed up the boat trailer, and we bumped our way home.

You know, it's not like I planned it that way. Just lost momentum. That damned bug and all those bushes and briars. A man shouldn't have to go out messing with such things. Makes me chuckle that Jig just sat there, stewing about how to go home, too chicken-shit to face his wife and mother-in-law.

Of course I had to go back. Didn't have much of a choice with all that responsibility bumping around in my pocket.

***

Ruth took one look at me and sent me to wash up. As I removed my jacket, I felt the book, and this passage popped into my head as I'd read it the night before:

> *More persons seek to live long, though long life is not in their power, than to live well, though a good life depends on their own will.*

I thought about those words. What about a good death? Shouldn't I be able to die well? Like I've said before, some things you don't choose; they choose you. At the top of the next page had been this:

> *Fiction seldom leaves a man honest, however it may find him.*

I opened the book to read that sentence again, just in case I had it wrong. What the hell did that mean? You know, some of the little book is old garbage. Looking back, my life seemed a miserable achievement for a man. I drank myself out of most possibilities. All my artistic attempts got lost. At least my kids weren't total failures, not like me.

Lou knocked on the door, and I told her to come in. She sat down beside me on the bed. "Dad, are you okay? Your clothes are a mess. I'll use bleach to get this stain out." She pulled on the knee of my pants. "Never mind the bleach, how'd you get this rip?"

"Don't worry about it, Lou." My hand reached out to hers. The book rested in my other palm, and I wished for the words to stream up one arm and down the other to get to her. I feared that too much of the book's history could be lost in my telling it to Lou. Not because she hadn't heard the stories, I'd told them all before. Maybe she even tried to remember them. But she was one more person removed from when the events had happened, so she couldn't see the orphan girl giving Mr. Sherman the book. Not like I could. She didn't understand the weight of Mr. Sherman's struggle to learn to read or how important it was that he had gotten rid of his slave name. Did I ever tell her that? And I knew I'd never told her about the gold. That thing felt like a sacred artifact hidden in the book's binding.

So much might be lost!

My breathing sped up. Suddenly, memories felt sketchy. When he'd told me stories, Mr. Sherman's words were vivid. But that was over sixty years ago. Could I remember everything? The history was dark, now, like muddy pond water. With all those years stacked up, my memories were probably wrong. Maybe I'd added or taken away details to fit what I wanted to tell. Hell, my drink hadn't helped. What I'd been told of Elizabeth seemed to suddenly feel like a weedy patch. How did Elizabeth become an orphan? Did Lou even know about her?

I'd never asked Mr. Sherman about the bookbinder, the one who'd signed the book first. I opened it up to the last page. Yes, there was his signature with its curly letters. More than cursive writing, more like calligraphy. Yes sir, I'd meant to ask about Alden Masters. I was too late. I read down the rest of the list. Elizabeth Rose Sherman, William T. Sherman, Johanna Kristoffersdatter Skauge Nyhus, J. Marcus Newhouse. Yes, I'd added my name and Mother's using a fountain pen and India ink.

A tear started to drip from my eye, but I wiped it away clean. No one cares, I thought, and slapped the book closed.

"I want you to have this," I said.

"What is it?" Lou asked, rubbing my back.

My speech came out like a streetcar on a crowded road, stopping for pedestrians, unable to get a smooth move on. "Do you . . . remember? I told you stories . . . about Mr. Sherman, and I read to you . . . from this book. His book. Remember?" I felt like yelling but my breathing was too shallow.

"Oh, sure," she said. "You still have that old thing?" She reached across me to take the book from my hand.

I held on tight, and for some reason, my breathing got better. "Hold your horses, young lady. Just sit here a sec. I'm going to tell you again. Listen up. When I'm gone, you'll need to keep these stories alive. Promise me. That you'll remember and tell Maren when she's old enough. You must remember!" I sounded desperate, and Christ, tears spilled from my eyes.

"Gees, Dad. Are you planning to die tomorrow or

something?" She stood. Gravy stains on her apron were evidence of the roast beef she'd fixed the Sunday before.

"Lou, you never know. So . . . so please, can you just sit still, for just one minute?" I patted the bed. My heart seemed to flutter then pound wildly.

"I'd love to Dad, but Mom and I have supper started. So maybe after we eat? Oh damn, but Maren needs a bath. How about in the morning. Okay?"

I stood and kissed her cheek. " I guess that's alright. But promise me, in the morning." Thinking of the gold piece, I added, "And Lou, remind me to tell you about the secret, in case I forget."

"What secret?"

"Not now. If you have to wonder, you'll be sure to ask me in the morning."

She hesitated a second then hugged me. "I really do want to hear, Dad. Honest." Lou's assurances sanded the edges off my worry. She walked toward the door. "We're having your favorite, macaroni and cheese."

"And they call it macaroni," I sang a verse of Yankee Doodle to her, and to me, to calm my nerves out of what I thought must be apoplexy. I smiled at her, waited until she was gone, shut the door, then stripped down to my skivvies.

Black-and-blue marks had formed on my legs, arms, and chest. My old bod' looked like it'd been in a brawl. "You're beat to a puddin', Marcus Newhouse," I said to my reflection. Hell, I was beaten by life, by the day, by bushes that wouldn't give me a break. Loads of time had passed since I'd looked at myself full-on naked in a mirror. A scary image of sagging skin, scant hair where it should be, some sprouting where it shouldn't.

I tiptoed down the hall to the john, opened the cupboard, and peered under the sink. No bottle, so I attempted to scrub off those dark marks. Most seemed to be bruises. The nail brush scoured off the grit from my hands. Returning to the bedroom and feeling somewhat better, I dressed in my best shirt and bow tie. "Damn, where did I put that bottle?" I searched under my socks. None.

Tying my tie, my thumbs seemed to have other ideas. Hadn't done that in maybe six months, or hell, maybe six years. Dapper? Ready for something new? A new life? I'd been given one when I blew my attempt to end it all at the lake. Maybe I'd pass on tonight's drink. Maybe give it up all together.

Ruth's table had an extra leaf in it. The blue casserole with the flowery white handles sat on the hotplate, and green beans, applesauce, and baked rolls rounded out the meal. My belly let out a growl as I plopped down on the chair at the head of the table. After pulling the cardboard plug off the milk bottle, I handed it to Maren and gave her a wink. She smiled back and licked off the cream. Everyone drank wine except Maren and me. So I poured us two glasses of milk.

Ah, milk, cream that's thin enough to drink. With a shot, it could go down easier. I left the table and walked into the garage, with milk glass in hand. Hidden under a pile of rags and on top of a metal storage locker was my garage stash. I held up the Kahlua bottle and peered through the brown glass. Nearly empty. One shot's enough. "Hell, if one's enough, two's better," I said, emptying the rest into my glass. The brown liquid swirled into the milk. I whirled it with my finger and licked it off.

One sip and then I'd go eat.

Kate Porter

VI

1958-1969
Louise Newhouse Spencer

Why do most people seem like experts, when I feel like such an amateur? Consider this example:

"Where's Dad?" I asked.

"In the garage," Mom and Jig said in unison, their voices dripping with impatience. Where do you think Dad is? Of course he's in the garage, you idiot, was what their tone implied. Didn't he always go there before sitting down to eat? The olive green Frigidaire started to hum.

"Lou, I'll check," Jig said and stood and walked toward the attached garage. He hesitated for a moment then opened the door. "Pop! Oh, God. No."

When I heard his words I knew.

I stood, but Mom raced to the door, and what she saw made her turn to me and scream, "Call the ambulance!" Her body seemed to melt with dread.

While crossing the room, I passed Maren. Somehow, even a one-year-old knew something was up. I marched with deliberate steps to the phone and dialed the numbers FA4-5000. "Hello, this is Mrs. Spencer, 2301 First Street . . . yes . . . it's my father . . . right away. Thanks."

I hung up the phone and looked back toward the table. My baby girl had a mini-furrow of worry between her eyes. I'd

211

wanted, no . . . needed, a child for years, but for some reason it hit home right then. My child needed me. Did she hope I would take away the panic she must have seen on my face? Was her life and happiness really up to me? She picked up her spoon and threw it on the floor.

After securing Maren's highchair tray and handing her spoon back to her, I walked into the kitchen, untied my apron, folded it, and tucked it into a drawer. The next morning, I would find it on top of the celery in the Fridge.

Like a slap in the face, the smell was the first thing to hit. An awful mix of booze and feces. I didn't flinch but stepped into the garage.

Mom held Dad's hand. "He's gone," she said.

Why do people say that when someone dies? They haven't gone to the store or gone to the bathroom or gone out to lunch. Why not just say he's dead?

Dad was dead.

Impossible, yet there he was deposited on the cement like a pile of dirty laundry. He'd just been sitting at the table, winking at Maren. Dad's dead? When he fell, somehow his glass, which wasn't glass but a plastic tumbler, landed on the cold, hard slab, still safe and upright and in his grasp.

I bent down and took it from him. My fingers brushed against his skin. And even though he was still warm, the rubbery feel of it told me there was no blood, no muscle, no life. Not like the hand that had stroked my cheek and patted my knee just a half hour before. I took a swig of his drink. Christ, Dad, you might as well have drunk directly from the bottle, I thought but said, "Mom, I'm so sorry."

At the sound of my voice, she started shaking. "He wasn't

coughing as much today," she managed as sobs overtook her body.

Jig stood there and wheezed.

"I thought the same thing. I thought maybe he was getting better," I said and stroked Mom's back.

"You know, ladies, a person doesn't die like this from lung cancer. He must have had a stroke or something," Jig said.

I glared at him.

"At least his suffering's over," he said and blew his nose into a handkerchief. With those tidy words, he tried to wrap everything up in a little package and throw it away. Jig had honed that particular skill, qualifying him as an expert.

Mom didn't answer. My husband's comment had sucked the will out of her. Dad's suffering was over, yes, but so was his life. "Uff da," I said.

Mom didn't flinch at the term Dad had used every day. The one I had adopted as a convenient, harmless swear. "Uff da" expresses exactly how a woman feels when she remembers her dad had wanted to talk and she had been too busy, and now it was too late. "Uff da, uff da, uff da," I whispered.

"Lou, it's okay," Jig said, patting my shoulder.

"No, it's not." I shrugged him away.

"He didn't suffer."

"Oh, shut up."

Jig looked hurt as he went to the door to leave. "I'll meet the ambulance and check on Maren," he said.

Maybe Dad hadn't suffered, but I would. Guilt washed over me like a fog bank at the beach. I would suffer if I wanted to, and no one could stop me. What if dinner was on the table at seven instead of my habitual six? Would that have me less of a perfect housewife? There are a few moments in a person's life when clarity strikes. Right then, I vowed to make time for what was important. Time for my child. Time for myself. I would become justifiably selfish—no more martyrdom for me. That hint of a possible shift leapt in along with a pain in my soul, one I recognized as I had felt it many times before. Scissors of grief sliced bits from my body, starting at my throat. Every time I'd noticed money missing from my childhood stash and realized Dad had stolen from me, I'd felt that pain. Each time I'd miscarried a baby, words had become stuck. The only way to speak was to force them out. No tears came that day, not a drop. If I had cried, the drops would have become torrents. I pictured myself being carted away in a straightjacket, a padded cell my future home. As I sat on the oily cement in our garage, looking at Mom's tears, why did earlier traumas come riding in like a sort of delayed Paul Revere? Grief is coming! Climb the bell tower! Through other dark times, I had simply kept moving, plodding along through the years, trying not to linger on any one hurt or disappointment. Was there anything left of me to feel? I don't remember the ambulance arriving, but I can see his body covered by a sheet, his arm falling out to the side, and Mom tucking it in. Dad was cremated. For years, Mom kept his ashes in an urn on her dresser, so they could be buried together. I could not cry. At the ripe-old age of thirty-eight, maybe I wasn't just an amateur, but a has-been. Or worse, a never-was.

***

To understand how my life drifted away from me, I look back to simpler times, like 1938, when I was a young woman. I wore red lipstick and fashions fit for the movie stars. That's what drew Jig in and snatched him away from the other interested gals. He was a frat boy, and I was the girl in a tight dress behind the handkerchief counter at Marshall Field's. He strolled toward me, flirting himself through the perfume department. I rushed to reline my lips. He'd been in the store bunches of times, couldn't pass up the lure of girls. One day, he picked out a gorgeous French-lace scarf, had me wrap it up, and paid extra for a silk-ribbon bow.

"Can we meet at Lucky's? Friday at six?" he asked.

I blushed and nodded and handed the bag to him.

With our first drink, he surprised me with that frilly kerchief and a kiss on my cheek. I nearly swooned as he tied the scarf around my neck. It was the most expensive one I'd sold all week.

My girlfriends would all be jealous, especially my best friend who looked like Ava Gardner. I'd thought she was the one he was interested in, but when Jig and I met at Lucky's Locker, he sent my fears packing. Unlike the dives my dad frequented, Lucky's was a swanky joint with real crystals hanging from the chandeliers and tables draped in white linen. We'd just sat down when Jig rubbed his foot up the inside of my calf and peered into my eyes through the smoky haze.

"Let's dance, Lou. I want to show off these legs of yours."

"No one's interested these skinny things," I said. My heart beat to the rhythm of the trio playing "Who's My Baby Doll, Baby."

"Tell that to those two sailors over there who can't take their eyes off you." He dipped me low then pulled me close.

"Should I call you Robert?" I asked when he gave me a twirl. His name was Robert John Spencer.

"My frat brothers call me 'Jig.' So after we're married, I suppose we'll be known as 'Jig a Lou.'" He laughed.

I laughed, too, even though it didn't seem all that funny. We danced at least one in every set that night and went out twice a week for the next three years. Jig was as handsome as Marlon Brando and as smooth a talker as Clark Gable. Most important, he was six inches taller than me. At my height, five-foot-nine, my beau being tall was very important. Style dictated I must wear heels, but I still needed to be shorter than him.

When he proposed, I said "yes." Come to think of it, I said "yes" no matter what the guy asked. Too bad I hadn't read this passage in Dad's old book; it could have saved me a lot of heartache:

> *Listen to no soft persuasion, till a long acquaintance, and a steady, respectful conduct have given thee proof of the pure attachment and honorable views of thy lover. Is thy suitor addicted to low vices? Is he profane? Is he a gambler? A tippler? A spendthrift? A haunter of taverns? Has he lived in idleness and pleasure?—Banish such a man from thy presence; his heart is false, and his hand would lead thee to wretchedness and ruin.*

***

Another year of fun sped by, and by 1940, when I was twenty-one, Jig and I got married. Dad's drinking was at an all-time high. Since I was the last to leave home and was saddled with the job of abandoning Mother to my drunken father, I have

Jig to thank for my rescue. Marriage was the only way to get out of there. I was sure we would have five children before I was thirty.

Yes, I jumped in with both feet, and for the first six years we had loads of fun. Nothing bad could touch us—except for the first three miscarriages.

I assumed pregnancy would amount to a baby someday and was able to squash my grief like an unwanted spider in the kitchen. For Jig, having a fun time came naturally, so we continued to laugh until our ribs hurt and insisted that everyone around us should join in. I wasn't the funny one, that was his expertise. But my laughing at his jokes, tasteless or not, kept the ball rolling. We did, in fact, become known as "Jig-a-Lou," and that name, forming a word so nearly describing my husband, made us a memorable couple. "Gigolo." Women seemed to fall over themselves to get to him.

"Jig" was fitting, he told me, not because of gigolo. "My frat brothers were right," he said. "I am a 'Jigaboo' lover."

"What does that mean?" I asked, kissing his neck.

"It means I love Negroes. But really I just love their music."

"Jigaboo lover, Jigaboo lover," I said playfully.

"Come on, Lou. I love you, not them. Can you imagine loving a Negro?"

I kissed his neck again and we forgot to finish the conversation.

Not until years later, when I realized what an awful, racist term that was, did I spit it out one final time and never again let it slip from my lips. My dad had taught me how hatred of others flashed like lightning from one person to another; how prejudice had nearly stopped his marriage before it began; how Mom had never let him forget that he was a "filthy Norwegian."

Supporting backward thinking was never going to happen near me, at least not if I knew what was going on.

Jig and I met all kinds of musicians and performers back then: Cab Calloway, Duke Ellington, even Billie Holiday. It was something the way Jig loved Negro music. In '46 we'd moved to California and lived in a cramped apartment over a bar on the corner of Hollywood and Vine. One evening, to the rhythms of thumping drums and horns bellowing up from below, Jig asked, "It's okay if I go down, isn't it? I won't be later than two. Duke's set is over by then."

I shrugged and didn't look up from my book. Jane Austen had a hold of me. "Do what you want. I'll be right here."

He kissed the top of my head.

Yes, smack-dab in the middle of Tinseltown. We fit in with the crowd: the drinking, smoking, partying crowd. With me tucked out of the way, Jig seized the opportunity to pick himself up a girl. I'm sure of it. Was she his first? Maybe. Most women say, when they found out about their husbands' affairs, they hadn't seen any signs or held any doubts in their hearts. I knew right from the get-go but didn't let myself think about the hanky-panky going on. As long as he was still married to me, I had a roof over my head, food to eat, and we were still trying to have a baby, I didn't let myself care.

The man flirted like a champ. He was an expert at that, too.

I occasionally joined him downstairs, and once I caught a glimpse of a girl, a girl with skin so dark it looked like tar. He'd patted her bottom as she walked by our table. Maybe the danger of getting caught, with someone he could be arrested for being with, gave him more of a thrill than staying with his White wife.

I never asked him, never saw the point. But the first time he touched someone in my presence, I should have called him on the carpet.

Here's what Dad's book had to say on the subject. Unfortunately, Dad still had the book in Minnesota, so it had no way of triggering my disgust toward my husband:

> *Art thou a wife? Respect thy husband; oppose him not unreasonably, but yield thy will to his, and thou shalt be blest with peace and concord; study to make him respectable, as well for thine own sake, as for his; hide his faults; be constant in thy love; and devote thy time to the care and education of the dear pledges of thy love.*

Even though that passage described me to a tee, I also saw the error in such an old way of thinking. It assumed "peace and concord" would follow the act of giving up all your rights. And "devote thy time to the care and education of the dear pledges"? Did this mean our dear children? With no method of stopping pregnancy, you'd think we'd have had a baby by then. Once, I'd bled so much after not having my monthly curse for three months, I thought I would bleed to death.

Much later, too late, I realized that no peace is ever found when someone can't live the way they were meant to live. Back then, though, what I could like or want, or what I could be, these things never crossed my mind. Wife-mother was all I wanted to be. Nothing more. I knew my place. Still, I began to have a healthy hatred of the never-ending, thankless jobs required of a housewife; it rose like the stench coming from the back-house.

My husband, though, didn't over-drink, and we had a roof over our heads. Other than a baby, what more could I possibly want?

***

"Lou, we're in desperate need of a good time. Don't ask. Just come along. I'll make our lives fun again," Jig begged.

My numb heart agreed to the ridiculous idea, and the next day, I was dragged away by the runaway horse, my husband— the horse's ass. I didn't really think that at the time, but looking back, referring to him that way seems perfect.

And so we were off. Off in a dilapidated camper, to Corpus Christi, Texas, for a swim in the Gulf of Mexico. Yes, that's right. We drove all the way from Hollywood to Texas for a swim. Then, we turned north and dashed to Minnesota to visit my mom and dad. Before I knew what hit me, we were barreling back toward the Pacific. I had another miscarriage, and we had seven flat tires on that road trip. I think someone was trying to tell us something. Stop running, you fools!

The distance between Jig and me grew. I'd become a bitter woman, one who couldn't keep a baby long enough for it to be born alive. I let almost everything important drop from sight. Even my dad's wanting me to have an interest in that old book faded from my view. But one day, he telephoned and said something about a rod being a unit of measurement. "Listen to this, Lou. Sit down," he said. "You might learn something."

I plunked down on my flowered divan and listened. Why didn't I say, "Dad, I love you, and I love that old book and how you love reading it?" Sad to say, I don't remember ever telling him I loved him, until the night he died. This is what he read:

How many inches are in a foot? Twelve.—How
many feet in a yard? Three.—How many yards in a
rod, perch, or pole? Five and a half.—How many
rods in a mile? Three hundred and twenty—How
many rods in a furlong? Forty—How many
furlongs in a mile? Eight.

I marveled at how much our language had changed in such a short time. "How many furlongs am I away from myself? Enough to quit wearing lipstick," I said and chuckled. Some things you can't fix—a set of frowning lips for one.

"What, Lou?" Dad asked.

"It's not important," I answered.

Jig was blindly throwing dice and hoping for that big windfall. He came up with a scheme to open a small bookstore in Big Bear, California. He spent his days talking books and flirting with the natives.

Going to church became my escape and one of the few ways I got out of the house. Even though religion had never been of any interest to me, I prayed every Sunday for a baby. I stared at Jesus's feet with that big, old spike stuck through them. Jesus's pain equaled my pain. The rest of the week, I tried to forget myself. Another miscarriage was my reward.

I thought that if I volunteered in the church's youth program, Jesus points would be granted, so I helped out by keeping the children attentive during bible studies. A woman named Delores was the Sunday school teacher, and the town seemed to revolve around her, as though she were the center post of a tetherball. She stood on a stage and spoke down at me and the little ones. If I paid this penance, perhaps a live child would be granted.

One Sunday, Delores asked me in a voice dripping with syrup, "Did I hear you'll be moving soon, sweetie?" Most of her questions didn't seem to need an answer because she moved on quickly. But that day, she lingered.

"Probably," I mumbled.

"Well then, 'happy trails to you,' as the song goes."

She planted that song in my brain, the one about meeting again, smiling, and not caring about the clouds. That little ditty turned into a royal pain in my ass. It was a reminder of all the false words people handed out when they wanted to cheer me up, all the while avoiding what pained my heart. So far, I'd had six miscarriages.

Other families pumped out children one after another, and no one seemed to be struggling to birth their own group. "Isn't it a beautiful day? How many children do you have?" they'd ask. Or "Lou, you'll be blessed with a baby soon, just quit worrying and one will come." Or "What a wonderful husband you have! Aren't you lucky. Planning any children?" There were no proper responses to any of their statements or questions, not when I'd just miscarried again and felt as though someone had amputated a body part. Some days, I considered taking a knife and slicing through the skin on my chest, just to relieve the pressure. My feelings couldn't be seen or felt or understood by anyone but me. I stored them away. At that, I did become an expert.

All those dead possible children. I'd given them names. Marcus, Erik, Jay, Suellen, Katherine and Natalie. I could almost picture who they would have become, but instead they were just gone. Only I remembered them.

How did Delores know we were moving before I did? Jig must have shared that along with other things. But we didn't move, not right then anyway.

Every Monday, I drove to the library and grocery store. After putting away the shopping, I parked myself on the couch and read and read and read, one novel every two days. Dickens perfectly described my life. "It was the best of times, it was the worst of times, it was the age of wisdom, it was the age of foolishness . . ." Yes, it was.

By the time Jig arrived home from work, most nights, I would have stockpiled more rage. It was heaped up high with resentment, along with the growing certainty of yet another woman, or women, in his life. Maybe that was why he had suddenly said, "I know you'll be happy about this, Lou. There's a guy, Bill, who owns a bar on Main. He's not doing so good, so we're going to start a little business." They invested the entirety of our cash, and Bill's, I presumed, and borrowed five hundred dollars from the bank.

Jig plunged headlong into a partnership with a bartender at a failing bar. They built a roller-skating rink. Did he see this as a blueprint for a stable future? Uff da, yes. But the tar they laid down was the wrong type for the weather in a mountain climate. On opening day, when we donned our skates and slid onto the surface, we landed on our asses. The surface was as bumpy as a giant washboard. Dripping with anger, I hopped into our Woody and drove for four hours around and around the oval, attempting to smooth out the rink.

The opening gala was a marginal success because he still knew how to have fun. However, the rink died a quick and ugly death. No one drove up to that town to roller-skate, not when fishing, hunting, and skiing had called them there.

"Lou, I'm going to the track," Jig said one morning.

"What? We don't have any money."

"Sure we do, twenty-five bucks." He pulled our entire stash out of his pocket and counted the bills on the table to prove it. "I can double this in a half-hour." He folded and fastened the bills in his money clip.

"No."

"What?"

"No," I said.

"No?"

"That's right. No. We can buy a week's worth of food with that. And fill up the gas tank. I suppose we'll be moving soon. Right?"

"Is that what you want?"

It wasn't. There was no chance, however, that I would let our last twenty-five bucks go to the ponies. So with my further insistence, he went to the bowling alley and got a part-time job cleaning sweaty shoes.

We stayed there and rang in a new decade, 1950. Maybe life would be different. Then, as if some greater power was sending me a curse, I woke up one morning with the certainty I was pregnant again. Two months later I miscarried, but this time I thanked God for the favor. After years of wanting a baby, I'd begun to feel a baby would complicate my marriage and life.

"You're better off, Louise," the doctor said. "Nature has a way of taking care of the unhealthy or unwanted ones. No need to cry." He threw a wad of bloody towels in a waste basket, washed his hands in the porcelain sink, and handed me a tissue.

His words were heartless, but I threw the unused tissue onto the bloody pile and didn't cry. I felt grateful. With my husband making excuses for coming home late every Saturday night, I didn't need to deal with a baby.

"Lou, I'm going to Vegas for a few days. I have a new system. I can't lose. We can't afford it, or I'd take you with me," he said one morning.

"Sure. Go to Vegas," I said, wondering if the blonde bombshell I'd seen him with was going too. They'd been sitting in the diner at the bowling alley, looking chummy.

"You'll see, Lou. This'll be different."

I was tired and had quit fixing my hair.

Then it happened. Jig blew back home on a Santa Ana wind, with $2,000 in his pocket.

"You should have been there, Lou! I would have made more if they hadn't kicked me out of town. If you win too big, they shut you down. On the way back through the valley, though, I heard about a job up in Bakersfield. Start packing, we're moving!"

My fatigue would grow with the move, but what I said was, "Okay, Jig," then placed my hands firmly on his shoulders, spun him around, and looked him square in the eye. "One more move. But don't ask me again." I hadn't unpacked most of the boxes from the previous move, so that migration went easier.

With his winnings, Jig put a down payment on a house. I was drawn to that little home because it had a great backyard for any kids we might have, someday. Yes, I'd shifted, once again, to wanting children. The property had a pomegranate tree and tall eucalyptus for shade. Across the alley behind the house was a cottage for sale. It would be perfect for Mom and Dad.

Jig started selling decks of cards and poker chips to businesses to give to their clients. He seemed born to sell. And I discovered I was born to buy, so I filled our home with beautiful things: reproductions of famous statues, a grand piano that might be played someday, and the latest dresses from New York designers. Buying stuff didn't really help. It felt like putting lipstick on your fingernails.

Jig didn't come home for dinner on Wednesday nights. He said he'd joined a bowling league but often left his ball in the front-hall closet. The signs were all but slapping me in the face. He'd become sloppy.

I confronted him.

He looked down at me with hurt puppy-dog eyes. "You're crazy. You know I like the ponies, Lou. Come on, you don't mind a little gamble now and then, do you?" He grabbed me around the waist and slid his hand up my dress.

Hard to believe it, but I giggled and we slid into bed.

He was providing us a home, and I got pregnant, again. I wanted to believe him. It's sort of like this little fable:

The Fox and the Swallow

A FOX swimming across a river, happened to be entangled in some weeds that grew near the bank from which he was unable to extricate himself. As he lay, thus exposed to whole swarms of flies, which were galling him and sucking his blood, a swallow, observing his distress kindly offered to drive them away. By no means, said the Fox, for if these should be chased away, which are already sufficiently gorged, another more hungry swarm would succeed, and I should be robbed of every remaining drop of blood in my veins.

What I had was better than what I would face, if I were a divorcee in the 1950s. Divorce was not an acceptable outcome for a marriage, and it was almost as bad as having no children. I felt the judgment of others who were living out their human responsibilities. They bombarded me everywhere I went. There were babies with mothers on every aisle in the grocery store. Women showing off their wedding rings like they were trophies of real accomplishments. Men telling each other how much they made in their stable jobs that would give them a pension for a secure life at the end of their days. My life had no meaning without the trappings of what society wanted of me. And I had no guaranty of security. I could not leave my cheating husband; he was earning a living. I lost that pregnancy too, but then a small miracle happened.

By June of 1957, I was three months along with a pregnancy that would finally produce a child. With Maren born on Dad's birthday, December 7, our family was complete and perfect in the eyes of others. I dove into diapers, cleaning, cooking, and doing everything for everyone. My dresses were classy, my hair stylish, and my lips red, again.

I'd always wanted a girl, and Maren's instincts seemed to have warned her. Go easy on your mother, or you may not survive. There'd never been a more agreeable baby. I loved everything about being a new mom: inspecting tiny, pink fingers and toes; sewing adorable sun dresses of my own design for her; dusting her with the sweet aroma and softness of talcum powder. These small pleasures filled our joyous days. Though I'd been focused on grieving my losses and worrying about how women with children saw me, Maren showed me how to be nurturing, accepting, and loving. I'd forgotten how to love. But still, Jig and

I barely concerned ourselves with each other.

No, I didn't pay much attention to him during those baby-filled years. He existed. He worked. He came home, most nights, and must have felt his obligation to his family was fulfilled. "I'll be more interested in doing things with Maren when she gets a little older," he said when I asked him to feed her a bottle. He chose not to get involved in her life. Not surprising since he wasn't involved in mine either.

His comment made my resentment rise like a pan of yeast-filled sweet rolls. Too bad Jig didn't read that page in Dad's little book. He could have learned something.

> *There are five states of human life: infancy, childhood, youth, manhood, and old age. The infant is helpless; she is nourished with milk—when she has teeth, she begins to eat bread, meat, and fruit, and is very fond of cakes and plums. The little girl loves her doll and learns to dress it. She chooses a closet for her baby house, where she sets her doll in a little chair, at the side of a table furnished with tea-cups as big as a thimble. The little boy enjoys any plaything that will make a noise, a hammer or a whip.*

When I read that, I thought, maybe I should have had a boy. I could have used a whip to force Jig to think about someone other than himself.

Following Maren's birth, I had my uterus yanked out. My doctor suggested it, and I heartily agreed. I knew there would be more questions from mothers who had more than one child. The first came from our neighbor when she dropped off a mushroom and tuna casserole because she'd heard I'd had surgery for my woman-trouble. "Now that you've had one child, you'll easily have another baby. You don't want to have an only child, Lou. They can be such demanding brats."

"Thank you, Mavis," I said. "I can't have more children, but now I know what to expect in Maren's future."

She winced, quickly apologized, and nearly ran from the house.

Recuperating on the couch, I became a stationary planet in a whirling universe. Mom stepped in to make order out of our chaos by doing laundry, shopping, laundry, sweeping, laundry. Even Dad came to lend a hand by washing dishes and telling Maren bedtime stories; though, she was too young to understand. If he staggered in drunk, or if I could smell booze on him even a little, I'd stop him.

"Go home, Dad," I'd say. "I don't care what gets left undone. I won't have you near Maren when you're sloshed."

"Sorry, Lou," he replied. He shed tears when I asked him to leave. He wanted to help. Sometimes, he might have even wanted to be sober. But he had been drunk so long that no one's needs were enough to change him.

When Dad died in our garage, his passing hurt more than I had imagined it would. That day was the end of what could have been possible for him. My child would never hear about his life, from him at least, and only Mom and I knew what had happened. His paintings, his pacifist ideas, and his connection to a slave named William T. Sherman had become muddy memories because they were one more person removed from anyone who'd actually been there.

Two nights after Dad's death, I walked across the alley to kiss Mom goodnight. She sat on their bed still dressed in her favorite lilac-colored dress. She held Dad's book in her lap. "Your dad wanted you to have this, Louise."

"He almost gave it to me that night," I patted her hand "but that's all right, Mom. You keep it."

"No," she said. "This is all that's left of the man your father went to for advice. William T. Sherman was closer to being his dad than his own. We don't have much. This is your father's way of giving you what he valued. Later, it should be Maren's too. Makes no difference whether you value it or not."

I picked up the book and felt its chamois-skin smooth surfaces. They'd been worn by years of hands and dirt and God-knows what. Flipping to the last page, to the list of signatures, I said, "I remember a few things Dad told me over the years. Do you, Mom?"

"Yes, dear, every word."

***

The Boy who went to the Wood to look for Birds' Nests, when he should have gone to School

When Jack got up and put on his clothes, he thought if he could get to the wood he should be quite well; for he thought more of a bird's nest than his book that would make him wise and great. When he came there, he could find no nest but one that was on the top of a tree, and with much ado,

he got up to it and robbed it of the eggs.—Then he
tried to get down, but a branch held him fast. At
this time he would have been glad to be at school,
for the bird in a rage at the loss of her eggs, flew
at him, and was like to pick on his eyes. Now it
was that the sight of a man at the foot of the tree,
gave him more joy than all the nests in the world.
This man was so kind as to chase away the bird
and help him down from the tree; and from that
time forth, he would not loiter from school but
grew a good boy and a wise young man, and had
the praise and good will of all that knew him.

While dusting one day, I picked up Dad's book and read that fable. I should have really paid attention to the words—not just looked at them. Going back to school might have been a good solution for what I lacked. College had never seemed possible. Jig had a degree in journalism, and it never got him any real job in that field. My dad only made it through sixth grade, I think, Mom through high school. And me? Sure, I'd earned my high school diploma, but further education to a woman who wanted to be a mother seemed frivolous. What could I do with more math, science, history, or literature while taking care of a house and child? I was a pretty good cook, cleaner, and seamstress. I'd even begun making some of my own clothes, following Vogue patterns and altering them to fit better, and even taking liberties with their designs to create my own. And childrearing turned out to be simple, at least while Maren was an infant.

Later that week, Mom and I snagged a chance to talk. "This book," Mom said, "is a member of our family." She rubbed the spine along her cheek. "Before your dad and I were married, he and I sat together in the library. He read to me. His whispers made me fall in love."

"See, Mom, I think you should keep it."

"No, dear heart. It's yours, and I'll tell you why. The story can't stop with me. What else do we have that connects our family to the past? When we lost everything in that storage fiasco, I thought I'd kill your father. Imagine, losing all our worldlies for the want of a twenty-dollar bill. You know, it's funny, after being boiling mad at him, I found myself thinking it was a little nice, not having all that stuff moving around with us. Less to pack."

She surprised me. Mom was smiling. We were dirt poor during my childhood. "Mom, don't you remember eating all those chicken gizzards and livers?" Dad had lost everything they owned because of his drinking. "Where's your anger, Mom?" I asked.

"I don't have time for that. Even the bad memories of our loved ones, they're all that we might have in the end. You'll take the book, then give it to Maren, and the passage will continue."

"But I don't remem—"

"You will," she interrupted. "First tell me what you do remember, then I'll fill in the gaps."

With dirty dishes waiting in the sink, Mom and I sat at the kitchen table, sipped at our coffee, and I told her. We smoked half a pack of cigarettes as the sunlight streamed in the eastern window. The black and beige checkerboard-linoleum floor remained in need of sweeping, and the day grew hot and desert-dry. Maren played on the floor with some plastic lids and spoons, and Mom told me the things that Dad hadn't.

"First there was Elizabeth Rose Sherman." She gazed at me to see if I recognized the name.

I nodded.

"Well, it turns out Elizabeth Sherman was quite a little troublemaker. While in school she met Elizabeth Cady. They grew to be friends, and when Miss Cady was married she became Elizabeth Cady Stanton."

I shrugged my shoulders.

"You know who she is? Or you should. She was a famous suffragette, friend of Lucretia Mott, Amelia Bloomer, Susan B. Anthony, and . . ." Mom flicked her long ash into the tray.

"I've heard of Susan B. Anthony," I said and yawned and puffed and sipped. Why should I care about who Elizabeth Sherman knew? I continued smiling at Mom.

"For years, Elizabeth Cady Stanton was Anthony's speech writer. Her powerful words made Susan B. Anthony famous. Ladies didn't talk like that. You know, Anthony was arrested for voting illegally in a presidential election. Don't you know?"

"Huh? No, I didn't." A recipe for potatoes au gratin started running through my mind. I wondered if I had enough cheese. I got up and looked into the refrigerator, saw the brick, and returned to the table.

"Come on, Lou," Mom pointed at me with her cigarette and glared. "All those forward thinkers met at Arlan Theel's house where Elizabeth Sherman lived. Amelia Bloomer, she invented bloomers, and without her we might still be wearing corsets and skirts that drag around in the mud. That particular fashion was the first outward sign of a new point of view. Of course people are always slow to change."

"Mom, how do you know all this?"

"When you kids were in school, I snuck out to the library and looked up those names. I never found mention of Elizabeth, but the rest of them made their way into a few history books. Lucretia Mott's house was a stop for runaway slaves. Mr. Sherman probably met her somewhere. They certainly knew some of the same people. There were a lot fewer people back then. They must have met. Mr. Sherman was an educated Negro, and Elizabeth never married, which was odd for the time. They wrote to each other over the years, and I suppose she was in a quandary to find someone who would play second-fiddle to her first love."

"Her first love?" I struggled to hide another yawn.

Mom drew in a large puff and blew smoke toward the ceiling. Our smoky kitchen made the sun's rays into a beautiful pattern of light and dark. She raised one eyebrow at me.

"Wait, you mean Elizabeth and William Sherman? Were they in love?" I asked.

"Dad didn't tell you that?"

"No . . ."

"You can bet they were," Mom said, "for their entire lives. Even though he married someone else. What was her name?"

"Wasn't it Diana?"

"That's right, Diana. Or was it Dinah? Oh well, no matter. Elizabeth even came to Minnesota after Mr. Sherman's funeral and visited with your father."

"Really? I didn't know that either," I said, feeling a little more enthusiastic.

"Your father told me she was very old, in her late eighties, but she was still quite beautiful. I guess she carried herself with confidence, nothing feeble about her. She was amazed to see the

234

book still existed. She wrote her name on the cover." Mom held the book in the sunlight. "See right here."

"It's so faded. I never noticed . . ." I sat up straight and dusted off my brain by taking a huge gulp of coffee.

"Yes, the years have nearly washed away any traces of value in that old . . ." At the sound of the Helm's Bakery truck tinkling down the block, Mom glanced out the window. She looked at me, seeming to wonder if I would dash out to buy some doughnuts.

I shook my head.

"Your dad received notice when Elizabeth died. She was over one hundred."

"Uff da."

"Uff da, indeed—pioneer stock. She'd had quite a life, except the poor dear never had a family."

"Maybe that's why," I chuckled.

"Why what?"

"Why she lived so long. No worries."

Mom smiled and reset a hairpin in her curls. "Just think, your father was only eleven or so, when he met Elizabeth. Of course, all his memories went south when he started drinking. It's a good thing he had told me, or the details might be lost. Elizabeth said the only true tragedy in her life was she couldn't marry Mr. Sherman. She held your father's hand and said, 'Always follow your heart. In all ways.'"

I walked to the oven and took out the pan of rising dough I had started earlier. After kneading it on the bread board, I placed it back to rise a second time. "Mom, you know what's the saddest part of that story? It's not that they couldn't marry back then, it's that even now they couldn't be together. No one seems

235

to think that black and white skin can be mixed, like it's oil and water or something. It's 1958, more than halfway through this century. You'd think it would be different by now."

"Maybe someday that'll change," Mom said. "But I've got to be honest, dear. If any of my kids had come home professing love for some Negro, I wouldn't have it. What chance would there be for happiness? I'll answer that. Not a lick."

"Mom!"

"Come on, Lou. Not today. With those people all heated up and fighting in the streets. You know, their children suffer. Those Mulatto kids, they don't know if they're Black or White. It's not natural." Mom drank down the last gulp of her coffee.

I glared at her and asked, "Didn't you learn anything from your parents? Didn't they hate Norwegians?"

"Yes, but that's different. I'm not proud of—"

"No, it's not different."

"But it is," she said. "Most people can't tell us apart, and they don't know about the hatred between our countries."

I shook my head. "All people are equal. That's what you should have learned."

"But it's not that easy. You can't change everyone and turn off years of history, just because you want to. It's simply the way it was."

"Listen to yourself, Mom. In you it still is that way. 'Yes but, yes but, yes but.' You're no better than a KKK member who burns crosses. Acceptance has to start here." I waved my hand around the kitchen.

Even though I was arguing this point, and feeling completely right about it, the truth was I didn't know any dark-skinned people. We played tons of their music in the house, but that didn't really mean I knew what I was talking about. If Maren brought a Colored home, a future boyfriend, what would I do? I liked to think that I'd be okay with them being a couple. But I also knew the truth. I'd lose friends over it. Maybe most. Maybe all.

"Let's just drop it, Lou," she said. "You sound like your father."

Fighting that battle would never go anywhere, so I checked the dough again. Five more minutes, and it would be ready to twist into sticky buns. I slammed the oven door a little too hard. The cookie jar rattled and the black cat-shaped electric clock shifted on the wall. "Mom, back to Elizabeth," I said, leveling the clock. The cat's tail swung evenly, to-and-fro.

Mom lit a new cigarette and told me how much she admired the work Elizabeth had done for women's suffrage.

"See, Mom. You're making my point. It wouldn't have worked if they hadn't stuck their necks out—against what everyone else thought. They stood up against society." I heard my words but knew I felt just as swayed by what other people thought. I had wanted to fit in and not stick out like a barren woman who couldn't give her husband a child. With Maren, I now fit in and the pressure of conformity was relieved.

Mom rolled her eyes but moved on. "Elizabeth died before we had the right to vote. The year after you were born was the first time I could cast a ballot. That morning, I got up early, took a bath, dolled myself up, and was waiting with my handbag when your dad came downstairs." She smiled and made a fist and pounded it on the table. "Finally, I could vote! And it was about time. It was 1920. Your dad thought my opinion shouldn't matter. But he couldn't do anything to stop me. I could vote how

I wanted. In that booth, I could do what I pleased. It only took our government seventy-two years to realize that it wasn't just the White and Negro men who needed a voice. Well, Darkies couldn't vote until 1869, but still, it shouldn't just be men."

"Darkies? Mom, really!" I shook my head and grimaced. But the amazing thing was that I'd never heard her talk about anything but cooking, cleaning, and shopping. "I didn't know you cared about stuff like this," I said.

"Well, you don't have to be political to see everyone should be able to vote."

"That's true. Thanks for remembering all this."

"When we were young, I hung on your father's every word. I was in love."

The sun had moved and now glinted off her silver hair. I stopped and stared at it.

"What's wrong?" she asked.

"Nothing. It's just that your hair looks really pretty this morning."

"My hair? Pretty? Uff da. Come on, where was I?" Compliments always flustered her. She combed her fingers along her temple. "Oh yes, the other thing you didn't mention was the *Insane Idea Index*."

"I remember that crazy, old genius. Dresden Withers, right? And that the Index existed."

"Mr. Sherman showed it to your dad."

"Really?"

"He read some of it. And a lot of it stuck in his mind: notions about machines to pick up horse dung and ways to talk over distances through vibrations. Sort of an early telephone, though, of course, they didn't know enough yet to invent those things.

And new ways to shave."

"Do you have the Index?"

"I'm afraid not. When Mr. Sherman died, your father went looking for it. The thing was gone. Turns out, there had been someone else visiting his room, the day before. Everyone assumed that man took it. There were a few other things missing, too."

"That's horrible."

"See how important the past can be? Now, no one will ever know what Mr. Withers' mind had cooked up."

"Speaking of cooking, I've got to get those rolls in the oven." I stood and put my arms around her.

"What's that for?"

"Do I need a reason to hug you? I'm going to write some of this down, so I don't forget."

Mom smiled and said, "Your father would like that."

I should have done the writing that day while it was still fresh. When time allowed, about a year later, shortly after Mom died, I had retained much of it. Maybe some wasn't right, though. After jotting down notes, I stuck them in a drawer, thinking I would place them along with the book in Maren's special box. But years later, when I actually put the book in the box, the notes were missing. I hunted for hours for that piece of paper, but in the end, I stored the book without my notes.

***

From 1958 to 1963, my feet stood firmly planted in the kitchen. The days melted together like homemade fudge—failed fudge—cooked but not quite to the perfection of the hardball stage. The days tasted okay, but there was something not quite right. Those years were a span of naive pleasures: summers at the beach house with Maren, reading a mountain of books, and Jig holding the same job for the entire six-year stretch. I spent mornings sewing while Maren dressed and undressed her dolls.

Evenings held an endless string of bridge games linked together with jazz concerts and Mensa meetings. I couldn't figure out why Jig wanted to mingle with all those smarty-pants stuffed-shirts. Although we both had passed the Mensa test, he on the first try and I on the sixth, rubbing elbows and small talking with people who thought, no, they knew, they were better than everyone else seemed the ultimate selling-out to a group to which I didn't want to belong. To everyone else, we must have seemed the perfect couple enjoying the perfect life. Healthy, intelligent, happy. At times I even believed it myself.

Attempting to keep up our façade, I made sure the front lawn was mowed. One extra-hot morning, pushing our rotary mower early enough to miss the midday heat, but still at eighty-six degrees, I looked down the block. All the other yards had men behind the mowers. I was the only woman.

"I hate it here," I said, wiping my feet on the welcome mat and peering through the screen door. Jig was on the phone and quickly said "goodbye" and hung up.

"Who was that?" I asked trying not to sound accusing.

"Wrong number."

"Another one? Who is she?"

Jig just stood there.

"Come on, tell me. Do you love her?"

"I never loved any of those women, not like you, well, except Belinda."

"Christ, Jig, Belle-of-the-Ball, Belinda?"

"I thought you'd understand. I've known her since grade school. Besides, she was the first woman who was as smart as me. She's a great bowler, and great in—"

"In what? In the sack? Let me see if I have it straight: Belinda, bridge, bowling. Next in line: Maren and me. It's completely understandable, really. Maren and I mess up your rhymed life."

"Lou, it doesn't rhyme. That's called an alliteration, and you don't have to be so—"

"So what? Stupid?"

"So sarcastic. Never mind, it doesn't matter," he said. "I was going to tell you tomorrow, but now's okay. Here it is. That's why . . . well . . . why we have to move. You shouldn't be mad at me. It's just . . . I have to get away from that woman. She'll ruin our marriage."

So a woman named Belinda Best, secretary of the Central Valley chapter of Mensa, ran us out of town.

We ended up in a place I thought of as hell on earth—Arkansas. Jig had been offered a partnership with a college buddy who was going into turkey farming.

"Lou, don't worry. We'll be rich! He says they practically raise themselves"

Again, I didn't speak up but simply remade myself into someone even I hated to be around. Holding anger in, each day I began with a martyr's attitude. Up to that moment, washing dishes had been pleasurable, soaking my hands in the warm water while quietly dreaming of other places. However, when I realized our kitchen was the only one on our block without a dishwasher, or without a Colored maid helping out, I began to resent dishwashing. When I asked Jig if we could splurge and buy a Kenmore on sale at Sears and Roebuck, he replied, "We have one, Lou. You." He held up a dishrag in front of my face.

Of course, I did dishes by myself, which created plenty of time for me to wallow in my bitterness. Soon, the same seething anger overtook every chore. My chores. My anger. My choice. Interesting things to do must have existed in Arkansas, somewhere, but in the summer of '63, I couldn't find any. Having just moved there from the mild, dry climate of Bakersfield, California, the South's bugs and humidity felt like terrible plagues.

And then there were the neighbors.

Jig had bought a two-bedroom ranch house because it was cheap, and because it was across the street from the city park. Almost daily, Maren and I put on our swimsuits and walked over to the public pool for a dip. The place was loud and crowded; however, one day everything changed.

"Mommy, nobody's here!" Maren flung off her towel and plopped down by the steps. She swirled her feet in the water. The color was the same blue as our '62 Buick Electra.

"Wait, Maren. Maybe there's something wrong," I said and dipped my right foot into the water as though I could tell by feeling it. "Nice and warm today. Oh well, let's take the risk and get in."

With Maren clinging to me, I was about to dunk under the surface when I spotted our neighbors, Sylvia and Anne. After marching across the grass, they stopped at the chain-link fence.

"Didn't you see the sign?" Sylvia asked. Her cigarette in a long holder was held by her impeccably manicured fingers. Her other hand sat squarely on her hip, her elbow jutting out to the side like a folded, de-feathered chicken wing.

"What sign?" I asked.

"In-te-grat-ed Fa-cil-i-ty," she said.

"Oh?" I said and shrugged, squinting across the water.

The two women looked at each other then back at me.

"You're going to let your precious baby get tarnished in this Nigger pool?" Anne asked. Even though she looked like someone I might want to know better, and she had a smile for everyone, always, she said those vile words in the same sappy-sweet voice she had likely learned in charm school. She used the same tone to say, "Lou, you have yourself a happy birthday."

"Sorry, Anne, but Maren can be friends with any child—yours or your cleaning lady's."

"You mean, Darlene? Why they don't even know who her daddy is," Anne answered.

"Why does that matter? They're just little girls."

"I declare, you're blinder than I thought," Sylvia piped in. "Suit yourself, but don't be knockin' on our door, my Emma Sue won't be home. Your Maren won't be sittin' on our chairs, not after she's been muddy-fied. Why, you don't know what might have washed off that Johnson family. They're divorced! I saw all of them kids over here yesterday afternoon. They were swimmin' in here, actin' like they owned the place. They have no right—"

"It appears they do, now," I interrupted. "I'm not worried about it." I lowered my shoulders under the water. Maren splashed with her five-year-old hands.

"Lou, I'd say 'have a good day,' but I won't waste the time. Come on, Sylvia," Anne said, linking her arm with Sylvia's wing. One of them murmured something about "crazy Californians" as they stomped off into the distance. Sylvia's high heels stuck on the melting blacktop as she stumbled across the street. Anne's hair bobbed about like a giant India-rubber ball bouncing on her shoulders.

There was no dust kicked up by their retreat. I'd have felt more at home if there had been. The only familiar signs of home were the heat ripples hovering on the horizon.

That's when I realized California was home. Wondering when I would feel at home enough to empty all our packed boxes, a panicky feeling arrived. Where is that old book? God, what if I've lost it in this move? That evening, after ripping open three cartons, I found it sandwiched between the lace scarf Jig had given me on our first date and the last electric bill from Bakersfield. I read this quote written so long ago but felt it had been written just for me:

> *The wicked flee when no man pursueth;*
> *but the righteous are as bold as a lion.*

***

The three of us were wayward refugees in that foreign land. All those Southern-belle mothers nearly drove me to drink. Their high-pitched voices grated on me. No public kindergartens existed in our town, and even though Maren had already attended one for a year in Bakersfield, she wasn't allowed to progress to first grade. My little blonde angel had made a dreadful mistake by being born after September first, and that fact set me back to filling my entire day with her needs. Of course, she didn't complain much—she barely ever talked. I could ignore that child, and she'd still stay out of trouble.

One dreary fall morning, while scouring the copper bottoms of my pans, I turned on the TV to keep my mind occupied. Around noon, Maren and I sat down at the kitchen table to eat our grilled-cheese sandwiches. In my head, I planned the afternoon: go to the market for lamb chops, cook chocolate pudding, clean the kitchen floor. I never filled the bucket and got down on my knees with my scrub brush. We ended up eating meatloaf that night, followed by nothing. No dessert.

Walter Cronkite's face came on the TV screen and my phone started to ring. I walked to the living room to answer the call.

"Louise, this is Etta. Etta Jackson?" It was one the Negro mothers who'd "dared" to let her children swim in the public pool. We were both new in town, and we had talked about our girls, wondering if they would get along. One afternoon, we'd exchanged phone numbers with promises to dial each other. Neither of us had called, until that day.

Her voice cracked as she spoke. "Lou, turn on your . . . your TV. I can't believe . . . just, please, call me later." She hung up.

I ran back to the kitchen and stared at the screen. A crowd of people milled around a conference room. The camera panned over to a dark-skinned waiter who dabbed his eyes with a white napkin. Cronkite's normally solid voice halted while he took off his glasses. He put them back on. He took them off again.

Everyone knows where they were that day—the day they shot President Kennedy.

"Why, it's about time someone picked up a gun. We're finally rid of that S.O.B.," I heard a man say to the checkout clerk at the Piggly Wiggly the following morning.

My heart dropped into my stomach, and I thought I'd either throw up or walk down the street to Woolworth's and pick up a weapon of my own. Many people whispered and chuckled but not Etta Jackson. Not me. She and I met in the park the following Tuesday afternoon to let the kids play, just as we had the previous week.

As she walked toward me, I saw the slump in her posture. Her skin reflected the bright sun. It reminded me of my black patent-leather pumps. I stood up and we hugged, but she backed away before my hug was finished.

"Raymond is . . ." she began, then stopped and placed her hand over her mouth. "I'm sorry . . . I can't believe it, Raymond's asking me, no telling me . . . we just can't meet here anymore. He's getting harassed at the plant. His boss threatened him. Land sakes . . . he could lose his job 'cause I'm lettin' our kids play here." She waved her hand around at the playground. With tears flowing down her face, she picked up her youngest, placed him on her hip, and grabbed little Jenny's hand, then turned to go.

Jenny struggled against her mom's grip, ran back to hug my legs, waved at Maren, and ran back to her mom. Etta walked as fast as she could across the lawn to the parking lot.

I watched them drive away, wishing I could run after her and stop her. Stop what I knew I had no power to stop. We could have been lifelong friends was how I felt, if we'd had the same skin color. Jig just said, "Well, now President Johnson will continue to fix it. The Blacks should be thankful; their lives are getting better."

Jig and I knew it was time to move back to California. He'd been struggling at work because he disagreed with his partner on just about everything. They were as different as the Beatles and Beethoven—not that Jig was anything like the Beatles—he just wasn't like his boss who was all responsibility and order. My husband was neither of those. He was rebellion and laziness, and his two-hour lunches didn't help.

Jig went ahead to scout out a house to buy, and with him gone, I was left to pack up. This time, tending to everything no one wants to do but everyone knows has to get done didn't feel like a burden. To be honest, my freedom felt luxurious. For once, I didn't care where Jig was, or why he wasn't where he should be, or who he was with. Jig would have to return to sign the paperwork when the house sold. After all, a woman couldn't sign anything without her husband's approval.

The day Maren and I waved goodbye to the moving van was the day after the Beatles appeared on The Ed Sullivan Show. Maren had sung "Love, Love Me Do" and "I Wanna Hold Your Hand" and jiggled around like jelly in an earthquake. She loved the Beatles. Her friend's older sister, Rosy, had been the first in the neighborhood to get all the early singles. In her garage, they spun those 45s for hours absorbing many of their afternoons. My then six-year-old learned all the lyrics, even though she was normally still silent.

On that February night, bathed in the gray glow from the tube, I heard joy in those young voices. They celebrated times to come, times soon to be altered by thudding bass rhythms. Their catchy songs seemed to leap into my body. I couldn't sit still, so I joined Maren in the raucous party we wanted to last longer than the two songs. "That's all?" Maren whined.

"Too bad," I said. "We'll stop at the record shop on the way out of town tomorrow." When we stepped into the store, the throngs of buyers forced the shopkeeper to pick up his bullhorn. "We're sold out," his voice blared. We hopped back into the

Electra, for the cross-country trip, and I promised to get some records when we got to California. "They'd probably melt in the car, anyway. Maybe it's for the best."

Maren smiled, opened her window, and let her hand glide along the air waves.

Many adults thought Martians had landed—or Communists. Hair length, sideburns, collar styles, and later skirt lengths, and bras—or no bras—became major topics of discussion. At first, I stuck to my same-old style. But the Beetles didn't just teach me how to dance differently, they taught me how far I'd moved away from my husband, even before he'd left for California.

"Lou, I asked you to cut my hair two days ago. Do I have to do it myself?" Jig had nodded toward the electric trimmer on the table.

I ran my hand up the back of his bristly head. "Do you always have to have a crew-cut? I like the longer style."

"What difference could it make how I cut my hair," he shot at me.

"Exactly the point."

"If it's okay for the military, it's okay with me."

I glanced at his crew-cut head. He did look like an Army Sargent. Perhaps that cut made him feel more powerful or commanding. "Sorry, but I think I'd rather you look like George," I said.

"Who?"

"George Harrison, the quiet, handsome one."

"One of what?"

"Never mind."

Poor Jig. He was lagging behind.

***

We beached ourselves in heaven—Santa Barbara, California. With terracotta tile roofs, adobe-like stucco buildings, palm trees, painted Mexican pottery, ocean shores, and mountain vistas, Santa Barbara oozed charm. Nearly every house was either a Victorian beauty or quaint California bungalow with a porch, patio, or bougainvillea-draped arbor. Jig had gone ahead to buy a house, all right. What he bought, though, was the county's ugliest one, a yellow stucco box sandwiched between twin neighbors, identical in layout and design except one was lime green the other aqua.

Maren and I drove into that suburban cul-du-sac, and I parked and sat in the car reading and rereading the address he'd told me over the phone. This was our new home? If you're not paying attention, you might walk into the wrong one, especially at night when all the pastels would look gray.

Maren clambered out of the car as Jig came toward us.

We'd been separated for about a month but I hadn't missed him.

"It's a brand-new development," he said. "Lou, we finally have a garage!"

"Who needs one here? We're not in Minnesota." I opened the door and stood up.

"And the school's within walking distance." He grabbed me around the waist.

"That might be true, but I'll have to drive a long way into town." I pushed him away. "There's nothing but dirt and sagebrush in the yard." Hearing my own voice, how resentment hung from every word, I tried to shift my feelings.

249

"You'll plant stuff. You'll learn to garden. It'll be nice." He reached for my hand.

I didn't want "nice." I kicked the gravelly dirt with my open-toed sandal. I wanted interesting, different, engaging. "How thoughtful of you, Jig, I was worried I'd have nothing to do," I said. Those words sounded the way our arguments often began. They had no hope of ever reaching a conclusion. I'd jab him with sarcasm. He'd attempt to smooth me over with condescending platitudes. I lifted my foot and removed a pebble wedged beneath my toes.

He ended up right about something. I did plant stuff: fast-growing juniper bushes, ice plant, and my own stubborn roots into the dirt. Every day, I swore an oath to someone or something, "I will never move again—unless it's on my own terms."

Jig acclimated. He had a pool dug, tiled, and filled. He located the local bridge and Mensa clubs, and he landed a job selling office furniture to doctors. Hobnobbing with all the rich men and their cute wives suited him beautifully.

Hold on tight boys, Jig, the Jigaboo-loving gigolo is in town.

We were living behind a pastel-stucco façade, teetering on a sandstone hillside. We didn't move, but nothing in California in the '60s stood still. Numerous earthquakes rumbled through, spilling the contents of my cupboards and sloshing water out of the pool. The massive fire of '65 roared across the mountains and sprang in fireball-flashes into the canyon behind our house. What saved our property was ice plant. That water-filled spiky foliage with roots as water logged as seaweed held the inferno at bay. Yes, I'd planted stuff and saved our asses from total destruction.

As I toiled, I sang, "Help! I need somebody. Help! Not just anybody. Help!"

***

My focus strayed away from my straying husband. I told myself that I didn't care what he did any more. He certainly didn't care what I was doing. His only comment was, "If it makes you happy, do what you want." That must have been what he told himself as well.

I started a little sewing business, Louise's Fashions, and created matching sundresses for mothers and daughters, for rich women, and I altered double-knit suit coats for their husbands. Life felt somewhat satisfactory, so I decided to finish unpacking the last three boxes still stored in the garage's darkest corner. Dad's decrepit book was in there under a stack of papers. I leafed through the pages and found this passage:

> *In cloth measure, two inches and a fifth make a nail—four nails, one quarter of a yard—thirty-six inches or three feet make a yard—three quarters of a yard make an ell Flemish—and five quarters make an English ell.*

I had never heard of an "ell" or "nail," not in relation to cloth. Looking further through the book, I felt like crying and wished my life was more my own. My dad had wasted his entire life. What if there was a better way to give to the world than raising a child and sewing? The world held so many things, and I only knew what was in my little life. What if I died suddenly like

Dad, and this was all that I'd done? I felt like a prisoner, a slave to a life I hadn't chosen. With my heart pounding in my chest, I shook my head and stood up. "When am I going to wake up?" The garage walls didn't answer. I held the book to my chest and brought it into the house.

***

Jig was turning fifty on September 16, 1967, so Maren and I decided to throw him a surprise party. He didn't seem deserving, but I knew my wifely obligation, and Maren talked me into it. Our daughter held onto old assumptions. You will have a dad you can count on. Your mom and dad will always be together. You will always live in a happy home.

Two days before the big event, I discovered lipstick on his collar. What a cliché, just like the Connie Francis song:

> ". . . You can bet your bottom dollar
> that you and I are through
> 'Cause lipstick on your collar
> told a tale on you . . ."

"Who is she?" I asked calmly. We were in bed.
"Janet."
"Janet fucking Farrell?" I didn't scream, not yet. I turned toward the window and stared at the full moon and felt like howling.

Janet Farrell. I hadn't seen that coming. She had bad teeth. She had nine kids. Nine! I had quit going to bridge games and knew he had picked her up as his partner. But I didn't see her as a threat. He and I had also been ignoring each other. No kissing for over two months and definitely no sex. He ignored Maren too, so I guess he had forgotten what he had said, that he would be more involved when she got older.

"Christ, Lou, when did you start using that word?"

"Just this minute. It seems fucking fitting when you're fucking mad. And call me 'Louise'. I like 'Louise' better."

"Keep your voice down. Maren will wake up."

"Maybe it's time we all woke up," I screamed. Yes, it was time to scream. I forced my hands to stay tucked in my armpits, so they wouldn't fly out to slap the bastard. "We are throwing you a big party on Saturday," I said with more control. "We're floating fifty candles in the fucking pool. I've invited about a hundred friends, so you better act surprised."

When I realized what I was about to say, nervous laughter became mixed with my words. "Oh, and on Sunday, Jig, I want you out." I turned to stare straight into his eyes.

"Out? Out where? Why?" he asked in disbelief.

My laughing grew louder. "I've had it, Jig. No more. Oh, and if I see that woman at the party, I might throw her into the pool." The week before, Janet had accepted my invitation, and I had been actually looking forward to seeing her.

"You've never talked this way," he said and crawled back into the bed and tried to touch me.

"No," I snapped. "I want you out of my house."

"Your house?"

"Yes, mine. I'm not going anywhere. And leave my bed. You're on the couch until Sunday. And every morning, you better be off it before Maren wakes up." As I turned away from him, I was shaking and didn't watch when he grabbed his pillow and left the room. Janet did come to the party, but I didn't throw her into the pool. Instead, I did spit into her drink. "Bloody Mary?" I asked with a smile, reaching the glass toward her, the red one with celery stalks sticking out the top.

"Thanks! Don't mind if I do," she said, and took a large, satisfying gulp.

The next day, as Jig backed out of our driveway, and Maren met him, "See you later," was all the coward said to her.

When she and I sat on her bed that night, and I explained how her dad had left for good, I threw her into a pot of boiling water when I said, "Your dad's gone, life will never be the same." And I tossed in a healthy dose of salt by adding, "The bastard! How could he leave you and not say anything?" As I fake sobbed on her shoulder, I made sure her pain would be preserved.

She stroked my hair and said, "Mom, don't worry. I'll take care of you."

I was determined to be the victim—not the bad guy—and I wore the victim's dress well. Like a hooker who says "I love you" to every guy, my lies came easy.

I saw to it that, from Maren's perspective, her dad abandoned her. He'd wounded her mother and destroyed her perfect family. I tucked her into bed that night saying, between her real sobs, "I know, sweetheart. What are we going to do? How could he do this to us?" Uff da, not my proudest moment. My daughter's eleven-year-old shoulders were successfully laden with responsibility.

The next day, I sat at the kitchen table with my pinking shears and snipped Jig's head out of every photograph we had of him and mailed them to Janet Farrell. I enclosed a friendly little note on lavender-scented stationary. In my best cursive writing, it read, "Here Janet, you can have him,"

Fear of being alone and poor festered in my gut. With no appetite for food, thirty pounds slid effortlessly from my body. I called it the "divorce diet" and continued lying to Maren and never stopped. That was the worst part. It seemed natural, since I'd been lying to myself for decades.

Adding to the drama, I had a near-fatal car accident. My shrink came to the hospital and said, "Well, you almost did it, Louise."

My head was immobilized and my jaw wired shut, so I raised my eyebrow to question him.

"You didn't put on your brakes. The highway patrol reported that you were going about seventy-five and didn't even attempt to slow down. What does that tell you?"

I couldn't speak. A single tear slid out of my eye and into my ear.

He continued. "Think about your child while you're stuck in this bed. I'm sorry to report this to you, but you will recover. Life will go on."

"You don't need a weatherman to know which way the wind blows." Bob Dylan's line popped into my head, and I repeated it until I went to sleep. Finally home, I wish I could report some shift in my behavior, but none came. Dad's book had a great quote in it that will never leave my mind:

A Persian writer finely observes:
"a gentle hand leads the elephant himself by a hair."

I needed to really pay attention to that because my need to be led by someone else had never left me. I'd just picked the wrong person to do it. I'd picked a professional philanderer as an expert.

For nearly two months, I recuperated flat on my back. On the first day out of traction, I called my shrink and he offered this advice: "Join a club, volunteer, and take Valium." I didn't listen, but time had a way of changing things, and the times they were a-changin'.

***

"Hey, hey, LBJ, how many kids did you kill today?" I screamed at the top of my lungs.

I was a fifty-year-old divorcee, and it was October, '69. Without me, the Summer of Love had come and gone. We, thousands of us, now marched toward Golden Gate Park, bathed in sunshine filtered only by marijuana smoke. It was a "be-in" and we were being-in all right. Being in-tolerant of the war, being in-spired to change, being tired of being in-active. I didn't feel in-sane any longer, and I don't know if that was what my therapist had in mind, but what the hell, I volunteered and joined the antiwar movement.

"Hell, no, we won't go!" the trio of men shouted. They hid behind their sunglasses. Two wore goatees and berets, and one had an Afro the size of a beach ball. Their black leather jackets had to be too hot, but their clothing made it obvious they were members of the Black Panthers. Sweat glistened on their foreheads. They marched to my right, Maren to my left. We were squashed together like chocolates in a candy box. To the front paraded a group of six twenty-something-year-olds, each with a braid of hair dangling down her back. At least I assumed they were girls. With their arms linked together, their feet kept pace like a giant centipede. They turned in unison to flip someone the bird who had yelled, "Go home, idiots! Get a job." I realized then, they were three boys, two girls, and one whose gender I couldn't quite tell.

Behind us marched a respectable looking couple with gray hair and glasses. At one point, the wife tapped me on the shoulder and asked, "Would you like a little water? We have some."

I smiled and declined, but Maren piped in, "Sure, man, cool."

The woman handed over an army-issue green canteen.

"I'm Louise . . . Louise Newhouse," I said, using my maiden name for the first time in over thirty years. We smiled at each other, and she introduced herself and her husband. They had traveled to San Francisco to voice their view that the Vietnam War was illegal. They carried a homemade placard that read, "Taxation without representation is tyranny." Their son, nineteen, was M.I.A.

We were an odd cluster of humanity. A group united, however, by a single cause.

Across the nation a "new generation" had grown up. The numbers gathered in moratorium that day, in U.S. cities alone, were about twenty-five million. The news had brought war-torn images into our living rooms for years. For me, though, the war began that day. Even the assassinations of Bobby Kennedy and Dr. King Jr. hadn't been enough, or the Tet offensive when we lost 2,500 troops in a forty-eight hour slaughter. Even Tricky Dick Nixon's inauguration promise of withdrawal, and then his swift escalation into Cambodia, had not moved me to action. Even the announcement, the previous April, that the numbers killed in Vietnam had exceeded the total lost in Korea didn't push me off my complacent ass.

No, the war didn't start for me until that October day in 1969.

Funny thing is, it was Maren who brought it to me. Amazing how the most vocal protester I knew would be quiet, no-trouble Maren. She didn't talk until she was three. I'd asked the doctor if there was something wrong with her.

"Yes, there is something wrong with her." He assured me with a pat on my hand. "I bet you and Jig talk for her. She can hear; she can make noise with her vocal cords; she'll talk when she's ready."

It did seem she had stockpiled words for years, so she could unleash them for a purpose. My newly found motto that year was, "if you can't fight 'em, join 'em", so I suppose our conversation should not have been necessary.

"Mom, if the war's not over, some of the guys we know will have to go. They have to register for the draft. Right?"

"Yes. But some will be 4-F and some will move to Canada."

"Oh," she said looking disappointed. "Well, so what about other guys who have to." Her expression returned to hopeful.

My mind shifted to two of my friend's sons with numbers that had already been pulled, to the one who had left for boot camp, and to the three who were coming home in flag-draped coffins. We were powerless. Why even think about it? If I'd said those statements, they wouldn't have made any difference—not to Maren, who at eleven had suddenly become opinionated and headstrong.

I shrugged and continued to chop tomatoes for a salsa then glanced at her.

She gritted her teeth, put her fists on her hips, and asked, "Didn't we move from Arkansas because of racism? Wasn't it your dad who knew a slave? If no one took a stand, nothing would ever change." Her determined look matched what she wore: military boots, Army-issue khaki shirt, a seagull feather stuck in her braid.

I washed my hands and turned toward her. "Hey, did I ever tell you that your grandpa Marcus was a conscientious objector to the First World War?" That lie just flew out of my mouth. Sure, Dad had objected to the war, but he didn't get drafted because Mom and he had three babies, all in a row.

"Wow! Really?" Maren's mood lifted. "Mom, we have to go march. If lots of people go, we can make them stop."

"They're not going to stop the war until they've won, sweetheart. America's never lost a war. And there's a lot of smart people who think we can win this one too."

"It's not a war, Mom. It's never been declared." Maren reached over, picked up a few scraps, and nibbled the flesh around the tomato ends. "I have friends who're going to march. You can't stop me," she said with a smile.

She was right. I couldn't stop her. I hadn't said "no" to anything she'd asked—not since her father left. I no longer called him "Jig." I called him "Robert Spencer." The man with that name could be removed from my heart. Especially since I'd returned to my maiden name. Using "Newhouse" buried any remains of our being married. I even tried to ignore that he was Maren's father.

That is why when we were marching, and I spotted a sign

259

which read, "Gamble on horses, or get a job," my heart skipped and then boiled as I realized who was waving it. Robert Spencer. Yes, Maren's father and Janet stood on the opposite side of the street in a doorway, watching the marchers.

Uff da, what were the chances of running into them? I didn't point him out to Maren. Instead, I took my cue from the six-headed centipede in front of us who made an obscene gesture in his direction. Janet said something into his ear. He looked at her. They laughed. They were married. He had her and her nine kids. Nine! I didn't need to share mine with him.

"All we are saying is give peace a chance." We sang and swayed and moved on.

The crowd was violently vocal but physically peaceful. The nonviolence was partially brought on by what was being passed among the assembled masses: numerous communal marijuana cigarettes. Luckily, the one nearest to us was commandeered by the caterpillar guard. It was sucked down by those six bobbing heads as they struck up a shaky rendition of "We Shall Overcome." They sang but not in tune. The backward passing of that hemostat-held roach halted at our doorstep. My heart had sped up as it approached. Would I have decided to say "no" to Maren, then? Maybe.

Maren, at not quite twelve-years-old, was still a virgin to pot smoking. I assumed. I'd tried it a few times but quit, even quit cigarettes and alcohol. While marching that day, I was relieved of having to choose between declining the stuff, snuffing it out, or taking a drag.

"One, two, three, four, we don't want your fucking war!" I spewed out the F-word as though it were normal for me. Maren looked at me in disbelief, and I shrugged and thought about my dad, about how Mom would have objected, but how he would have found a way to march with us. When Maren and I returned home exhausted, I tried to go to sleep but couldn't get Dad out of my mind. I dug up his little book. In it were these words written long ago, but they were still appropriate 140 years later:

> **_Q. How does cruelty show its effects?_**
>
> *A. A cruel disposition is usually exercised upon those who are under its power. Cruel rulers make severe laws which injure the persons and properties of their subjects. The effects of cruelty are hatred, quarrels, tumults, and wretchedness.*

We were more than a little tired of our "cruel rulers" and their "severe" decisions. War hardly seemed a fitting answer. "Wretchedness?" When was the last time I heard that word said aloud?

> **_Q. Who are the peace-makers?_**
>
> *A. All who endeavor to prevent quarrels and disputes among men, or to reconcile those who are separated by strife. The man who keeps his temper will not be rash, and do or say things which he will afterwards repent of. And though men should sometimes differ, still they should be friends. They should be ready to do kind offices to each other.*

We should not be rash? Instead be friends? To hell with that! And what are "kind offices"? I had no idea. We were peaceniks who were not interested in keeping our tempers. It was Eldridge

Cleaver who said, "You are either part of the solution or part of the problem." As I lay in bed and tried to fall asleep, it became obvious. Being a nice, quiet, compliant housewife from the suburbs no longer worked for me. I stuck the book back into a box marked "Things for Maren" and shoved it into the darkest corner of my closet. The hems of my long dresses draped over the carton top, making it all but disappear.

I decided to "go where you wanna go, do what you wanna do" and sold the house and bought a 1920s bungalow on East Valerio Street. It had a front porch with a bougainvillea draped over one corner, French doors, a fireplace, built-in hutches, a window seat, a yard with canna and calla lilies, birds of paradise, peach and persimmon trees, and a fuchsia with a trunk as big around as a ten-inch frying pan. The yellow stucco façade where Jig, Maren, and Lou had lived became a fading memory.

***

My sewing business brought in a small supplemental income to Robert Spencer's monthly one hundred in child support and one hundred for alimony. I looked forward to the day when I could write to the bastard and tell him to keep his damn money. But when Maren turned eighteen, in just a few short years, the loss of half my income would be devastating. Who could support a house, a car, feed themselves, buy clothes, and pay taxes on one hundred a month? Forget about insurance. I'd just have to stay healthy and create other ways to make money.

I started playing bridge again, this time with rich women who didn't mind playing for money and losing to me. I became one of their weekly expenses like their Mexican maids and gardeners, and their Black cooks. I'd come home with over fifty dollars in winnings. Sometimes, an extra twenty dollars would be tucked inside a pocket. It had to be Dorothy who'd slipped me a little extra. The other two ladies were rather stingy, coming from inherited money: one from her railroad-owning great-grandfather; the other from her father who invented some shock absorbers or struts of something else found on the underbelly of the automobile. Dorothy a self-made woman, a talented composer and musician, she'd known her own poverty in the past. She hadn't forgotten her lean years. Maren and I became one of her charities.

Even when the others began to judge me, I still kept meeting with them. I had to. "Louise, you've got to get control of that daughter of yours." It was Nell, the one who had eaten caviar before she was three. "Just take away her privileges."

What she didn't realize was that we didn't have privileges. I couldn't take the car away; Maren rode a bicycle. I couldn't stop giving her an allowance; she didn't get one. I couldn't stop buying her clothes; she shopped at thrift stores. We'd become what I never wanted—poor.

Pride shall bring them low;
But honor shall uphold the humble in spirit.

Kate Porter

VII

1969-1975
Maren Spencer

Nestled between the sheets, I listened to Mom's coffee pot percolating. "Good morning, good morning, I love to see you smile," Mom sang, walking into my room. My eyes popped open to see gray smoke puffing from her lips. Sometimes, I thought Mom's promise to quit smoking had worked, but other days she didn't even try to hide it. "Good morning, good morning, your smile makes life worthwhile." She took a long drag, the ember sizzled. "It's 7:45, Thanksgiving eve. Do you want eggs or French toast?"

Mom didn't believe in cereal. We lived on Dad's alimony and child support payments, but we would always have "the best" in everything, in this case, a real breakfast. She wanted us to also wear fancy clothes, so we wore hand-me-down silk shirts from her wealthy friends, and everything else we bought at thrift stores. An ancient baby-grand piano came from a yard sale and sat neglected in the living room. Mom pestered me to play, but it seemed to me that if it was so important to her, she ought to play. Someday soon, I would go to "the best" college. Better yet, she hoped I'd find "the best" husband. No good-enoughs in my life. Mom wouldn't have it. She gave me that gift—her expectation of perfection—difficult to live up to while we scraped by well-below the poverty line.

"Eggs," I mumbled.

"Scrambled or fried?"

"Whatever." My commitment to being the family's eleven-year-old decision maker had its boundaries. I refused that role before 8:00 a.m.

The next day, after peeling potatoes, basting the turkey, and chopping two onions, I escaped to my room to read until it was time to eat. Soon, she called, "Dinner's on."

"One more page," I yelled back. My hands held that worn-out scrapheap. The book. The all-important one Mom had handed me, insisting that I read it. Some stuff was interesting:

Let thy words be plain and true
to the thoughts of the heart.

But that old thing also contained some ridiculous passages:

The path of duty is always the path of safety.

True bullshit, if you asked me. I knew my grandfather had owned the book, and it had been given to him by someone, someone who had gotten it from someone else. Their names were written in the back. The book maker had signed too, which was sort of cool. But to me, it was mostly a waste of time to read any of it. Who cared about old crap? Not me. Not when important things were happening, like war, over-population, the Civil Rights movement.

I should have kept reading, but a whiff of roasted turkey yanked at my senses. It smelled of what family should be. But this was Thanksgiving, 1969. Dad had left us, and I chose to read more than join in. Reading was easier, even the other book I read that fall, *A Short History of Vietnam*. The three-hundred-fifty page book was misnamed, you bet. "Uff da," is what Mom said when she saw I was reading that one.

The turkey's aroma called again. I couldn't stall forever, not when cozy-family possibilities, like sage rice stuffing, were steaming on the table. There would be gravy, homemade cranberry sauce, green beans, and dessert—not traditional pumpkin pie—but the custard-filled, meringue-topped one I had requested.

I dog-eared the page, stuck the book under my pillow, and headed for the dining room.

Plopping down in my chair at the corner, I wondered if saying our oval table had a corner was correct. My knee whacked a table leg. "You won't mind sitting there, will you sweetheart," Mom had said, not asked, while we set the table and discussed where everyone would sit. She still talked for me, assuming she knew what I thought.

I smiled, remained silent, and sat down in my assigned seat in front of a dish of dull-orange, overcooked carrots.

The cranberry sauce was that jellied glop with can-embossed rings. "Mom, where's the regular cranberry sauce?" I asked. No one answered since my mouse-of-a-voice was barely audible. Everyone laughed, not at me, but in a tone that seemed out of tune. More like a pack of hyenas than a clan of Homo Sapiens. I looked around the table at all the barely known faces. Mom was familiar, of course, but then there were five others. A bunch of college kids Mom had found drifting downtown with no homes to go to. Five guys, all with flowing locks and facial hair.

One passed a cigarette to Mom.

"Mom, why are you smoking again?" I blurted out, wondering what was that weird smell?

The laughter stopped. Someone had pushed the eject button on the eight-track tape deck of my life. Six sets of eyes stared at me. The room seemed to close in. Blood rushed to my ears and splashed onto my cheeks. I had to be as red as the canned cranberries.

Mom put the tiny thing to her lips and inhaled until I thought she would pop. She sat there, her lips pursed. Little lines formed around her mouth, just like they did when she kissed me good-morning and asked what I wanted for breakfast. No one answered my question. Mom passed what was left to the guy who sat on the other side of her. The acrid smell and what I was seeing collided. Mom's smoking a joint? She's into pot?

I wasn't completely naïve. I knew drugs existed. After all, no one in sixth grade in Southern California in the late '60s didn't know. One of my friends had even brought a joint to school, and we had passed it around pretending to smoke. No one had lit it though. Not while I was there. The gray cloud mixed with the turkey steam.

I peered under the table. The cave with intruding root-legs invited me below, so I slipped from my seat and joined the safety of shoes. When I was little, I'd spent hours under there, content to be near, yet disconnected, while tying everyone's laces together. When someone would stand up, I wanted them to be unable to walk. The adults had always created a big commotion when they got up, but they hadn't fooled me. They obviously could feel their shoes being retied. I wondered if they thought I was stupid. Did they still?

Glancing around that day, though, all I saw were clogs,

sandals, and flip flops. No laces. Nothing to keep me busy. My pink sneakers had laces, and didn't fit in. But I didn't want them to. They were like me—a pair of pink Keds among the hippy-shoes.

The laughter picked up again. Only Mom peeked under the table to see me and to ask, "Can Jeffrey have the skin off your drumstick?"

Not knowing which one was Jeffrey, I still nodded yes. Words are unnecessary when you want to be invisible.

A strong whiff of that foreign smell wound its way between the chairs and through the cracks where the two table leaves didn't quite meet. Only when all the table leaves were used did the table have a crack large enough to spy through. I could see Mom. Her eyes looked sleepy. I wished Dad was here. His minty gargle wasn't in the bathroom. I had eaten dinners and completed homework without him. Sometimes I was glad he wasn't there, other times not. At least they weren't arguing any more. If he'd come for turkey, Mom wouldn't be stoned.

The day after Thanksgiving, Mom came into my room and sat on my bed and told me secrets, the ones I was the last to know. "Come on, Maren. You didn't know Ricky is a drug dealer?"

"Little Ricky?"

"How could you not know?"

I wondered how that could be true. Ricky was a small person, and the Good Humor man, not a likely person to sell drugs. I didn't think so, anyway. But he did. Clingity-clang-cling. Come and get some treats, kids. Weed, snow cones, blotter acid, ice cream pies, LSD, popsicles, heroin. The chances were slim that any of us kids on the cul-de-sac would escape his jingle-bell call to participate. In my neighborhood it paid to be a quiet loner. My choice was the chocolate cone topped with nut sprinkles.

***

Christmas morning, the phone rang and I answered it.

"Merry ho, ho, ho," Dad said in a deep Santa-like voice. "Are you looking forward to coming up?" I would be spending the rest of my winter break at his house, being expected to romp around with his other kids, all of my nine step-brothers and - sisters.

Looking forward to it? Hell, no. "It's okay," I answered, but hated spending any time with him and his new family. He seemed different when he was with them, and I wanted no part of that family. The first sign of his changing was when he dropped his terrycloth robe by their near-Olympic-sized pool, and he wasn't wearing a swimsuit. I swam only when he was at work and swore to never swim too late in the afternoon. I might have to see his penis. As he sauntered to the deep end, he let it dangle free like an obscene flag. "Look at me," it said as he stepped onto the diving board and dove in.

Hiding and avoiding, I became so good at both I called myself "the best" at them. Better than anyone I knew. A piece of guilt hid along with me, under the bed, in the back of the closet and, at one point, in an empty refrigerator box in the garage. That cavernous space felt a little like home; it could make a good house for someone. No one disturbed me in those places, so I was left to my own thoughts and feelings like this one: It was my fault Dad had left . . . well, not the first time, but the second time, absolutely.

Mom and I had taken in a stray dog. After we nailed "found" posters all over our neighborhood, the dog's owner picked up the mutt, but left a healthy infestation behind. Fleas seemed to like Mom, and she couldn't keep from scratching. The bites on her legs became infected, and blood poisoning took over. Dad felt guilty that I was taking care of her, all by myself, so much that he moved back to live with us. In Mom's delirium she didn't refuse him. Sometimes, I wondered if she even remembered he was there.

He said, "We'll be a family again. You'll see."

She smiled a little and closed her eyes.

This happened in the summer when I was twelve, so I hung around the house to nurse-maid Mom back from death's door. I slathered ointment on bites and dispensed her daily doses of antibiotics and painkillers. While feverish, she ended up divulging more than she should have. "Your Dad slept around, honey . . . starting about a month after . . . after the wedding. I couldn't . . . he slept with my friends." Those words slipped off her tongue and slithered into my brain, planting hate where they landed.

When Dad came home from work, my gaze sped to everywhere but toward him. I couldn't force myself to look at him. Standing in front of my dresser mirror, I said to myself, "I hate you, Dad."

Our interactions became requests from him that I do something. "Maren, walk down to the five-and-dime and grab a paper." "Come on, Maren, someone's got to mow the lawn or it will be up around our ankles." I felt like his slave—not his daughter.

"Yes, sir. Massa, sir," I whispered. Maybe he heard me because he slammed the door right behind me when I went into the garage to get the mower.

One day when Mom was fully recuperated, she blurted out, "Should I take him back? For good?"

"No!" I punctuated the word with a slam of my fist on the kitchen table. "He's married! What about his wife?!" Mom's wine glass had toppled over and the crystal shattered on the floor. The next day he drove away, for good. I'd decided—not Mom.

What I learned was that a single word, "No" if properly placed, could contain power—actual power to cause actual change.

***

After I entered junior high, Mom sold our home and bought a bungalow with a bougainvillea-draped porch. Located on a street on the eastside, near the Santa Barbara Mission, all the houses were much older than where we'd lived with Dad, and the little brown pellets along the foundation proved to be evidence of termites. Mom loved it, but I hated that house. Old stuff gave me the creeps. Sometimes when I couldn't sleep, I'd stick my fingernail through the paint on my windowsill, in search of the underlying cavern tunnels. Never found any actual termites, but the windows were so damaged they rattled for the slightest reason. For my next birthday she bought me a bicycle. The rusty ten-speed disappointed me because it wasn't new and the handlebars didn't have tassels.

My freedom was born, though, in the form of two wheels, a

chain, a derailleur, and wind in my hair. After grabbing my lunch at the local tortillaria, I'd sit on the courthouse lawn to eat fresh tacos with beans and guacamole. When peace rallies happened there, I met people who were actively calling for the end of the Vietnam conflict. And, like me, some were eighth graders.

We began writing, printing, and distributing an underground newspaper, The Star Spangled Revolutionary Press. My new friends didn't see me as the ever-quiet member of a family. They saw an organizer: the one who knew a lot about Southeast Asian history; the one willing to spend Saturday afternoons mimeographing copies in some guy's basement; the fearless one who distributed leaflets in the quad, even though it would mean detention or worse.

"I'm disappointed, Miss Spencer. Your grades are slipping, and now this," the principal, Mr. Dwyer, said. He waved that week's canary-yellow handout in my face. "Did your parents put you up to it?"

I laughed and twirled my braid around my index finger. "My parents have nothing to do with it."

"They didn't write this?"

"You think they wrote it? Wow! No they didn't." A feeling of pride washed over me.

"Kids your age don't write lines like 'civil disobedience,' 'male chauvinism,' and 'fascist capitalist pigs.' Who wrote it, really?"

"I wrote some. Other kids write, too. Our names are printed on each article. See?" I pointed to my byline and smiled.

Mr. Dwyer did not smile back.

"This isn't a trial, is it?" I asked, feeling the power of integrity and righteousness.

Mr. Dwyer scratched his bald head and wrote something on his dreaded pink pad. "I'll let it go this time, Miss Spencer, but you can't distribute this thing at school. If I catch you again, I'll be forced to suspend you."

I ditched my last period, gym, and rode to the courthouse and then to city hall. There, I learned we could pass out our papers on the sidewalk because it was public property. The school had no legal jurisdiction over those gray squares.

The next Monday morning's announcement began with Mr. Dwyer. "Anyone caught reading The Star Spangled Revolutionary Press in school will get detention." So Friday afternoon the detention hall was standing-room-only, and the following Monday there was a walkout from third period. In a democracy, even thirteen- to fifteen-year-olds have some rights, if they know how to fight for them.

Then Dad called. Again. His calls, his interruptions, felt exactly like a summons to Mr. Dwyer's office. With a four-day weekend coming up, I was supposed to take the bus to the bay area for a visit. My father wanted to take me to a baseball game. His other family was "looking forward" to seeing me. All I can report is that I frowned through thirteen innings, the stadium was freezing, and whoever Dad was cheering for lost the game. To me, games were irrelevant while napalm fell on babies, while apathy reigned, and while the Black Panthers wore arm bands and held their fists high.

Back at home our next area to attack was the school's antiquated dress code. Girls couldn't wear pants. The rule dated back to when the school had opened, in 1875, when skirts had to cover ankles. The rule, modernized only once, read that our hems needed to touch the ground when we knelt on the floor. "If rules can be changed once, they can be changed again," I wrote on a poster and tacked it near the auditorium.

After homeroom, six of us were called into the principal's office, again. Mr. Dwyer held up his ruler, swiveled his chair to face us, and made us line up on our knees in front of him. My friend, Colleen, and I had tested the rule on purpose, so our skirts were found to be two inches too short.

"Miss Spencer and Miss McIntyre stay. The rest of you are only about a half inch off, so you may go back to class. See, I'm reasonable," he said, grabbing the edge of his desk and sliding his chair backward. "One of you made that poster. Which one!"

I started to get up.

"Stay where you are, Mary," he barked. "I haven't released you."

"My name's Maren. Miss Spencer to you. And I'm going to stand and you're not going to stop me." I stood, rubbed my knees, and lifted my blouse a couple of inches to reveal my waistband that I had rolled up to make my skirt shorter. After quickly unrolling it, the skirt fell to the proper length. Colleen did the same. "Now what did you say, Mr. Dwyer?" I asked.

"This doesn't change anything. You're suspended for the rest of the week."

"Do you have a witness? Your secretary can come in. She'll see our skirts are the right length. Let's go back to class." I grabbed Colleen's hand and backed up toward the door.

Mr. Dwyer was a military-type, a real square. He coughed into his fist. The tips of his ears turned red. I thought about how he must have longed for the "good-old" days when children respected their elders, deserving or not. He reminded me of my dad. They both had crew-cuts. Most men who were squares had hair that short.

Colleen and I literally sprinted from his office and back to class.

Two weeks later, after some serious organizing, half of the students wore floor-length skirts in protest—even the boys. Long flowing dresses of various styles and colors swirled through the hallways and classrooms: caftans, Madras dresses, paisley skirts, a few ball gowns, bathrobes, and two boys in my fifth-period debate class wore black negligees. The long-skirt protest brought media attention, and after a series of articles appeared in a national magazine, our school's dress code was permanently amended.

From then on, my uniform became an army-issue shirt, Navy-blue wool bellbottom pants or Oshkosh bib-overalls, and huarache sandals with rubber-tire soles. I bought a beautiful leather journal and began writing down my thoughts. This was my first entry: "True words, combined with action, hold great power." I knew that sentence was the most profound ever written by a teenager. But the next day's entry was: "I think Cindy's in love with Brian. I'll ask her today in chorus."

***

Being a political activist didn't stop me from being the quiet, sulky type. I liked to think my mood was because of what I knew to be the truth. Most people didn't know enough about the world to understand the depth of the world's problems. And most, even if they did know, would never act to change them. In those high school years, my convictions were who I was.

After school, I simply flopped on my bed and read until

dinner. What I saw to be worthy of my time mutated. Mom and I had gone to that huge peace march in San Francisco, so I said goodbye to books like *The Secret Garden*, and hello to Jerry Rubin's *Do It: Scenarios of the Revolution*, *Soul on Ice* by Eldridge Cleaver, and Chairman Mao's little red book. The Black Panthers who had marched beside us knew what they wanted. They'd fight for what was right. I had a mission to learn everything I could, in order to change what I saw was wrong.

During my next visit to Dad's house, our conversation slid into an argument when I told him that cattle were a poor use of our resources. "Beans, corn, and rice form a perfect protein," I screamed at him. "I believe in non-violence and I'm vegetarian and I'm going to be in high school next year. You can't tell me what to do."

"If you don't eat more food than that, you're going to die. You'll get sick, Maren. Listen to me, I'm older. I know the facts."

"That's not all I eat, Dad. Oh, never mind." Then I mumbled, "I'm healthier than you."

Being there in his four-story A-frame house, the hours dragged on. I could never do anything important—not with Dad's nine step-kids all asking me to play games. We had mounds of dishes to wash. Twelve people eating three meals a day produce a mountain of them.

During that visit, Dad patted his knee and said, "Come on, Maren. Make your old dad happy. Come sit on my lap." That's when I started calling him O.D. for short. Old Dad, the one who never would change.

I glared and frowned and walked away. Didn't he see the yellow button with the black peace symbol displayed prominently on my breast pocket? I'm a soldier, a woman of the counterculture, a revolutionary member of the working proletariat.

In the '70s, most high schoolers were piss-faced. My peers hung out on the lower field smoking, popping, or drinking whatever they could get their hands on. That made classes easy for me since everyone else was stoned. It didn't take much effort to be on the good side of the bell curve, so I skated through by keeping my head down and my mind clear. Better to be pissed-off than piss-faced or pissed-on.

In my sophomore year, though, Patty Stamp came into my life. She and I had many classes together, and with alphabetical seating assignments the teachers sat me in front of her. At first, I tried to talk with her, about plans for the weekend, about where I lived, asking where she lived. She never answered that. Our mostly one-way conversations always felt awkward, but I loved the challenge.

One day, I forgot my biology notebook and said, "Hey, Patty, do you have a piece of paper I could borrow?"

"Borrow?" She glared at me as though I was the stupidest person alive. "Here, have one. But don't ask again, lame ass."

Her angry answer didn't make sense, until she started to pinch me and pull my hair throughout every class period we had together. "Your hair's so pretty," she said. "Just give me a few for my collection." She yanked out a handful.

I winced and thought about how POWs might have to endure a similar torture. "Please stop it," I whispered. Why would a Black girl want to pick on me? I understood the plight of the poor, of the underprivileged, of the discriminated against.

"You don't really care do you, White girl," she whispered.

Between classes I could usually avoid her. But one day while hiking from American History to Spanish, I had to travel from the main building to a temporary classroom, which was down a long hill. Sure enough, Patty was walking toward me. I breathed a sigh of relief, though, because a teacher was following close behind her.

Patty wouldn't do anything with Miss Barnes right there.

That was my thought, anyway, until she slugged me in the stomach, forcing me to drop to the ground, similar to what we'd learned to do in the duck-and-cover drills in elementary school. While on the ground, she kicked me twice. Muscle spasms forced me to gasp for air. I looked up in time to see Miss Barnes step around me, glance away, and continue up the path. What the hell was that? Apathy? Fear? I wasn't sure which, but I knew how indignant the assault made me feel. Betrayed by an adult who should have protected me, my heart raced, and I tried to figure out what to do. I felt violated. Powerless. Me. The one who had marched shoulder-to-shoulder with the Black Panthers.

"Why do you pick on me?" I moaned.

"You love it," Patty said.

"I've never done anything to you."

"You were born," she said and started walking away but turned back and kicked me again. "That's because my hair will never be blonde."

"I'm White and you're Black," I said and started to get up. She shoved me back down. That's when I heard several people laughing. It was a group of her friends. They were Black too. One girl was in my biology class. She sat at the same lab table. We had shared petri dishes. "Please help, Savannah," I said to her. She whispered something to Patty and they laughed louder.

"Why are you doing this?" I pleaded.

"That's why—because you don't know why."

Right then, I learned something about myself. Hate could form in my heart for more people than just my dad. I hated Patty. Even worse, racial prejudice was born. I don't know, maybe it had already been rooted, before Patty. Perhaps it had been lying in wait, like a tiger ready to pounce, because it came on faster and easier than I thought possible. Maybe because some people I knew seemed to feel that way already. My mom called Brazil nuts "Nigger toes," even when I'd begged her not to. And O.D. talked about loving "Jigaboo" music. I had told him I couldn't stand any of his music, even though I secretly loved Billie Holliday's soothing voice. I'd laughed at some horrible jokes, despite the fact that I knew they were tasteless and promoted prejudice.

After the attack, I felt powerless and never talked about it. My shame and anger grew, got all mixed up, then solidified in me. Everyone was prejudiced, as far as I could tell—unless they were trying to be a "liberal" like my mom. She put all Black people on a pedestal, and when I tried to tell her about Patty, her response was to point out how much she wanted to go on an African safari and that she loved afros. "The bigger the better," she said. She sewed a caftan from fabric with an African tribal print.

"Mom, you're embarrassing," I said the first time she wore it. "How can you ever leave the house wearing that?" She'd been out to a parent-teacher night at my high school, wearing that bright orange sack.

"What are you talking about, Maren? Mrs. Stamp wore one too. I think it's cool to wear something ethnic."

"Cool? Really?" Moms shouldn't say words like "cool." My heart started to leap about in my chest in anticipation of how Patty might react, if her mom told her about my mom. "She probably thinks that you don't have the right to wear an African dress? You're not one of them."

"One of them? Oh, you mean Black? But she and I had a great talk. Her first name's Ebony. Don't you love that? She changed her name when her husband divorced her. Maybe that's why Patty was giving you a little trouble last month. Her father split. Just like yours did. You two probably have a lot in common. I'm sure everything will be okay, now that I've talked with her mother."

The next week the attacks escalated. Another girl, one I didn't even know, grabbed my books and threw them into a trash can. My humiliation ramped up when I scrounged around in the barrel, then wiped off scraps of a PBJ and gooey bubblegum from my book covers.

Patty and her friends became part of my avoidance routine. I sped from class to class, trying to not look at anyone, knowing other violence could come at any moment. The in-class bullying never slowed down. One beating was on my walk home and contained two punches to my face and a broken finger, when Patty crushed my hand with her patent-leather boot.

I felt angrier than I'd ever felt, and worse, humiliated and ashamed. Even though I knew judgment of their entire race was wrong, I couldn't change my raging feelings. Why are they, of all people, discriminating against me because of my skin color? My blonde hair? The growing hatred sickened me, so I started ditching school and writing excuses and signing Mom's name to them. I saw no other way to fix the problem.

One night, Mom came to dinner carrying that old book. She showed me a table of U.S. census figures from 1790 to 1820. In 1810, one in every seven people had been slaves.

"Maren, Patty's just showing you how unfair the world can be. You need to ignore her. Just walk away."

"So what, Mom. They're all the same. A bunch of them laughed at me while she kicked me. Besides, slavery was abolished a long time ago."

"Do you know, it's still legal in Mississippi? I'm sure you're exaggerating about Patty Stamp. Her mother's so nice. If it happens again, just go to the nearest teacher. They'll help you."

I shrugged. Miss Barnes didn't do anything. There would be no help from anyone at school, and I didn't bother to tell Mom because she wouldn't do anything either.

***

One Sunday, I woke up and read for an hour, took my weekly shower, then walked into the kitchen where Mom was chopping vegetables. They were ingredients for Ugali, which was some sort of African meal she was making for breakfast.

"Mom, I'm not going to eat that glop. It smells terrible," I said, braiding my wet hair in tight pigtails. I had begun pinning the braids up across the top of my head since that style slowed down Patty's torture of me. She couldn't grab my hair easily; though, she'd begun pinching the back of my neck instead since my hair no longer flowed over my shoulders. Which was worse? Both hurt like hell.

Mom didn't react to my complaint, so I blurted out, "And I'm not going to O.D.'s, I mean Dad's, this summer."

"That's okay, sweetheart. You don't have to go to your dad's. But you do have to eat this." She nibbled a little glob of corn meal. "I wonder if I have this recipe right. There's no real way to know. That's another reason I need to go over to Africa."

"I can't stand him," I said, staring at the food. "I hate my dad." There it was. With no pre-thought, those words had just popped out of my mouth. Mom, please tell me you love me, anyway. Please tell me I'm not a terrible person to hate him, I was thinking as I stuck my finger into the food, scooped up a glob, and licked off. I opened the under-the-sink cupboard and spit into the garbage.

"Well, I guess it'll be okay," Mom said.

I turned to look at her, but she didn't raise her head to look at me. She didn't see my tears.

***

It's odd for a sixteen-year-old to notice what's in her fifty-year-old mother's closet, but my mom's clothes were an eclectic mix of trendiness, classic lines, and artistic flare. It was 1970 after all. The lines between ages had faded like blue jeans. They were no longer dark blue, they were stonewashed. Her clothes weren't my style, whatever that was, so even though I wore the same size, going in there to choose something to wear wasn't ever the point. I just loved to see and stroke the fabrics. She wore things made from the softest cotton, silk, or wool. At the remnant store, we'd weave our way through the bolts, looking for bargains. We'd hunt for the right color; however, vastly more important, we required the right feel. I stroked a fabric and instantly knew if it contained a hint of synthetic fiber. If it did, even if the colors were perfect, we would never buy it.

Mom had untangled the mysteries of the fabric world: wool- and synthetic-blends "pilled up"; if you wore a cotton-polyester blend shirt on a hot day, it would make you sweat; the proper needle in the machine was as important as the cloth; and you must absolutely use the right thread. This knowledge was passed from Mom to me, as it had been to Mom from Grandma Ruth. I swore to uphold the rules as though they were the Ten Commandments: Thou shalt sew straight seams; thou shalt not covet polyester; thou shalt not bed down with thy neighbor's Singer lest ye forsake thy Bernina.

One morning, when we hadn't been to the laundromat for two weeks, I searched through Mom's closet, looking for the shirt she had sewn in a silk crepe-de-chine fabric printed with a Chinese woodcut. The shades of purple and blue would show off my long blond hair, and since I wasn't leaving the house that day, I wanted to wear it. She'd sewn on seven mother-of-pearl buttons each with a tiny bird carved on it, which I had found on a '40s era angora sweater for sixty cents at Sam's Thrift Store.

I removed the shirt from its hanger and continued to feel my way through the luxurious fabrics to the back of her closet. There was the wool-challis shawl, the cotton-sateen sundress made from a '30s Vogue pattern, the silk cut-velvet jacket that felt like angel's hair. When I reached the far corner, my foot kicked a box. My name was written on the top of it in black magic marker.

In those lean years, I didn't get many presents and hated to spoil this one by possibly uncovering a future gift. I asked Mom what was inside.

"Oh, just some special things I've kept for you," she said as the phone started to ring.

"Can I look in it?"

"Sure, just put everything back." She waved her hand in the air, picked up the receiver, and said "hello" to who was on the line.

I returned to the closet, lifted the lid, and as expected, found cloth: an embroidered piece of linen I had sewn in second grade. I removed this treasure and uncovered other things a mom might save: report cards, old cards I'd drawn, and a watercolor of a whooping crane I'd painted. Among these was a mixture of the unexpected: a 1969 peace-march button with a map of Vietnam on it, overlaid by the words "OUT NOW"—I remember this!; a few issues of *The Star Spangled Revolutionary Press*—She knew?; an essay I wrote about apathy and hypocrisy entitled "The Two Things I Hate Most." I had forgotten about that, but she hadn't.

I put on the crepe-de-chine shirt and pinned the protest button on its lapel.

The box contained a childhood—mine. But wasn't I invisible? Maybe not to Mom. I could still hear that she was talking on the phone. At the bottom of the box was something else. It took me a minute to realize it was that old book. When opening the cover, a few page corners fell to the floor. I read, wondering why Mom had put it in a box of things she thought were special to me.

Formation of verbs in the three persons

I grant   thou grantest   he granteth   we grant
you grant   he grants   ye or you grant   they grant

On the following page was this:

> *Let truth only proceed from thy mouth—despise not the poor, because he is poor; but honor him who is honest and just.*
>
> *Envy not the rich, but be content with thy fortune. Follow peace with all men, and let wisdom direct thy steps.*

"Typical old bullshit," I said. Do this, do that, written by and for men. I carried the book into the hall where I could hear Mom's words.

She wasn't saying much, mostly "no" or "yes" or "I'll think about it." As I entered the kitchen, she hung up.

"Who was that?"

"Jig."

Why did she call him "Jig" not "your idiot father" not "Robert Spencer, my S.O.B., lying, cheating, son-of-a-bitch ex-husband?"

"What did he want?" I asked, dreading that she'd say I had to go visit him.

"He wants me to come up and visit. And well . . . I don't know, maybe try living together again. Or something?"

I leaned against the wall. My hands started to shake.

"Oh . . . I don't know . . . but I am thinking about it." Mom poured a cup of coffee.

"Why?" I managed to say. A headache began to form. She couldn't be thinking I'd move too. Could she? Could I live on my own? My friend, Colleen, was an emancipated minor. Maybe

I could be too.

"There's a part of me that still loves him," she said and pulled the gold tab off a pack of Kools, threw the cellophane end into the garbage, placed a cigarette between her lips, and lit up. "I know you think I'm nuts, Maren, but maybe he's changed." She hadn't been smoking anything for the last few years.

Sometimes, I liked the smell of the lit match and that first puff of smoke, but as I inhaled, the odor made me want to puke. "Mom, you've got to be kidding. And why are you smoking again?"

"No, I'm not kidding. I don't know. But I am thinking about it." She took a deep drag and avoided looking in my direction. "It's different for me," she said and exhaled. "I miss having a man around. You'll be leaving in a couple years. What am I supposed to do? Be alone the rest of my life? And poor?"

"Wait, Mom. You've been divorced from him for seven years. No really, you're joking. O.D.'s married to Janet. What about that?" Then I added these whispered words as though they didn't matter, but I knew they mattered the most: "Mom, I hate him. We hate him."

She inhaled and exhaled several times forming a small cloud. "You don't know what love is like, Maren. Maybe your dad and I can . . . well . . . just move on. Maybe we've mended the hurt."

"Mom, you're crazy. He has a new family." The tone in my voice was a cross between a mad dog and a confused little girl. I cleared my throat and asked, "What are you going to do, be his mistress?" I felt like someone had punched me in the stomach and hated myself for what happened next. I began to cry. Not a slow buildup of silent tears to gentle weeping. I wailed like a widow at a Sicilian funeral.

Mom put her arms around me and said, "Didn't I tell you? Dad and Janet are getting divorced. They've filed the papers. It just isn't final, yet."

"So what?" I pushed her away. I had never pushed Mom away before. Without asking her about the old book, I threw it on the floor and ran to the back door.

For years, she had been mothering a sizable hate for my father—in me. I thought the same hate lived in her. "It's better to live alone than with him," I screamed as I slammed the door behind me. "Not just for you. But for me!"

I ran down Olive Street, trying not to slip on the fallen fruit, until I stopped in the shade between a prickly pear cactus and a yucca plant with its towering bloom. For the first time, I understood that she didn't know how I felt. How could she? When I was younger, I'd thought Mom knew everything in my mind. She'd certainly talked for me and answered her own questions before I had a chance to speak for myself. "You don't mind if we skip your birthday party this year, do you, Maren? Of course you don't. Thanks, sweetheart." She didn't know how I felt about Dad. The feeling was mine to bear, my own burden. No one else knew what it felt like to hate their own father, at the same time as wanting nothing more than to love him.

***

On August 10, 1974, Mom did move out. So did Richard M. Nixon. He left the White House and flew off in a dark-green helicopter. Mom drove away in a dark-green Volvo. Both were leaders of their houses. Both resigned from their commissions.

He was no longer President of The United States, a.k.a. POTUS, and she was no longer My Own Mother, a.k.a. MOM. Well, technically she was, but she drove away to live with my DAD, a.k.a. Dear Adulterous Dad. The mom I had loved shouldn't have done such a thing. I started calling her Mizz Spencer even though she had gone back to her maiden name. In my opinion, she was no better off than a slave. And she'd left me alone.

She called weekly to tell me when she'd mail me a money order, so I could buy food.

"That be you, Ma'am? How be da Massa, Mizz Spencer?" I asked in what I was sure was a southern drawl.

"Maren, stop it."

"He be cheatin' on ya, yet?"

"Maren, I won't call you again. Now, stop it."

"You cookin' up dem grits-an-gravy in da big house, Mizz Spencer?"

"I'm hanging up."

The dial tone hummed in my ear. "That's okay," I said as I replaced the receiver. If she came looking for a pardon, I would not grant one. Not like President Ford would later pardon Nixon. Mom and I had spent nearly every day the previous summer, watching the Watergate Hearings and discussing the President's complicity in crime. We knew the bastard was guilty. Just as guilty of a crime as O.D. had been when he cavorted with Mom's friend whom he had married. His divorce from her wasn't final yet. I pictured Mom seated in front of that same Senate panel answering for her crimes. They'd have a scarlet letter "A" sewn to her silk blouse, the one with printed turtles running down the sleeves. Guilty? Yes, indeed.

"I'm sixteen, I can take care of myself," I had said to Mom

as she drove away.

"Just lie to them, you know, if the school calls," she said, during a phone call a week later. "Don't tell anyone you're alone. I mean it. Or they'll make you come up and live with us. I know you don't want to." She hesitated but added, "It's not perfect up here, but Jig is trying."

"Trying, Mom? Give me a break."

I spent my senior year alone. All alone. Graduation was approaching and my grades remained borderline, but passing. The one thing I did that year, which gave me any pleasure, was what I did most Sunday afternoons. I jumped on my bike and rode down State Street. The rushing air seemed to blow most of my worries away. Twenty minutes later, I arrived at the beach along Cabrillo Boulevard where a large group of people gathered to do international folk dancing. Artists and crafts people sold their work nearby.

Seascapes drew crowds of tourists. Weekend shoppers could also find other items they might desire: macramé bikinis, tie-dyed tee shirts, leather belts, beaded roach clips, and paisley printed everything in sizes from newborn to age ninety, including pants, shirts, dresses, rolling papers, and condoms. If you knew who to ask.

Folk dancing there felt like a performance for tourists. It often didn't seem worth the bother because beginners, drawn by the romantic idea of frolicking on the beach, could turn a graceful dance into a traffic jam. After riding my ten-speed off the bike path, through the throngs buying and selling crafts, then over the lush green lawn dotted with palm trees, I struggled through the hordes already gathered. Some were sitting to watch, others not. Sit down, assholes! I silently willed the rest to obey.

A few did. Sit. Now stay. Good humans.

I parked my bike and took my customary position against the chain-link fence. Like a corner booth in a restaurant, from that spot, I could see who came and went. In front of me was the circle where the grass was worn down to dirt from years of trampling feet. I could also avoid the dust storm that arose when the dancing and sea-breezes converged.

The music started up from the record player, which was run by a Greek disk jockey. A circle of dancers formed and moved slowly to the simple steps of the first couple of easy warm-up numbers, the horah and the debka. Like a runner who stretches before a jog, I joined in. The more complicated dances, mostly Balkan, would come later. In the lulls between songs, the sound of pounding surf mixed with the rotting smell of beach-thrown seaweed. I grew bored and returned to my spot.

"Why are all these people jumping around?"

I turned to see who was speaking. A guy, a Black guy, with a head as clean shaven as a bowling ball, looked at me with deep-set sorrowful eyes. Mom would have liked what he was wearing. "This is folk dancing," I said.

"Yes, the folk be dancin', but why aren't there any of us folk joining in?"

"Us folk?"

"You know, Black folk."

I laughed nervously and said, "I don't know." I hopped up and danced a few more and was surprised that he was still sitting there when I returned to my spot. I gathered my nerves and asked, "Do you want to try it?"

He looked at me and raised his eyebrow in a questioning glare.

"You can follow my steps," I tried to assure him.

It was his turn to give off a nervous laugh, but we stood, walked over to the circle, and joined hands with the other dancers. The easy back-and-forth chain steps allowed him to learn a little. When the music stopped we sat back down.

"I'm Curtis, Curtis Jones."

"Maren, Maren Spencer."

"Right on, little sister," he said and held up a fist.

I wondered if his calling me "sister" would have come so easy, if he knew about the hate smoldering in my heart. Silence descended. What could I say to this guy. He was at least fifteen years older than me and smelled like sweat and garbage. I noticed the POW emblem sewn on his army jacket.

"You see my POW patch. That's for Prisoner Of War. You know that, right?"

I nodded.

"Well I never was one, not really. But might as well be now. I'm still living that hell, inferno, torture."

"Sorry," I said, wanting that word to mean more than just "sorry you were in Vietnam." I wanted it to say, "I'm sorry I've been hating all Black people." But I wasn't sure if I still did, or not. No one had threatened me for about two weeks. At least I was able to talk with this guy because he seemed harmless, but I wondered what he wanted from me. Should I worry? Maybe he was planning to steal my bike or follow me home, or something.

He stood up and walked over to a grocery cart. It was loaded with old stuff including a pile of dark clothes, odd junk like alarm clocks and pans and silverware, and heaps of cardboard. "These are my things. I work at Sam's Thrift Store," he said.

"Oh, I know that place. On Milpas, right? It's close to the

high school, sometimes I stop there after school . . . oh, never mind. What do you care?"

"That's the one. Stop by if you ever need a hand."

"What? Oh, no thanks," I said, shaking my head. "I don't need a hand."

"Little sister, you look like you need one more than I do."

Kate Porter

VIII

1975
Curtis Jones

B umping his grocery cart along the sidewalk, Curtis jogged eight blocks to Ruby's Market. After checking out the side alley for thugs, he parked the cart and walked through the store and into the back. He entered the room marked "Women Only." That's where Ruby kept her best soap. He rubbed two healthy globs of the aloe-rich cleaner into his palm then slathered it onto his three-day chin stubble. Some he rubbed along his temples where he still grew a little hair. Scraping the semi-sharp razor *scritch, scritch, scritch*, he knew he'd need to spend his money on new disposables, not on that pinstriped shirt he had his eye on at Sam's Thrift Store. The shirt was the one thing he really wanted. The one that would maybe get him off the street.

—Can I afford that shirt? Not yet, hell no. Got to buy me some damn razors.

For over a month, Curtis had been working at Sam's, so now the ten-percent employee discount was his. He thought of Sam as an uncle, but the guy had never let anyone shave in his shop's bathroom, even the one with "Niños" over the door.

"Shit," Curtis said as he nicked his upper lip. He walked into a stall to get some toilet paper but spotted a dollar bill on top of the empty dispenser. He tore a corner off the George

Washington, placed it on the blood spot, crammed the rest of the bill into his pocket, threw the dull disposable into the garbage, then swung the door open into Ruby's Market.

Since Curtis was a paying customer, Ruby's charity came without strings. He didn't steal from her like some did. He'd seen her give money to other homeless folk and watched them grab candy bars when her backside was turned. And what a fine ass it was; Curtis thought so anyway. He always loved a sister with a nice high behind.

With perfectly placed mirrors, Ruby could watch the counter, and some of the crazier guys thought she could actually see out of the back of her head. Many thieves she caught; some she didn't; others she probably ignored. Curtis saw the look of disappointment she gave one brother who came in almost every day and left eating an apple—an unpaid-for apple.

"Hey! That didn't grow on any tree I know of," she yelled. "Get back here and pay for that thing." The guy just shrugged and left.

On his way to the front of the store, Curtis grabbed a razor pack, a small box of granola, a cup of that new stuff called "yogurt," and a plastic spoon from the deli counter.

Ruby met him at the register. When she began to talk, he stood still and looked straight at her. Her smile grew with each word. "Oh, granola," she said. "I meant to put that on sale. This week, it's buy-one-get-one-free. Just watch the front for me, would you, Curtis?" She tore her gaze from his face and stepped away from the register. He noticed how she glided among the racks and returned with a second box.

He pulled the dollar out of his pocket. "Hey, this was in the head. Must be yours, and I'll say you're looking fine today, Miss

Ruby."

"Why thank you, Mr. Jones." She touched her eyebrow with a manicured fingertip. "Can't say that's mine. No name on it, is there? Seems to be your lucky day."

—Lucky day? Shit for luck. I hate to think of what unlucky is, luckless, jinxed, hapless, unfortunate, wretched.

Curtis kept his mind-lists to himself. At least he tried to. They rushed in uninvited and might linger for hours. Today was no different. When he came to the end of one list, he often shifted to a new but somewhat related thread. Or he might repeat the same string linking it to a drum beat. He needed lists ever since he returned from Vietnam. The minute he stepped off the plane he'd said, "Home," and added "house, hut, hovel," as a scene from the last skirmish he'd been in flashed into view. The Santa Barbara landscape of palm trees, tiled fountains, and land meeting the blue Pacific had faded to rice paddies and muddy bomb craters.

He gave a quick smile, paid for the goods, and then asked, "Can you double bag, please?" His fingers were tapping on the counter. "Sure thing," she said. The bags would come in handy as he could cut a few layers to put in his shoes. Loafers, sneakers, boots, spats *Tap tap tap tap . . . tap . . . tap* Loafers, sneakers, boots, spats *Tap tap tap tap . . . tap . . . tap* Loafers, sneakers, boots, spats. He picked up his bag, paid, and thanked her.

She asked, "Any plans?"

"Just trying to stay warm."

"Know what makes me warm?"

"What?" His tone not only said, "I want to know the answer," but also "did I hear you right?"

She looked at her fingernails. "Hugs from a handsome man."

"Miss Ruby, are you flirting with me?"

"Only if you want me to. Good day, Mr. Jones," she said.

"I will now. And I wish the same for you, Ruby," he said. Her

flirtation took him by surprise. They hadn't ever talked much, but he walked to the beat of his internal rhythm back to his cart. His head bobbed to that last list until he shifted to his favorite Stevie Wonder song.

—You are the sunshine of my life, yeah. Ruby is the sunshine of my life, yeah.

He could hear the words, but he was never a brother who could sing in tune, so he no longer belted out music in public. Didn't want to freak anybody out—no more than he already did. Even if he didn't see it happen, he could still feel when women swung their purses to their other shoulder, or when men guided their dates to the other side of the street, or when children stared and pointed.

The chilly sea breeze, colder than the previous night, had left a heavy dew that morning. It reminded him that he'd need more layers for his entire body, not just for his feet.

—Or find a second job, asshole.

This time, he would be determined to keep whatever work he could get. He'd been homeless for four years, and though he had become an expert at it, he still had further ambitions. The thrift store didn't pay enough to feed and clothe him, or more important, to get him rent money.

After arriving at Sam's Thrift Store, Curtis parked his cart where two others already sat wedged within an alcove. When he walked through the back door, he held his head high. His face was clean and he didn't stink. At least he didn't think so. Not like some of the other vets.

Sure, he'd been in Nam too, but that wasn't the problem. He had those lists. But lately, they rarely sent him into screaming fits where his mind went dark and his memory hurtled into horror. He'd never hurt anybody or himself when he'd sunk into those holes. Curtis noticed the other vets' stench, saw their rage, and swore to change his life.

His downward slide had come as fast as a cheetah on speed. All it took was the car accident, the concussion, being laid off from his job as a reporter, having money and marriage troubles, losing his wife and home, and here he was a backdoor Nigger at a junk store. He remembered the final thing he had said to his ex when she drove away in her paid-for-by-him VW van. "Christ, Aggie, I'd've given you the shirt off my back. The least you could do is leave me a few t-shirts."

He headed to the men's rack. Good. It was still there. The pinstripes would make him seem taller, and the cut would give him a broader appearance, and the collar, cuffs, and buttons would let him look like a professional. Even though he meant to not say his lists aloud, this one he let fly, "Capable, competent, able, skillful, masterful."

"Shut the fuck up, Jones. You'll drive me to drink," Sam said, grabbing his arm and giving his clean head a friendly slap. "Come with me, you old hound dog."

"Sorry boss-man, you know I don't want to be drivin' your sorry ass nowhere."

A huge pile of donations had arrived over the long weekend. Boxes of good stuff, sure, but also garbage. Some people must have thought Sam's was the local landfill. After one rainy weekend they'd found an entire bedroom set out back, from a rug on the bottom, all the way to the sopping wet mattress and red floral bedding on the top. Two end tables with lamps and a wind-up alarm clock rounded out an illusion of suburban bliss. Curtis had stripped off the linens and washed them in Sam's industrial washer. Then he'd driven the rest of the sopping mess to the actual landfill. Sam had let him drive his truck that day, but the poor guy had also lost good money on the load. "Got to take the good with the bad, poor, awful, distasteful—"

"Hey, I want you to move these boxes over there," Sam interrupted Curtis' list. "Sort through 'em. You know the drill." Sam hung clothes on hangers while Curtis got busy.

Most boxes held the regular crap: chipped and incomplete sets of dishes, old clothes, single balls of yarn, a tool or two, empty candy wrappers. Halfway through the morning, however, he looked up to see the young girl he'd met the day before out on Cabrillo Boulevard. The California sunshine had made her hair appear almost white, but now her blonde braids were strapped tight atop her head.

She held a box in her arms but didn't look directly at him. "You said if I needed a hand to stop by," she said.

"Yep, I did. What can I do for you?" Curtis hadn't expected ever to see her again. She'd said that she didn't need help, and her tone had expressed complete defiance. She looked to be about sixteen, but those sad eyes said, "I've seen a world of hurt." He knew what that felt like, and what it looked like too. He saw those same tired eyes when he looked in the mirror, only hers were blue and his as dark a brown as brown could be. For a kid to have bags under her eyes and a permanent frown too, what could have possibly happened to her?

"Look, don't ask me why," she said. "Just take this crap. Okay? I don't want to have to throw it away myself." Her face was red from rage or tears. Her jaw muscles pulsed from teeth clenching. "I'm done with this," she said, "and with my damn parents."

Throwing his hands up in surrender he said, "You got it, little sister." He lifted the box from her arms and felt its weight, about the same as a bag of oranges. The lid flaps were folded closed, so he checked the sides of the box On one, in black magic marker, it read, "Things for Maren." Oh yeah. "Maren, Maren Spencer. That's what you told me," he said and looked up to see that she was halfway down the aisle and moving fast. "Hey, anything good in here?" he called to her.

"Not really," she said but didn't turn around.

He shrugged, set the box down, and unfolded the lid. It appeared full of papers.

Curtis wasn't paid for his lunch hour, but like a lot of businessmen he took pride in his work ethic, so he often worked through lunch by sorting through boxes while he ate. He felt obligated to read the paper discards, especially those that once might have been important.

Noon rolled around, and after eating half his yogurt, he opened the granola and mixed some into the remaining yogurt tub. He wiped his hands on his pants and reached into Maren's box. The pile was topped by a canary-yellow mimeographed page with a heading, *The Star Spangled Revolutionary Press* and was dated, Sept. 13, 1970.

—Do I want to read this? Shit, yeah.

He placed it, and a few others with the same title, into a pile that he planned to pack into his grocery cart to read later. Next, he found a political button, and he traced his finger over its surface, outlining a map of Vietnam. Over it were bold letters, "OUT NOW."

—Being a soldier, shit, I wish I'd made a different choice, selection, decision, judgment.

The rest of the pile consisted of what looked like book reports and report cards. Trash. Under the stack, the box contained a few books. Curtis had read almost all of them, so he placed those in the book bin for later shelving.

—But then here's this other thing. Not a book, not exactly. A scrap pad? Musty mess? Forgotten relic?

A book with no cover, just crumbling cardboard sewn to a leather spine. He flipped it over and opened the back cover. A few pages were stuck together, so using his fingernail, he carefully separated the paper and discovered a roster of signatures and dates. This list contained writing in a wide range of script styles, from perfect calligraphy in faded ink to the final entry scribbled in ballpoint pen.

He finished off the rest of the yogurt-granola mix and read the names from the top:

Elizabeth Rose Sherman 1820-1825
William T. Sherman 1825-1880
Johanna Kristoffersdatter Skauge Nyhus 1880-1896
J. Marcus Newhouse 1896-1957
Louise Newhouse ~~Spencer~~ 1958-1969
Maren Spencer 1969-

Maren's signature contained no second date but was written in the capital letters of a small child. He pictured her in pigtails, her frown plastered on her face, even at the age of six. He wondered if the names and dates were when each of the signers owned the book, but there was no way to know.

On the facing page, he read an inscription:

> *To whomever shall open my pages and read my words,*
> *may thy life be abundant with beauty and grace.*
> *Alden Masters, Bookbinder, Virginia, 1820.*

—Beauty and grace, my ass. Maybe in 1820.

Curtis didn't know if he'd ever held anything as ancient as this battered thing. He opened it to a random page and read more:

> *Here is a carpenter, he squares a post or a beam; he scores or notches it first, and then hews it with his broad-ax. He bores holes with an auger, and with the help of a chisel, forms a mortise for a tenon. Each timber is fitted to its place. The sills support the posts and these support the beams. Braces secure the frame of a building from swaying or leaning.*

He appreciated the list-like format of that paragraph. While he read and munched through the rest of his hour, he thought that maybe Sam would let him have the old book since it was obviously in horrible shape.

—Dented, damaged, dilapidated, decapitated. Oh shit! Don't go down that fucking hole. Please! Killed, executed, murdered, dismembered...

He lunged from where he sat into the murky black. Dropped

deep to where the past swirled. The figure suddenly appeared in the dirt, cowering. His heart pounding in his ears. A hand reached for what seemed to be an AK-47. The weight of his M16. A drop of sweat stung his right eye. His finger on the trigger. The blast. His gun firing. The recoil. The person turning. A woman. The baby's face appeared from under a cloth. The woman's scream. A bullet sliced through its mark.

"Hey, Jones. You're here now, man," Sam was saying, his hands resting on Curtis' shaking shoulders.

Curtis fought to step away from the murky hollow. Tried to halt the sound of the woman's shrieking. He could still hear her. Why didn't she stop? In memory, the sound always lasted longer than when the shot actually left her writhing, then dead in the dirt. He sat as still as he could. He stared into the florescent lights overhead. Memories began to fade, again. Even the look of horror on the woman's face when, for an instant, she saw the bloody, mangled flesh where her baby's face had been. Even that began to fade. The mother's eyes, dull then blank, that image ended too. Two lives gone with a single shot. It wasn't the first or the last bullet Curtis had sent from his weapon during his time on the Mekong Delta. But it was the one he relived over and over, when awake and in his nightmares.

The horror slowly unwound from his vision. Until next time. Would there always be a next time? His lists—his escape—worked to lessen the frequency.

—This day might be different. Lucky? Fortunate, favorable, felicitous.

"Now, there's a good list," Curtis mumbled, bringing himself back. He remembered where he was and tossed the empty yogurt container toward the garbage barrel. It dropped in.

"Two points," Sam said, his voice reassuring.

Curtis looked at his left hand. He held the old book that had seemed to push him off the edge.

—I'll just toss this too. Don't want more stuff shoving me over.

Stepping toward the rusty oil barrel used for trash, though, he opened the book again. He didn't know why he did. Maybe it was the paragraph he'd read, and the list of names and dates it contained, he closed it again. Lists were his life. The book was garbage, but that barrel was destined for the landfill. He didn't feel right about throwing away any book, even one as old and worn out as that one, not into the landfill.

He looked over at Sam and asked, "Okay if I take this home, boss man?"

Sam glanced at the thing and nodded. "You know where I'd throw it, but suit yourself."

Curtis stashed it in his pocket for the rest of the day. On his way home that evening, he felt the book's soft cover and thought there seemed a potential for the thing to be a kind of mascot, buddy, friend, comrade, pal, brother. Those gentle words relaxed his worries the way mashed potatoes could. On the prior Easter, the soup kitchen had served a full meal including ham with all the fixings. He wondered if a traditional Thanksgiving turkey dinner would soon be served, or if the next holiday meal would just be chicken stew like the previous year. Potato and carrot soup, consommé, broth—he cut the food list short. It would only make him hungrier.

***

The roar of cars and trucks filtered through the night to where Curtis sat under the freeway. Four concrete columns loomed overhead resembling the legs of a massive creature. His home, a shelf of rock and dirt, contained room just big enough for his grocery cart and refrigerator box. After crawling through the cardboard-flap door, he hung his flashlight on a brass staple. The bent metal, which was the only built-in fixture, made life bearable. He could read.

"Don't hook my scalp," he said. "Be a useful hook, clip, catch, fastener." Curtis found comfort in this list, so rooted in solid, non-threatening nouns.

He threw himself onto a three-inch stack of his past corrugated houses that now served as a bed, then struggled with the flashlight's metal on-off switch that was corroded by four years of exposure. At forty, he didn't believe he was old enough to feel as achy as he did, but the same four years had taken their toll on his ankles and knees.

—Jones, my boy, you need a good lube, like the axles of your old VW. I'm way too sick of this shit.

When he'd lost everything, that van had been taken too, by his ex-wife, even though it was the first thing Curtis had bought after his tour in Nam.

With the light emitting a dull beam, he retrieved the hand-sized book from his pocket. The shabby remnant didn't have a leather or cloth cover but wore two crumbling ancient boards for protection. He opened the book and saw the first page number, 16. Printed in bold type along the top edge was the apparent title, *An Easy Standard*. Curtis chuckled and said, "Doubt that's the whole of it. More like *An Easy Standard of Bullshit*." Down the page these words caught his attention:

Art thou a brother? Is thy brother in adversity?
Assist him.

"Hell, yeah, this Black brother's 'in adversity.' So, where the fuck's my assistant?" A screech of brakes broke his concentration. He sat still, awaiting the inevitable crunch of metal. None arrived. Not this time. And no accompanying scream from his neighbor, either. Curtis had seen her leave when the sun began to hit her box, limping away in her unlaced army boots, pushing a baby stroller, same as every other morning. But her hour to return never followed a pattern. Not one he detected. Was she dead? He scratched his stubbly chin.

—Will anyone care when I'm dead, departed, lifeless, a rotting corpse?

Feeling rage slithering into his throat, he veered his attention from the danger of that menacing list and back to what he held in his hands. The book's floppy pages had rounded corners and were broken by many splits and tears. Its mildew odor blended with the riot of smells emanating from his bed. He stifled a sneeze and read more.

In troy weight, twenty-four grains make a pennyweight—twenty pennyweights, one ounce — and twelve ounces, one pound. These are the divisions used by the metal smith.

"Smith, Jones, Johnson, pecker, dick," he said mixing his words with a raucous laugh.

"Shut the fuck up!" his neighbor screamed.

"Ah, she lives on," he whispered and clapped the book shut.

"Should've let Sam throw you away." While he wondered how many other people had almost thrown the old thing away, he ran his fingers along the book's spine and counted five thick stitches. Who the hell had fixed the thing? And why? He poked a finger through a hole in his pants. He'd never considered sewing up his jeans—not when a better pair could be found at Sam's. Newer books could be found there too. Curtis knew because he was one of Sam's homeless vets hired to do odd jobs, and his task was to shelve the paperbacks, 8-track tapes, and cassettes.

He opened the book again and ran his fingers over the paper. It felt as soft as his faded jeans. "You were made to weather a shit-storm." He turned to a new page. Half of it fell onto his lap. "Man, you're as pathetic as I am."

But he knew words, written or not, held power. His lists kept him sane and, before the war, he'd been a reporter. Just four years earlier. Clutching the crumpled book to his chest, he wondered what story the book would tell if it could.

He yelled toward his neighbor, "You've survived this long. Who am I to judge your sorry ass?"

Curtis knew about being judged. A black man pushing a grocery cart along a sidewalk parted pedestrians like Moses parted the Red Sea. He waited for his neighbor's response. None arrived. After placing the book in his shoe box where he kept toothpaste and toilet paper, he shut off the flashlight and rested his head on a folded jacket. In the morning, he'd read more. His eyes closed as the freeway roar retook the night.

He hoped no rain would hit tonight in Santa Barbara County. On a TV at Sam's, a clean-shaven guy had said there was only a thirty percent chance of precipitation. He could trust those meteorologist dudes. They were always right. He chuckled. His box was marked "Frigidaire" on the outside, and it had twice as much room as the last one. The old box was now under him, an added inch to his three-inch-thick cardboard bed. Even if it rained he should stay dry. This was his final thought before sleep arrived.

***

Cold toes woke him up in the morning since he'd kicked off his one blanket, and he'd forgotten to wear socks to bed. He pulled the book from his shoebox and switched on the flashlight. Crude linen stitches lashed the calfskin spine together.

—Too bad someone can't fix my brain that easy. He sent a wish into the night: I want a home with a shelf for books. My life is shelved, suspended, postponed, delayed.

"*An Easy Standard*. Damn! A real creative-thought killer, slayer, murderer." He sat up. When a bad list began, sometimes changing positions helped to stop it. His heart pounded against his ribs like a jackhammer, so he knew he'd come close. But the list did stop. This time. He ran his fingertips over a page, a rougher texture than the paper in modern bestsellers. More rag content. Nineteenth century paper. Curtis flopped a few pages over. That's when he discovered this text:

Coins of the United States

> *Ten dimes make a dollar, ten dollars an eagle, which is a gold coin, and the largest which is coined in the United States. Dimes and dollars are silver coins.*

On another page was a heading: Inhabitants of the United

States. Below this, a list of census figures for the years 1790 to 1810. The column for 1820 had no figures. He realized it must have been made sometime between 1810 and 1820. Yeah, that was right; it was signed in 1820 by the bookbinder. In the column dated 1820 three states were listed: Alabama, Missouri, and Floridas. Floridas with an "S"? Curtis made a mental note to look up Florida history in Sam's 1959 encyclopedia. The complete Britannica was on sale for five bucks.

He sneezed.

"Shut up, asshole!" invaded his space. Even though they hardly spoke, Curtis kept track of his neighbor. She had the right to live as much as the next person.

Curtis took a whiff of the book, smelled the problem, mildew, and stifled another sneeze. Returning his attention to the 1790 census figures, he read that 3,929,326 people lived in sixteen states and the territory northwest of Ohio. To the left of those numbers he quietly read this:

Of these are Slaves—697,696

A cold chill scurried down his spine. Images raced to his mind of beatings, iron chains, the horrors of slavery he knew his ancestors had endured.

Two columns over, the figures for 1810 showed a total population of seven million, and the slave count had risen to more than one million.

—One in seven were slaves, hostages, captives, prisoners.

Curtis stiffened his back and waited. Another dark list stifled. He hoped.

"You're a hundred-fifty years old, my friend," he whispered, set the book on his chest, and noticed how old he felt. His bed seemed to grow more uncomfortable, no matter how many layers he managed to add. He picked up the book again and looked at its worn-out cover. There, in ink faded to a soft brown, was a name, Elizabeth R Sherman. A new image leapt into view, of a girl studying in a stuffy parlor. The writing style, full of curly letters, was not like anything done in the 1970s. Calligraphy took patience and practice, much more than any kid seemed to have. In spite of its title and dilapidated condition, the book was turning out to be interesting. "You have a story to tell," he said.

The wail of a siren snatched his attention, but no screams blared to go along with it. Perhaps she'd left early to find a fix. Sometimes, because he had his eye on her grocery cart, he hoped she would just disappear. Her cart's four wheels rolled straight, and its plastic handle still commanded "RETURN TO THE STORE." No rust either. She'd obviously grabbed hers from some parking lot. Rust fell from his cart's underbelly like soot falls from a dirty chimney pipe. He'd found it at the landfill when he'd taken a load there for Sam.

Curtis said, in a near yell, "I ain't never stole nothing from nobody. Ain't gonna start now, just 'cause times are hard."

He wondered if times were hard in the early 1800s, maybe not for some, but for most Black folk, definitely. Bummer that he couldn't travel to that time. He thought it would be a gas to talk with that Elizabeth Sherman. As a reporter, Curtis had interviewed people when he'd written profile articles for a weekly rag. He enjoyed finding out about local people doing local things. Then, during an interview with an heiress to a shock absorber company, he'd ranted aloud a mind-list that should have stayed inside: "Wealthy, rich, prosperous, bourgeois, money-grabbing bastards." The woman was an interesting interview and accepted his apology. He returned to the office and wrote a great piece about her collection of pewter tankards, but the next day his editor called him into his office. He handed him a box of stuff from his desk, and told Curtis to pick up his last paycheck on Friday. The woman had demanded he be fired.

It stung because he loved to write. All of what he loved then began to be pulled away. As Curtis recalled the day his life had dumped him in the gutter, he said to himself, "That day was terrible, awful, shocking, staggering." Writing rode out on a current of surrender, submission, resignation, compliance. A new truth slithered into his mind. "I didn't have any fight left. Shit, no. Already had too many battle wounds that weren't scarred over yet."

His hand holding the book dropped onto a metal box, which he kept beside his bed. *Clink.* His heart seemed almost to skip a beat. He sat up straighter and flipped the book onto its back and reopened it.

He again read silently the Alden Masters inscription then the opposite page: Elizabeth R. Sherman, William T. Sherman, Johanna—

—Wait, William T. Sherman? William Tecumseh Sherman. Isn't that right? Hey, maybe you're worth some actual money.

He recalled learning about the Civil War general, the guy who'd been so hated by the South for burning Atlanta. He scanned down the list again. Long ago, Curtis had interviewed a guy who bought and sold old books in a dingy, crowded store on lower State Street. The shop-keep, Jeremy, had some prized first editions, many of them signed by the author. One was by Curtis' favorite jazz poet, Langston Hughes. Curtis had stayed in touch with Jeremy because the guy had shown him some charity, by treating him like a human being—not like a worthless bum.

"Are you rare, uncommon, precious, valuable?" He drummed the book with his fingertips. "I'm gonna see my friend, my old bearded friend. Jeremy's his name. Be waitin' for him, waitin' on his steps, a-waitin' and a-holdin' my book in my hand."

After pocketing the book, he put on his shoes and crawled through the flap and into a morning shimmering in Southern California sunshine.

***

Limited-N-Rare, Jeremy's store, was supposed to open at 10:00 a.m. That's what the sign said, but Curtis was there and Jeremy wasn't. He sat in the two-feet-wide space between buildings, in front of his grocery cart, and watched a bird hopping along a roof gutter.

—You live on the street too. But you get a lot more respect than I do, brother.

He whistled and drummed the Aretha Franklin tune, R-E-S-P-E-C-T.

From the inside, Jeremy finally unlocked the door. As he walked through the doorway, Curtis noticed the distinct odor of musty paper, permeating the air. He waited at the counter while the shop owner propped the door ajar with a wooden sign that read, " Sunday Sale 25% off—paperbacks 25¢" Curtis knew Jeremy bumped up prices so he could lower them for his perpetual sale. He also knew the guy could be haggled with. In fact, Jeremy's scowling expression seemed to say that anyone

313

who didn't haggle was an idiot.

—Imbecile, moron, stupid ass.

"Jer, I've got something here, poor condition, but signed," Curtis said.

"By the author?"

"No, but somebody famous, William T. Sherman. It's here in the back."

Jeremy's left eyebrow shot up as he held out his hand. He took the book from Curtis and placed it in a velvet-covered wooden stand, which supported both covers. With the book opened, he reached for a set of weights and quickly chose the correct one: just heavy enough to keep the book open and not so heavy it would harm the fragile spine. With his magnifier that hung around his neck, he peered through the curved glass at the page Curtis showed him. "Huh. Easy to see it isn't printed—it's an actual penned signature. But I've got to look up what Sherman's handwriting looks like. It'll take a minute. Is it really General Sherman's? That's the question." He stepped around from behind the counter. "Remember, Mr. Jones, don't touch just dream." Jeremy walked down a shelf-lined aisle and out of sight.

Curtis stepped behind the counter to look at the "rare" books. Some were large leather-covered tomes about polar exploration, some ragged Civil War diaries, and others books about female etiquette. He loved the spines because all had that weathered, old-color hue. No psychedelic greens, reds, or blues like the books he shelved for Sam. One spine here had a woman in a floor-length Victorian gown, and many contained gold-leaf border designs and titles.

—Too bad my book isn't fancy like these. Probably would be worth more dough.

"Okay," Jeremy said, walking back. "We don't have General Sherman's signature here."

"Shit," Curtis said under his breath, trying to not let his shoulders slouch as he stepped to the customer side of the counter.

"Yeah, too bad. But we do have one of possible interest— Alden Masters." Jeremy placed an open reference book on the counter. "Says here Alden Masters was one of England's finest bookbinders. Who knows if this is the same guy, or what his signature is worth. Maybe a couple hundred, maybe three? You know, in the right auction. Makes you wonder, though, how in the world did his inscription get to be in this ratty old thing? Or if it's even him." Jeremy gave Curtis one of his scowls.

"A few hundred?" Curtis said, with indignation. "This thing's old, man. I wouldn't let it go for less than five."

Jeremy's you're-an-idiot-if-you-don't-haggle scowl disappeared. "Well, you see it's obviously made in America, and was a product that was certainly produced in large numbers, by hand, but it wouldn't be considered rare. The signature might be historically significant. If you could prove it was that Alden Masters fellow, well . . ." He pointed with his white-gloved hand at the signature. He always wore a glove if a book might be valuable. Curtis saw this as a good sign, but it made him chuckle inside because a few more fingerprints weren't going to ruin this book.

"Who knows? I could give you . . ." Jeremy began again and scratched his thick, brown beard with his ungloved hand. "Well, I can part with a hundred bucks."

"What? No way, man."

"Look, I'd be taking a risk. You just don't know."

"What about the other signatures?"

"Well, none of those seem to be anybody significant. Definitely has got some age to her, made in 1820, but the condition, that makes all the difference. But then, Mr. Jones, you know that."

Curtis looked down at the book, at its worn-out pages, at the signatures ranging from old script written in ink dipped from a well, to the final name—Maren Spencer. He knew he couldn't sell the book, even though one hundred dollars would be an amazing windfall. "I'm going to keep it, Jer," he said and slipped it back into his pocket. "Sorry, man. Maybe next time."

"If you change your mind, you know where I am." Jeremy shrugged but added, "It could be good enough for a collector, somewhere. Maybe of interest in England, or to a university or something. Stuff at auction's kind of slow right now, so you might be smart to hang on to it until things turn around. When it feels right to you, stop back and I'll let you know if things have turned around."

As he left the shop, Curtis felt the book thumping against his leg and noticed the comfort it gave him. He pushed his cart back to the overpass, feeling grateful that it was Sunday. Sam's was closed, so no work. He'd read and go to that church where a free meal could be had. He crawled back into his box and tossed the book onto his bed. That strange sound, a muffled *clink* hit his ears, again. Earlier, he'd assumed it was something else that had made the noise, so he hadn't checked it out, but now he scanned the area. Nothing could explain the noise. No bottle caps, no soda cans, no trash. Not in his box. Curtis kept a clean house.

He lifted the book, opened it, closed it, and dropped it on the cardboard floor. *Clink.* He ran his fingers over the covers and spine then noticed a slight thickening of the surface along the back. He sat down, opened it, and probed the inside of the back cover. Tucked into a flap running the length of the book was a folded paper. He took it out and felt its surprising weight. Inside the creases lay two coins. He turned the flashlight on and held them close to the beam. One was a Buffalo nickel.

—What's this? This other one, maybe . . . wait . . . maybe it's gold?

Reading the raised letters on the coin's surface, he whispered, "One Stella 400 cents, four dollars." His heart sped up. He'd never heard of a four-dollar coin. Curtis held it in the palm of his hand. The weight was much heavier than the nickel, but the gold piece was only slightly larger. "Gold? I think so," he said, staring at it until he remembered the paper. The page, a letter, was handwritten on both sides in tiny uniform script. The letters were so tiny he had to shine his flashlight directly at the script, hold it close to his face, and squint to read it.

My dear Maren,   22, Feb. 1958

Since you're the only baby in my Lou's family, I figure you're the one to receive these treasures, my only precious things.

This little old book has a history all its own. I don't suppose anyone will think it's valuable, but I can't live another day knowing that it could be lost, you know, if I were suddenly pushing up daisies. This is all I know, along with how important it was to me when a friend, William T. Sherman, gave this book to me.

Long before I was born, this old thing belonged to a dirt-farmer and his wife in Virginia. On their daughter's birthday, they gave it to her when it was brand-spanking new. Her name was Elizabeth, and because her parents drowned less than a year later, I was told that she treasured this thing something fierce. She later became one of those Suffragette ladies, just like my Aunt Maren, the one you were named for. They paraded all over town and carried signs for their right to vote. But before Elizabeth got that far along, she gave the book to a Colored boy, my friend William. It was a secret, you see (and would have been a big fat scandal) but they were in love. I just can't imagine a Colored boy and a White girl together, but he told me she called him Willy T. The T was for Turnbull (his slave master's name), and he said that he'd gotten his new last name from her along with this book.

Curtis leaned against a cardboard wall. It shifted, so he slouched onto the bed. Well, there it was; the "T" was for Turnbull. He thought about how his common last name, Jones, had always felt like a dead weight. Maybe that was sort of how Willy Turnbull felt, like that name was a chain around his ankle, keeping his soul working for the boss. Curtis continued to read.

You can bet he had a terrible childhood living in Virginia in the early part of the '20s, that's the 1820s. His being a slave on the Turnbull plantation. From way back, his kin were slaves. But he got freed and educated all the way up through high school. He even went part ways through college and married another ex-slave just like himself, a girl named Dinah.

Years later, he ended up rooming at our boarding house in Minnesota. I think about when I was a boy, and I can see him plain as day, sitting by his window telling me stories. I was so lucky to know the man, to spend a good part of my childhood hearing his tales. Some of them seemed far-flung. Like him claiming to write for a Negro newspaper. Whoever heard of such a thing.

Anyways, a more gentle, caring soul I have yet to meet. I only wish I could have become a better man. I could have made him proud. He showed me how important an education was. But then, I wasted my life on drink. It's just mighty unfortunate to have never made it past the sixth grade.

Didn't stop learning, though, I'll give myself that. And I have Mr. Sherman to thank for it. You see, his love of books, of learning how people think and how they choose to live, and the fact that he read more books than most folks, all that did impress me. I have no excuses. Maybe it's guilt that drove me to read lots. In my sixty-plus years, I don't know how many books, but there are more than I care to count.

One last thing about my old friend. He was missing something big—one of his legs. Don't know how it got lost because he'd never tell me that particular business. He seemed pretty much embarrassed when I asked about it.

Mr. Sherman passed the book along to my mother Johanna Skauge Newhouse. He wanted her to learn to read. She'd came on a ship from the old country, and when she first got here, she didn't know a word of English. None. She and my father arrived with their families on the docks, carrying a few trunks. But they lost them. Imagine stealing from folks when they're in the pox quarantine. Uff da.

"Uff da," Curtis said, trying on this strange word. "Shit, yeah. It feels good, flinging it out of your mouth like spit." He listened again for sounds of his neighbor, then he remembered. It was Sunday, and the first Sunday of the month was fish day at the shelter. "Uff da, I missed it." He wondered if that was a proper usage of the word. Wondered if a Black brother using that word would be kind of like a White guy trying to talk hip. He chuckled. "Back to reading, you fool."

Anyway, she was the one he gave the book to, and the one who sewed it to its present cover. Hard to believe it was in worse shape before.

My mother never learned to read enough to value words. Seemed kind of ironic since folks like her were probably why the book was written in the first place. But I made up for it. There were many years when I slept with this old rag tucked in bed with me. When Mr. Sherman passed to the world beyond, what was printed in the book kept him close to my heart. Hate to admit it, but he was more my dad than my own.

I've told my Lou all the stories. Check with her. Your mother may be able to fill in somewhere I'm lacking. I'll be surprised if she remembers much, though. But don't blame her. Life just gets in the way sometimes. She's been so wrapped up in moving, trying to have babies, and putting up with that husband of hers. Sorry, but I see right through that frat-boy. Course no man would be good enough for my Lou. He's not all bad I suppose. He's a mighty fine card player and provider for you. Better than me. So who am I to be the judge and jury? Sorry, I shouldn't talk about your father that way.

Another thing, the gold coin I'm stowing away here, it was Mr. Sherman's too. There's an important thing about that coin. It was bought from some congressman with slave money, so that means somebody earned it by selling slaves.

"Cool," Curtis said, letting out a long breath and grabbing his jacket to put it on. "Colder tonight," he said.

"Shut the fuck up, asshole!"

Curtis, so enthralled with the letter, hadn't noticed her return. "Sorry, scumbag!" he yelled back, feeling glad she had alerted him she was back before he'd had a chance to say something he would have regretted.

—Regret. I bet my ancestors had themselves some powerful regret. Those who'd been slaves.

He didn't know much family history, except that some of his people had lived in Georgia. After emancipation they'd stayed on a plantation, until his great-grandpa finally left at the age of twelve, then later he'd made it through high school. He was the first, and was the one who'd headed west.

—This book's gone west too, with a piece of slave gold tucked in its pocket. Bet great-grandpa Jones didn't have any gold in his pockets.

Curtis felt he'd inherited something from that man, a want for more education. "Shit. I was going to be the first one to get myself a college degree." Maybe it wasn't too late. Feeling a sense of urgency to get on with the job, he quickly read the rest of the letter.

> So this little thing's yours now, Maren. You're only a baby, but we share our birthday. So think of me as you grow up and when you grow old. You and I are stuck together in a special way and to the past that came before. Through this book, through these pages, I pass what I know to you. Where this book travels, on its next journey, is up to you.
>
> Yours,
> Grandpa J. Marcus Newhouse

Curtis turned the letter back over and reread the first line, "My dear Maren." The girl might have her own regret, having donated the box of her things. She might end up like him, someday, without anything but the junk that could be pushed around. This letter from her grandfather was so full—so full of love. He wondered if she'd known it was tucked inside the book. How could anyone leave a gold coin at a junk store?

What he owned was worthless: a collection of cardboard,

brown bags, books, toilet paper, shaving stuff, and used-up clothes. He felt no connection to these things. None. His thoughts drifted to his deceased parents and to Sam and his thrift store, and to Ruby, the beautiful Black sister who ran the market. He longed to be closer to people and to have the support of others. Living alone seemed inhumane. "I-N-H-U-M-A-N-E," he spelled the word aloud but didn't feel compelled to make a mind list. He lived like an animal in a cardboard cage. "Sam and Ruby are my friends, more than friends. They are my family. My chosen family." He knew he loved them, but they didn't know.

He looked at the Buffalo nickel, dated 1938. He turned it over to the Indian head side of the coin and felt sure it wasn't worth anything. He refolded the coins into the letter, tucked them back into the book, slipped it into his jacket pocket, and laid the bundle under his head for a pillow. If the gold turned out to be worth a lot, he'd find a way to share the wealth with Sam and Ruby, his chosen family.

—Wealth? Who am I kidding?

Later that night in his box, he devised a plan. After working at Sam's, he'd go to the phone booth by the Santa Barbara Hotel. It still had a phone book attached by a chain because it sat in the open where tourists ambled by. Most booths had books with missing pages, but that one was reliably intact. He hoped "Spencer" wasn't too common a name. Also he had a second name to try, "Newhouse." The year before, the cost of a call had gone up from ten to fifteen cents.

—What a rip-off. I'll need quarters. Maybe I should scrap the whole idea, could get expensive. What do I care?

But he pictured Maren's sad, tired eyes. How he instantly felt that the girl's life was shit. Maybe worse than his. He knew

323

he'd at least give her back the letter.

—The gold coin? Well, maybe I'll keep that and just give the little sister the nickel. It's cool with the Indian head on one side and the buffalo on the other.

His hand started moving to the rhythm of Aretha Franklin's song, "Chain of Fools."

" . . . Every chain, has got a weak link
I might be weak, yeah,
But I'll give you strength
Chain, chain, chain,
Chain of fools . . ."

***

Curtis placed another quarter in the slot and dialed the second number listed for L Newhouse. A dime slid into the return slot, he retrieved it for the next call. He'd already spent ninety cents and twenty-five minutes, on the Spencer listings, and hadn't found her.

"Hello?" a female voice answered.

"Hello, is Maren there?"

"She's . . . um . . . she's visiting her sick grandmother. Can I take a message?"

He started drumming his fingers on the white pages. "So this is the right number?"

"Yep, but she's . . . she's not here . . . wait. Who's calling?"

"My name's Curtis Jones. I'm—"

"Oh," she interrupted but hesitated. "I thought I should pretend that I'm my mom. It's me, Maren. I'm alone, so, um, what do you want?"

Curtis heard irritation in her voice, but he sighed with relief. "Little sister, listen. There's something in your box you might want to have. I know you said to just chuck it all, but there's a letter. It's from your grandfather. And a coin." Curtis sighed again, this time heavily. "I meant to say, two . . . two coins." He wasn't quite able to lie about it. Just because his great-great grandparents had been slaves, and the coin had been bought with slave money, those facts didn't add up to make it more his.

"Coins? You can have 'em. Why should I care?"

Curtis wondered what to add to make her understand. He knew if she'd just see the things, they'd show her what he already felt. This crap was some important shit. Silence descended and he waited.

"Um, okay wait . . . " she hesitated. "Did you say a letter?"

"They were all stuck together in an old book. It's one from the early eighteen hundreds, a really messed up thing."

"Sure. Yeah, I remember it. Mom kept trying to make me read it. But it's just filled with garbage about how people should live and what they should think—and mostly about what they shouldn't do. I called it 'An Easy Standard of Bullshit.'"

Curtis couldn't believe she'd just said that. He'd given it the exact same title. But then he'd discovered it held lessons in disguise. "That is one way to look at it, but the letter talks about the book's journey and who owned it. A slave had it for a while, then your great-grandmother. Seems like it meant something to them. Maybe it's a family treasure. I think you should keep the letter at least, it's addressed to you and . . ." He realized he'd just said "should," right after she'd complained that the book told people what they should and shouldn't do. Again, silence. He knew she was still on the line, but wasn't talking. "Look, I can

325

bring them to you, if you want," he said. "Or better, let's meet somewhere. You don't know me, but I won't mess with you, little sister. I promise. Let's meet at the coin shop on De La Vina near Mission street. Do you know it?"

"Why?" Her voice quavered. "I just don't want . . . don't want to have anything to do with my family . . . ever."

Curtis wished he knew how to deal with a teenager's feelings. But he didn't. Soft crying sounds came over the phone. He'd grown up as an only child, he never had kids, and he certainly never experienced being a girl. "I hear you, and I'm sorry. That's cool. Hey, I have a friend, her name's Ruby, and I'm sure she'll come with me if you want her to." As he pictured Ruby's soft smile and gentle ways, he felt a longing he'd forgotten existed. He wished he could hop in a car and ride over to her market, that she'd want to go for a ride and have a talk, one that would lead to more.

He halted his fantasy and took a couple of seconds to reconsider keeping the gold—could be worth enough to buy that car. But he couldn't lie—not about slave money. "Look, one of the coins is gold, a four-dollar piece from 1879," he said. "It's a 'Stella,' whatever that means." Glancing to the left, Curtis saw he wasn't alone. A guy with a camera around his neck, tan shorts, and black socks and loafers stood behind him. The tourist mouthed something that ended with the words "filthy Negro" as he glared at Curtis.

"Listen, Maren, it might be worth a couple hundred. Don't you want to find out? At least you should—" He waved his middle finger at the guy behind him and collected his thoughts before continuing. "You gotta see it. The girl on it reminds me of you. She's really pretty and her hair's all wrapped up on top of her head and—"

"I'm not sure if I want any of it."

"Little sister, are you always this stubborn, or just with us Black brothers?"

"I'm not stubborn," she said. "Can we just hurry up? I've got something to do."

"What's so important that you can't hang on a sec?"

"Not that it's your business, but finals are next week. I might not pass English. If I don't, I won't graduate." Then she whispered, "Did you say a letter?"

"Yes, I did." Curtis knew then that she would meet him. "Hey, bring your books. I meant to be a journalism major, before I got drafted. Reading and music are what I groove on. Bet I could help." He heard a click, and an operator's voice interrupted, asking him to deposit another fifteen cents. He obeyed with two dimes, even though it seemed like a waste since the call was probably almost over.

"Well, okay," Maren said. "What's the name of the place? Oh, and could we meet on the weekend? My mom isn't, um, never mind. I'll get there. Not during school hours though."

Curtis mentioned Ruby again and how he'd need to arrange a time with her, too. He glanced toward the tourist and saw that the guy must have left but was now returning with a bellhop from the hotel.

"Bye, Curtis," Maren said. "And . . . well . . . thanks for drinking with me." At least that's what he thought he'd heard. Her voice had become almost too soft to hear. He thought about it, though, and knew she must have said, "Thanks for thinking of me."

"No sweat, little sister," he said, hung up, checked the coin slot and grabbed the nickel, jangled the three quarters still in his pocket, opened the phone-booth door, stepped out, and walked quickly away.

"The next time I see you here, I'll call the cops," a gruff voice yelled as Curtis turned a corner toward home.

He parked his cart for the evening behind his box and sat beside the outer cardboard wall to read the letter again. He squinted in the half-light and held the paper close to his face. The tiny letters were as even as letters typed in a book. They reminded him of the copy of *A Tale of Two Cities* he'd borrowed from the library—the one he'd later returned, unread. The print had been too small. Sure, he owned a flashlight for reading, but he would have used up an entire six pack of batteries to get through that book. Batteries were valuable—like gold—to a man with no other light source. Too expensive for something that gets used up. Instead, he'd borrowed a copy of Steinbeck's *The Grapes of Wrath*. Now that was an old book he'd enjoyed reading, so much so that he'd kept it for a few months and read it several times.

He picked up the scrappy old book and opened it to the back, again. William Turnbull Sherman, Willy T. He liked the guy's name, felt like it had good rhythm to it.

—Willy T's a comin' to my rescue. Yes, Willy T's a man I wish I'd known.

The gold piece rested in his hand, and he marveled at its weight. It was little but defied its size and felt similar to a small lead fishing weight. "As heavy as my heart," he said and thought about Maren who had a mother who loved and cared for her.

—She'll grow up, get married, have kids, and never live alone. Living alone is inhumane.

Just then, Curtis realized his mind hadn't drifted to a mind list. The word "alone" often drove him to that dark hole and buried him there, sometimes for hours. "Solitary, lonesome, abandoned . . ." he said, his voice barely audible. This time, the list floated outside his body, not just because he'd said the words aloud, but because this time he didn't hold them captive in anger and regret. He didn't feel any fear of stepping into the dark hole of memory.

That same list, just the week before, had swirled him in brain fog, right when he'd been crossing a street. The traffic had stopped, horns had honked, and a young mother holding a baby in her arms had stepped around him and slung her child to the far side of her body. He knew why she did that, but if she'd actually known that he'd killed a baby, she would have shrieked with horror.

"Today, I haven't made a single mind list. Not one drummed list.".

***

On Saturday morning, Curtis put on the new-to-him pinstriped shirt. The day before, he'd splurged and bought it. With his discount, it had come to only $2.70. And he'd dabbed on some cologne from a bottle he'd spotted mis-shelved in the pots-and-pans department.

Maren had arrived at the coin shop first and was sitting cross-legged next to her bicycle. Her long, blonde hair flowed down past her shoulders. Curtis nodded toward her and said to Ruby, "There's the little sister."

"She looks older than I thought," Ruby whispered as she placed her hand on Curtis' arm.

They'd never touched before, except when his fingers grazed her palm while paying at the market. She gently squeezed, sending a shockwave of pleasure through his body. His anticipation of what more he wanted grew. His skin felt her skin. Curtis smiled, picked up her hand, and interlaced his fingers with hers, relishing the radiating warmth. Four years had passed since he'd felt the urgent rush now speeding deep within his body. He also felt the old book, with his other hand, resting in his pocket.

His hands were both occupied, right then, but he felt a need to reach out in a third direction—to Maren, if her need would allow him. Someday. He wondered if this is what a dad might feel, being pulled in many directions, each one needing, no, requiring his attention.

Maren stood up. Her eyes stared at the ground, not at them, even when she said, "Hi." Her shoulders seemed drawn together toward the front by some cold worldly weight.

He introduced Ruby to Maren then added, "We're all here. Let's see what we can make of it."

They walked into the coin shop and up to the counter. "Jeremy, sent me. Bruce around?" Curtis asked the guy behind the counter.

"Yep. In the back. I'll get him," said the kid with greasy hair, then he walked through a door, slammed it hard, and disappeared into an unseen room. "Dad," he yelled. "There's people out here. Jeremy sent 'em." Some incoherent response was heard, then the kid's loud voice, again. "No. It's a Black couple with a White kid."

Curtis glanced at Maren. She had her arms crossed and a deep furrow creased her forehead.

The door flew open, and an older man with a loupe up to one

eye strode in. "Jeremy sent you?" he asked with no hint of a salesman's pleasantries. "What do you people want?"

Curtis cringed at "you people" and wanted to walk away, but Jeremy had said the guy knew his stuff, more than anyone else in Santa Barbara County, so he shrugged it off. He knew how. He'd had a lifetime of practice. "I have two coins. One's a Buffalo nickel, the other's gold. It's a Stella," he said.

Bruce's loupe dropped from his eye. It swung like a pendulum from its cord. He gripped the side of the glass case in front of him. Rows of coins on a rotating louver system began to turn slowly within the display. The levels contained multiple little cardboard sleeves, each holding an individual coin. Curtis watched the shelves as they changed, level by level.

The shop owner pushed a button to stop the movement and cleared his throat. "Did you say, 'a Stella,' sir?"

Curtis nodded. "Dated 1879. We might want to sell it."

"Holy crap," Bruce said, pulling up a stool but nearly falling to the floor as he attempted to sit down. "I never thought a Stella would walk into my shop, not today. Not on any day, no sir." He shifted to be perched squarely on the stool. "Is she with you?"

"Right here." Curtis let go of Ruby's hand and brought out the book. He freed the letter and the two coins. After handing the letter to Maren, she slid to the floor, carefully unfolded the paper, and began to read. He recognized her immediate reverence of the thing. Her eyes quickly moved down the paper, and he couldn't stop watching her. She paused, looked up at him, and beamed.

—Look what her mother was missing. Why didn't she come?

Curtis carefully laid the coins on a purple felt pad, which had obviously been placed on the glass countertop for that purpose. The nickel, though almost the same size, looked worthless next to the glittering gold.

"Holy crap," Bruce repeated. "Her hair's up in a coil. You know what that means?" He glanced at Curtis, who shook his head. "You, sir, are about to get a whole lot richer." He spun around, grabbed his son by the arm, and brought him closer to see the coin. "Only about fifteen or so of these suckers in the entire world. One turns up now and again, but rarely. Not in my shop. This here's what we numismatists call a 'white whale.' She only weighs in at about six grams, but it doesn't matter. It's the rarest coin I've ever been . . ." Sweat slithered down Bruce's temples. "Man, I never thought I'd be in the same room with her. Never. Seen pictures of her, sure, but to be in her presence. This here's a holy miracle."

Curtis picked up Ruby's hand again and held tighter. He didn't know what to think. The coin really belonged to Maren, or maybe to Sam. After all, it had been donated to Sam's store. Sam had bills to pay and helped many homeless people, so it might be a fitting place for the money to end up. Besides, right there, with Ruby beside him, feeling sane in the head with no lists pushing him around, he didn't feel poor enough to fight for it.

"Do you hear me, man?" Bruce asked. "You're rich. I have to look her up, but I'd guess about half-a-mil richer."

Maren jumped up from the floor. "Half a million? Is that what you said?"

"Yes, Miss, half-a-million bucks. Five-hundred big Gs. Maybe more! Depends on the price of gold, what someone'll pay, the condition of her surfaces, what auction you decide to place . . ." Bruce put the loupe back up to his eye and glanced at the coin. "A few imperfections, but not too bad." He paced behind the counter. "Everyone's going to want her. Have to call Christie's or maybe Sotheby's. Get her insured. Put her in a safe. Can't let her walk down the street." Bruce strode behind the counter like a caged mountain lion, all the while ranting about how the coin had been pulled from circulation by Congress, and how the weight of it didn't match some coin in the Latin Monetary Union. And he mentioned his ten percent finder's fee six times while pointing his finger at the coin.

Curtis and Maren searched each other's faces. Bruce's words drifted to a droning background.

"It's really yours, little sister," Curtis said, placing a hand on her shoulder.

"We should split it in half," she said. "My grandpa said it was slave money."

"Well, bought with slave money, sure, but that's ancient history. I have no real right to it." He watched as Maren's face turned a bright, embarrassed red. "What's the trouble?" he asked.

"I've been hating people. Hating, you know, Black people," her voice sounded hollow as though almost no air pushed through her throat. It quaked like a tree blown by the Santa Anas. "I got beat up. I couldn't help it. Hate took over. I felt so alone. It got to be too much."

"Do you hate me?" Curtis asked.

Her chin quivered as she got up from the floor. "At first I was afraid of you, just like the others. But now? No, I . . . um, I don't think so."

Smiles began to form on both their faces. "The book and gold and letter can change our lives, little sister. That's what I think," he said. "You've got some serious speed to your reading, even with the print being so small. You were enjoying it, no doubt. Did you bring your English books?"

Tears began to stream down her cheeks. "No."

He started to reach his hand toward her but stopped. "Why the tears?" he asked.

"I'm . . . I'm all by myself," she said. "Mom and Dad both left."

Curtis longed to hug her tears away, but if she was even a little afraid of him, he didn't want to scare her.

"I was born on . . . on my grandpa's birthday," Maren continued. "I love him. Can't explain it, just do. Mom was mad at him because he was a drunk. She said he stole money from her to buy alcohol. But he was a pacifist and an artist, too. He died on our garage floor." She wiped her nose on her sleeve and looked down at the letter. "I don't remember him. I was too young. Oh, my God, his letter's dated February 22. He died just two days later." Her tears turned to sobs.

Curtis ignored the part of him telling him to not hug her. He drew her into an embrace and salty tears fell on his new shirt. He didn't care.

When she stepped away from him, she patted her chest and said, "I've had a hole. It's right here. Sometimes it hurts so much I think I'm going to die. But now, I don't know . . . maybe it's getting filled up." She turned away from him, but then swiveled back to face him. "Thanks for finding me, Curtis." Tears still streamed from her eyes. "Maybe I do need a hand—from a friend."

He felt another urge to embrace her but held back. "I suspect, you're stronger than you think," he said.

Ruby slipped her hand back into his. "You're right," she

said. "But much of our strength comes from who's around us. You two can be friends. You've got to find a use for that money, one to fit its history. Seems like it weighs more than it does in ounces. Let your fear and anger wash away, and you'll be free to walk together." Ruby placed her gaze on her sandals, on her red toenails. "Both prejudice and tolerance begin at home. Just give yourselves a little time, and you'll find the path you need."

Curtis felt his chest swell with emotion. He couldn't seem to catch his breath for a moment. He hoped Ruby was right, that he could let fear and anger go. Maren's tears began to slow.

"And what were you talking about?" Ruby asked. "There's an old book?"

Curtis and Maren looked at each other, hoping the other would answer the question. "The book is garbage," he began. "It's all trashed up by life, kind of like me. But it's worth more than the gold it hid, at least to me. That ratty, old thing contains the lives of people who've owned it before. Don't you think? They gave it a life by reading it, by treasuring it. And more important, it's brought Maren to me."

Maren sniffed, but her tears had stopped.

Bruce wrote up some paperwork while the three friends continued to talk. Curtis felt uneasy about the coin's possible value. Maren reassured him that she wanted him to have half, no matter how valuable the coin ended up being. He decided to bring up the issue to Sam, and maybe they'd split his half in half. He had saved the book and coins from the trash barrel, after all. He began to agree that some of the money felt right for him to keep. Whatever he ended up with would certainly get him into an apartment and feed him until he found a job. He shook his head. All of his plans and doubts about how to get off the street hadn't amounted to anything. This unexpected thing happened, and *bam*, it had chased much of his worry away.

He turned to Maren. "No more worries, little one. No more hate to fill your heart." Her broad smile warmed his soul. "Fortune's come a-knockin'," he said and placed the Buffalo nickel in her palm. "Keep this and the letter, for now. But, if you don't mind, I'd like to read the book for a spell. It's yours when you want it back. I think you will someday."

Maren hopped onto her bike and rode away as Ruby and Curtis, arm in arm, watched until she turned a corner and was out of sight. "I'll be waiting for you to stop by," Ruby said, squeezing his hand.

"I know where to find you," he said and placed a kiss on her cheek, but she turned and passionately kissed his lips.

"Remember, now, you can choose to let the hurt wash away or drown you. There's people that need you, Mr. Jones. I need you."

She looked into his eyes and he could feel his heart thumping wildly in his chest. His breath deepened. "I know where to find what I need," he said. Their second kiss held them together. He wanted to drown in her embrace. They found a bench under a giant pepper tree where they sat and hugged. Again, he felt the softness of her mouth and longed to feel more of her. Finally, Curtis said, "It's safer if I leave before dark, Ruby."

"Will I be seeing you soon, Curtis?" she said and stroked his cheek.

He loved the sound of her saying his first name for the first time. "Nothing can keep me away." He didn't want to leave, but finally they did go their separate ways. He turned toward the freeway and she toward her beat-up Datsun.

Later that night, in his box, Curtis knew if any rain began to fall, he'd wake up and move to higher ground. Storms were a problem only when they really poured, and there was a prediction of a storm that could drop three inches overnight. He settled in, imagining how he was just as much a part of history as the next guy.

—Slave gold, huh. Might as well buy me some freedom.

He felt responsibility—not to himself—but to the people who'd owned these things before, and to Maren. And to Ruby.

"My great-great-grandparents were slaves. But I'm free and always have been. I'm lucky. And I won't fail."

He looked at the book resting in his hands, now empty of any loose objects. The letter and nickel were home with Maren. The gold was safe at the coin shop. He folded his jacket, rested his head on it, and held the book close to his heart. The sun descended below the horizon, and a new feeling arose.

"No more darkness. I am content, grateful, free."

The End

Kate Porter

Questions for book clubs, readers, and students:

1) If you could go back in time, what era portrayed in *Lessons in Disguise* would you most like to visit to better understand the people who lived then?

2) With which of them do you share feelings about racism, bigotry, or being judgmental toward other people?

3) Which of them best describes your family of origin and their attitudes? Why are yours the same or different?

4) Are racism and bigotry mostly fed by society or by families within their own homes? Or both?

5) Have you ever told a racist joke or laughed at one? Have you stopped someone from telling one or asked them to stop and apologize for what they said? What is an effective way to say something?

6) Were you surprised by any of the negative actions or feelings of one group toward another in this book?

7) Why did the author choose to write from the characters' points of view?

8) Do you love books, or do you think books are ancient garbage and electronic media is better?

9) Do you have any books that were owned by a parent or grandparent? Do you have memories of reading one or having it read to you as a child? Will you keep any for your own children or grandchildren?

10) Do you think antiquarian books are destined for the landfill? Is preserving them a waste or does it have value? Has this story changed your feelings?